MW01199426

BEYOND JEALOUSY

To Kim,
It's an O'Kane thing.
Kit Rocha

kit rocha

This book is a work of fiction. The names, characters, places, and incidents are products of the writers' imaginations and are not to be construed as real. Any resemblance to persons, living or dead, actual events, locales or organizations is entirely coincidental.

Beyond Jealousy

Edited by Sasha Knight

ISBN-13: 978-1499115277
ISBN-10: 149911527X

For everyone who celebrates love, no matter what shape it takes or how it comes to people.

1

SHE'D TURNED INTO a creeper, and it was all Ace's fault.

Rachel drained her third shot of tequila and fought a losing battle to drag her covetous gaze away from the cage—and the man inside it.

Of course, everyone was watching. It was hard not to when Cruz was setting a Sector Four record by taking on three opponents at once. And he'd apparently decided to go big or go home, because not a single one of the poor bastards had managed to land a solid shot on him.

It wasn't fair when even three-on-one odds couldn't bring a man down.

Rachel half wished she'd laid money on the match, just to have an excuse for her galloping pulse, not to mention the tiny drop of sweat that rolled down the small of her back. But she'd never been good at lying to herself, so there it was. The truth, in mesmerizing

Technicolor.

Lorenzo Cruz, stripped to the waist and fighting like his life and dark mood depended on it, was a beautiful sight. Damn near enough to make a woman come from thirty feet away.

A tug on her shirt drew her attention away from the cage. "Show me where you want this?"

Shit, she'd forgotten all about Gunner, their conversation—and, frankly, anything that didn't have to do with licking a path straight down the center of Cruz's chest. "Uh, yeah." She lifted her hands automatically, allowing Gunner to pull her shirt higher. "I know the ribs hurt, but I was thinking my left side?"

"Sure, sure. No problem." He grinned at her. "I can put it anywhere you want."

"A tattoo," she said firmly. "Don't get your hopes—or anything else—up."

Gunner winked, a gesture more playful than suggestive. He knew better than to push his luck with an O'Kane, especially in the heart of their compound. "I'll be a perfect gentleman," he assured her, crouching to get a better look at her side. "So you want a fallen angel right across here?"

"Falling," she corrected. Not just an angel, and not one lying on the ground, her wings broken. That wasn't her. What she wanted to capture was the journey, the dizzy, spinning descent. "I want—"

Someone reached around her waist and jerked her shirt back down into place. Even before she looked down at the brash, beautiful sleeves of ink covering those arms, she knew who it was from the zing of awareness that rocked her.

Ace.

She slapped his fingers and turned to face him. "Hands off, Santana. I'm having a conversation here."

Ace's gorgeous face twisted into a scowl. "Not with him, you're not. *Hell* no."

It wasn't enough for him to dominate her thoughts, her fantasies. He had to own her skin, too. "Seriously? You think I'm gonna come to you for this?"

He shifted his gaze to Gunner, as if she hadn't spoken. "I thought we had an understanding, man. You got a sudden death wish?"

Gunner raised both hands in clear surrender, and Rachel shoved him out of the way. It wasn't about him anyway, not really. "If you have a problem with my life choices, Ace, have the respect to take it up with *me*."

Now she had his attention, one hundred and ten percent of it. He was usually so easygoing that she forgot how intense it could be when he fixed his dark gaze on her. "Letting that bastard ink you isn't a life choice. It's a *fuck you*."

She swallowed hard. "Don't you think you've earned it?"

"Maybe, but there are better ways to say it." He leaned in, the air between them heavy, electric, and even the roar of the crowd around them couldn't shatter the illusion that they were trapped in their own tiny world. "Did you think past sticking it to me? About how long it would take, how much it would sting? How high you'd be flying, with only some fucking outsider there to catch you if you fell too fast?"

"I hate you." The words slipped out, and she immediately wanted to snatch them back. Not because they weren't true—he'd hurt her, more than once, in ways that couldn't have been accidental—but because they revealed too much. How much she cared, when she shouldn't have, not at all.

Her cheeks burned. She turned on her heel and fled, heading for the back hallway and its maze of rooms and exits. Plenty of places to hide until the waves of mortification settled. She'd blame it on the tequila, laugh it off the way they did everything else—

"Rachel, wait."

"No way."

Ace caught her arm and hauled her to a stop. "Fucking hell, woman, *stop* for a second!"

"What?" She jerked away and smacked her shoulder against the hallway wall. At least the darkness would hide the sudden tears of pain that stung her eyes, though it did nothing to conceal her stupidity. "What do you want from me, Ace?"

"Fuck." His hand hovered over her shoulder. "I want to stop hurting you. But it's the one thing I manage, no matter what I do."

Did he stop to wonder why? To think about all the ways he was in her face, every day, showing her there was nothing he couldn't have if he wanted it? Nothing and no one, including Cruz.

Including her.

"I don't—" Her voice failed her, and she fought to speak past the thick, painful lump in her throat. "I don't want to do this anymore. We should just stay out of each other's way, okay?"

"Easier said than done," he whispered, dropping his hand to her wrist. He slid a fingertip over the cuff obscuring her city bar code, the first tattoo he'd ever given her.

The moment was burned into her memory. Ace had set her at ease with his friendly jokes and warm smiles, turning a terrifying moment into something simple, almost sweet. She'd clung to it, the only solid thing in a whirling storm of uncertainty.

He pulled away. As light as the caress had been, its absence was a punch to the gut. "If you don't trust me with your ink anymore, fine. But Emma's got more talent in one toe than that bastard will ever have in his life. And she's one of us."

"Okay, you win." The words caught on a hitch, and Rachel shook her head. "You always win."

"Sure as hell doesn't feel like it, angel."

"That's your own damn fault." She looked away, toward the low red light glowing at the end of the hallway. "You didn't even ask me why."

"Would you have answered?"

He was leaning closer. She could feel it, and she steeled herself against the seductive tug before she looked up and met his gaze. "Anything."

The space between them was too precise not to be deliberate. He should have been touching her somehow—an accidental bump of his hand, his chest grazing hers when she dragged in a breath—but the prickle over her skin was nothing but pure anticipation.

He let her hang there forever before closing his eyes. "Maybe I don't want to hear you say how much you hate me again. Once a night is all my wounded, delicate heart can handle."

Instead of temper, the words sparked a tiny frisson of guilt. "I meant it. But not the way you think."

The corner of his mouth kicked up. "My mistake. It's the good kind of hate."

"The frustrated kind." He always found a way to hide behind his joking words. Exasperated, Rachel reached down and grabbed his belt buckle, curling her fingers beneath the warm metal. "I know what sorts of games you and Cruz are playing these days. How come you two haven't knocked on *my* door yet? Think I can't handle it?"

"And what do you think you know?" Ace demanded, his eyes snapping open. His hands hit the wall on either side of her head, caging her. Trapping her. "Don't skimp on the filthy details. You know how I love dirty talk, angel."

She'd lost her mind—it was the only explanation for why she didn't retreat. "You've been sharing your women." She leaned closer, her mouth next to his ear. "Is it about pleasure or conquest, Ace? And do you take turns, or fuck them at the same time?"

"Conquest?" His eyes narrowed, and a new expression darkened his features, one she'd never seen directed at her before.

Anger.

Good. She could work with him hating her, too. At least that made sense.

Rachel snatched her hand back. "Sorry, I forgot the rules. Everything's a joke until it's not, and words don't mean anything until you want them to."

The arms on either side of her tensed, muscles flexing under ink. "We fuck them at the same time, because that's what they want. What *he* wants. Is that what you really need to know? What your city boy's doing now? How filthy he's gotten? Because you sure as fuck don't seem to give a shit about me."

If only.

Her eyes burned, and she bit the inside of her cheek until she tasted blood. It didn't stop the first hot tear from spilling down her cheek, or the ragged sob that tore through the knot in her throat.

"Fuck. Fuck, fuck *fuck*." Ace cupped her cheeks, a warmth on her skin that lingered for only a heartbeat before vanishing. "Ignore me, angel. You're sweet and you're perfect and Cruz is in love with you. You're both too good for the likes of me, so don't cry."

The only thing that hurt worse than his censure was his pity. Desperate for escape from both, Rachel stumbled blindly toward the door. Any place was better than standing in front of Ace, hearing awful, hurtful words spill from her lips, when all she'd ever wanted was—

It doesn't matter. She repeated it like a mantra, a tiny whisper under her breath until she was outside, her breath puffing out into the frigid night air. She was heading in the wrong direction, toward the warehouses instead of the living quarters, but she didn't give a damn.

She had to get away.

It wasn't difficult to track down Rachel. Cruz had successfully stalked more elusive prey across far more expansive terrain, and had done so with less intimate knowledge of his quarry. When Rachel was rattled, she fled to higher ground, to fresh air and open skies.

So he wasn't surprised to find her on the roof. She sat with her back to the low wall edging the rooftop, a nearly empty bottle nestled between her knees. "Emergency tequila," she explained, holding the bottle aloft. Her teeth chattered, and her lips were several shades darker than their usual pink. "To keep me warm."

Liquor didn't work that way. It opened the capillaries, flushed the skin with what seemed like a rush of warmth, but in the end it only hastened the loss of body heat. Especially now, when they were well on their way to winter. It got cold in the desert at night, and for all that Eden had fought to hide the fact with irrigation and reservoirs and carefully cultivated greenery, that was exactly where they were.

"Here," he said, slipping out of his jacket. His blood was still pumping from the fight, but the icy wind cut easily through his thin T-shirt. He could only imagine how chilled she was, huddled against the stone.

He dropped the jacket around her shoulders, and she relaxed into the fabric with a soft moan. "You're so warm. And I'm so stupid. I shouldn't have come up here, but now I can't leave."

It didn't make sense, but she was so wasted it probably shouldn't. Rachel could match any O'Kane drink for drink, which made him wonder how full that bottle had been when she'd come up here. She might have even started drinking while he was in the cage, before he'd claimed victory only to discover a guilt-stricken Ace hitting the whiskey hard enough for it to hit back.

It wasn't a surprise that the two people he cared for most couldn't exchange two words without shredding each other to ribbons. That had been his life forever—the agony of divided loyalties. His orders or his conscience, the sectors or Eden...

Rachel or Ace.

Ace would have to fend for himself tonight. Cruz crouched and held out a hand. "Share the tequila?"

"Take it. My head is spinning." She passed him the bottle, then pressed her palms over her closed eyes. "You talked to Ace."

"He didn't have much to say." It wasn't a lie, because Cruz hadn't needed words to know. The pain in Ace's expression had told him who, and enough of what. Only a fight with Rachel could put *that* look in the man's eyes.

She changed the subject. "Congratulations on your win. That's a record, you know. I hope you were smart enough to bet on yourself and clean up."

"I've got some cash now, yeah."

She leaned her head back against the brick. "Good."

"Rachel, honey. It's too damn cold to be out here. Why don't you go back to your room?"

"I don't want to be alone." Her eyes fluttered open and fixed on him. "Up here, I'm killing time. If I go home, I'm alone."

The offer hung heavy on the tip of his tongue, but he bit it back. It would be too easy to cross this line. He'd crossed so many others lately, stumbling across them in blind pursuit of pleasure.

He could stumble into her, too, but not like this. Not drunk and sad and shivering from the cold. His words had to be careful, precise. Comfort with no hidden strings, no temptation. "You don't have to be alone. There are plenty of places you could crash tonight."

She smiled—slow, with no hint of amusement. "Everyone feels sorry for me these days."

"I don't think that's true."

"Maybe not. Fine." She reached out. "If you're not going to let me sit here and feel sorry for myself, the least you can do is help me up."

Now it was safe to smile as he straightened and took her hand. "You promise to go somewhere warm, and I'll let you brood all night long."

"I don't *want* to." She tripped over her feet and pitched against him, bracing her free hand on his chest. "I don't know what else to do. This isn't how things were supposed to turn out."

His lines always blurred when she put her hands on him. But this was the first time she'd touched him since he'd killed Russell Miller, and that had been a turning point. The moment he'd given up on some impossible idea of being a hero.

Of being *her* hero.

He gripped her shoulders to steady her and ignored the way even that small contact stirred arousal. "Turn out? That's awfully final."

Her fingers tightened in his shirt. "Yes, it is."

Careful. "Your life's not over. Anything could happen tomorrow. You and I both know that better than most."

She looked up at him, her expression serious. Her eyes clear. "I'm glad you're happy. Doubt anything else, but not that, okay?"

He wasn't happy. He was falling, losing himself in vice because fucking and fighting were the only things that gave him a taste of pleasure. But she looked so somber, so fucking *sad* that only a monster would take that small comfort from her. "All right."

She huffed out a laugh and hid her face against his chest. "You're a terrible liar. Just wretched."

It wasn't funny, but his lips twitched as he gave himself permission to touch her hair. He'd missed running his fingers through it, feeling the slippery blonde strands slide over his skin. It was longer than it had been during their brief time together, long enough that he could imagine wrapping it around his fist—

No. "I'm actually a damn good liar," he said, mostly

to distract himself. "Just not with you, I guess."

"Not with me." She arched closer, rubbing her cheek against his shirt. "I miss you."

"Yeah?" His heart kicked into his throat—an amazing fucking feat with all the blood rushing to his cock.

But Rachel didn't respond, and she wasn't just leaning into him for support anymore. He allowed himself a single sigh before scooping her off her feet. She barely murmured as her head tucked itself neatly under his chin.

She'd be feeling the tequila tomorrow, and chances were good she wouldn't remember a damn thing she'd said to him tonight. That was the only reason he let himself speak at all as he carried her toward the stairs.

"I miss you, too."

2

JADE DIDN'T LIKE the needles.

Not that she gave any sign—she endured being tattooed with a quiet stoicism practiced enough to be depressing—but Ace knew women. He knew their bodies and all the ways they could tense and tremble, especially when pain was involved.

Jade didn't like the needles, and he didn't like putting the hurt on a woman who already seemed terrifyingly fragile. "You still with me, honey? Last thing I want is a gorgeous lady bursting into tears in my chair."

The corners of her mouth twitched in a whisper of a smile. "You're right, Trix. He's a flirt."

"Told you." The redhead leaned over, bracing her elbows on the table. "It looks good, Jade. Real good."

Usually Trix leaning over anything made for a banner day. The redhead had a killer rack and a wardrobe meant to show it off, and Ace had always enjoyed ogling her tits.

Today, he was too hung over to summon more than a sad echo of his usual grin. “So, you two like to talk about me, huh?”

“Don’t start,” Trix advised. “You were drunk as shit last night. Even if we wanted to bask in your attentions today, you’d be no good to either of us.”

“Baby, I’m an O’Kane. My drunk attentions would still rock your world.”

“So I hear.”

It was Trix at her sultriest, flashing a knowing gaze and a teasing pout, and he supposed he was lucky she was still talking to him at all. The O’Kane women were harder to get between than an Eden virgin’s thighs, which meant he’d been getting a lot of cold shoulders since he’d pissed off Rachel.

Last night sure as hell wasn’t gonna fix that.

Swiping the spot he’d just been working on, Ace spent a moment admiring the clean lines swirling across Jade’s brown skin. The O’Kane emblem was always the centerpiece of a member’s cuffs, but the framing had to fit the person. Trix’s were among his favorite—lace and swooping curves, just like her—but something sassy and flirty wouldn’t work with Jade.

She was elegant, and she was tough. Lex had hauled the woman out of Sector Five, drugged out of her skull and so past addicted that even Doc hadn’t thought she’d pull through. Her fragility was skin-deep at best, an illusion that would fade as her health came back.

No lace for her. Nothing delicate. Strong roots twining around the emblem and twisting down, forming an unshakable base. Strong branches rising above, dotted by tiny leaves. He’d spent most of a sleepless night sketching it, and a good part of the morning refining it.

Yeah, he’d been drunk off his ass, but he was still a fucking genius.

Jade tensed as he started the next line, her stoicism wavering, and Ace filled the silence quickly. "So, there must be a party in the offing. Noah and Six haven't had their big O'Kane welcome yet, and now you'll be needing one, too." He shot Trix a meaningful look—*Help me distract her*—before resuming his work.

Trix winked and stroked Jade's hair back from her forehead. "You and Ace should help me convince Scarlet to get her band out here for it. Her bass player's delicious."

"*She's* delicious," Ace replied, flashing Trix a teasing grin. "Better watch out, Trixie-girl. I bet you're just her type. I heard she likes her girls all pretty and curvy."

Trix blushed. "She's too into power games for me, thanks."

"Everything's a power game," Jade murmured. "Sometimes we don't realize we're playing, and sometimes we're not playing the game we thought...but if there's trust, there's power. And if there's no trust, it's just a more dangerous version of the game."

Trix propped her chin on one hand. "Do you really believe that?"

"Mmm. That's all my training was, at the heart of it. Learning to recognize what game a person wanted to play, even if he didn't know it himself."

An elegant way to put it, but Sector Two trained their courtesans to be refined and clever. Ace's mentor had tailored his lessons to his student, and Ace had learned the blunt version. *Almost nobody knows what they really want. Figure it out before they do, and you own them.*

Great advice, if you could follow it. The two people he'd trained with had. Jared and Gia could spend five minutes with anyone, man *or* woman, and know a half-dozen paths straight to their soul. Ace had always preferred games where the rules were set in advance—games where they had to be set in advance, because you couldn't play them if everyone wasn't on board.

Maybe if he'd studied better, he'd know what games Rachel wanted to play.

"What if you love someone?"

Jade hesitated, and Ace glanced up in time to catch a flicker of sadness before she schooled her features again. "I imagine it's a much scarier game with far higher stakes."

He had blunt words for that concept, too—*too fucking much to lose.* They were the words that pounded through his skull every time he pictured Rachel tied to his bed, naked and hungry and *his.*

Or, more often than not lately, *theirs.*

His fantasies about her had never been tame, but they'd flown off the rails since the night he'd gone down on Cruz. That was as far as they'd taken things that night, though they'd tag-teamed Jeni so hard she'd been incoherent with glee for a straight fucking week. She kept begging him to bring Cruz back for another round, but Ace couldn't do it. He couldn't fucking do it.

He wanted Rachel between them. Rachel helping him suck Cruz's dick. Rachel wrapped in chains, bound immobile and groaning around Cruz's cock as Ace laid stripe after stripe of pink across her creamy skin. And that was just the warm-up, the foreplay. They were both shaky-legged innocents, barely dipping their toes into carnal vice. He could drag them into the deep end so fast, so hard.

Too fucking much to lose.

So damn much to gain.

A soft touch on the back of his neck. "Ace?"

Starting, he swiped at Jade's wrist and repositioned her hand for his next set of lines. "What, I'm making art here."

Frowning, Trix stroked her thumb just above his collar again. "You seem worried. Did you hear about Ford?"

Jade sucked in a breath when the needles pierced her skin, but she covered it with a question. "Ford? I don't think I've met him."

"You wouldn't have," Ace replied, mostly to distract her. "Ford's the man with the plan, and all that. Uses his big brains to get us in good with the illegal farms and communes that sell us grain. It keeps him on the road."

"Until he crashes his bike." A cloud of concern darkened Trix's eyes. "Lex said he walked back. Is that true?"

"Nine fucking miles." Ace fought a shudder at the thought of it. Bad enough to go down in a tangle of fire and steel, but to claw your way back to your feet and walk with a broken, splinted leg spiking agony through you with every step? "Doc was furious with him. Dallas, too. He did so much damage walking on it, the regen wouldn't take, and now he has to heal up the old-fashioned way."

"Goddamn stubborn O'Kane men." The gentle hand on his neck softened Trix's words. "You're all impossible."

"That's why you love us." He finished the outline of the O'Kane symbol and glanced up at Jade, who had fallen silent and was staring ahead, her gaze unfocused. "You still with us, Jade?"

"Yes." She hesitated before tilting her head. "I was just thinking... If he needs help while he's recovering, there's a girl—a refugee from Sector Two. I've been hoping to find her a job, something uncomplicated she can do while she gets her feet under her."

Ace could read between those innocuous words easily enough. *Something boring to do while she gets whoring out of her head.* And he was sympathetic as hell—the mind games they played in Two made his tenure in Eden look mild by comparison, and he'd needed a solid year before he'd been ready to mix money and sex again.

But sending some emotionally wounded waif to play nursemaid to *Ford*? Might as well find a lion and shove her head between its jaws. "Is she tough?"

"She trained at Orchid House."

Just that, as if it was the only answer anyone needed—and maybe it was. After all, Lex had been trained by the same people. "Well, couldn't hurt to run it by Lex and Dallas. If it matters to you, they'll figure something out." He tapped her wrist. "You're family now, girl."

"We can find her something to do," Trix said resolutely. "Everyone's so busy these days, we need all the help we can get."

"Tell me about it," Ace grumbled, because it was the honest fucking truth. They'd been working too hard since taking over Three. Good work, worth it, and they'd be rolling in the sweet rewards eventually. But it didn't make it any less work.

And it made the time to play so much more precious. Too bad Ace was losing his grip on that, too. Sex worked when everyone followed the rules and knew what to expect, and he couldn't hold up his end anymore. Not with Cruz and Rachel crashing in on him from opposite sides, screwing with his sense of balance.

Something had to give. Soon.

Trix's fingers stroked over his jaw, and he caught the edges of his name in that warm, husky voice of hers. "Huh?" he asked, looking up. "Did you ask me something?"

She laughed and shook her head. "I wouldn't want to interfere with your art." She leaned down and whispered something in Jade's ear.

Too low for him to hear, but Jade's lips curved upward and her gaze flicked over Ace with the sort of assessment he was used to dishing out.

Ace glared at Trix and returned to his work. "What sort of tales are you telling, Trixie?"

It was Jade who answered. "Oh, she just reminded me about a story Noelle told me. About the day she got her ink."

Noelle had started off as such a good, good girl who

wanted to be so, so bad. Strapping her into his chair while Jas played with her and the pain got her hot and squirmy had been one of the better afternoons Ace'd had in his studio.

If he *didn't* flirt, Trix would know something more than Ford's accident had him spun. So he leered at Jade and nudged her leg with his knee. "Just say the word, pretty girl, and I'll strap you down. Trix isn't usually into pussy, but I bet she'd make an exception if you asked real pretty."

Jade laughed, the sort of low, throaty sound that usually set his blood pounding toward his dick. "It's a sweet offer, but pain isn't my vice. And I don't think I'm yours."

Trix's smile was a little sad, as if she'd noticed his heart wasn't in the teasing. "We're not wild enough for Ace these days, that's what I hear."

He glanced up to find Jade watching him, and for one moment those dark eyes could have belonged to Jared or Gia or Lex. All of them had training and instincts, and all of them could peel back a person's armor and see what it hid.

The sympathy in Jade's gaze ached, but she tempered it with another of those dirty-hot laughs. "I'd offer to prove you wrong, Trix, but if we start kissing, he's never going to finish my tattoo."

"Not in time for the party," Trix agreed.

"At least it would keep you from trying to be smartasses," he muttered, but he tossed Jade a wink before bending over her wrist again. Maybe he had been working too hard, if he didn't have the energy to work up a good, juicy fantasy about the two of them tangling tongues. A party would fix that. Lots of booze, lots of dancing, lots of people willing to fuck in dark corners—or well-lit ones.

Strong liquor and hard fucking cured most ills. Unconsciousness would cure the rest—for a while, anyway.

It would have to do.
For now.

3

THE NIGHT WAS alive with promise, a throbbing Rachel could feel in her blood, her bones.

It wasn't just the music or the booze. There was something in the air, amid the writhing bodies on the dance floor, something that zinged up her spine anew when she glanced at the couches lining the perimeter of Dallas's party room and caught sight of Ace and Cruz.

Watching her.

A smooth arm slid around her waist, and she caught a flash of wild brown hair before Noelle rested her chin on Rachel's shoulder. "Can I dance with you?"

"Better than dancing alone." And getting distracted by broody, untouchable men. "Where's Jas?"

"He and Mad had one last delivery to make." Noelle's fingertips brushed the skin bared by Rachel's dress, tracing along the leather straps in a teasingly light caress. "This is pretty. You look amazing."

"We're not the only ones who've noticed." Lex stepped up in front of her, and her casual words belied the fire in her dark eyes. The awareness.

Lex's loose, silky halter teased Rachel's exposed skin, and she closed her eyes as she leaned back into Noelle's embrace. She didn't want to think about Ace or Cruz—or Ace *and* Cruz. She wanted...

Her eyes snapped open, and she laid one hand over Noelle's.

Noelle stilled. "What is it?"

Rachel shook her head and turned in the woman's arms. Wanting and not having had somehow become normal, an unbreakable habit that seemed to define her life now. She wasn't the sum total of her experiences but her desires.

But she couldn't explain it to Noelle. If the words even existed, they wouldn't come, and Rachel was left staring at her in frustration.

It didn't matter. Lex pressed closer to her back with a warm laugh. "We've got this, don't we, baby girl?"

"Oh yeah." Noelle swayed closer, brushing her lips over Rachel's in the softest kiss. "Do you trust us?"

"You know I do." It was herself she didn't trust. How far she'd go if those last walls fell. If she'd beg. "But I—"

"Just watch them." Lex turned her head with a hand on her jaw.

She couldn't *not*. Ace and Cruz filled her vision the same way they filled her thoughts, edging out every damn thing until nothing else existed.

Cruz met her eyes, held them. There was a wild sort of hunger there, an intensity that had seemed closer to the surface lately. It only brightened as a soft touch brushed the edge of Rachel's bodice. The tiny straps holding it up gave way under someone's fingers—Noelle's or Lex's, she couldn't tear her gaze from Cruz's to be sure.

It was Noelle's tongue that swiped across her newly

bared breast. Noelle's mouth that closed around her nipple.

Rachel bit her lip, but she couldn't stop her shiver of arousal, the way her skin tightened at the wet heat. And she didn't *want* to, because she was tired of being locked up, even when she let go.

"You can have anyone you want." Lex's voice vibrated against her ear, and her hand drifted from Rachel's hip to her bare upper thigh. "You don't need them."

"Mmm." Noelle licked a path to her opposite nipple and teased it with quick flicks of her tongue before smiling against Rachel's skin.

She could feel good if she wanted. And holy *shit*, she wanted. The whole room was fuzzy already, a jumble of aching lust and mounting pleasure. Cruz was still watching, his eyes on Rachel, and she could feel that resistance slipping, see it in the way he shifted his body, a restless reaction in a man usually so controlled.

Then she made the mistake of looking at Ace, and the lazy pleasure winding through her cooled. A frown played around the edges of his mouth, as if he didn't like what he was seeing, not even a little—

Noelle slid up Rachel's body and turned her face with a gentle hand on her cheek. "Ace has to make his choice," she murmured, stroking Rachel's lips. "He doesn't get to lock you away from pleasure because he's all tangled up. You're made for joy."

There was a smart answer to that, a defiant, strong one, but Rachel's head was spinning too hard for her to think of it. She'd assumed both men had the same problem—that opening their fragile new relationship to include her was risky, dangerous—but the truth was exhilarating, horrifying. Tragic.

Cruz wanted her, and Ace didn't *want* to want her.

She opened her mouth, and Noelle's thumb edged between her lips. Moaning her approval, Lex eased her hand higher, under Rachel's skirt and panties, between her thighs.

Hazy pleasure gave way to liquid desire, wet and hot and centered on Lex's fingers. Rachel arched, her answering moan muffled by the pressure of the pad of Noelle's thumb pressing down on her tongue.

"Her fingers feel good, don't they?" Noelle traced her tongue around Rachel's ear. "Sometimes Jas and Dallas pin me down so Lex can see how much I can take."

Lex was unabashed in her pursuit of sexual ecstasy. Sometimes, Rachel wished she could lick that abandon off of her, like sweat off her golden skin.

"Rachel?"

Speech was impossible, so Rachel tilted her mouth over Noelle's in a rough kiss. This was all that mattered anyway, not words but action. Intimacy.

"Naughty kitten." Dallas's voice rumbled over the three of them as Noelle's mouth vanished. Dallas had a hand twisted in her hair, and he was grinning at Lex. "You trying to get her in trouble with Jas, love?"

"If he wants her mouth for himself, he should come and get it," Lex shot back. "It's a lesson quite a few of the men around here could stand to fucking learn."

"Mmm." Dallas stroked the thumb of his free hand over Rachel's cheek. "Lex loves to put Noelle's tongue all over pretty people. No wonder she couldn't resist."

Dallas held Noelle's hair in a tight grip, as nonchalantly as he would have held a door for her, and a spark of jealousy arced through Rachel. Of course he'd assume she hadn't started it all. Everyone saw her as the shy good girl, and months of dancing at the Broken Circle hadn't changed that. Maybe nothing ever would.

She reached up and traced the cleavage bared by the plunging neckline of Noelle's gauzy white dress. "Maybe we're just killing time until Jasper gets back."

"I'm sure you are." He tugged on Noelle's hair, urging her toward the couch. "Why don't you come kill time all over me, if Lex can bear to take her fingers out of you for two seconds?"

"Doubtful," Lex growled, but she pulled her hand out of Rachel's panties with a whispered, enigmatic promise. "Soon, honey." Then she followed him.

The couch on the dais was Dallas's place of honor, the closest thing he had to a throne. From it, he would command everything—the music, the alcohol, even the more carnal revelries. Rachel could follow, insinuate herself into the midst of what would soon undoubtedly be a tangle of naked limbs.

She'd been invited. They wanted her there, wanted her happy and sated.

But they didn't *crave* her.

She shivered, pulled the top of her dress back into place, and turned for the door, only to find Cruz blocking her path.

He was wearing a tight white T-shirt that molded to his frame, emphasizing every muscle beneath the supple fabric, and faded jeans that did the same damn thing. Rachel stared at him, struggling for words. But the only ones that sprang to mind were the three she vaguely remembered whispering on the roof.

I miss you.

Her throat ached. She took a half step back to keep from reaching for him, cursed herself for her lack of control, and ducked past him in a rush.

The halls outside Dallas's rooms were dark, and she welcomed it. There was no one here to see her misery, no one with good intentions who would try to drag her back to the party, make her smile.

Two corners. One more, and she'd be home free.

"And here I figured you'd be riding Lex's tongue by now. Or maybe Noelle's. Probably both."

Oh God. "Ace."

He was propped next to an open window, a cigarette dangling from his fingers and his face hidden by shadows. "Don't tell me Lex let you go easy."

"I wasn't in the mood." It was all too true lately. "If you hurry, I'm sure you can catch up."

He took a long drag and leaned forward to ash out the window, giving her a glimpse of a serious expression. "Maybe I'm not in the mood, either."

"I'll believe that when I see it." She took his cigarette—because she could, and because he'd taken so many things from her. "What do you care if I spend the night fucking my way through that whole room?"

"Do you really want to know?" he asked, his voice dry. "Or will you keep on not believing my answers?"

She'd trusted him with the truth once, but they'd been back and forth and up and down too many times now for words like *truth* to mean anything. "Honestly? I think you never say anything real to me unless I'm crying."

He plucked the cigarette back out of her hand and crushed it against the wall. "Here's a freebie, no tears required. Loving the hell out of sex doesn't mean you're always in the mood. Even when you have a cock."

A little sliver of the real Ace, and Rachel hated herself for clinging to it so fiercely. "Then why do you spend so damn much time trying to convince everyone it's all you give a shit about?"

"Maybe that's just all you want to see." The cigarette butt went out the window, which squeaked loudly as he dragged it shut. "I care about art. I care about keeping the whores safe and their pimps honest. I care about the gang and everyone in it. I care about how much I make you cry."

"But you don't know how to stop." Second verse, same as the first.

He sighed and closed his eyes. "We spark, angel. We spark so bright, and I always thought I'd woo you nice and slow and you'd adore me. But you only ever see the worst in me, and there's so much worst to see."

She'd wanted the truth, but there was too much of it

now. It stripped her bare, left her shaking, and she couldn't stop the flood of words. "I loved you, Ace, from the very beginning. But you kept pushing me away. Nothing I did seemed to matter, and now I don't know if anything ever can, because it's all too fucked up."

His lips twitched. "Yeah. It's easy to love me in the very beginning. Prolonged exposure usually fixes that."

"That's not what I *said*." She turned away from his sad, self-mocking smile. "God, you're such an asshole."

"I never meant to push you away." He caught her arm, his fingers loose, as if he was afraid of hurting her. "But maybe I let you go too easy."

If she let him, he'd pull her in, whether out of desire or comfort, or even something he couldn't begin to express. And they'd be right back where they started, unable to have the simplest conversations without misunderstandings and hurt feelings.

Rachel looked down at his fingers, then met his gaze. "If you can let someone go at all, you probably should, right?"

"Is that why you went after Cruz?"

Maybe she was finally starting to get Ace's morbid sense of humor, because she had to laugh. "*Went after* him? Fuck you, okay? Cruz showed up, and I wasn't expecting him, but you know what? I care about him, and I don't regret that for a goddamn second."

He flinched. Just that, a tiny reaction, but it was as real as the pain in his eyes. "Because it was easy to let me go."

"No." If she'd been able to let go of Ace, things with Cruz could have turned out differently. "Because I never had you in the first place. Whatever you were looking for, it wasn't me."

Ace's gaze roamed her face, as if he was trying to unlock a puzzle. "If I had fucked you that night, would things be different?"

She stiffened. They didn't talk about that night. It

seemed like years ago—Noelle had been new, Lex had still been avoiding taking those last few steps with Dallas.

Everything had been so fucking simple.

She'd danced with Ace, a dance that had turned into more—his hands on her body, then on her bare skin beneath her clothes. She shuddered just thinking about it, the slow build of lust that had rumbled between them like a thunderstorm, implacable and unstoppable—

Except he'd done exactly that. Gotten her off and *stopped*, left her standing alone in the middle of the room, flushed and dizzy and confused.

He was still staring at her, so she licked her numb lips and shrugged. "I doubt it. I'm not big on pity fucks."

"Pity?" Ace took a step forward. So precise again, close enough that she could feel the heat of him, but not quite trapping her, even though his voice had dropped to something low and dangerous. "You inspire a lot of things in me, angel, but pity? Not in a thousand damn years."

"Whatever." She turned and tried to edge past him.

He pressed a hand against the wall, barring her path with one tattooed arm. "Damn it, Rachel, don't run away."

A hysterical laugh fought its way free of her aching throat. "This is perfect. Fucking priceless."

His other hand slapped against the wall, and now she was trapped. Penned in on all sides, and he lowered his face until it was inches from hers. "You can knee me in the balls and spend the rest of your life hating me if you want, but not until you hear this. I didn't walk away from you. I ran, because sometimes you scare the hell out of me. And then I turned around, and you'd gone and found yourself a fucking hero."

It was the last thing she expected to hear, and she blinked up at him stupidly. "What the hell are you talking about? What did I ask you for that was so terrifying?"

"Not what I had to give," he whispered, holding her gaze. "What I had to be. Worthy. Of you and everything you offer. You're fucking fearless."

"Fearless?" she echoed. "Then why do I feel like such a fucking coward all the time? Why can't I stand in front of you and stop letting you run?"

He shifted one hand to smooth over her hair, tracing the lock down to where it curled against her bare shoulder. "Watching someone run doesn't make you a coward. Letting them come back makes you too brave for your own damn good."

"Brave or crazy." The ache spread to her chest, and she tried—and failed—to look away from those dark, dark eyes. "But I'm done, Ace."

His fingers followed her shoulder to the curve of her neck, fingertips ghosting over her skin like a whisper. "Maybe you're not seeing the worst in me. Maybe I fucked up so bad I made you see shadows in yourself that weren't there."

"What does that even mean?" She pressed her palms against his chest, but instead of pushing him away, her fingers clenched in his shirt. "That you made me feel like shit? I could have told you that a long time ago."

His thumb came to rest over her pulse, stroking back and forth. "I made you feel unwanted."

The way he said it, like it was some kind of guilty revelation, made her face burn. "No. You broke my fucking heart."

His thumb froze. Pain twisted his features until he bit off a curse and closed his eyes. "Jesus Christ, Rachel. I'm not worth that."

"Shut up," she whispered thickly. Her head throbbed already, the only part of her that hurt worse than her heart. "Don't you dare say that. Don't run yourself down, and don't call me stupid on top of everything else."

Groaning, he pressed his forehead to the wall next to

her head. "No wonder we're tied in so many knots. You think I know what to do with a woman's heart? That's not the part they want my hands on, angel."

She couldn't stand there and justify her ill-advised feelings, especially with him looming over her, so warm and so close. "Let me go, Ace."

His breath shivered over her ear as he turned his head. Not far, just enough for his groan to fall against her cheek. "I can't."

"You have to."

"I tried." His fingers slid into her hair, tangling in the strands. "The only thing I haven't tried is taking you."

In that moment, she felt so, so weak, because she wanted him to, even if it left her shattered beyond repair this time. "I'm tired of fighting. I'm just *tired*."

He lifted his head, tilting hers back until she was staring up at him. A stolen moment, wrapped together in shadows, and he whispered as if he didn't want his words to carry to the world beyond. "I know, Rae. I know."

The nickname shivered through her, a reminder of a time when she'd harbored hope along with her need for him, and she relaxed her hands, let go of his shirt—and slid her arms around his neck. The inches separating their lips became one inch, then a fraction of that.

So close to touching. So close to *more*. "Tell me to stop," he said, "and I will."

The breath she was holding tore free on a whimper. "Don't."

His hand drifted up, settled around her neck with his thumb pressed against her skittering pulse. A menacing touch, just like the fingers still twisted in her hair, but his tongue flicked lightly across her lower lip, a playful prelude that turned taunting when he didn't close the final distance between them.

"Ace." The word shook because Rachel did. She tried to close the gap herself, to taste him, but he held her tight for what seemed like forever.

Then he kissed her.

She only had a heartbeat to process the softness of the caress, the gentle pressure of his lips on hers, the slow exploration, because the sparks were there. They jolted through her, bringing every sense to life, and Ace groaned and pushed her against the wall, his mouth slanting over hers, his tongue venturing into her mouth.

Yes.

Too much buildup, too much expectation and yearning that reality couldn't possibly survive—except that it did. Kissing Ace was every bit as good as her feverish fantasies. Better, because she'd never imagined that he'd tremble under her hands, or that he'd kiss her like her breath was life and he'd never survive without it.

She clung to him, her heart pounding, her senses alive. He tasted like cigarettes and bourbon, and she drank in the heat of him along with the soft noise he made when she slicked her tongue over his.

He tilted his head, luring her deeper into his mouth only to toy with her, closing his teeth lightly on the tip her tongue. His own made lewdly suggestive circles, slow and lazy and so hungry she could feel the need along every inch of their bodies even though his hands stayed carefully above her shoulders.

What the hell was she doing?

Lightheaded, she broke the kiss and dragged in a rough breath. "Stop."

Ace lifted his head, breathing every bit as heavily. "Christ, you taste sweet."

She swallowed a moan. Only a crazy woman would do this, open herself *again* right after his blatant warning. *You think I know what to do with a woman's heart?* "We have to stop."

"Stop." He shuddered, his eyes dark. "I can still feel you on my tongue. It's taking everything in me not to slide to my knees and see where else I can lick you.

Damn near everywhere, in this dress. It's nothing but leather straps and sass."

"Why do you think I wore it to Dallas's party?" She'd been planning on forgetting everything else, if only for a little while. "Turns out, I'm not as fearless as you think."

The hand at her throat drifted lower, tracing the edge of one strap where it circled her waist. "Bullshit. Everything about this is brave. You're halfway to tied up and so damn strong."

She didn't feel strong, not even when she braced her hands on his chest again and pushed this time. "I didn't wear it for you," she lied.

Ace let his hand fall away. "If you wore it for Cruz, you should try ribbons and silk next time. Leather and chains are my thing."

Oh God. Cruz, who'd stumbled into the middle of this whole mess, who'd never been anything but careful, gentle. It wasn't fair, that she was so reckless, clueless, standing in the dark hall in Ace's arms. But she'd lost track of who they were hurting, because pain was all she knew anymore.

Pain and anger. Ace had to bring him up, had to remind her that none of his pretty words mattered, because any way she turned, someone's heart would break. Rachel gritted her teeth against a wave of guilt and anguish, but it only built higher with every passing heartbeat.

So she squeezed her hands into fists and met his brittle tone with one of her own. "You both know way more about what the other likes than I would. I'm just a spectator."

"And I'm invisible. Cruz could fuck his way through all eight sectors, and you'd still be the only person he really sees."

Jealousy. It wreathed every word, hung in the air between them like a low fog, and Rachel swallowed as she tried to process his words. It was hard enough, being the woman caught between two friends, but life wasn't that simple.

And neither was Ace. He was circling them *both*, like a wolf drawn to a fire but afraid of getting close enough to burn. He'd been telling the truth—they fucked women together because it was what Cruz wanted, and Ace went along with it, because why not?

He could have what he wanted, after a fashion.

She shuddered and choked out a laugh. "It's a fucked-up little triangle, isn't it?"

"No, it's an *actual* triangle." He traced the shape on her arm, his finger burning into her skin. "Three lines. No one in the middle."

The heat from his touch skated up her arm—and down her spine. Rachel shuddered again and ducked past him. "I'm sorry, I gotta get out of here."

"Rachel."

She skidded to a halt and turned to find him watching her, carefully intent. "I'm not running," she whispered. "I—I need some time."

For a second she thought he'd reach for her, but he hooked his thumbs in his belt instead. "I won't push. But I'm not walking away this time."

For the first time in months, the possibility that he was hiding his feelings—or, worse, *lying*—hadn't even occurred to her. It was a sobering thought, one that chased her down the hallway and the stairs and finally left her alone, with only one conclusion.

He meant every word.

4

CRUZ HAD LOST track of how many times Jeni had come.

When he'd fallen into her bed, he'd been set on fucking away his frustrated confusion before letting the liquor knock him out. He got her off twice before he realized no amount of gratified moaning would distract him from thoughts of Ace and Rachel, so he made her come again out of guilt.

Not that Jeni cared why he was fucking her. She cared about having a good time and giving him one in return, and that was what kept him going. It was what the O'Kanes were supposed to be about, after all—shameless pleasure with an edge of fondness, all of the fucking and none of the feelings.

No one seemed to believe he could get it done. Maybe that's why it had seemed so important to get Jeni beneath him, shaking from the intensity of the final orgasm building inside her. He could render a woman every damn bit as insensible as Ace—

Even when Ace wasn't there to help.

Jeni turned her head, pressing her cheek to the bed, and flexed her hands in his grip. "Harder," she gasped, the word already twisting into a desperate plea. "Fuck—"

Ace had been the one fucking her the last time they'd visited. He'd cuffed her wrists to her thighs, wrapped that wild hair around one fist, and ridden her hard, every thrust pushing her mouth down Cruz's shaft until she gagged. It had taken him a while to believe she really wanted it like that, rough and choking, but Jeni had just laughed and promised to suck the Eden right off him.

Ace had helped with that, too.

Jeni went silent, not even breathing as her pussy clenched around him, gripping his cock in hot, wet pulses.

His body was poised on the edge of release, a physical response he automatically distanced himself from. Then he closed his eyes and imagined all the things he was here to forget—Ace's teasing smile and Rachel's soft hair, the play of tattoos along Ace's skin and the way Rachel moaned and leaned in to Cruz's kisses...

He came too fast for it to feel better than nice, but he still groaned and rocked his hips, dragging it out until the last shudders of Jeni's release faded. He stroked her arms as he eased away, rubbing the reddened skin of her wrists where his fingers had dug in. "You okay?"

She collapsed to the mattress with a noise that was half giggle, half groan. "You're an intense motherfucker, aren't you?"

Coming from a woman who liked to have Ace flog and fuck her to giddy completion in front of an audience, Cruz figured he should consider that a compliment. He stretched out on his back next to her and ran a hand over his face. "I suppose I am."

She groped on the nightstand and came up with two

cigarettes and a lighter. She lit them both at the same time and passed him one. "I've been after Ace to bring you back. Didn't figure on you showing up alone."

He stared at her ceiling, because closing his eyes again would invite the image of Ace leaning into Rachel, his hands all over her body. "Guess he was busy tonight."

"Mmm. Trouble in paradise?"

"Is that where we are?" He stared at the cigarette without putting it to his lips. He'd smoked when necessary for cover, but he'd never much seen the appeal. "I thought Eden was supposed to be paradise."

Jeni laughed and rolled to her side. "Eden's a giant fucking cage. Sector Four's the closest thing we've got around here to real freedom." She ran her toes up his shin. "It's a hundred if you want to leave soon. Three for the night. Though something tells me I enjoyed myself more than you did."

It was twice what she charged Ace, even when he brought Cruz—and half what Ace usually left tucked under her jewelry box. Money never seemed to matter to him, and it had taken Cruz a while to understand that Ace had a far more valuable currency to trade.

Cruz couldn't offer her a tattoo, but he'd count three hundred a bargain if it kept him out of his rooms and clear of any awkward apologies. "I'll stay, if you don't mind."

She arched one eyebrow. "Jesus Christ. What did they do, fuck right in front of you?"

Only practice kept him from flinching, and he took a drag from the cigarette to cover his momentary discomfort. Exhaling, he watched the smoke drift upwards. "You're blunt. I don't know if that's refreshing or irritating."

"If you want me to stroke your ego, too, it'll cost you way more." But she grimaced. "I could've warned you, though. Ace and Rachel. That's some sort of crazy, epic shit right there."

"That's what everyone says," Cruz agreed, turning to study her more closely. Jeni worked shows at the Broken Circle, but she wasn't an O'Kane. A position like that gave someone a good vantage point for observation—familiar but invisible. Trusted, but not intimate. "If they're so epic, why haven't they been a thing forever?"

Jeni's eyes locked with his. "You'd have to know Ace. More importantly, you'd have to know what he used to do before he joined up with Dallas."

Most of Eden knew of Ace, though fewer people would associate Alexander Santana with Dallas O'Kane's tattoo artist. "I know some of it. He slept with a lot of prominent women in Eden and broke up a few marriages when their husbands discovered the paintings he'd given them."

One corner of her mouth ticked up in a rueful smile. "Slept with them? Sure, he did—after they paid him. He was a high-class whore, sweetheart, and those proper Eden ladies chewed him up and spit him out."

Maybe it should have surprised him, but it was only a more pragmatic assessment of what most people in Eden thought—that Ace had seduced those women into being his patrons, trading sex for access to a comfortable life and high quality art supplies.

That had been scandalous enough, in part because his rumored lovers had already made similar bargains with their husbands. In Eden, it was a woman's place to exchange infrequent access to her body for the comforts of a secure life, making Alexander Santana a disruption to the natural balance of power.

Cruz rolled over to stub out the cigarette as a few more pieces of the puzzle slipped into place. "Jared and Gia. That's how he knows them?"

"Yeah. They all had the same mentor, Eladio."

"And the good ladies of Eden don't chew Jared up?"

"He can hold his own." Her smile faded. "He's not like Ace. He's not looking for love."

Ace would be the first to turn the words into a joke, one about how artists fell in love every day before noon and got their hearts broken by dinner. Cruz could never tell how much truth lay beneath the words, and that bothered him. Once upon a time, assessing motivation had been easy for him.

Or maybe it had only seemed that way because he'd always been objective.

"Rachel probably knows," he murmured, rolling onto his side so he could study Jeni's expression. "She's from Eden, too. Those sculpted paintings he used to do are infamous."

She hesitated. "I don't know Rachel very well, just from around the club and backstage, but she seems pretty open. I think maybe she can't read Ace because she doesn't get how much he's hiding. She expects everything to be on the level, and it's not."

"But you know Ace?"

"Enough to know he plays it off, but he's got some fucked-up shit going on."

Cruz caught a strand of her disheveled hair and wrapped it around his finger. "If you were me, what would you do?"

She held his gaze. "You want pretty words to make you feel better?"

Pretty words wouldn't make him feel better. "I like you blunt."

"Then I'd run like hell. Get as far away from both of them as possible, before they could break my heart." Jeni finished her cigarette and passed it to him to crush out. "But that's Ace's move, right? He's scared out of his mind, Rachel's oblivious... Let's face it, you might be the only one who can take them in hand and make something happen."

Take them in hand. Simple words. Filthy ones. They wouldn't have seemed possible even a couple months ago, but he'd crossed so many lines. He'd betrayed his oaths, turned his back on his city, killed his former commanding officer.

This was nothing. A little fucking, and what was more harmless than that in Sector Four, the carnal playground of Dallas O'Kane? Rachel and Ace had been on a collision course since long before he'd met them. If he didn't want to end up left behind, he had to be between them when they finally crashed together.

The last hour before dawn was a dangerous time for anyone to be out and about in the sectors, even a man wearing O'Kane ink.

Ace didn't give a shit.

Jared's house might have been in what passed for the nicer part of Sector Four, but you could split the difference between *nice* and *slums* and come up with two big hands full of nothing. Even here, close to Eden and the well-patrolled brothel neighborhood, Ace kept his attention focused and his hand close to his gun.

He turned the corner and bit back a frustrated curse. A silent black car with tinted windows idled in the street, which meant there was nothing to do but lean back against the building and pull out a cigarette. He knew Jared always shooed his clients out before dawn, but tonight, with the wind biting through his jacket and his guts twisted in knots, Ace wasn't feeling patient.

He'd never understood how Jared could entertain Eden's richest adulteresses in his own bed before rolling over for a peaceful night's sleep. Ace had always gone into the city, meeting in secret apartments or sometimes in their own beds under the noses of their oblivious husbands. It was easier that way, easier not to get too attached. Easier to remember that fucking them to their first real orgasm might put wide-eyed adoration in their eyes for a few weeks, but he was still the paid help.

The front door opened as Ace discarded his cigarette, and he watched from the shadows as a rumpled Jared dropped a kiss to an equally rumpled brunette's cheek before leaning against the doorjamb. The brunette swayed a little as she walked to the car, her giddy flush a sharp contrast to the stone-faced man who climbed out to open the door for her.

She paused, glancing over her shoulder, and Ace bit back an amused snort. Jared was still on, playing the moment for all it was worth—barefoot with his shirt hanging open to reveal a perfectly sculpted body, ignoring the bitter temperature to present a flawless picture of lazy contentment. The pretty brunette would carry that last glimpse of him into her flustered dreams and be calling him again before the week was out.

No wonder the bastard was so fucking rich.

The car pulled away. Jared glanced at Ace with a rueful laugh before clutching his shirt around him with a shiver. "Goddamn, it's cold. My nipples could cut glass."

Ace should probably summon a leer for that—it wasn't like he hadn't had his hands and mouth all over Jared's nipples and every other damn part of him—but the swiftness of the transition set him off balance. "Then it's a good thing you put them away. You gonna watch until her car makes it through the gates, or can we go inside?"

"She'll be fine." Jared jerked his head toward the dim interior of his apartment. "Make yourself at home."

Yeah, the woman would be fine. Some dumb fucker had rolled one of Jared's clients on her way back to the city a couple years ago, thinking she'd be an easy mark and that Jared wouldn't care if it happened away from his street.

And he hadn't seemed to—until a week later. The thief had been celebrating by trying to find the bottom of a bottle of pricey O'Kane bourbon when Jared strolled into the bar and caved in his skull with a crowbar.

Another quality Gia and Jared had in spades that Ace had always lacked. He'd killed a lot of fuckers out of protective rage and self-defense, and more than a few in stone-cold vengeance, but he'd never been good at practical ruthlessness.

Inside, Jared waved him toward the couch and poured two stout drinks. "Should we pretend you were just in the neighborhood?"

"Like I don't always come crawling over here before dawn for the same fucked-up reason?"

"In recent memory? Yes." The reason was always the same, even when the catalyst changed. Ace came to Jared because he was safe. Because he'd been there for most of Ace's life, charging ahead and excelling at every challenge while Ace foundered behind. But Jared had never abandoned him. He was the one who'd walked away and found a home and a family with Dallas O'Kane.

Ace knocked back the liquor just to feel the burn. "I was so busy trying not to break Rachel's heart that I didn't see it shatter. I've been walking on the pieces for months, grinding them into fucking dust."

Jared watched him, his eyes shadowed with sympathy. "That sucks."

It drove a choked laugh from him, one that warped somewhere in his chest and came out as a pained noise. Everything inside him was pain, and he didn't know how to let it out. "Yeah. Yeah, it fucking sucks."

"All that time, and she didn't say anything? Kick your ass, cry at you, *something*?"

"She started running around with Cruz," Ace ground out, tossing the glass to the couch cushion so he could shove both hands into his hair. It was like everything after that night had split into two worlds—hers built on the agony of rejection, his twisted by the pain of watching her pick someone else.

They'd been living alternate lives, crossing just close

enough to grind salt into the wounds because neither thought the other was bleeding.

“We’ve had this conversation before,” Jared chided gently. “She hooked up with Cruz. She also dropped him. And instead of asking her why, you picked him up.”

He hadn’t meant to, not at first. Jasper had stepped up to take some of the weight of the sector off Dallas’s shoulders, and Dallas had shuffled Cruz into the empty space at Ace’s side with a stern command to put aside their personal shit and get the work done. The gang came first.

And then... Emotional decisions. Muddled rationalizations. He had vague memories of spewing some of them on this couch, drunk off his ass and trying to convince Jared he was in control of the situation. That he had a plan.

He hadn’t been lying to his friend. He’d been lying to himself. He’d been lying for months, because the truth was fucking terrifying. “I have no goddamn idea what I’m doing.”

“That’s a start.” Jared retrieved his empty glass and refilled it. “I’m guessing you talked to her.”

The memory of her mouth surfaced, her lips parted, her tongue slicking against his, bold and hungry but still nervous. Open, the way she always was, brave even in the face of her own terror. “Yeah. We talked.”

“And?”

“And I need to...” Ace waved a hand at Jared. "Fuck, man. I need to do something. Make a move. *Not* making one hasn't kept me from hurting her."

Jared shrugged. "You don't sound too sure about it."

Because he'd started to make a move last night, and she'd bolted. "She's nervous now, because I fucked up. And wooing skittish women is your specialty. I like the ones ready to take a running leap onto my dick."

Jared choked on his whiskey. "I'm not sure what you want me to tell you, since she's in love with you already.

She didn't get that way because of pretty tricks. She fell for *you.*"

He asked Jared the question he couldn't ask Rachel, because it would have sounded mocking or condescending or, worst of all, fragile and terrified. "*Why?*"

"Love is blind, right? I mean, I think you're swell, but it wouldn't matter if you were the biggest fucking asshole left on planet Earth." He shrugged. "Why her? What's so great about Rachel?"

Ace stiffened, more irritated than he wanted to admit, even if all Jared had done was turn the question around. It felt like an insult, one he wanted to answer with a little brotherly face-punching, but Jared was watching him, waiting for a response.

Except the truth might be as harsh as a fist to the face, because the thing that had first entranced him about Rachel was the thing that terrified him. "She's not like us. She never learned how to lie."

But Jared only nodded. "Makes sense. It was never your favorite part of the job."

Maybe not, but maybe he was still lying to himself. It wasn't like all the other women in his life had been experts at deception. Some had been as guileless as Rachel. Some had been smart and some had been funny, and others still had given him big eyes while being both. And he loved women. He loved the filthy temptresses and the newly, earnestly horny and the women who fucked for money. Rachel wasn't special because they were *less...*

She was special because they were all fucking amazing, and she still felt like more.

There was no one trait, no logical reason. Nothing he could point to and say, *This, this makes her better than those other women.* No defining moment where his honest lust for everything she represented had slipped over the line into this gnawing, obsessive hunger he couldn't escape.

She was a work of art. Jared saw the paint and the

canvas and a few pleasant shapes. Ace felt the earth move.

Jared made a soft noise of indulgent amusement. "A rhetorical question," he declared. "All I meant was that you may never know her reasons, and does it really matter? Unless you doubt what she feels, that is."

He might have, if the hurt in her eyes hadn't been so damn real. "I guess not."

"Don't even start. I've seen her look at you." Jared paused and tilted his head. "What about Cruz?"

The question stopped him cold. He'd been running on adrenaline, on the horror of realizing what he'd done to Rachel, and fucking *hell*. Hurting the man would be like sinking a knife into the back of a brother. Worse, because somewhere in all those muddled rationalizations, Cruz had started looking like more than paint splattered across a canvas, too.

No matter which way he turned, he was crushing something fragile. "I don't know."

"But you need to figure it out."

Yeah, he really did. And maybe, for once, he needed to make a decision while he wasn't strung out on booze and self-indulgent angst. Ace drained his drink and slumped back on the couch. "It'd be great if you'd go get stupid over some sweet little piece of ass. Then you could be the idiot for a while."

Jared grinned. "I have my idiotic moments. I keep them to myself, that's all."

"Come on, brother. Solidarity. Tell me one."

Silence. Then a rough sigh. "I fell in love once. It didn't work. That's why I don't recommend it."

Ace had never seen evidence of it in all the years he'd known Jared—but then, he might not have. That was the one lesson they'd all learned, even Ace—you showed the world your strengths because they earned you respect, and your flaws because they earned you trust. But your weaknesses you held tight in your heart.

Gia struggled to remember she couldn't rescue every wounded woman she stumbled across. Ace couldn't stand seeing hookers mistreated, because paying for someone's body didn't give you the right to leave marks on their heart and soul. And Jared didn't trust himself with feelings, as if he was convinced that dropping his pragmatism for a few moments would end in an emotional bender he'd never survive.

They were all broken, right along the lines drawn by their respective fucked-up childhoods, and for the first time in his life he didn't envy Jared. Because whatever was going on between him and Rachel and Cruz hurt like hell, but the pain was a pinprick compared to the satisfaction when Cruz growled his name or Rachel whimpered it.

If he could just figure out a way for both of them to do it at the same time, they could tear his heart out of his chest and burn it to ash, and he'd still go to hell happy.

5

AVOIDING ACE WAS easy. Avoiding Cruz turned out to be harder.

When Rachel edged through the warehouse door, she almost dropped the box of bottles she held. She managed to catch them—barely—between her hip and the door-jamb, then stood there stupidly as Cruz did one-armed pushups in the center of the cage. His torso gleamed with sweat under the harsh lights, and his dark hair clung to his temples. He grunted softly with every push off the rough concrete, a noise that made her stomach clench and the back of her neck prickle.

She considered turning around and walking back out, liquor restocking be damned. But fuck that—she was an O'Kane, dammit. She wasn't a coward, not even when presented with this. So she got a better grip on the box and let the door slam shut behind her. "Good morning."

He looked up without breaking his rhythm. "Rachel.

Need some help?"

The situation was too ridiculous for words. An ill-advised laugh bubbled up in her chest, and she bit her lip. "I wouldn't dream of interrupting your incredibly difficult workout, not when you're making it look so stupidly easy."

His mouth quirked. Barely a smile, but the warmth in his eyes had more than her neck prickling. "Let me finish this set, and I'll haul boxes for you."

"You don't have to."

He polished off five more pushups in quick succession before rocking to his knees. "I want to."

A bead of sweat rolled down the center of his chest. Rachel dropped the box on the bar with a clatter. "I'm just making sure everything's topped off before the party in a couple of days."

Cruz hopped out of the cage, snagging a towel tossed over the door on his way by. "That's right. Six is drinking in. And Jade, too?"

"Yeah. Should be a good time."

"Hey."

She paused with her hand around a bottle of tequila and looked up at him. He stood there, watching her, his hands locked around both ends of the towel around his neck. "What?"

He met her eyes squarely, and the warmth was still there, but so was something else. Something darker, that dangerous edge she'd never seen in him until she'd tried to shove him away for his own good. "You don't have to keep running from me. If you and Ace have a thing now..."

Oh God, he must have heard something, even *seen* them. "It's not like that. He and I have always had a thing—just like you and me. It's always there, no matter what."

After a moment, he nodded. "I know how much it hurts to be pulled in opposite directions. I don't want that for you."

"But you can't stop it." No one could, not since the beginning. Maybe not even then. "It's not about what you've done or might do, Cruz. It's about who you *are*. What it does to me when you—"

She bit off the words, but he wouldn't let her hold them back. "When I do what, Rachel?"

It felt like balancing on a ledge—and one wrong move would tip her off it. "When you look at me." She had to close her eyes. "When you touch me."

The bar stood between them, but that wasn't enough protection when he could just reach over it. His fingertips grazed her cheek, warm and electric, and she sucked in a breath. "What if I stopped pulling you away from him?"

No matter what either of them did, it would hurt. "I don't know what to do," she confessed.

"I do." His touch returned, lower this time. Brushing the corner of her mouth, so close to her lips. "But I need to know one thing."

She swayed toward him. "What?"

"Did you ever want us both? Or did I just get in the way?"

That brought her back to reality. She jerked away from him, snapping her eyes open. "Do you really think that?"

"No." He let his hand drop. "I'd be stupid not to make sure, though. Arrogance is a liability."

He deserved the truth, not hints and scared, half-hearted admissions. "If I didn't love you both, this wouldn't be so fucking hard."

She caught his smile, just a flash of it as he planted one hand on the bar. All those bare, gorgeous muscles flexed as he vaulted over it in a move so effortless, he had his hands on her before her brain caught up to what was happening. He gripped her hips and hoisted her with the same ease, depositing her on the bar with his body wedged between her knees.

"Tell me what you want," he whispered, cupping her cheeks. "Don't think about what's easy, or even what's possible. Tell me what you'd want if you could have anything in the damn world."

She was the embodiment of greed, grasping and hungry. Covetous and insatiable. She would have been ashamed of herself, except that there was no room for that. Not here, and not now. "I want you *and* Ace," she whispered. "It's not fair. Other women have had you both for sex. Why can't I have you to love?"

Cruz smiled, his thumb smoothing back and forth across her cheek. "Ask me what I want."

He wasn't angry or sorrowful, and Rachel caught her breath. Only one reason for him to smile at her words, and his answer had the potential to change everything. "What do you want?"

"To have both of you to protect."

Her stomach fluttered. "What the hell did you see last night? I mean, I know what happened, and that you must have been there, but...what did it *look like* to you?"

His thumb shifted course, the rough pad dragging across her skin in slow motion before rasping over her lower lip. "Like getting left behind."

"Hardly." Her mouth moved beneath his thumb like a kiss. "Haven't you figured it out? Neither one of us can stop thinking about you."

"Even with his tongue in your mouth?"

Not an accusation—arousal. The way his voice heated as it wrapped around the words kindled an ache between her thighs, and Rachel moaned. "Even with his tongue in my mouth." She reached for his hands and guided them back to her hips. "With his lips on my skin. His fingers under my clothes."

His hands tightened, and he swayed forward, his lips so close to hers. "If I put *my* tongue in your mouth, will you think of him?"

Nothing short of a challenge, and Rachel felt herself

responding to it, melting closer to him. "Every. Damn. Second."

"Maybe only half of them." He murmured the words against her mouth, and if Ace's kiss had started slow, Cruz's was the opposite. Fast and hot, lips parting over hers, his tongue slick and commanding, thrusting in search of hers with no mercy and no restraint.

Oh God.

He blocked out the world, but he sent her spinning so wildly that clinging to him would provide no purchase. So she wrapped her hands around the edge of the bar and held on.

When he bit her lip and growled—*growled*—even that wasn't enough. She whimpered, and he eased back, dragging his teeth along her lip until it popped free. He soothed the spot with one last lick before straightening.

That got her moving. She reached for him, but her fingers slipped across the sweat-slicked skin of his abdomen, and she swallowed. Hard. "You do this on purpose. Walk around half-naked."

His lips twitched. "Maybe."

"Definitely." She leaned in and teased her tongue over the muscled line of his chest. Salt, heat, and lust roared up, almost drowning out his groan as he sank his fingers into her hair.

Rachel choked on a moan and wiggled, trying to ease the tense ache. The only thing better would be Ace's fingers bumping his, tangling tight as he urged her to lick lower.

Cruz shuddered and pulled her away. "Not yet. Christ, this is hot, but I need you to trust me. I know what to do."

She trusted him more than herself and Ace put together, more than anyone. Cruz would always do the right thing, no matter what. "Okay."

He tilted her head back, and at least she wasn't the only one breathless and flushed. "Soon. I promise."

Oddly, it soothed her trembling. He'd never lie, never make a promise if he didn't know he could deliver. "I trust you, Cruz. With my life."

"Good." He brushed a final kiss against her forehead, carefully unwound his fingers from her hair, and took a step back. "Are you working tonight?"

"Taking the stage at ten." Her cheeks heated. "You gonna come watch me dance?"

His smile promised everything she'd asked for, and a whole world she could barely imagine. "Count on it."

Ace was prone to sadism, not masochism, so he usually didn't watch Rachel's performances.

Tonight had to be the exception. It was Six's first night working the floor as a bouncer, and Ace would bet he wasn't the only O'Kane lurking in the shadows, ready to back her up if necessary. She'd kick his ass if she found out, and maybe he'd deserve it for insinuating that she couldn't clean the floor with a few drunk motherfuckers just because she was short and sweet-faced and had a half-decent rack hiding under her no-nonsense black tank top.

If it had been anyone else on stage, Ace wouldn't have thought twice. But Rachel...

She gave away too much of herself, too recklessly. She'd fallen from her family's protective grasp straight into Dallas's outstretched hands, and he'd had too much invested in his relationship with Liam Riley to let anything happen to the man's favorite child.

Rachel might be the only damn person in Sector Four who'd never had to be afraid. She'd scoffed at the idea of her own bravery, but it lit up the air around her on nights like tonight, and drew the men in the crowd like flies to sweet, naked honey. They could tell they were getting the real deal with every vulnerable whimper, every trembling flush.

The crowd turned Rachel's crank in a way that turned Ace's, but the thought of her flinging herself out there with no one to catch her when she came crashing back to Earth cranked him up in a different way. And until he figured out what to do with her, he wouldn't be able to unwind.

"Jeni was right," Cruz murmured behind him. "Rachel doesn't know how to hide, does she?"

Ace tensed, torn between guilt and jealousy—and not over Jeni. "Is that where you disappeared to last night?"

"Yeah." No apologies, no explanations—just a tilt of his head and a soft smile. "Didn't think you'd mind where I stuck my dick, as long as I kept it out of your angel."

"Jeni would feed me *my* dick if I tried to tell her who she could fuck." Ace struggled for a casual tone as he watched Rachel slide her hand out of her panties to untie the ribbons securing her black fishnet bra. "So would Rachel."

Cruz moved fast. He grabbed Ace by the back of the head, holding his gaze fixed on the stage, and leaned in to whisper in his ear. "Rachel would give you big eyes and say *yes, sir*."

Surprise held Ace frozen, but only for a heartbeat. It wasn't like it was the first time he'd had Cruz's fingers on the back of his head, but he'd always had to lure the man over that line, daring him to do the things he'd imagined but would never admit.

The fingers pressing into Ace's skull didn't belong to a man inching toward a fantasy he didn't want to want. They belonged to a man who didn't give a shit anymore. A man who had every intention of taking what he needed.

Who he needed.

It kicked Ace's heart into his throat and made his dick ache. "I think you got your wires crossed, brother," he whispered hoarsely. "That's *your* fantasy."

"You have no idea." Cruz angled his body against Ace's side, his mouth touching his ear. "You think it'll be good. But then she watches you, stares right into your eyes while she wraps her fingers around your cock. Bites her lip when you start fucking her hand. Moans when you come."

Jesus *Christ*. Either he'd gotten farther with Rachel than Ace had given him credit for, or he had one hell of an imagination.

Cruz eased closer, and Ace wasn't the only one turned on now. It was the first time he'd gotten his dick anywhere near Ace without a woman between them—

Except she was still between them. She always was, whether she was there or not, and never so much as now, when they could both hear her moan as she pinched her fingers tight on her nipples.

Cruz's breathing hitched when she did it again. "I saw you last night."

Ace froze. He hadn't heard a sound, but he'd been so focused on Rachel, and Cruz could move like a ghost. There was no telling what he'd seen—or misunderstood. "Listen, brother—"

"Don't." Cruz leaned in until his beard scraped Ace's jaw and his breath was a hot tickle that whipped arousal higher. "Just admit it. Admit you can't stay away from her."

He couldn't, but that didn't matter. Rachel had a choice between the man who'd shattered her heart and the hero who'd do anything to put it back together. If she really wanted Ace, she'd have ended up in his bed, riding his tongue to an orgasm as hot as the one she was headed for now.

But she hadn't. She'd asked for time. She'd run away. "Who says it's up to me?"

"Isn't it?"

"Look at what she's wearing." It couldn't be a coincidence, not after last night. Thick black ribbons crisscrossed her torso, dragging the eye down to the lace-edged panties secured at her hips with more satin. "Last night, I told her you like ribbons."

Cruz laughed, low and rough, and his hand slipped down to the middle of Ace's back. "Did you whisper it in her ear nice and dirty, like this?"

Nothing he said would ever be as dirty as this. Casual filth tumbled from Ace's lips, waking or sleeping, because it was fun and easy and pretty fucking effective at scaring away nervous virgins looking for Jared's specialty—tender sexual awakenings. His dirty words came cheap.

Cruz's were precise, each one slamming home with the impact of a hundred of Ace's, and doled out in servings so small you were ready to beg for the next taste. But Ace didn't beg. He taunted, though it was mostly bluster now. "You think this is dirty?"

Any answer he might have made was swallowed by a roar from the crowd. Rachel had shed her panties, everything but the dark ribbon tied around her midsection. It made her look like a gift as she lay on the stage, back arched, so naked, so exposed—even her pussy was bare, something Ace wouldn't have realized was new if he hadn't had his hand in her pants before she'd taken up dancing.

She was on display, breathlessly, fearlessly vulnerable as she slipped one hand between her thighs. The audience quieted in time for her to part her lips on a long, trembling moan of pleasure, one Ace felt in his bones.

Cruz shuddered, his hand creeping lower to settle at the small of Ace's back. "You don't waste resources on overkill. You focus, and you do just enough to accomplish your mission. Dedicated, effective strikes." He glanced down, his voice dropping to a rasp. "Are you that hard from watching her dance? I'd believe it, but I don't think it's true."

His fingers burned, even through Ace's shirt. "Am I your mission? Or is she?"

"I think it's more complicated than that." Cruz eased his hand beneath the cotton and brushed the backs of his fingers over the bare skin above Ace's belt. "She may be in ribbons now, but she was in leather last night. And she looked like she was ready to let you eat her alive right there in the hallway."

A day ago, Ace would have sworn nothing could drag his gaze from the sight of Rachel with her fingers in her pussy, fucking them in and out with a rhythm he wanted to memorize. But he twisted to stare at Cruz from two damn inches away, and he still had no clue what to do with the dark recklessness in the other man's eyes. He had wanted to break Cruz free of the bullshit he'd learned in Eden, but he'd never considered he might not be up to handling what was lurking underneath.

Fuck that. He was Alexander fucking Santana. He was *Ace*. He wouldn't get knocked off his feet by some wobbly-legged dominant still fighting to hide his city-boy shine.

"Is that what you want?" he asked, keeping his voice low and seductive. "Rachel, all soft and sweet in between us?"

And then, a glimmer of truth behind the dark eyes and lust. Cruz glanced at the stage, and the hard set of his jaw relaxed a little. "You want to take care of her. You need it as much as I do. This way, no matter the fallout, she'll have someone, right?"

The fallout.

Ace should have cared more about those words, the truth of the inevitable ending. Wasn't that the most terrifying part of imagining Rachel as his? He could play her body a hundred ways, bring her up so high the fall would be endless. He knew how to catch her when it was all about physical pleasure.

Maybe Cruz could catch her when it was something

more. And if it all fell apart—

—*when* it all fell apart—

Ace wasn't naïve. His illicit allure would wear thin eventually, and the hero always got the girl. As long as Ace was the only one who came out of it with a bruised heart, the gang would be okay. No ugly fight, no mess to clean up. Cruz and Rachel could have their happy fucking ending, and Ace would drown his sorrow in the sympathy of willing partners. Everyone loved a broken-hearted bad boy.

Christ, he barely had a heart to break. And the rewards...

Rachel's moans grew louder, more intense, and Ace looked back to find her watching them with helpless longing. She gave everyone everything, and now she was giving him this, the unvarnished, messy truth of her deepest desires.

It wouldn't be a fucked-up triangle if they met in the middle.

It would be straight-up fucking.

Ace shifted his hand, found Cruz's belt. "How far will you go for her?"

Cruz hissed in a breath. "Find out." His teeth scraped Ace's ear, then dropped to his neck and closed in a hard bite.

Pleasure sizzled straight to his gut. No amount of Jeni's begging had convinced Cruz to get sincerely rough with her, but he didn't seem to mind manhandling Ace. Maybe he'd be like that with Rachel, too. Soft and gentle, all strokes and pets that would drive her crazy when Ace mixed in a little pain. They could drown her in alternating sensation, shove her to the edge and woo her back, over and over...

She was on the edge now. Her gaze had fixed on Ace's hand with fevered need, so trembling and hungry she'd probably come the second Ace wrapped his fingers around the other man's dick.

Teasing all three of them, Ace stroked his thumb over the well-worn leather before easing it open. Cruz's breathing turned ragged, and he tugged Ace into a hard, desperate kiss.

Teeth and tongue, that was his style. Rough, and usually that could hold Ace's attention, but he'd never had Rachel ten feet away, moaning her approval.

Cruz bit him again, a quick nip at his lower lip, and growled. "Watch her," he commanded, "but keep your hands on me."

"Bossy motherfucker." Jesus, he sounded *proud*, and maybe he was. Proud enough to obey, dragging Cruz's pants open as he looked back to Rachel. Simply slipping his hand inside wouldn't be enough, not for her, so he eased the other man's cock free and wrapped one hand around it. "I'm not gonna be as gentle as she was."

"Gentle?" he echoed breathlessly, the word overlaid by Rachel's soft groan.

Humor and disbelief, which had Ace imagining Rachel with her fist around Cruz, jerking him off with the same impatient tempo he was ready to employ. "No, she wants you too bad to be gentle, doesn't she? Look at her now. She can't take her eyes off your dick."

"And your hand." Cruz moved, just a little, thrusting against his grip.

Out on the stage, Rachel came with a shuddering cry. So open, so fucking *beautiful*, and the audience's shouts didn't bother Ace this time because nothing she was doing was for them.

Her legs trembled as she rode the orgasm—but she didn't stop. If anything, her hand moved faster, fingers plunging deeper. Ace groaned and squeezed Cruz's shaft hard. "Too bad she's not over here to lick you until you're nice and wet."

Cruz braced one hand against the wall with a hoarse laugh. "A little rusty on your jerk-off etiquette? Spit in your fucking hand."

They were standing backstage at the Broken Circle, which meant they could find better lube without taking a step. "Don't be so goddamn barbaric. There's a drawer right there."

He reached past Ace and dragged open the drawer on the metal cabinet. On stage, Rachel grinned and rolled to her knees, her ass to the crowd. She braced herself on one hand while the other stayed put—fingers curled inside her pussy, the heel of her hand rocking against her clit. Under the lights, her skin glistened with sweat and maybe a little of the oil Cruz pressed into Ace's hand.

"That's right, angel," he whispered as she watched him spill the oil across his palm. She was too far away to hear him, but next time she wouldn't be.

God, let there be a next time.

He gripped Cruz's cock and slicked his hand up and down. He responded by wrapping his fingers around Ace's to guide the pressure and movement—a quick pump, all the way down to the base, followed by a slow, leisurely glide back up to the tip. Cruz shuddered, his shaft growing harder with every stroke.

"Not too fast," Ace warned, swiping his thumb across the crown when their fingers reached the tip again. "You time it just right, maybe you can come all over those gorgeous tits."

Cruz groaned, his hand squeezing tight for the span of a heartbeat. "Fuck."

"You like that, do you, brother?" Maybe his dirty words worked on Cruz after all. "She'd still be an angel, you know. Even with come all over her face and her lips swollen from sucking you off, she'd be my sweet angel. Everything they told you in Eden was bullshit. Sex is messy, not dirty."

"Can't be both?" Cruz gritted his teeth, but his hips jerked whenever Ace moved his hand.

"Not until you're sure dirty's not bad."

He opened his eyes to watch Rachel as she rocked

and swayed on stage. "Nothing about her is bad," Cruz murmured. "Maybe nothing about you, either."

"Maybe," he agreed, a friendly lie because he couldn't give less of a shit about the truth right now. Cruz's cock was hard under his hand and Rachel was headed for a big finish, her lips parted, her breaths panting.

Teetering on the edge, because they were already playing the game, even without discussing the rules. "Tell her to come," he told Cruz, stilling his hand. "Watch what happens."

Tense. Hungry. But before he could open his mouth to form the command, Rachel tipped over the edge with a stifled shriek. She bucked and shivered, fucking her hand until the shudders faded and she collapsed to the polished wood.

Spent. Helpless. The roar of the audience smashed into Ace, shifting pleasure to spiky hot rage. He leaned forward to wrap his hand around the rope that controlled the curtain and jerked hard, swinging it into place and cutting Rachel off from the world.

The cheers shifted to disappointed shouts and one or two boos, and Ace didn't give a fuck. They'd go back to drinking soon enough, or Six would smack their heads into the stage until they learned manners.

Ace didn't give a fuck about that, either. The whole damn world could burn itself to the ground, as long as no one interrupted this moment. Rachel, sprawled naked and sated, her sleepy gaze following Ace's hand. Cruz, tense and hard, his rough breaths falling against the side of Ace's neck.

"Forget about coming on her," he said, speeding his strokes. "Come for her."

Cruz groaned and parted his lips. His tongue stroked over Ace's skin, a fraction of a second before his teeth closed in another bite. Pain slid over him in a fiery wave, but Ace didn't let it distract him.

The bite turned into rough suction, and Cruz held

on, moaning desperately as he stiffened. His cock throbbed, heavy and hot, and he came with a grunt that melted into a shuddering sigh as he spurted onto the floor.

Ace stilled his hand and watched as Rachel touched her hand to her trembling lips. She sat up, came to her knees, and crawled a half step toward them—

"Ace! Cruz!"

Jasper's voice, and it shattered the spell around them. Cruz jerked away, fumbling for his pants, and Ace wasted a precious moment hating his old friend.

Jasper rounded the corner backstage and drew up short when he caught sight of the three of them. "Rachel." He nodded, then turned his attention to Ace and Cruz. "We're rolling out. Mad found another still."

Cruz scrubbed his hands over his face. "Bootleg O'Kane liquor?"

"Looks like."

Ace had too damn much experience getting his dick under control, and it was still a struggle to shift gears. He *had* to shift gears, because if Mad hadn't just burned the place to the ground, it meant complications.

Complications meant danger. "Where is it?"

"Way the hell over in Three." Jas shoved his hands into his pockets and took a step back. "Meet us in the garage. Five minutes."

Jas vanished, and Ace blew out a rough breath and rubbed a hand over his face. "I guess the good life has a price. You okay, angel?"

She'd already reached for her robe. She slipped her arms into it and rose up to kiss him, soft and quick. Then she turned to Cruz and did the same. "Be careful. And I'll be here when you get back."

Cruz grabbed her hand. "Rachel—"

"It'll keep." She glanced back and forth between them. "I mean it. Watch yourselves out there. Come back to me."

The other man was still staring at her, conflicted and clearly reluctant to leave, so Ace caught him by the back of the shirt. "Come on, lover boy. Clear your head on the way to the garage. It's time to make war."

One look at the shack beside the half-collapsed factory, and Cruz knew this couldn't be the base of operations.

At first glance, it was just like the one he and Bren had stumbled across the first time—small, nondescript, hastily assembled. But those things had been a cover, a way to hide the real treasures within. This one didn't even have a sophisticated lock on the door, and he'd stake his life on the certainty that the interior would reflect that. Sparse and minimalist, the product picked up as soon as it was bottled, with only the necessary supplies on hand and no surplus.

They'd changed their game plan.

Resources were a precious commodity—when he'd seen their lack at the first location, he'd assumed that was all they had. But no one who had lost everything would have been able to set up a second location this quickly. And from the looks of things, instead of wasting time and money this time around, they'd accepted the inevitable.

It was brilliant, insane—temporary stills that popped up out of nowhere. Unprotected and totally disposable, like the men running them. Dallas could swat them down as fast as he wanted, and it wouldn't do a damn bit of good. One batch of passable swill in counterfeit O'Kane bottles could pay for the whole operation. Everything after that was a bonus.

Jasper kicked at a broken crate near the door. "Bets on whether it's outfitted the same as the last one?"

"No deal," Ace drawled, crouching to retrieve a crumpled piece of paper. He smoothed it out to reveal a label, too crooked to be useful, but otherwise a pretty close approximation of the legitimate design.

To Cruz, at least. Ace scowled, glaring down at it. "They could have at least gotten someone who could trace in straight lines. I'm fucking offended."

Bren returned from his recon around the building. "Truck out back. Either they parked it here, or there are men inside."

Jasper shook his head. "They wouldn't leave it unattended. Only question is how many bodies."

"Not enough." Mad was checking the sheaths on his wrists, a tight smile curving his lips. "The building's not big enough for a still *and* a dozen guys, and that's what it'd take. The five of us can handle it."

Jas nodded, satisfied. "Bren, you and Cruz take the back. Mad, Ace, and I will go knock on the front door and say hi."

Ace straightened, still looking murderous and distracted, and the first twinge of anxiety stirred in Cruz's chest. He'd started something they hadn't been able to finish, opened that door Ace had been pounding on forever.

God only knew what lay on the other side. The three of them in a tangle of sweaty, naked limbs, fucking in configurations Cruz was still ashamed to have dreamed up. Probably fucking in a few he *couldn't* have dreamed up.

On his own.

And now he was thinking about naked bodies when he needed his head on straight. Worse, he didn't like following Bren around the side of the building. Ace was out of sight—and Christ, it wasn't like the man was helpless. He'd been navigating more dangerous situations than this long before Cruz came along, keeping himself safe with his wits and a ruthless edge.

Bren took up position at the back door, and Cruz fell in next to him, forcing his focus to the task at hand.

"Where do these guys come down on the scales of O'Kane justice?"

"You mean, are we warning them or killing them?"

He remembered the last time, barging in on men who honestly thought they were working for O'Kanes, nearly getting his ass blown off. Killing them had been instinct, a survival response that had come too easily.

Not knowing whether or not he cared made trying to give a shit that much more important. "They could be dupes."

"Could be," Bren agreed. "Minimize the carnage at initial contact, and we'll follow Jas's lead. Good?"

Just follow orders. The easy way out, and he'd taken it for a hell of a lot longer than Bren had. The time was coming when he'd have to decide if he trusted Dallas O'Kane enough to just follow orders.

It was coming, maybe, but not here.

A crash sounded at the front, and the time for thinking was over. Bren burst through the door, gun raised, and Cruz had his back, like he had a hundred times before. They knew the rhythm of this. How to clear a room, how to divide and conquer.

Bren thundered down the short hallway and cleared the corner as the first shots echoed through the cavernous building. Cruz followed in time to see Jas and Mad take cover behind a stack of packed crates.

"It's O'Kane's men!" The harsh shout came from the metal catwalk crisscrossing the walls above them. "Take 'em out!"

So much for that question.

Cruz had always preferred close combat, hand-to-hand. There was something raw and satisfying about it, a primal thrill he'd never felt with a ranged weapon.

But sometimes a gun was the only smart move. Cruz's was in his hand without thought. Everything inside him was calm, sharply focused. His gaze found the first target—two men firing on Mad—and his finger was already squeezing the trigger before the thought had fully formed.

Two bullets. Two dead men. The rest of the guys hadn't even realized the enemy was coming at them from behind when Cruz lunged to the side, trying to get an angle on the men in the catwalk.

Instead he caught a glimpse of a man with a knife lunging toward Ace's unprotected back.

Clarity shattered. The steady beat of his pulse turned into a pounding roar, and the chaos of the room crashed in around him. Shouts and curses, shots and grunts, sounds of pain and men fighting and dying. His feet moved, carrying him forward, into the crossfire.

But Ace was already turning, gun in hand. He didn't even look worried as he squeezed off two rounds, both at close enough range to blow out the back of his attacker's head.

Stupid. *Stupid.* Ace knew how to handle himself in a fight. Cruz was the one fucking up, darting out from full cover in a fucking panic, not trusting his brothers to have shit under control. He checked his advance and lunged to the side—too late.

Fire bloomed across his ribs, a graze that could have been lethal if he'd been a fraction of a second slower. He made it behind another stack of boxes and pressed a hand to his shirt. It came away bloody, a silent recrimination.

He'd been fast enough this time. If he couldn't keep his shit together when the bullets started flying around Ace, next time might be a different damn story.

6

Rachel had never been the one at home, waiting out an O'Kane raid.

If she'd realized how difficult it would be, how worry could stretch the seconds into minutes and the minutes into hours, she would have found some way to occupy herself from the start, even if she had to manufacture a task. But it was only after her shower and two solid hours of sitting, perched nervously on the edge of her sofa, that she fled her room in search of distraction.

She went to the place she knew best—the bar.

Trix greeted her with a smile and an open bottle of beer. "You gonna help clean up?"

"Yeah, why not?" Rachel set aside the beer and grabbed a broom.

Zan, the regular bouncer, grinned over his shoulder as he lowered the solid wooden bar across the front door. "Chase Six around the room while you're at it. Girl's wound tighter than Dallas in a church."

"I won't be any help with that tonight."

Trix grinned as she turned chairs up onto the tables. "So it's true, then?"

"Is what true?" Six came out of the back room and hopped onto the bar before waving her middle finger in Zan's direction. "And I heard that, bastard."

He laughed, his usually gruff demeanor gone now that there were only O'Kanes in the room. "Ace and Cruz were backstage when Jas went looking for them. Backstage watching Rachel dance."

Trix abandoned the chairs and wrapped her arms around Rachel. "I'm not teasing," she promised. "I think it's perfect."

Perfect? Rachel barely knew what *it* was, and she sure as hell wasn't ready to talk about it. That moment backstage felt so fragile, as if the slightest wrong move could dissolve it all like smoke. "It's not..." Words failed her, and she tried again. "I mean, I don't—"

"Message received." Trix gave her one last squeeze and backed off. "I get it."

Zan leaned against the bar and wrapped a huge hand around Six's ankle, stilling the anxious bounce of her foot. "Don't even think it, girl."

Guilt flashed through the brunette's eyes, then vanished with her scowl. "I don't know what you're talking about."

"Sure. You're not sitting there wondering if you can give us the slip and trot over to Three to back up your boyfriend. And you can't. Hell, unless there's a fucking army there, Cruz, Bren, and Mad together are already overkill."

True words, reassuring ones, and Rachel clung to them, even as she spoke without meaning to. "Back in Eden, on nights like this, my mother always made sure there was something going on. A big project to keep all my aunts and cousins busy. I never wanted to be there, canning vegetables or making wedding quilts. I wanted to be out there, too."

Six's other foot stilled on its own as she studied Rachel. "Your family brewed beer, right?"

"They still do." Rachel dragged the broom idly across the floor. "Monday night collection runs, Wednesday night deliveries. Those two are the dangerous ones."

"Because it's illegal?" Six twisted to lean behind the bar and surfaced with a bottle of rum. "I still think that's crazy. Eden has slums. And *crime*. Aren't they supposed to be shiny and perfect?"

Eden had a lot of things it professed to condemn. Men were men, whether they lived in the city or the sectors or out in the goddamn wilderness. They had desires, and forbidding those desires didn't diminish them. It just turned them into vice.

There was good money to be made in catering to those vices—liquor and women, chief among them. Rachel's father had been content to let sector leaders supply what he considered the harder markets. He'd only allied himself with Dallas because his own products, the beer and other malts, sold to the same customers, and it made sense to work together.

Beer. Against her mother's wishes, Rachel had been making it since she was ten years old. In the grand scheme of things, it seemed so *harmless*, and yet Six's words held truth. It was against the law, and that made it dangerous.

She shook herself and set aside the useless broom. "That's how I wound up here," she told Six. "Special Tasks busted a joint shipment—Riley brew and O'Kane liquor. My father couldn't risk admitting to the partnership, because our whole damn family would have been exiled."

"Hypocrites," Zan grumbled, folding his beefy arms over his chest. "Like those stiffs in Eden thought you were the damn ringleader. They just wanted to hit your dad hard enough to scare him into line, but not so hard he stopped making all that beer they pretend to hate."

"Pretty much. Not that it matters." Only a fool would overlook how lucky she'd been. "I never fit in there, anyway. I'm happier here."

"Who wouldn't be?" Six asked, passing the rum to Zan. "Eden's like living in jail, and all the other Sectors are pits. Except One, I guess. Don't meet many people who ran away from One."

"Just Mad," Zan said, his rough face twisted into a thoughtful look. "Not that it matters to the people who live there. People in One stop him on the street and ask him to bless their fucking babies and shit."

"To them, he's royalty," Rachel mused. "Here, he can just be—"

"Mad." Trix rose as he walked in through the door behind the stage, Bren at his heels. "How did it go?"

"About as expected." Mad slapped Bren on the shoulder and propelled him toward the bar—and Six. "We're all in one piece, more or less. Jas has a split lip and a few bruises for Noelle to fuss over, and Cruz got winged, but he just needed some med-gel to be good as new."

"Winged?" With Cruz, it could mean anything from a flesh wound to a fucking amputation. "He got *shot*?"

Mad winced. "A graze, sweetheart. Barely shot at all."

The sudden burst of adrenaline began to subside, leaving Rachel's hands shaking. "Right. Barely."

"He'll be just fine," Mad assured her. "Ace was looking for you. I think they're in Cruz's room."

"Thanks." She paused long enough to peer down at a nasty scrape on Mad's hand. "Get Trix to look after that, okay?"

He kissed the top of Rachel's head with a rumbling laugh. "Go make yourself feel better."

She couldn't settle down until she'd checked Cruz out

herself, until she saw his injuries were really as minor as Mad claimed. That goal held her attention so completely that she was out the door, through the back, and hurrying past the garage before the import of the rest of Mad's words hit her.

Ace was looking for her. And they were in Cruz's room.

A fresh wave of nervousness assailed her. She'd given them an implicit promise, but she'd been too wrapped up in worry for their safety to really consider what would happen if—*when*—they took her up on it. And there was no time now to center herself. To think.

By the time she raised her hand to knock on Cruz's door, she was shaking again.

Ace dragged open the door and hauled her inside without so much as a greeting. "Thank God you're here. He was about to stomp over me to go find you, and I can't talk any sense into the bastard."

Cruz stood in the middle of the room, his T-shirt bloody and torn over a six-inch span on his side. He looked irritated more than anything, annoyed and frowning.

"Mad said..." But the words died on her tongue as she reached for him, pulling his shirt up his rib cage until she could see the already-healed skin beneath. "Does anything hurt? Did you crack any ribs?"

"No." He caught both of her hands and glared at Ace over her shoulder. "He wasted time slapping med-gel all over me."

"That doesn't sound like a waste to me," she argued.

"We get it, brother. You're tough." Ace's voice came from just behind her, only a moment before his hands slid around her waist. "I'm sure she's impressed."

She turned to face him. He seemed unscathed, though a little disheveled and a lot exasperated. "Are you all right?"

"I'm fine, angel." He smiled and tugged at her hips,

forcing her to rock against him. "Unlike *some* people, I don't charge armed men. I shoot them in the face, like God intended."

Cruz made a choked noise of amusement, so Rachel tilted her head back against his chest. "It's not funny," she whispered. "If Mad hadn't told me you were fine and that Ace was with you..."

His smile was different than Ace's. Quieter. Rarer. He cupped a hand under her chin, his thumb sliding up the side of her jaw. "I'll always come back to you. And I'll always bring him with me."

Always. The word soothed her nerves, but with the two of them standing so close, another kind of tension twisted up to take its place, delicious and hot. Low in her belly for now, but ready to unfurl at the slightest touch.

With Cruz's fingers still on her face, she raised her head. Her gaze locked with Ace's, and he edged a thumb under her shirt to stroke her skin. "I was horny as hell *before* I got pumped full of adrenaline, so someone else better make some decisions here. I can't think past your mouth and all the things I want to do to it."

"Decisions?" They both had their hands on her now. Rachel's mind stumbled over that fact, only to circle around and hit it again. They were *touching her*. It wasn't an accident, and they weren't going to stop.

Cruz lowered his mouth to Rachel's ear. "Only one decision. We owe Ace an orgasm. Do you want to be the one to give it to him?"

Until Cruz had come into her life, she'd wanted nothing else, so it only made sense that he was behind her now, offering her the chance to savor the hot desire sparking in Ace's eyes.

She answered by lowering her hands to his belt and holding on to the warm leather as she sank to her knees.

"Wait." Ace folded his fingers over hers, trapping them against the leather. "Just...let me savor this sight. You're a vision."

Two years of waiting. One more minute was torture, so she flexed her hands beneath his. "Please."

His eyes darkened as he released her and stripped his shirt over his head, letting it fall away. "Who could resist you on your knees, begging to suck him off?"

He was beautiful, leanly muscled and covered with ink. She worked his belt buckle as Cruz knelt behind her, so close his body was half-wrapped around hers. Between his heat at her back and the anticipation of the moment, her fingers fumbled, and she jerked at Ace's pants with a hiss. The zipper slid down, and she looked up at him as she eased down his jeans and the cotton beneath to free his cock.

She'd seen him like this before—you couldn't be an O'Kane and not know what everyone looked like, naked and aroused—but never hot and hard and waiting for *her*. She wrapped her hand around him and shivered when he bit off a sharp moan.

Cruz leaned in until his breath tickled her temple. "Let go, just for a second." Warm fingers slipped under the edge of her shirt, stroking her bare skin. "No shirts in my room. It's my new rule."

She lifted her arms. "Is that for your benefit or mine?"

He didn't answer until her tank top had joined the growing pile of discarded clothing. Gripping her wrists, he guided both of her hands to the small of her back, where her fingers brushed the hard planes of his abdomen. "Wrap your hands around my belt. Don't move them."

Ace's breath hitched, and he fixed a blistering look above her head. Enraptured, she watched him stare at Cruz as she obeyed the harsh command.

Cruz stroked her arms, following them up to her shoulders. "So obedient. Did you know she'd be like this?"

"I knew she'd be perfect." Ace cupped her chin and pressed his thumb to her lips. "How much of my cock can you take without choking, angel?"

Another prickle of heat washed over her, tightening her nipples until they ached. "I don't know." The whispered confession moved her lips under his thumb like a kiss, so she opened her mouth wider and licked him.

Cruz reached past her to grip the base of Ace's shaft, dragging another of those hissed breaths from Ace. "Let's find out," Cruz murmured against her ear.

Rachel leaned in. The tip of Ace's cock glistened with the evidence of his intense arousal, and she caught a tiny drop with her tongue before teasing him with a soft kiss.

"Christ." Shuddering, he sank both hands into her hair, twisting the strands around his fingers. "Lick me. I want to see that tongue again. I want it all over me."

Intoxicated by his words as much as his taste, Rachel gave in. She started at Cruz's hand and drew her tongue up Ace's shaft, a slow glide that ended with a gentle flick at the underside of his crown. His fingers tightened as his breathing hitched again, and his gaze followed her tongue as if he'd never seen anything half so riveting.

This was pleasure. This was *power*, bringing Ace to his knees while she was on hers.

"He's had enough teasing," Cruz said, and something in his voice had changed since the last time she'd been with him. He'd always been strong, but there was an edge of command now, the kind of steely dominance Dallas wore with ease.

Cruz expected to be obeyed—by both of them. And judging from the hot look in Ace's eyes, he had no problem with it, especially when Cruz lowered his mouth to her ear. "Open your mouth for him, Rachel. He's dying to see your mouth around him."

She whimpered, too desperately turned on to be nervous. She licked her lips, parted them, and strained forward.

Ace held her head with his grip in her hair. "Look at me."

The way he stared down at her was more painfully intimate than her tongue on his flesh. Rachel shuddered, and he rocked forward, pushing the head of his cock between her lips with a groan.

Yes.

Cruz lifted his free hand to cup her breast, toying with her nipple. The sparks of sensation echoed through her to center on her clit, and she squirmed against him as she took Ace deeper, gliding her tongue along his shaft.

“Faster,” Cruz rasped, his hand moving ever-so-slightly, in time with her mouth. “See, sweetheart? He’s already shaking, because you feel so good.”

“Sweet and hot and perfect...” Ace tugged at her hair, bringing her head forward until her lips brushed Cruz’s hand. “You’d take it all if you could, wouldn’t you?”

She whimpered again before drawing back, and her cheeks heated as she confessed, “But I can’t.”

“He’ll teach you.” Cruz guided her mouth back to Ace’s cock, then tugged at her jeans, popping open the buttons until the denim was loose enough for him to slide his hand inside, under her panties.

She jerked at the first graze of his fingertip over her clit, and the flames roared up as Ace muffled her moan with a slow thrust.

Cruz was touching her, touching Ace, but connecting them in ways that went beyond mere contact. Separately, the two men drove her crazy, twisted her into knots of longing and thwarted desire. But together—

Together, they’d give her everything.

“Fucking hell, Rae.” Ace guided her head, forced her to bob up and down. “I’ll teach you later. Tonight I just need you to suck.”

“Hard,” Cruz whispered, another of those commands she couldn’t help but obey. It made a dizzy sort of sense now, why the two of them had been fucking women together. Cruz was letting go of the last of his inhibitions, and Ace was teaching him, too.

It would have been so easy to believe this was one more lesson, that she was just another woman between them. But Cruz's hands held a fine tremor now, and Ace's face as she stared up at him—

Pure, naked *need.*

Ace shuddered, his fingers pressing tight to her scalp. "Is this what you want, angel? For me to come on your tongue?"

To answer, she'd have to stop—and she couldn't, not when he grew more rigid in her mouth with each passing heartbeat. Not when he'd gone so *rough,* from his breaths to his movements, his caresses to his words.

She sucked him harder, her cheeks hollowing out as she drew him in as far as she could before bumping into Cruz's hand. Suddenly, he pulled his hand away. Rachel pitched forward, then gagged as the head of Ace's cock hit the back of her throat.

"*Fuck.*" Ace jerked back, sliding free of her mouth. "Not like this, not the first time. I'm not coming on your tongue until you've come on mine. Cruz—"

Cruz slipped his hand free of her pants. "I want both of you in my bed. Naked."

She almost whimpered at the loss of his touch, then climbed to her feet and kicked off her shoes instead. Ace stripped even faster, his boots smacking against the wall as his socks followed.

By the time she'd wiggled her pants and underwear down her legs, he was naked except for the tattoos etched into his brown skin. So much ink—his O'Kane cuffs bleeding into colorful dragons and fanciful flames, and that giving way to the designs on his chest. A pair of guns. Flowers and vines. Five playing cards spread to show a royal flush, with the ace of hearts on top.

Words written in Spanish crawled up his left side, wrapping around an intricate skull, and she knew what they said because she'd gone digging to find the answer.

Strength in pride. Weakness in oblivion. Not the exact translation, Mad had said, but that was what it meant.

For the first time in what seemed like forever, she didn't have to look away. She was free to stare, so she did, her gaze roving over his body until he caught her face between his hands.

Then he kissed her, hard and deep, fusing his lips to hers like he'd been waiting ten thousand years to do it. A million. His body bumped hers, flesh against flesh, and he eased her backwards until her legs hit the edge of the bed.

He didn't stop kissing her. His mouth shifted to her lower lip. Her chin. He nipped the underside before licking and kissing his way down her throat, lingering on the hollow at its base as his hands swept up her sides.

She shuddered and slid her fingers into his hair. So illicit, tipping her head to meet Cruz's gaze as Ace kissed his way across her collarbone and teased his tongue over the curve of her breast.

Cruz smiled and wrapped a hand around his erection, drawing his fingers up in one lazy stroke. "He can't keep his mouth off you."

The same arousal that had lit his eyes in the warehouse was burning again. Her skin prickled with awareness, and her nipples hardened. A split second later, Ace circled one in a slow lick that fanned heat into fire.

She bit back a moan and closed her eyes, but that only brought the sounds into focus. The whisper of skin on skin. Ace's heavy breaths. The rasp of his tongue over her nipple and his groan when she pulled his hair in response.

She heard the rustle of sheets, the quiet groan of the mattress. Ace's mouth vanished a second before he gripped her shoulders, and he turned her to face the bed.

Cruz had gotten naked, too. He lay stretched out, miles of muscle and luscious skin just a shade lighter than Ace's. His ink was sparse but perfect, from his cuffs to the piece on his shoulder—dragons, like Ace's, but done in black and gray instead of color and winding down toward his elbow. The utmost care had been taken with each and every intricate line, a mark not only of skill but of attention.

"You've always wanted him," she whispered.

Ace gathered her hair off her neck and kissed his way to her ear. "Michelangelo couldn't have built him finer."

No, and he was *theirs*.

His eyes had always been expressive, but now they were something else entirely, commanding her without a word to come closer. Close enough to touch.

Rachel slid to her hands and knees on the end of the mattress. Ace released her hair only to run his hands down her spine and over her hips, and he groaned before slapping her ass teasingly. "Get over there, sweet girl, before I do something about how good this view is."

Cruz held out a hand. She crawled over to kiss his wrist, following the strong line of his inner arm to his elbow before sinking to the bed next to him. "Tell me," she urged softly. "All those things you were thinking backstage earlier."

The bed dipped as Ace knelt behind her, but Cruz held her captivated as he traced his fingers over the curve of her breast. So gentle, but the shock of it had her trembling long before he circled the tight tip. "I was trying to decide where I'd touch you first."

"Where did you—?" Ace's nimble fingers skipped down her spine again, cutting off the question along with her breath.

Cruz closed a finger and thumb on her nipple, pinching just hard enough to arch her back. "I don't have to decide. Because he'll touch you anywhere I tell him to. Won't you, Ace?"

"Mmm." Ace squeezed her hip. "Especially if you

promise to use all the dirty words."

Every single syllable shivered through her like a filthy, secret caress. "Please."

Cruz caught her chin and leaned so close that all she could see was *him*, his intense expression and his dark eyes and the tiny spattering of silver hair mixed in with his beard. "Work your fingers into her pussy. Slow and easy, one at a time, until she can't take any more. And then you can suck her clit until she comes on your face."

Anticipation pulsed between her thighs. Every coherent thought drained out of her head, and she stared at him as Ace slid his hand across her trembling abdomen.

They moved together. Not smooth or practiced, not like this was something they'd done before. Ace pulled too soon, urging her to roll to her back before Cruz released her chin, but it didn't ruin the moment.

It made it hers.

Cruz loomed over her, propped up on one elbow with the other hand cupping her cheek. And then he was kissing her, lips warm and a little rough, delicious as sin but still not enough to distract her when Ace's fingers slicked between her legs.

She parted her thighs without thought, opening for him the moment one fingertip grazed her clit. It ricocheted through her like a shot, rocking her so hard that she was still shaking when he stroked her again, more firmly this time. She arched her hips, and he slid deeper, thrusting one finger inside her.

He groaned against her stomach and pumped his finger, working it deep. "Christ, you're so damn tight. But you can take it, can't you?"

Cruz moved his mouth to her throat, and she dragged in a ragged breath. "Anything you'll give me."

"I know." His finger slipped away, returning as two. He worked them into her, rocking bit by bit as her muscles stretched, and his low, dirty laughter tickled across her abdomen. "But I've had Cruz's cock in my mouth. I know how big it is."

"So do I." They weren't the only ones who had filthy words. "The one time I almost got him out of his pants, I had to use both hands to jerk him off."

It was Cruz's turn to groan, and Ace bit her hip with a hum of approval before curling his fingers inside her. She jolted up at the caress, only to have Cruz press her gently back to the bed. He held her there, watching silently.

It was too much exposure, falling apart at Ace's touch while Cruz held her gaze, but she couldn't look away. Not even when Ace increased his pace, plunging his fingers in and out as filthy encouragement tumbled from his lips. "That's it, angel. Squeeze that sweet pussy all hot and tight around me. Show me you can take one more."

All bravado aside, she couldn't—and yet she knew she would. Nothing about being trapped between the two of them was safe, easy, but it was the only place she dreamed of being. She clenched around Ace's fingers and moaned when it heightened the sensation, contact so close and distinct she could feel his fingertips glide across her G-spot, bringing her hips off the bed.

"Easy, sweetheart. Slow and easy." Cruz spread his fingers across her belly as he pushed her back down. His leg hooked over hers, urging it wide, holding her open. "Ace..."

"On it."

She didn't have time to wonder what *it* was. The bed dipped as Ace shifted positions, pushing her other leg even farther before settling his shoulders between her thighs. "Look at me, Rae."

She tried to answer, but all that came out was a whimper that sounded like his name, far away and trembling. Lifting her head required too much coordination with her limbs trembling, but Cruz did it for her, sliding his other arm behind her neck so that he was cradling her, holding her in place, pinned, unable to look away—

Ace met her gaze across the bare expanse of her body, and she could have fallen into his eyes. They were always dark, but now they were glazed with arousal, the black of his pupils threatening to swallow the brown irises. He moved slowly, stroking his thumbs over her pussy lips before using the pads to spread her wide.

"I've been waiting forever for this," he whispered, his mouth so close she felt every word as a puff of air over her too-sensitive clit.

Her hips jerked again, and this time the scratch of stubble over her inner thigh shuddered through her. She was still stumbling over the sensation, struggling to make sense of how such a tiny thing could shake her so thoroughly, when he lowered his mouth and his tongue touched her.

Slow at first, just the wet tug as he teased his tongue all the way up to just shy of her clit before retreating. She tried to chase his mouth, and he did it again, slower, taking his time to explore, to *torment*.

Cruz rubbed his fingers in soothing circles across her abdomen without lifting the unyielding pressure of his palm holding her in place. "I could watch him lick your pussy all night."

And he would. The words were a promise that, at some point, he would hold her just like this—captive to the sinuous lash of Ace's tongue, not letting go until she screamed. Tense anticipation curled even more tightly inside her, not only at the prospect of such unrelenting pleasure, but at the thought that Cruz wanted it so badly.

"But not tonight," she murmured, sliding her hands into his hair.

"Not tonight," he agreed. "Tonight, we're both going to be in you."

A pulse of pleasure flashed through her, jagged and bright, rebounding when Ace closed his mouth around her clit and sucked. She cried out, and he groaned his approval and worked his fingers back into her.

Three fingers.

She couldn't stay still, even with the firm, commanding pressure of Cruz's hand on her belly. She thrashed, and he shifted over her, pressing her into the bed under the weight of his body. Being pinned down sparked an even more primitive response, a satisfaction that crashed into arousal and sent her into a free fall of pleasure.

She came with a louder cry, a scream that spurred Ace to rock his fingers deeper. So wide, stretching her until the first lick of pain sizzled through her release, turning it hot and heavy. "Good girl. Good, sweet girl, taking everything we give you."

"Please." It was all she could do not to sob. "*Please.*"

But Ace's fingers didn't relent, and then the large hand on her abdomen shifted down until the calloused tips of Cruz's broad fingers rasped over her clit.

Blood roared in her ears, her pulse galloping like the trains that used to run beneath the city. Their passing would shake the lamps and rattle the silverware, vibrate up through the floor to tickle her feet. This wave built inside her, its force spinning tighter and higher until the pressure exploded, shattering her in one perfect moment of bliss.

It lingered, hazy and warm, until their kisses cleared it—Cruz's on her shoulder and Ace's on her forehead—two sets of warm lips dropping lazy caresses over her skin.

She reached out as Ace's mouth descended on hers, winding one arm around his neck. Cruz slid closer, his hot skin flush against her side, and she twined her fingers with his, as well. Anchored by the two of them, just like before, but in a quieter, gentler way.

He rested their joined hands on Ace's side. "Don't be

so greedy, Ace."

Ace bit Rachel's lower lip. "Who wouldn't be? She's perfect."

"Hungry," she countered, rubbing her bare legs against his. It made no sense. She should have been exhausted, spent, but she craved her next taste of him already.

Of *both* of them.

She tilted her face to Cruz's and nuzzled his jaw, drawing a growl before he found her mouth. His kiss was different—deeper, more demanding. He groaned against her lips as he reached down to curl his hand around the back of her thigh.

One tug and she was facing him, her leg draped over his. "You've been waiting for Ace for a long time, haven't you, sweetheart?"

Her answer didn't matter, because they all knew the truth. She felt it in the way Cruz watched her—and in the way Ace's breathing quickened as he positioned his cock. No more teasing, no hesitation, just the broad head pressing into her as Cruz held her open for him.

As wet and ready as she was, it still hurt a little, just enough of a stretch to awaken nerve endings that tingled in anticipation of more. "Oh, God."

"I know, angel." Ace withdrew a couple of inches before thrusting forward, driving deeper with a choked snarl. "*Christ*, you're still so fucking tight."

The edge of pain faded under a sudden throb of pleasure so sharp it stole her breath. She reached for Cruz to steady herself, bracing her hands on his chest, but that didn't keep her hips from grinding against his when Ace thrust again.

For a moment they were frozen there, tangled together, panting, Ace so deep it curled her toes and Cruz's thick shaft a tormenting pressure against her clit.

Cruz hissed, sliding his hand to grip her ass, holding her there with no escape. "Fuck her just like this," he rumbled, low and rough, clearly expecting Ace to obey.

And he did, driving her against Cruz's erection over and over, until the man's shaft was slick, and every hard rock turned into a glide that sizzled through her. Ace turned her face with a rough hand on her chin and caught her gaze.

"Watch me." He rocked harder, and they all moaned as the movement ground her hips against Cruz's. "I need to see this. You. Coming around my cock. *Finally.*"

"Ace." Her voice was so damn dizzy. "I need you."

"You have me, angel." His face was so close, but he didn't cover the distance and kiss her. He watched her as if she was the only thing he wanted to see, the only thing he could ever need. "You'll always have me."

The tension swirling through her wound tighter, and she curled her fingers, digging her nails into Cruz's skin. It would be so easy to believe Ace's words—with that look in his eyes, that intensity, how could she doubt him?

No, there was nothing false between them right now, no lies and no hiding. She drew in a shaky breath and released it with a near-sob. Her limbs were trembling, every nerve ending in her body on a collision course with orgasm—and she couldn't look away from those eyes.

Not until he used the hand on her chin to turn her face again, and Cruz was watching her, too, the affection he'd always given her so easily tinged with a darker edge, one echoed by the bite of his fingers digging into her skin. "You've got both of us," Ace rasped in her ear. "No holding back."

No, none, not even if she wanted to. The tension shattered, and Rachel bucked between them. Every movement swept away all sensation, replaced it with something hotter, sweeter, until she was sure she'd die if it got any better.

And then it did.

Ace groaned and dropped his hand to her shoulder, pinning her upper body to his chest. He slammed into her again and again, rough and fast and out of control until he came with a hoarse snarl.

Ace had always talked about how good he was, teasing jokes that turned out to be nothing but the truth. As he moved, she tried to ask him if he was ever wrong about *anything*, but all that came out was a broken plea, one that Cruz answered by rolling her over and pulling her up to her knees.

He stroked a soothing hand up her spine, urging her to relax her upper body on the blankets. "You still with us, sweetheart?"

She turned her cheek to the bed and grasped the covers in her fists. "No."

Ace's hand joined Cruz's on her back, warm and strong but different, and not just because every inch of her skin was hypersensitive. Cruz's fingers were broad and rough—both in texture and the way he touched her, hands shaking, fingertips digging in too hard. He was anxious and needy, still too hungry for the lazy path Ace traced along her side and across her belly.

But he didn't stray lower. He lingered there, circling her belly button over and over as anticipation drew tight within her again. "Tell him to let go," Ace whispered. "You're the only one who can."

The idea of Cruz surrendering his self-control, even for a heartbeat, was unfathomable. But the *possibilities*, holy shit. Her elbows gave way, and her upper body sank fully to the bed. "Cruz?"

"Ace sent you flying. I want you back on the ground before I fuck you the first time." He rocked his hips, and the tip of his dick slicked between her folds, tauntingly close and not nearly enough. "I want you to feel how empty you are before I fill you. I want..."

The words trailed off, and she shivered. "Tell me."

He did, low and harsh, as if he hated himself for admitting it. "I want to fuck you so hard you feel me for days."

Another wave of lust tempered by tenderness washed through her, and she looked back at him. "Then do it. Don't let me forget."

And maybe that permission was all he needed, because he took his cock in hand and guided himself into her. He was *big*, so wide he only made it a couple of maddening inches before stilling with a groan. "Fuck."

Again, the pain seethed with an irresistible promise of mind-blowing pleasure. "Don't stop." Rachel bit her lower lip, but a whimper escaped.

Ace smiled and cupped her cheek, freeing her lower lip from the sting of her teeth with his thumb. "You want it, don't you, angel? That beautiful damn cock. I know it's big, but you can take it, can't you?"

"Y-yes—" Rachel panted. Then Cruz pushed deeper, and her answer melted into a moan.

"That's it," Ace soothed, his voice low and warm. His words spun around her as Cruz worked into her body, both of them forcing her to feel everything. "Next time we'll suck him off together, and I'll show you how to take him all the way. I love a good face-fucking, but that bastard'll blow in five seconds if you get on your knees and part these pretty lips for him."

The mental picture may as well have been *contact*, a lick or a pet that had her clenching in response. She opened her mouth but lost whatever she was going to say when Cruz growled and surged forward, dragging her hips back at the same time to turn a short thrust into all-out warfare against her senses.

It was possession, no less than Ace's hand in her hair or his demanding words, and it tore away the last of her protective walls. Cruz claimed her, branded her inside and out, not only with his body invading hers, but with the fine tremor in his hands. The rough rasp of his breath. The way he clutched her closer, grinding against her.

How was she supposed to survive this?

As if he'd heard the thought, Cruz growled again, hauling her hips up so his next thrust went even deeper. "Your fingers," he snapped at Ace. "Let her lick them."

Ace lifted two fingers to her mouth. She parted her lips and drew her tongue over his fingertips, gratified to see her own lightheaded astonishment reflected in Ace's captivated expression. He kept poking at Cruz, demanding the man unleash his darkest desires, and he couldn't handle them any more than she could.

Nothing had prepared them for what they'd get when Cruz let go.

Cruz freed one hand from her hip and ran it up her back to curl in her hair, and she was shivering even before he tightened his grip and pulled her head back. "Now rub her clit, and don't stop until I do, I don't care how many times she comes."

Sucking in a breath, Ace reached beneath her. The wet tip of his middle finger slid between her pussy lips and circled her clit as Cruz thrust into her again, harder than before, hard enough to drive her several inches across the bed, and somehow, Ace knew to follow.

She wrapped her fingers around Ace's forearm, relishing the play of muscle as he worked her. The now-familiar heat flared to life, and Rachel threw back her head with a cry that turned into words. She was trapped between them again, only this time she didn't fight it, she embraced it.

She *begged.*

And they gave her everything she asked for. More, deeper, harder, and when Cruz's cock bumped across her G-spot and drove a cry from her lips, he answered her plea—*right there*—and fucked over the spot again and again, rough and relentless and growling encouragement as Ace's fingers stroked and teased.

She came with another scream. It didn't stop, one shudder after another, until she was hoarse from crying out, but Cruz didn't follow her over the edge. He pumped his hips in shallow strokes while she shivered and panted for breath, and just when she thought she'd found purchase on the world, he shattered her reality with a deep thrust—the hardest yet—and the startling, *terrifying* truth crashed into her.

This wild ride, all the passion and hunger, and he was still holding back.

"*Fuck!*" Her free hand clenched in the bedspread, then slipped, ripping the fabric.

He hauled her back into his next thrust with a grunt. The sound wasn't enough to drown out the slap of skin against skin, their bodies colliding in every way possible as Ace pressed his forehead to hers. His fingers were still moving, faster now, three of them working her clit as he groaned. "Now he's just showing off, isn't he? Does it feel as good as it looks?"

Answering meant words, and words meant thinking. Rachel couldn't think, couldn't *breathe*. Everything felt tight, hot, like she didn't fit in her own skin anymore. Like she was dying, and she never, ever wanted it to stop.

Then Cruz reached down and pressed Ace's fingers hard against her clit. The slippery friction vanished, replaced by a low, deep throb that shattered through her in prickles of light and heat.

The world was on fire, and so was she.

She shuddered, screamed, clutched at every bit of both of them she could reach, until a tortured noise rolled out of Cruz. He rode out his final jerky thrusts before collapsing, one hand braced above her head to keep the bulk of his weight off her. "Holy *hell*."

Every shift in position rubbed against nerve endings that were already overloaded. Rachel whimpered and wiggled onto her side, wrapping one arm around his. He settled behind her with a sigh, leaving them in a sprawl of tangled limbs and sweat-slicked skin, with her at the heart of it.

Her breathing began to slow, but Ace was still panting. She opened her eyes and allowed herself the luxury of a long, lazy appraisal of his bare skin—damp hair, broad chest, the muscled planes of his stomach—

And his prominent erection.

"You're fucking kidding me." Christ, with all the screaming, she sounded like she'd smoked two dozen cigarettes and downed a fifth of rough moonshine. "Again?"

Cruz's chest rumbled against her back as his laughter tickled her neck. "Christ, Santana. You horny bastard."

Ace grinned. "What, was I supposed to yawn while you fucked her cross-eyed and made her come all over my fingers?"

This was what elation felt like, warm and light, like it could carry her right off the bed—*if* she ever wanted to leave it. "Horny bastard's right." She snuggled closer and licked a line of ink running between Ace's collarbone and his nipple. "Or dirty bitch. No—filthy motherfucker."

"Talking like that's not going to make me any less hard," Ace murmured, lifting a hand to weave lightly through her hair. "Neither's licking me."

Cruz leaned over, and Rachel heard the drawer on his bedside table slide open. "Oh, I don't know," she drawled, buying him some time. "What if I bit you instead?"

"You angling to mark me, angel?"

"It'd be fair," Cruz replied, tossing a bottle to the bed. Oil slicked his palm, and he curled his fingers around Ace's shaft. "You've marked both of us."

"Fucking hell, man." Ace tilted his head back and arched, thrusting against Cruz's hand. "Fuck."

Witnessing this sort of unbridled sexuality could be addictive. Riveted, Rachel stared at him before leaning in to graze his nipple with her teeth. Then she stretched up, put her mouth right beside his ear, and sighed. "Is it this sexy, watching me get off?"

Ace parted his lips, but a groan spilled out as Cruz sped his strokes and answered for him. "Every damn time."

Her body was too spent to ignite into arousal again, but that didn't stop her heart from pounding or her hands from shaking as she clenched her fingers in Ace's hair and pulled. "I like it."

"Of course you do," he choked out, clutching at the back of her head. "My dick's fucking mesmerizing."

"No lie." Hard and thick, jerking in Cruz's hand. Rachel reached down to help, marveling at the contrast of hot and even hotter skin, slick and unyielding. "Come on me. I want you to."

And he did, spilling across their fingers with a moan, the only sound until Cruz shifted their fingers to rest on Ace's trembling abdomen. "Too bad we won't all fit in my tub."

"We will if we stand up." Giddy, Rachel laughed. "If we *can* stand up."

"Fuck it," Ace groaned. "Kick the blankets onto the floor and we'll sleep under the sheets. My mesmerizing dick and fine-as-fuck ass aren't moving."

"Until the next time you get excited?"

Ace rolled over, trapping her against Cruz's chest. "Bite your tongue, woman. I earned at least an hour of sleep."

Cruz wrapped an arm around both of them, and Rachel's heart skipped a beat. Together, the three of them filled the bed, with no room between them for things like doubt, no time to second-guess what had happened. Maybe that would come later, when the afterglow had faded and sense returned.

Or maybe, just maybe, they fit together so perfectly there would never be room for regret between them at all.

scarlet

IF ONLY THE bastard wasn't so damn hot.

Scarlet brooded into her fourth drink—vodka, neat—and watched Jade smile up at Dylan Jordan. What she had to smile about was anyone's guess, not to mention a mystery. Every time Scarlet herself had spoken to the man everyone called Doc, she'd come away irritable. Hot under the collar, in more ways than one.

Doctor. Back in Sector Three, there was no such thing, not really. People assumed the title, of course. Some were even good at healing, provided they'd apprenticed with someone skilled in folk medicine. Other, more affluent sectors had real doctors, older men and women who'd trained for years in the formal schools that had existed before the Flare.

And then there was Eden. Rumor had it Dylan Jordan had learned his trade in one of the city's state-of-the-art facilities. Exiled since then, no doubt, but that didn't change facts. He wasn't some back-alley job with a bag full of drugs smuggled out of Sector Five. He was the real deal.

And a real asshole. Scarlet's stomach flipped over as Jade leaned closer to him, her smile widening. Whatever knowledge and skills Doc possessed were practically buried beneath a drug-fueled haze. He spent half his time high and the other half doing suicidal shit that would get him killed sooner rather than later.

Scarlet would be damned if she let him take Jade with him when he went down.

A drink thudded next to hers, liquor sloshing over the edge of the glass as Adrian Maddox leaned against the bar beside her. "When did that start?" he asked, jerking his head toward Jade and Doc. "He never sticks around to unwind after a visit."

Scarlet shrugged. "Beats the shit out of me."

Mad considered the pair for a few moments before shaking his head. "It's not going to happen. I don't care how pretty Jade's smiles are. Doc's not going to start smiling back."

He sounded almost jealous—though of which one, Scarlet couldn't begin to guess. She nudged Mad with her hip and snorted. "You know better than to go there. Just like I do."

He exhaled sharply, and it almost sounded like the start of a laugh. "Yeah, that's you and me, Scarlet. Smart."

"Liar." Her gaze drifted back to the dance floor, where Doc had laid a hand on Jade's waist. "We're both stupid as hell."

Mad's gaze followed hers, and she felt the sudden tension roll through him. "Stupid," he agreed. "But never selfish. You just met him. You don't know how good he was, how good he could be again. I tried to make him see it, but..."

He sounded so damn *sad*, and the answering twinge

in Scarlet's chest pissed her off more. "The man's a fucking burnout, Maddox. Everyone knows it."

"Do they? Everyone *knows* you collect lovers, even though you're stone cold." He leaned closer, his voice dropping lower with every word. "Everyone *knows* you like the easily controlled, submissive ones. The ones you can play mind games with." He straightened abruptly. "And everyone in Sector One knows my grandfather performed miracles and I should bless their kids. *Everyone* knows shit."

Adrian Maddox on a defensive tear was a sight to behold, all clenched jaw and fiery, dark eyes. Scarlet smiled and fished a cigarette out of his pocket. "Stop trying to convince me your boyfriend is a prince and give me a light, would you?"

One thing was for sure, at least Mad could laugh at himself. He slid out his lighter, a nice, shiny silver one engraved with an intricate logo she didn't recognize. "I thought you knew, honey. I'm the prince."

"You're something close." Scarlet lit her cigarette and turned the lighter over between her fingers. "Are you gonna break up the party on the dance floor, or should I?"

Mad frowned and said nothing.

"It's okay to want to, you know. Whatever your reasons."

His frown deepened, and Scarlet knew what was coming. Anyone who'd known Mad more than five minutes would have. "If she can make him smile, I'm not about to get petty."

"Saint Adrian." Scarlet slipped her cigarette between his lips and raised both eyebrows. "Maybe you should go bless some babies, after all. Me? I think I'll go get laid."

She made it two steps before his laughter rolled over her, deep and warm, because Mad could be a stuffy martyr but he never took himself seriously for long. "Show me how it's done, Scarlet."

"Yes, sir."

Scarlet eased up behind Doc, running one finger up his back a heartbeat before dancing a hip-swinging circle around him to slide her arm around Jade.

Jade wasn't stingy with her smiles. She laughed and turned her head, and Scarlet got the full force of one as Jade leaned back into her. "Am I not dancing with enough enthusiasm?"

"You're doing fine, sweetheart. Doc's technique could use some work, though."

The man smiled, easy and blurred around the edges, a perfect match to his red eyes and flushed skin. "Scarlet likes to tease me," he said, his tone lending a lascivious double meaning to the word.

"I think she teases all of us." Jade eased closer. They were the same height, and the movement thrust her ass against Scarlet's hips. Gone was the fragile woman whose body had suffered through all the worst rigors of addiction. She was solid now, curves filling out more and more as the weeks passed.

Scarlet wanted to touch her, so she did, drawing one hand slowly up Jade's thigh. "Sometimes it's not a tease," she mused. "It's a promise."

Jade shivered under her fingers, turning her head just enough to whisper against Scarlet's cheek. "So which do you give him? The tease, or the promise?"

"Who, Doc?" Scarlet rolled her hips, urging Jade to move with her. "Nah, he's a special case. The tease doesn't work, and he's not interested in the promise." She looked up, her eyes locking with his. "Right?"

Tension had straightened his back, but that was the only sign anything she said affected him at all. His mouth curved into a lazy smile, and he shrugged. "You're not my type. No crime there."

It stung. Not his type...because she didn't need him to save her. Scarlet bit her tongue. The words wouldn't touch him, but they could cut Jade to the bone, and she'd be damned to hell before she did that.

Jade slid her hand over Scarlet's, twining their fingers together as their hips swayed in a slow, taunting mimicry of sex. "Maybe you haven't found the right promise," she murmured, turning them both in a lazy circle.

Mad was watching.

Only *watching* didn't cover it. He was fucking them with his eyes, his face shadowed with lust, and Scarlet's heart skipped a beat. The only thing keeping him from touching them was the space between them, and that could be gone in a few insistent strides.

She'd assumed Mad was carrying some kind of torch for Doc, but the truth hit her in a rush.

It was much, much more complicated.

7

THE SOUND OF water woke her.

Rachel stretched and bumped into Ace, who grumbled an incoherent protest and threw his leg over hers, pinning her in place. “No wiggling.”

“Grump.” She felt blindly at the empty expanse of bed behind her. “Cruz is in the shower?”

“Mmm.” He tossed an arm across her body, too, his skin warm against hers. “He probably has a meeting today.”

“Then shouldn’t we clear out?”

“Does that involve moving?”

“Probably.” Not that she was any more excited by the prospect than he sounded. So she rolled on top of him and kissed his chin. “Good morning.”

Ace didn’t open his eyes, but his lips curved up into a lazy smile. “Now this is the kind of wiggling I can get behind.”

"Or under?" One last wiggle, and she sat up. "The etiquette here is a little mystifying. Maybe we should talk about it."

He cracked one eye as his hands settled on her hips. "Funny thing, angel. Straddling a man's dick when he's half-awake doesn't really get him thinking deep thoughts about etiquette."

A flush of awareness prickled over her skin. She braced her hands on his chest and levered herself back until she was sitting on his thighs instead. "Better?"

He raised an eyebrow and peered down at his undeniable erection. The flush spread up her face, but before she could respond, he tightened his grip on her hips and hoisted her with an effort that made his arms flex enticingly. He dragged her up and dropped her to sit on his stomach. "There. You have my undivided attention."

Only now hers was shot to hell with his abs rippling beneath her. "Etiquette," she repeated blankly, then shook herself. "You're big on rules. Surely a situation like this has some."

"Probably," he agreed, rubbing his thumb over her hipbone. "If I'd ever been in a situation like this before, I'd tell you all about them."

The idea that this was different for him was intoxicating. "So we're all flying blind."

"Mmm. But we're doing it together."

And it was good, damn good. So good it felt like she must be missing something, overlooking a crucial piece of information that would make her second-guess it all. "It feels so right that it makes me wonder," she admitted. "Whether there's some drawback I'm not seeing because I don't *want* to."

"Well, I can think of one..." Ace chuckled softly and tugged on a lock of her hair. "After last night, we'll be lucky if that bossy bastard doesn't chain us both to his bed. Or maybe that's not a drawback."

She shivered as a thread of the now-familiar sexual

tension snaked through her, and she leaned over Ace, her mouth close to his ear. "I'm glad you want to be here just as much as I do."

His lips ghosted over her jaw, a teasing caress before a sharp bite that elicited a zip of pleasure. "Right now I want a whole lot of things."

"Like...to see if Cruz was right about us all fitting in his tub?"

Ace swatted her ass. "Bad girl. Don't tempt me to distract him from whatever serious fucking business he's headed out on."

The shower cut off, and Rachel grinned. "We could wait right here until he gets back."

"*Right* here? Have mercy and scoot up a few feet. Or down. Either direction works."

"For fuck's sake, Ace." Cruz stepped out of the bathroom, naked except for the towel he was using to dry his hair. Droplets of water rolled down his skin, playing peekaboo over ridges of muscle and through hair.

Rachel swallowed. Hard. "You heading out?"

"Yeah." He stopped next to the bed and cupped her cheek. "Wish like hell I didn't have to, but I've got a meeting with my contact in Eden."

The word around the compound was that Cruz's contact was high-level, someone who shouldn't have been talking to him at all, even before his exile from the city. The fact that he still had that source of information was invaluable—to Dallas, to the gang. Maybe to their lives.

But it was dangerous. She covered his hand with hers. "Take care of yourself."

He bent for a brief, warm kiss, then rose and tossed his towel across Ace's chest. "You two can be lazy in here for as long as you want, but don't let Ace ride you hard, or I won't let him touch you next time."

His tone was easy, but there was nothing casual about the words. They were as precise as Cruz himself, with layers of information you could spend all day peeling back. That he had accepted their relationship, that he intended it to continue. That he planned to control it, even when he wasn't physically present.

Ace's fingers tightened on her hips as he drew in a ragged breath and spun the game out. "Do you want me to ride you after he leaves, Rae?"

Her mouth went dry. So many possibilities, and she had to trust her instincts, her *desires*, because there weren't any rules here—except for the ones they made. "Maybe not," she whispered. "Unless you could do it soft and slow."

Cruz made a sympathetic noise as he hauled on his pants. "Are you sore, sweetheart?"

"A little." She turned and met his gaze over her shoulder. "I like it."

He smiled as he slipped his belt through its loops. "Then Ace keeps his dick out of you for the morning."

Ace's warm, aroused laughter tickled up her spine. "You see that spark in his eyes, Rachel? It took me forever to get him to admit that giving orders rocks his world."

"I see it." He'd probably never understand why getting them could be sexy, but all that mattered was that he accepted it. "Proper motivation, that's all. If we do what he says, he gets off. And so do we, right?"

"Mmm." Ace ran his fingers lightly up and down her thighs. "I might need more explicit orders though. We all know I'm an asshole with a short attention span. Maybe he should give me a list."

Cruz's glare broke as he dragged a tight black shirt over his head, covering all those beautiful muscles. "There's only one thing on it, and you were going to do it anyway." Cruz shrugged into a shoulder rig but left it unfastened as he crossed to sink a gentle hand into Rachel's hair. "Give her anything she needs."

It was permission, not for sex but for intimacy, the chance to get close to Ace in a way she craved, a way that was just as real as him being inside her. Rachel closed her eyes and leaned in to Cruz's touch. "Tonight?"

He nodded. "Why don't we meet at Ace's studio before the party?"

"Fine by me," Ace murmured, still stroking her legs. "We can make bets on how many people are making bets on whether we all show up together."

When an O'Kane hooked up with someone, word got around. With three of them? Gossip would be flying. "Do we care?" Rachel asked.

Cruz's fingers tightened a little. "I care. I want everyone to know."

A possessive touch, one that curled Rachel's toes. "Then we don't wait for them to talk. We tell them instead."

Ace showed his possession, too, but not with anything as simple as a rough hand in her hair. His fingers wrapped around one side of her throat, his thumb stretching across the front to rest over her pulse. "You know how O'Kanes make that announcement, angel."

The same way they did everything else—with ink. But before that came the collar, a mark that was a step below the permanence of a tattoo. "You like leather and chains, and Cruz is all about ribbons and silk. You'll figure it out."

Cruz released her hair to cover Ace's hand with his own. "This is what you want?"

"It was inevitable, right?" This was why their hesitation had been so awkward—they'd spent months dancing around each other because there was no going back once they crashed into one another.

"Maybe it was." He bent to kiss her again, slower this time, his lips warm and firm. But he lifted his head before she could deepen the kiss, smiling down at her as he shifted his grip to Ace's wrist. "Only sweetness for her this morning. We've got a big night to look forward to."

Anticipation joined the arousal swirling through her.

She laid her hand over Ace's and twined their fingers together as they watched Cruz check his knives and tuck his handgun into its holster. "I'll be back by noon for our run," he told Ace, giving them both a final smile before he slipped out.

The door clicked shut behind him, and Ace's easy smile faded a little. "Fuck, I wish he'd take some backup on these trips."

The gentle arousal twisted into concern. "You think he needs it?"

"It's Eden." Ace caught her hips and resettled her in his lap as he sat up. "Everyone needs someone watching their back in that snake pit."

She wrapped her arms around his neck and nuzzled his cheek. "You have to trust him. He'd know if it was too dangerous."

"Maybe," he murmured. "But sometimes I wonder if that bastard thinks anything's too dangerous. Maybe it's all those years of knowing Eden would put him back together."

"You could mention it to Dallas."

"Oh, he knows." Ace caressed her back, and the warmth returned to his voice. "Maybe Cruz'll be more careful now that he knows you're waiting for him to come home."

It wasn't the first time he'd downplayed his importance to Cruz. "What about you? You're here for him, too."

"Of course I am." In a pretty flex of muscle, Ace rose with her tangled around him. "Wanna go see how big his shower is?"

She ached at the carefully concealed pain in his voice. He was trying to distract her—and the moment felt so new, so delicate, that she let him. "Only if you remember the rules, Santana."

He chuckled against her temple. "I'll be a perfect gentleman. Just clit-sucking and jerking off, no funny business."

He was incorrigible. She muffled a laugh by dropping her face to his shoulder for a sharp bite. He hissed, tightening his arms, and hurried his steps.

The bathroom was as tidy and sparse as Cruz's bedroom. Shaving supplies lined the counter in a neat row in front of a stack of precisely folded towels and a few bars of unused soap, each an equal distance from the next.

Ace let Rachel slide to her feet in front of the mirror, which was still fogged over from Cruz's shower. "You bite me again, pretty girl, and I'll bite back. And then we'll both be in trouble tonight."

"We wouldn't want that." Ace's erection pressed against her hip as she reached past him to cut on the water, turning it hot enough to billow more steam up around them.

Groaning, he lifted her with an arm locked around her waist and swung her around. "In. Now. Unless you want me to bend you over the counter and see how deep I can fuck you with just my tongue."

"Uh-uh." She stepped onto the warm tile and let the water stream down over her hair and face before wiping it away. "Come here. I want to kiss you."

It turned out the shower wasn't so big after all. Ace seemed to take up all the space as he climbed in and pulled the door shut, trapping them in a world of hot mist and steam. Droplets splashed off her skin to land on his shoulder, and it was impossible not to follow their path as they sluiced down his inked flesh.

He slid his fingers into her hair, gathering the damp strands up high on the back of her head. "Too bad Cruz only has the unscented shampoo in here. I like the shit you usually use. The coconut."

He'd been as painfully aware of her as she had been of him. The knowledge made Rachel bold, and she skated one hand down over his stomach. "A lady on the other side of the sector makes it for me."

"Yeah?" His lips hovered over hers, so close she could taste them.

A little lower, and her fingers grazed his hipbone. "Yeah."

"Are you going for my cock, dirty girl?"

His approving tone sent shivers racing through her, even under the hot spray. "It's not against the rules."

He licked her lower lip, dragging his tongue from one corner of her mouth to the other. "Let's hope it never is."

"Mmm." She wrapped her hand around his shaft.

He groaned, his hips jerking, and she barely had time to shift her fingers before his mouth was on hers, open and firm and *starving*, his tongue coaxing her lips to part in time for her to swallow another rough growl.

Rachel pushed off the wall, sinking her teeth into his tongue as she rubbed one leg up along the outside of his, relishing the slick glide of wet skin. Ace was hard under her fingers, rocking into her touch as he embraced her.

He spun her in a dizzy circle, her hair flying everywhere before her back hit cooler tile. He braced his hands above her head and rested his forehead against hers. "Do you know how many times I've jerked off in the shower, imagining your hands on my dick?"

"No." She stroked her hand over his length, twisting lightly, and swallowed a moan when he thrust against her palm. "Tell me."

"Damn near every time." He closed his eyes. "When it wasn't your hands, it was your lips. And when it wasn't that, it was about getting inside you. And those were the quick fantasies."

Oh God. She watched him, rapt, as she slowed her movements, then stopped entirely and squeezed her fist tight around him. "Give me a not-so-quick one," she teased, "and I'll keep going."

"You sure you can handle it?" he rumbled, tilting his head back. "Because it starts with you in my tattoo chair. Strapped in."

The strong column of his throat beckoned, and she licked a rivulet of water from his skin. "You want to tie me up?"

"Fuck, yes. Though maybe I wouldn't have to. I bet Cruz would hold you down for me."

It flashed through her like fire, the thought of Cruz's steely hands locked around her wrists or ankles. She'd glimpsed that unyielding strength the night before, when he'd held her helplessly still while Ace pleasured her with his fingers and tongue.

Yes, he'd hold her down, hold her up. Hold her spread open to Ace's eager, questing mouth.

Ace tipped his head forward and grinned. "There's those big eyes. You like that, don't you, angel? Thinking about Cruz pinning you in place so I can play. But you've seen my shows. You know what comes next."

Pain—and more pleasure. "You think I wouldn't want that, too?"

"I know you would." He ducked his head and licked a few drops of water from the curve of her breast. "You're not like Noelle. She's flash-fire. You barely hurt her and she's coming all over you. Jas lets her flame out fast because that's the part he likes. The big finish. He doesn't need what I need."

"What do you need?" Rachel asked, though she already knew the answer. Control, the same as Cruz, with his careful strength and meticulously ordered life, only with a different focus—the precise, measured application of pain.

"The slow burn." He thrust against her hand again, fucking her fist. "Waiting for that moment, the one where you stop taking the pain for me and start wanting it for yourself. When you don't know if it hurts or not anymore, but you'll die if I stop."

Blood pounded in her ears. Her nerve endings sizzled. She pumped her fist and leaned closer. "Touch me?"

He worked a hand between them without moving,

his fingers sliding across her belly before grazing her clit. Soft, easy, so gentle that she instinctively rocked against him, seeking a more forceful caress.

But he held back, quieting her with a soothing noise. “Careful, Rae. So careful. Because Cruz will ask. He’ll demand every fucking detail, and I’ll tell him.”

She stayed still this time as he explored her slowly, his fingertips slicking through her folds, though she couldn’t suppress a whimper. “No secrets, right?”

“Not a damn one.” He whispered the words against her forehead as the very tip of his middle finger arrowed in, stroking with enough pressure to arch her back. “You’ll be ours. Just ours. And we’ll give you everything.”

She tilted her head back to meet his eyes. “Do you like it? Having him decide how you get to touch me?”

“You think that’s what he’s doing?” His touch shifted again, finger swooping low through her folds. “He’s not deciding how, angel, only how far. He won’t let me take too much, too fast.”

Too much of *her*. Rachel shuddered. “Do you want to?” she asked softly.

“Yes.” It tore free of him, a confession and a warning. “Christ, the things I would do to you. All my damn life I’ve been good at playing games, but you make me want so hard I forget the fucking rules.”

Tenderness kindled a different kind of warmth. It crashed into the rising pleasure, heightening both, and she nestled her face in the wet hollow of his throat. “Wanting that much?” She moved her hand faster, jerking over him as she teased the edge of her teeth against his skin. “I know how it feels.”

It was his turn to shudder, and his caress sped. “Show me,” he groaned. “Let go, angel, and fly for me.”

Steam billowed around them, blocking out the rest of the world. They were locked together, flesh gliding against flesh as they strained toward release. Rachel came with a cry, her hips snapping against Ace’s hand of their own volition, Cruz's words echoing in her ears.

Only sweetness.

And sweetness was what Ace gave her. Soft strokes that soothed her through her shaking without driving her higher, and his lips against her ear, whispering encouragement and affection. When she started to drift down, he dropped his free hand to cover hers, pressing her fingers tight around his cock.

Christ, he was trembling. She licked his lips, then slanted her mouth to his, capturing his groan as he thrust into her grip and came on her belly.

She wrapped her arms around his neck and kept kissing him. This was a brand-new world—having instead of wanting, feeling so much instead of merely the hollow ache of loss.

No wonder the earth was still quivering beneath her feet.

There were a dozen ways to bypass the secure walls that guarded Eden from the end of the world, and Cruz knew them all. He knew the blind spots in the security system, the easiest places to scale the walls without being noticed, and how to slip beneath them using the tunnel system few outside the Special Tasks force even realized existed.

He also knew the guards manning the gates. Not just their ranks and names, but their lives and stories. It was the most subversive rebellion he'd allowed himself in all his years of obedience, the choice to make connections with people who should have been beneath his notice.

Howard McGrady worked first shift on the Sector Four checkpoint. He was forty-three years old, with a wife and one daughter—Aileen would be twelve by now, undoubtedly growing as pretty as her mother. Howard had shown Cruz a vid of the three of them on her tenth birthday, seven full minutes of family bliss. Watching had left a hollow ache in his chest, though the fact that the video existed at all helped to ease it.

Aileen would have died before her fifth birthday if Cruz hadn't procured the medication necessary to save her.

It had been nothing to him. A minor inconvenience. But it had meant everything to Howard, and sometimes the strength of his gratitude had unnerved Cruz. Before he'd defected from the city, there'd been no one in his life who could evoke that level of intensity. He understood fondness, and companionship, even brotherhood—

Love was something else. Dangerous. Terrifying.

Powerful.

Love was what allowed Cruz to join the line at the checkpoint. Howard had a scanner in hand, one linked to the computer just inside the gatehouse. It tracked not only who entered the gates, but who left Eden and how long they were gone. When Cruz's turn came, Howard pretended to wave the scanner over the leather cuffs covering his O'Kane ink before waving him on with no other sign of recognition.

Love, or loyalty. Maybe there wasn't a difference.

Being inside the walls should have felt like coming home, but Cruz had been a shadow here. Home—if he'd ever had one—was the Base, the military outpost where Eden trained its elite soldiers. It was a rough place, a bluntly honest one. Everyone openly acknowledged your rank and status as everything, not like here where they tried so hard to pretend the shiny buildings and fancy lives were within your grasp, if you only worked hard enough.

Cruz cut through a middle-class residential district, skirting the high-rise skyscrapers that lined the river. Eden's elite lived in those buildings, with councilmen's families enjoying the lavish penthouses while their maids and cooks huddled in crowded barracks in the basements and counted themselves lucky.

Maybe they were. Not everyone could stumble into Sector Four and survive the experience.

A dozen footbridges spanned the narrow river, most crowded with people rushing to work. Cruz joined the crowd headed toward the market district, drifting along until he was sure no one had followed him from the gates. Only then did he peel off, ducking into an alley between two warehouses.

The street on the other side was decidedly dingier. He wasn't far from the neighborhood where Rachel had grown up now—a few streets over and he'd stumble into her family's territory.

Not that he particularly wanted to look Liam Riley in the eyes right now. Not after last night—and all the things he'd considered doing to the man's daughter this morning. God, all the things he *still* wanted to do to her.

Some fucking hero he was.

Coop fell in beside him, straight-faced and casual. "In town for a little shopping, my boy?"

"Maybe." Some of the tension knotting Cruz's shoulders eased at the older man's appearance. Coop might have aching joints and bones that had been broken far too often, but there was nothing wrong with the man's brain. His presence meant a degree of safety. "Maybe I just wanted to visit an old friend."

It elicited a deep laugh, one that came from the man's gut and trailed off into a delighted wheeze. "Haven't lost your sense of humor, have you?"

It was impossible not to smile, even if it meant poking fun at himself. "Fine. I *needed* to visit an old friend."

"Now, that's more like it." Coop turned his twinkling blue gaze up to study Cruz's face. "How are you making out, running with O'Kane? He's treating you right, I hope."

"No complaints. O'Kane's not stupid. He likes having guys like me and Bren around." Dallas was too smart not to respect their training—and their contacts.

“Good to hear it.”

Silence fell, carrying them to the end of the street. The bartering district was to their right, forming a quasi-respectable front for Eden’s thriving black market. Coop wouldn’t blink if Cruz swung in that direction and wasted the next half-hour on small talk and fake shopping.

He wouldn’t blink, but he’d know. Cruz had come into the city early because Coop was the only person he fully trusted who wasn’t wearing Dallas’s ink, and he refused to be too damn cowardly to ask the man his hard questions. “Do you mind going straight to your place? We could catch up before our mutual friend drops in.”

“Sure.” The old man pulled his tiny handheld tablet from his back pocket and activated the screen. His finger slid quickly over the reactive surface as he wrote out a message. “You promise to stay for lunch?”

“Only if Tammy’s cooking. I need all my teeth.”

“You getting so fancy you can’t choke down burned biscuits?” Coop teased.

Cruz snorted. “I still think you mix them with cement. I burn twice as many calories as they have just trying to chew them.”

“Uh-huh.” Coop stowed the tablet and squinted up at Cruz. “Liam stopped by the other night.”

Masking his renewed tension, Cruz took the left turn that led to Cooper’s building. “Liam Riley?”

“The same. He heard you got booted out of the city and wound up over in Four.”

God only knew what else he’d heard. Hunger for rumors about the sectors—and the O’Kanes—was at an all-time high, thanks to Noelle exchanging her cushy life as a councilman’s daughter for life as an enforcer’s woman. Most people couldn’t get more than a shred of the truth—

But most people weren’t Liam Riley. Coop was still studying him with those careful, knowing eyes, so Cruz exhaled roughly. "Did Bren tell you? Last time he was here, I mean?"

Coop snorted. "Bren? Volunteer information?"

"It could happen. Have you met that girl of his yet?"

"I try to hand you a job, and you change the subject?" Silver hair flew as Coop shook his head. "You want to hear Liam's offer or not?"

Offer, not threat. "What does he want?"

"He doesn't much like what's been going down in the sectors. I mean, he trusts O'Kane, obviously, but that only goes so far where the man's daughter is concerned. He's looking to put a little extra security in place. For his own peace of mind, understand?"

Jesus *Christ*. So much for absolution for his guilt. He'd given in to the need to take, and this was the universe kicking him in the balls over it. "He wants a bodyguard for her? She's not likely to put up with that."

Coop shrugged. "Who says she has to know? He doesn't want a shadow, just an insurance policy. If the shit hits the fan, Rachel's protected."

She already would be—but men like Rachel's father had zero faith in anyone they weren't paying to do a job. Too bad. "I can't take his money, Coop. Rachel and I... It's complicated. And not in any way Riley's going to like."

Coop didn't even have the decency to look surprised by Cruz's confession as he passed the tunnel access and took a left down the alley that led to his building. "Don't be so sure he wouldn't like it. The man lives in abject fear his baby girl's gonna get marked by one of O'Kane's true-blue soldiers. Or is that what you are now?"

Cruz traced his thumb over the leather cuff covering his ink, and for the life of him didn't know how to answer the question. He'd killed for Dallas already. Too blindly, too easily, because that was the only comfort he'd ever known. Obedience was supposed to mean it wasn't your fault.

It had always been bullshit, but now he couldn't pretend anymore. Not when he'd already shifted his allegiance once. "I respect what O'Kane's trying to do. I'm his man, as long as he keeps trying to do it."

"But you still have *Eden* written all over you, and that matters to Liam," Coop said matter-of-factly as he opened the hidden panel beside the door and keyed in the code to open it. "He busted his ass, you know. Scrounged out a tiny little empire from nothing, and he always thought Rachel was his ticket to taking it legit. Plans change, but expectations die hard."

Cruz frowned as he followed Coop into the narrow hallway. The only way Rachel could have changed her father's fortunes was by marrying someone with power and influence. Someone who had to follow all of Eden's rules on the surface, which meant chilly, sterile perfection. No love, no pleasure, no affection.

He could barely imagine her surviving it, much less enjoying it, but maybe that was love again. Howard could lose his job or his freedom for letting Cruz into the city. Rachel might well have married some cold-blooded bastard and died a little inside every day if it meant protecting the people she loved.

But the people who loved *her* shouldn't have been willing to let her.

Coop clapped him on the back. "Don't look so down. Rachel's got a good head on her shoulders. She's not gonna fall for the line of shit. She'll go her own way, always has."

Cruz managed a smile. "Sounds like her, yeah."

Grinning, Coop led him into the living room. "No reason we can't win you some points. I'll tell Liam you'd be happy to watch Rachel's back, free of charge."

It had been too long since he'd stood in this room. There was a comfort to it, something almost like home. Sinking down into one of the worn chairs felt like putting down a burden...or at least being able to share it. "You could do that. It'd be true enough."

"Done. And the rest is between you and me."

"The rest." Cruz closed his eyes and leaned his head back. There was no good place to start, because everything felt so raw and fragile. If Coop recoiled from the revelation that his involvement wasn't only with Rachel...

Cruz sighed. "Can I ask you a question? A personal one?"

Coop bent with a grunt to fetch two cold beers from the tiny refrigerator behind his chair. "Shoot."

"Why are you still in Eden? With all the help you've given people, you could live well in the sectors."

"And what, retire?" Coop chortled and passed him a beer. "I've got plenty left to do. And Tammy's here. I'm not sure I could get her to cross the wall with me."

Tammy was young compared to Cooper, Cruz's age or a little older, and as far as he knew, the two were still living the chaste, companionable life of a housekeeper and her employer. But Coop had been sweet on Tammy forever, and as long as she resisted the sectors, there was no power on either side of the wall that would make him abandon her.

Tammy was a believer. Not like the men who ran Eden and mouthed empty words about sin and a God they barely credited. She had faith, both in the rules and in her own unshakable moral code—a code Cruz had violated in half a dozen ways last night between kissing Rachel and jerking Ace off.

At *least* half a dozen. "She wouldn't like the sectors much, would she?"

"Oh, I don't know. She might, once she got used to it." He tilted his head. "Why?"

Cruz rubbed a hand over his face. "Maybe I'm just...getting used to it. Doing things I never would have expected."

Coop raised his eyebrows as he cracked open his beer. "Waiting on me to judge you for it, is that it?"

"Don't you think someone should?"

"Nope. But I'm starting to think you do." He leaned forward and braced his elbows on his knees. "What's really bothering you, Lorenzo?"

Cruz reached for his beer and drained half of it, but it only made him think of the first time he'd kissed Rachel. He'd just won his first fight, and she'd dragged him up to the roof. He'd kissed her with the taste of beer on his tongue and promised himself he'd treat her gently, softly.

Right.

Except he hadn't known what *right* was. "Do you believe in all the sins they taught us?"

That knowing gaze sharpened. "The sex stuff? Nah, it's bullshit."

"I know the Council doesn't believe it or even live by it, but that doesn't mean—" Cruz clenched his hands. "I crossed the one line you *never* cross, Coop. And I'm not talking about Rachel."

"What line?"

The line that got men killed. A Special Tasks team could grow as close as the O'Kanes in some ways, but feelings deeper than trust and brotherhood were a distraction and a liability. Fucking your teammates was against the rules, and it went double for your partner. "I fraternized."

Coop paused with his beer halfway to his mouth. "Dangerous game. Makes it hard to do your job."

The proof of his words lay in the tender length of skin over Cruz's ribs. Med-gel wasn't as perfect as regen technology, but the faint scar from last night's lapse in judgment was already fading. Too bad it couldn't take his fear with it—or the memory of those three terrifying seconds when he'd seen a bruiser twice Ace's size coming up behind him with a knife and hadn't paid attention to his own surroundings.

Ace had shot the guy in the face without blinking,

and Cruz had barely gotten his head back into the fight in time to avoid a gut wound. "I know."

"What does O'Kane have to say about it?" Coop asked. "It's his army, after all, and he's your CO now."

Cruz choked on a laugh that felt desperate, even to him. "O'Kane's a big fucking fan of fraternization. You have no fucking *idea*, Coop."

"You got no worries, then." He paused. "Or do you?"

"Not enough of them to stop me, I guess." And those were the truest damn words to come out of his mouth. Appealing to Coop was a last-ditch effort, a desperate attempt to make the man step down hard on him until he could figure out how to put on the brakes.

But there *were* no brakes on this ride. Just the adrenaline rush and the pleasure before they skidded off the cliff all three of them could see.

Coop smiled almost wistfully. "When you're as old as me, it's hard to remember what it's like, the first time you open up and really start to *feel*. Scary. It gets better—or worse. Hell, I don't know. But the world doesn't end, Lorenzo."

"It already did that," Cruz agreed. "I'll manage. I'm living a damn soft life these days, all things considered."

"Mmm." Coop polished off his beer and waved the empty bottle. "You want another?"

The back of his neck itched. Cruz was opening his mouth to mention it when he heard the slight creak of a floorboard followed by the whisper of fabric. He was on his feet in the next heartbeat, reaching for his knife by the time a familiar voice drifted in from the hallway. "Stand down, soldier."

Cruz let his hand drop as Ashwin Malhotra stepped into the doorway. The new head of Special Tasks was only a few inches shorter than Cruz but built like Bren—solid and unmovable. He had dark hair with surprisingly light eyes, along with skin almost the same brown as Cruz's own. But the stern, emotionless expression Cruz often struggled to maintain sat naturally on Ashwin's sharp features.

It should. He was a part of the Makhai Project, the most elite soldiers the Base had ever turned out. The Base had taken Cruz from his crib to train, but they'd taken Ashwin to a lab, where genetic drug therapy and endless surgeries had turned out the perfect emotionless warrior.

He wasn't constrained by feelings like guilt or empathy. Mercy. He cared about logic, his mission, and the personal code of ethics shaped out of the space where the two intersected. The fact that he considered Cruz a friend and ally was useful, but Cruz wasn't stupid enough to imagine things could never change.

Cruz nodded in greeting before sinking back into his chair. "Good to see you, Ashwin."

The man ignored the greeting and offered no pleasantries in return. "I have information for O'Kane."

"All right."

"Some of the bootleg liquor he's been tracking has turned up in the city."

A chill snuck over Cruz. Bootlegging the shit was ballsy enough, but bringing it into the city was dangerous—and not just to the idiots doing it. If Liam Riley decided Dallas was going behind his back and dealing with another distributor, things could get ugly real fast—assuming the move didn't bring Eden's wrath down on Sector Four.

Ashwin was still watching him, unblinking, so Cruz nodded his understanding. "Any other pertinent details?"

Ashwin finally looked away, his gaze tracking over the room. "I'll run it down if I can do it quietly, find out who's behind it. But if O'Kane figures out how they're getting it in, that's just as good."

"I'll pass it along." Cruz hesitated, hyperaware of the ink wrapped around his wrists and the promise it entailed. Dallas trusted Cruz to keep O'Kane secrets while trading for intel, but he probably had no idea just how highly placed—and dangerous—Cruz's contact was. "Anything you need to know?"

Ashwin spared a quick smile for Coop, then nodded. "What are O'Kane's plans for Sector Three?"

"Short term? Cleaning it the hell up."

"Long term," Ashwin corrected. "Someone's been talking to the Council. Hinting that your new boss might be planning to rebuild the factories in Three."

Not too difficult to draw the lines there. Mac Fleming ran the Sector Five factories that produced drugs—medical and recreational—while Jim Jernigan had a chokehold on all other manufacturing in Sector Eight.

Both had necessary relationships with Eden, but only one possessed the subtlety to hint instead of accuse. "Jernigan has nothing to worry about. Dallas is interested in expanding Four's current businesses, not dumping money into infrastructure that won't pay out for years."

"If he did, the Council would move on him. Fair warning."

"Understood."

The man vanished without another word, and Coop shuddered. "Makhai. Freaks my shit out."

Cruz had grown up on the Base with them, sometimes working and training alongside them, and he couldn't disagree. "They should. Ashwin's pretty much as personable as they get."

"I believe it."

The front door rattled open, followed by Tammy's cheerful greeting, and Cruz grabbed at the chance to change the topic. "I heard she moved into the spare bedroom."

The old man's cheeks reddened. "Spare bedroom is right. Didn't make sense for her to keep paying for another place, not when I have plenty of room."

And not when the shadier parts of Eden were getting more and more dangerous for a woman living on her own.

After all, Ashwin Malhotra had gotten his new gig after the previous head of Special Tasks was caught kidnapping Eden's poor to sell as forced labor. No doubt Coop slept better knowing Tammy was safe under his roof.

Which didn't make pestering him any less fun. Cruz grinned as Tammy clattered around in the kitchen, the noise loud enough to cover his teasing whisper. "I'm sure your intentions are honorable."

Coop's smile softened his harsh reply. "Fuck you, Lorenzo."

No, Cooper's intentions weren't innocent, but Cruz was all out of stones. Dark or not, *wrong* or not, all he wanted was to get back to Sector Four, to Ace and Rachel. Back to the moment where they were naked and open and *his*.

Fuck the brakes. If it was too late to stop, all that was left was to see how fast and far they could go.

8

SHE HAD ALWAYS been comfortable in the distillery, with its shining copper and steel pots and its familiar smells. It reminded her of home. Maybe that was why Dallas had let her carve out a corner of it as her own, even though the beer she produced wasn't distributed and didn't pull in a fraction of the revenue earned by Nessa's barrels of delicately aged whiskey.

Rachel counted on brewing to help center her. She'd been handling the grains, yeasts, and fragrant hops for years, and experience left her plenty of room for distraction. So she relaxed enough to let half her brain focus on what had happened with Ace and Cruz—

No panic assailed her, none of the worry or second-guessing she'd expected in the cold light of day, only the pleasant ache she carried with her like a secret.

Rachel lifted the lid of her mash tun and smiled at the earthy steam rising from the bubbling mixture. Part summer wheat, part caramel malt, raised by a man out in the communes just for her. Not even her father could get it. This batch would be light, almost sweet, nothing like the darker brews Dallas preferred.

But she was working on that, too. She checked the fermenter next, climbing the short wooden ladder to peer in at the steeping liquid. Its gentle bubbling had slowed, so she grinned and called out, "Hey, Nessa! You get the stuff I asked you for?"

"Yup, just a sec!" A clatter came from the far side of the room seconds before Nessa popped out of the room she'd claimed as an office. "I had a couple bottles left from the summer we got too much corn. It's a little more sugary than our usual bourbon, but it should work for your recipe."

"Thanks." Rachel took the bottle and rattled it. "Oak chips?"

"Yup. Put 'em in the day after you asked."

"Sweet." The oak would enhance the flavor of the bourbon enough to offset the vanilla and chocolate. "Happy birthday, Jasper."

"He's gonna love it." Nessa picked up one of the empty bottles she'd collected. "Maybe Ace would make a label for it. He does it for my small runs sometimes, so I can trade them to Eden."

Rachel's cheeks grew hot. Of course Nessa hadn't heard, because she spent most of her time holed up in the distillery. "I'll ask him."

"You can charge as much for the packaging as—" Nessa turned back to her and stopped abruptly. Her eyes narrowed. "Oh my God, what happened? What did I miss? No one tells me anything!"

"What? Nothing. We're working some stuff out, is all."

"Yeah, whatever. Last time you turned that pink, you'd been all up in between Lex and Dallas in the porn adventure of the century. A good friend would let me live vicariously."

True, except Rachel wasn't used to being the one with tales to tell. "When they finished their run last night, Ace and I went back to Cruz's place."

"Wait, you went—" Nessa blinked, then broke out into a triumphant grin. "Fuck yeah, Riley. Okay, get your ass off that ladder. We're breaking out the good shit."

Still blushing, Rachel followed her over to the sitting area in the corner, dropped to one battered couch, and covered her face with her hands. "I know O'Kanes aren't shy about sex, but I can't help it. Maybe I have more Eden left in me than I realize."

Nessa made a sympathetic noise and swung an arm around her shoulder. "Hey, it's me. It's not like I'm gonna ask all the dirty details, because Lex would probably glare at you for telling me anyway."

Nessa had been there for years, practically since childhood. It made it hard for some of the older members to see her as anything but the gangly thirteen-year-old girl she'd once been.

But that wasn't Rachel's problem. She shook her head. "It isn't that I don't want to tell you. It's just so new, and I don't even know what to call it. And I mean, the sex was good—*really* good—but it feels like..." She struggled to find the words. "Like it's not the most important thing that happened last night." Or that morning.

"Then call it fantastic." Nessa squeezed her again before leaning forward to snag a bottle of bourbon. "I mean, there's no way it was just sex. If Ace was gonna *just sex* you, it would have happened years ago."

"Maybe."

"Totally. There's *zero* Eden in him." Nessa hesitated and tilted her head, studying Rachel's face. "Hell, do you need me to shut up? The last time I saw someone looking this dazed was the morning after Flash went all caveman on Amira for the first time."

Rachel shook her head and opened her mouth to reassure her friend, but what came out instead was a desperate confession. "I don't know if this is the best or worst idea ever, and I don't think I care. Is that bad?"

"No. Fuck, no." Nessa laughed as she poured two generous shots and offered one to Rachel. "Someday, the right hot bastard's going to show up here, and I'm gonna get every bad idea I can think of all over him. Anything awesome that doesn't kill you is worth the risk."

Except that wasn't exactly true, was it? An ugly blowout between two—or three—O'Kanes could be worse. It could have everyone else choosing sides, squaring off against one another, shaking the very foundation of the brotherhood that was vital to the gang's existence.

But it didn't matter. This *was* worth it. Rachel would walk through fire just for a chance to make it work, would risk everything, because the moments she spent in their arms made it all...

Perfect.

"Damn," Nessa whispered. "It can't be a bad idea, not if you get that look on your face just thinking about them."

Rachel touched her flaming cheeks again. "You know how Mad always says he loves everyone he can, for as long as he can?"

"Yeah."

"This is different." It was the one thing she knew with certainty. "It's about the three of us. I don't think it'd work any other way."

Nessa nodded. "It makes sense, kind of. I mean, Ace has never really been like Mad. I don't think he's ever fucked another O'Kane one-on-one. Well, except Emma, but it was already happening before she got ink, and it stopped pretty fast after she did."

"He hasn't been looking for anything permanent. I know."

"No, it's not just that. I think..." She shrugged. "Ace

talks a dirty game, but sometimes I wonder if he really believes it. He tries too hard, you know? Like he's scared being himself isn't enough, which is stupid. He's fucking irresistible when he's being sweet."

The rare glimpses she'd had of *Ace*, unguarded and uncensored, had left her grasping greedily for more. "I haven't helped matters on that count. But I'm going to, because no one should ever think it, least of all him."

Nessa passed the liquor to Rachel and flopped back with a groan. "Ace is cute and all, but I'm dying of jealousy over Cruz. I can't even look at his cage fights straight on. I might get spontaneously pregnant or something. Tell me he's that hot in bed."

"He's..." Cruz was *Cruz*, focused and intent. Himself, only more, somehow. Open, maybe, to all the things he usually bottled up to hide.

"Lord save me, it's so dirty you can't even say it." Nessa nudged her leg. "Don't you dare feel bad about this. Be smug. *I* would be."

She planned to—once she'd wrapped her head around it. "Trust me, it's fucking awesome. But my brain's still playing catch-up."

"Then I'll have mercy on your brain. Tell me someone else's gossip."

Rachel's humor vanished. "The run last night? They found another still."

Nessa swung upright, her boots slamming into the floor. "Fucking hell. I hope they burned those bastards to the ground."

The fake O'Kane products were a financial threat to them all, but the sting was much more personal for Nessa. She poured her heart and soul into crafting her liquor, and for someone to take that brand over... "Only ashes left."

"Motherfuckers. I'd love five minutes alone with whoever's pouring toilet swill into our bottles." Nessa rolled her eyes. "Which'll happen when the world stops spinning. The guys won't let any of us near them."

"Only to patch them up so they can kill them some more."

"Some things are the same on both sides of the wall."

"No doubt." Rachel considered the bottle on the table in front of them before retrieving it and knocking back a bracing gulp. "You going to the party tonight?"

"For a little while, anyway." Nessa reclaimed the bottle and swirled the liquor in it. "Gotta be there when Six and Jade drink in. Especially Six. I promised to lend her some clothes."

"Clothes, not hair dye?" she teased, reaching out to flick a purple-hued lock of Nessa's hair.

"Give me time." Nessa grinned. "She'd look badass with bright red streaks in that hair."

"Agreed." Rachel hesitated, then forged ahead. "Is it so bad here? With everyone thinking of you as little Nessa, I mean."

"Bad compared to what?" The younger woman leaned back, the bottle still cradled between her hands. "Pop and I had to get here from Texas. The shit we saw on the way... Hell, being everyone's little sister isn't the worst thing."

Uncertainty lurked beneath the words. "But?"

Nessa half-smiled. "But I guess sneaking out to screw some hot piece of cage-fighting ass feels kinda lonely sometimes. Stupid, huh?"

"Not to me." Sometimes, there was nothing more isolating than being untouchable in a group defined by a whole hell of a lot of touching. "Be careful?"

"What, with the hot pieces of ass?"

Rachel took the bottle. "You wouldn't be the first to get burned." Plenty of the fighters who dropped into the warehouse on fight night were looking for ways in, and wouldn't hesitate to think that romancing an O'Kane woman was an easy ticket.

"I'm careful." Nessa's voice grew serious. "Shit, I was

fifteen the first time someone tried to find the secret to O'Kane whiskey inside my pants. I let Bren take a pass at anyone who wants to get to second base."

Rachel almost choked on the whiskey. "That'd scare off anyone who wanted to do anything more nefarious than pin you to a wall."

Nessa's good humor never stayed quiet for long. Laughter lurked in her eyes as she leaned into Rachel. "Hey, if I'm stuck with all these big brothers, they can fucking well earn their keep."

"It's their solemn duty," she agreed, unable to keep her own grin in check.

"And *your* solemn duty?" Nessa rose and snatched the bottle, holding it out of Rachel's reach. "Get your head around the dirty details, baby, because I am dying for some girl talk so filthy those boys start blushing and don't even know why."

"Hey, if you really want to know? Stick around after Six and Jade drink in. You know Ace isn't shy at parties."

Nessa solemnly lifted a hand, and Rachel hit her with a high-five. Maybe it wasn't much, but it still felt like a small victory for the untouchable girls.

As proud as he was about always rolling with life's punches, there was one thing Ace wasn't sure he'd ever get used to.

Sentimental Bren.

Not that the man looked like he'd gone soft. He was sprawled in Ace's chair, his face as stony as ever, but the simple tattoo Ace was finishing up on the inside of Bren's left forearm screamed its own sappy message. Today's date—the date Six was drinking in as one of them—under a single word.

Hope.

Truth in art, man. If Brendan Donnelly could fall

cross-eyed crazy in love, maybe there was hope for all of them. "Almost done. Is your fighter-girl excited about her big night?"

"Oh yeah." He smiled. "She's going for double shots. Can't let the men show her up."

Rachel was the only woman who'd ever done the full sixteen shots, and Ace had fallen a little in love with her that night. "No wonder you got stupid, brother. That girl's as crazy as you are."

"I know." Bren eyed his fresh ink. "It's gonna be one hell of a party."

Ace rolled his tray closer to retrieve a tube of med-gel and savored the potential of a party. Rachel got off on a crowd, and tonight's onlookers would be perfect. They'd be O'Kanes, men and women who would protect Rachel with their lives and revel in her pleasure.

In *their* pleasure. Because she sure as fuck wouldn't be the only one getting off.

"How's Cruz doing?"

Bren was watching him with a too-observant look, the one that saw everything. "He's good. He had another meeting in Eden today with that secret contact of his."

Bren nodded. "Six said Rachel was upset he got himself shot."

His heart rate spiked before he realized Bren wasn't talking about something that had happened in Eden, but during the raid last night. The memory of Rachel's initial concern had been drowned out by what had followed.

Christ, half of Ace's life to date had been drowned out by what followed.

"She got over it," he said wryly, and because Bren would find out soon enough, Ace grinned. "Nakedness will do that."

"I bet." The other man flashed him an appraising look. "Is that how it is now?"

"I guess so." Ace smoothed some gel over the finished tattoo and barely managed to keep the smug fucking smile off his face. "Serious enough about it that I paid a visit to Stuart's shop and bought some jewelry from his sister."

Another rare smile curved Bren's lips. "Congratulations, man."

"Yeah, I'm a lucky bastard. And you're all done." Ace rolled his stool back. "Let me grab you a bandage, and then you know the drill. Should be able to take it off before the party."

"Thanks." Bren flexed his arm, his smile lingering. "Did you ever think you'd see the day?"

"Which day?"

"This one. Me, with a woman's name on my skin."

Ace studied the tattoo again before placing the tightly woven gauze over it. *Hope.* Not just a feeling, then, but Six's mysterious real name. It was almost tragic when you knew the sort of shit the girl had survived to make it to Sector Four—or maybe that made it all the more appropriate. No one lasted in hell for as long as she had without hope burning in their gut.

And hope spread. Bren had touched the spark of it, and now he burned so bright it hurt to look at him straight on.

Taping the gauze into place, Ace returned Bren's smile. "Just had to find the right one. You know you're hot stuff, Donnelly."

"Uh-huh. What about you—buying a collar?"

Ace caught movement out of the corner of his eye—a glimpse of blonde hair through the barred window—and threw Bren a wink as he smoothed down the final edge of tape. "You know I'm hot stuff, too."

"Yeah, you're—" The bell on the front door jingled, and Bren snapped his mouth shut as Rachel walked in.

"Uh-oh." She leaned over the chair to kiss Bren's cheek. "My ears are burning."

"They should be." Ace patted Bren's shoulder as he rose—and got his first good look at Rachel.

The dress she'd picked wasn't fancy. It could have been—God knew Jasper had damn near kick-started a new trade in ruffles and lace, buying Noelle all the pretty things she liked—but Rachel had gone for something plainer. Something...*her*.

Simple white knit fabric, and it could have looked like she'd stolen one of those muscle shirts Cruz liked to wear when he worked out, except she would have been drowning in that. This gorgeous thing clung to her breasts and skimmed her curves like it had been made just for her.

She folded her hands in front of her, a gentle blush rising on her face. "Hi."

Bren coughed and stood. "Well, I'm out of here." He paused long enough to brush his thumb over one of Rachel's reddened cheeks. "See you tonight."

"See you." She watched him go, her teeth set into her lower lip.

When the door had swung shut behind him, Ace gave in to temptation and laid his hands on her hips. "So he gets a kiss and I don't?"

"You get a different kind." The corners of her lips turned up in a small smile, and she slid her arms around his neck. "Unless you want me to start making out with Bren. Six might kick my ass, though."

It had been so long since he'd had Rachel like this. Smiling at him, open. He'd killed her trust in bits and pieces the last time, crushing it so slowly he hadn't seen the light go out of her. But it was back now, so vivid he was almost afraid to touch her.

Almost. He smoothed his hands around to the small of her back and traced one up her spine. "Nah, she likes you. You'd get a warning."

"Not much of one." Her smile grew wicked. "Especially if I liked it."

Ace tried to imagine Bren and Rachel tangling tongues, and for the first time felt a hint of sympathy for

Six's possessive tendencies. Playing could be fun, but he'd finally gotten his hands on Rachel, and sharing didn't appeal to him—with one exception.

That exception came walking through the door, clutching a package wrapped in brown paper. Cruz met his gaze with a short nod, and Ace dropped a quick kiss to Rachel's lips. "Now we're all here."

She raised one eyebrow at the parcel in Cruz's hands. "What's that?"

A miracle. Stuart did good business in leather and steel work for the O'Kanes, but his sister was the one with the delicate touch when it came to accessories. She'd accepted all of Ace's requests with a gleam in her eye at the money coming her way, but he'd had to promise her any tattoo she wanted to get one project done before tonight.

"This is an offer," Cruz answered, holding the package out to Rachel. "What happens next is your choice."

She took it and peeled away the paper wrapping slowly enough to reveal the fine tremor in her hands. By the time she opened the white box inside, the tremor had intensified. "I didn't know we were doing this right away. Today."

It had been Ace's idea. His safety net. The collar came with a set of rules he could wrap his brain around, and expectations he could handle. And Rachel would be *his*, for however long they maintained this precarious balance...

If she'd wear it.

Ace was still struggling for the right words—the ones that wouldn't push, wouldn't demand—when Cruz stepped into the silence.

And his words were as perfect as always, just like the way he delivered them. Strong and firm, as he cupped Rachel's cheek with one big hand. "It's like I said, sweetheart. It's an offer. Ace had it made, but we didn't discuss the details. Not without you. Whatever we make this, we decide together."

Rachel melted, her eyes drifting shut as she leaned into his touch. "I want it. It surprised me, that's all."

Cruz met his gaze over her head, and Ace's momentary prick of jealousy vanished under the naked hunger in the other man's eyes. Not guarded, not reluctant—and not all for Rachel this time.

Something had changed.

Smiling, Cruz slipped his hand into Rachel's hair and gathered it off her shoulders. "Ace?"

He reached around Rachel to retrieve the box, and damned if he didn't owe Stuart's sister *two* tattoos for the masterwork inside, because it was fucking perfect. Three strands of chain interwoven with thin black ribbon, not the cheap stuff they sold in the market but soft, nubby silk.

Ace lifted it out of the lining fabric, and Christ, his hands were close to shaking, too. "Turn around. It latches in the front."

When she complied, he looped the choker around her neck. The toggle clasp rested in the hollow of her throat, a perfect silver circle with another pair of beribboned chains trailing down between her breasts. Ace traced his fingers down their length with a smile. "Ribbons and chains."

Her eyes locked with his. He'd never settled on a color for them. Sometimes they flared a smoky gray that was almost blue, and sometimes they seemed more like hazel ringed with tiny flecks of gold.

He had a whole damn pre-Flare palette of colors memorized, and not one did justice for the way her eyes looked as she beamed up at him and whispered, "I love it."

Ace wrapped the ends of the chains around his fingers and gave them a teasing tug. "Me, too."

She gasped in a breath and reached back, steadying herself with one hand on Cruz's thigh. He locked an arm around her waist and met Ace's gaze again. "You two have been around the sectors for a while, so maybe this goes without saying, but I need it nice and clear. This means we're all-in? Exclusive?"

Exclusive. The word fit as awkwardly as another man's boots, carrying with it too many unpleasant memories. *Exclusive* had been his specialty in Eden, because that was what women wanted when they paid to be a man's muse—total, unshakable devotion.

After years of being owned, even the O'Kanes' definition of monogamy felt almost claustrophobic. But that's what a collar was—a promise that things were serious, that there would be no friendly visits to hookers or casual fucking with other friends.

Well, or at least that they'd visit the hookers and fuck the friends together.

"Rachel's still got her shows," he said slowly, buying time and covering his nerves with an easy smile. "Work shouldn't count. But I've been thinking of cutting back on mine, anyway. Too much shit to do in Three, and I'd rather spend my time spanking Rae."

He said the last with another teasing tug on the chain, and she swayed toward him. Then she leaned her head back against Cruz's shoulder. "You've already figured it out. Anything we want, so long as we all agree. But I..." She trailed off as she wound a hand in the front of Ace's shirt. "I don't want anybody else."

Beautiful fucking words, and they distracted him from his lingering unease. So did looking at her. She was gorgeous like this, her back bowed, chin up, chains—*his* chains—around her throat. He wanted to draw this moment, capture the way she was trapped between them, eager.

Theirs.

Cruz splayed a possessive hand just beneath her tits and smiled at Ace. "I'll have my hands full with the two of you."

"Especially Ace." Rachel tugged on the thin cotton he wore until he took a step forward. It aligned his hips with hers, and he felt the warmth of Cruz's arm through his shirt.

The other man smiled at him, and who could blame the girls for throwing themselves at the bastard's feet when he got that look in his eyes? Ace had created a monster, and that monster wasn't thinking *ours*.

He was thinking *mine*, and he was thinking it about both of them.

Ace stroked a hand up Rachel's arm and kept going, along Cruz's chest and up over his shoulder. "That's right, brother," he murmured, answering the unspoken words as much as the ones Rachel had given voice. "We'll keep your hands busy, won't we, Rae?"

Her hand drifted lower. "In the very best ways."

Cruz's eyes narrowed, and he caught Rachel's wrist. "Was Ace gentle with you this morning?"

Her breathing hitched, and her smile was pure bliss. "Excruciatingly."

"Tell me."

Ace opened his mouth, but Cruz shook his head, lifting Rachel's hand to press her finger against Ace's lips. "Not you. I want Rachel to tell me what you did to her."

"We took a shower," she whispered. "He used his fingers to make me come. God, it was so slow. Hot."

He'd wanted to use his tongue, but then he wouldn't have been able to watch her face as she drifted into bliss. So he used it now, drawing the tip of her index finger into his mouth and dragging his tongue in a slow, suggestive circle.

Her gaze clashed with his, and she shuddered in Cruz's arms. "I tried to push him," she confessed. "He wouldn't let me."

"Good," Cruz rumbled, releasing her wrist. Ace scraped his teeth along her finger as he pulled away, reveling in the flush climbing her cheeks. Christ, the two of them together could make her flush all over.

No, not could. *Would.* He pressed a kiss to Rachel's palm before taking a careful step back. Patience. She was warm now, soft and melting, but by the time the real party started tonight she'd be burning up. "Time to head over to the warehouse. You've got shots to pour, angel."

She blinked, then moaned faintly. "You play dirty. Both of you."

Cruz stroked his fingertips along the ribbons and chain at her throat and smiled. "No, for now we're playing it safe. Dirty comes later."

"Could have fooled me."

Ace couldn't leave that unchallenged. He leaned in and let his breath dance across the skin beneath her ear. "You know better, don't you, love?"

Her tongue touched her bottom lip, just for a moment, then she sighed shakily. "I have drinks to pour."

"Lots of drinks," Ace agreed, straightening. He broke the tension by tossing her a wink. "Better look out. Six is gunning for your record, angel."

"I hope she pulls it off." Rachel's smile took on an edge of shyness that did nothing to dull her happy glow. "This should be everyone's best day ever."

She didn't see his doubt, and Ace was glad. She burned so bright, with so much hope, he didn't have the heart to tell her it didn't get better than this.

So he touched her cheek and told her a version of the truth. His version. "Too late. It already is."

9

THE LAST TIME Cruz had attended a welcome party, it had been his own.

He'd been the one downing shot after shot, trusting his training to keep him steady on his feet. And it might have, if the alcohol had been the most affecting part of the initiation. It *should* have been—there was nothing about booze and hugs that should have been more than quaint, maybe even innocent.

But there was a cunning sort of brilliance under the tradition. You took a shot—two, if you were a guy, or stubborn like Rachel and Six—and traversed a gauntlet of back slaps and embraces. Over and over, with the liquor chipping away at your defenses and the welcome sneaking its way under your skin. By the time he'd choked down the rotgut at the end of the line, he'd been grateful for his blessedly numb taste buds, not to mention drowning in the seductive allure of what Dallas

O'Kane was offering.

Belonging. Family. The sectors were lousy with orphans, and Dallas knew just how to bind them to him. Not with fear or threats, but with loyalty and affection and the promise of comfort and companionship.

Lord knew it had worked on Six. She'd done her double shots and was still flying high, dancing with Rachel and Noelle in a tangle of long limbs and laughter. And that wasn't even the damn miracle.

Bren was watching her with a soft smile so at odds with his rough face, like everything worth having in the world rested on one wary-eyed brunette. Cruz had known the man for years, years during which he'd been sure there was nothing soft inside Brendan Donnelly.

Of course, Bren might have said the same about him.

Cruz fell in beside his friend as Noelle whispered something to Six that made her dissolve into husky laughter so wild that Rachel had to steady her. The chain around her throat caught a glint of light, stirring a longing he'd indulge. Soon.

For now, he smiled. "I have to admit, I figured she'd be throwing those shots back up by now."

Bren laughed—an honest-to-God fucking *laugh*. "Hey, there's no shame in that. Happens to the best of us."

Six would probably disagree. There was a pride in the girl that the entire brutal weight of the sectors hadn't been able to snuff out. It hadn't been evident in her earliest days, but that was another thing Dallas nurtured in the people he gathered close to him—stubborn, breathless pride.

And fuck, it was addictive. Far more habit-forming than the whiskey that supported their lifestyle. "Congratulations, Bren."

"The way I hear it, I should be congratulating you."

Oh yeah. Pride was addictive, all right. It filled his chest with the uncivilized smugness of a barbarian showing off his conquests. "Maybe, yeah."

"What, you're not sure?" Bren teased.

Cruz snorted. "I'm not sure what the rumors say. Not sure I *want* to know."

"No rumors. I heard it from Ace earlier today, and I've got eyes." Bren scratched his thumb over his forehead. "I know what you're thinking."

That made one of them. "And what's that?"

"That I'm going to tell you it's wrong. That you can't do this—no way, no how. That you're going to hell, or someplace worse. That you need to stop thinking with your dick."

Maybe he was, somewhere deep in his gut, because the words still held power. "I keep waiting for someone to," he admitted quietly. "I don't know why, because it wouldn't stop me anymore."

"Then you shouldn't let it. Full stop."

"Even if I want them both?"

Bren surveyed the crowd. He nodded to where Rachel was dancing with Six and Noelle, then over to where Ace stood. He was talking to Jasper, but his gaze was fixed on Rachel. "From where I stand, it looks like those two are down with it. What else matters?"

"That simple?"

"Does it have to be hard?" Bren shrugged. "You want to know what Six has really taught me? That everyone needs to be loved."

Love again. Everything came back to it.

As if to prove that, Six broke free of the laughing dancers and prowled toward them, weaving dangerously and blind to anything but Bren. She crossed the last three steps in a drunken stagger and hopped up to lock her arms and legs around Bren. "Hey."

He stroked her hair back from her face. "Hey yourself, sweetness. You ready to bug out yet?"

She grinned at him. "Told you I wouldn't puke, old man."

"That you did." Bren turned, but not before casting one last pointed look at Cruz. "You have what you want. Don't lose it over bullshit. Trust me."

How could he not? Bren had a woman who adored him wrapped around his body, but the real truths were in the details. The way prickly, prideful Six turned her cheek to Bren's shoulder as they walked away, tucking her face trustingly against his neck.

Not that Rachel was prickly or prideful—hell, she was the opposite, so blithely vulnerable it wrecked him—but Ace was both. Hell, Ace was broken in places he still wouldn't let Cruz see, much less touch. Rachel was the only one with a chance of reaching him, and only if Cruz could keep those sharp edges from slicing her to the bone.

A dangerous tangle that could explode in a dozen directions, but Bren was right. If it went bad, it shouldn't be over bullshit.

And it wouldn't be tonight.

He turned back to find Rachel making her way slowly across the floor, her eyes on him. She wound her way around writhing bodies and kissing couples, finally drawing close enough to speak. "Dance with me?"

"Always, sweetheart." Though calling what the O'Kanes got up to *dancing* was generous, at best. He pulled her to him with a hand at the small of her back. "You having fun?"

"Not as much fun as you and Ace promised me." She slipped one hand under his shirt at his side and stroked her thumb over his skin.

Fire raced through him at her touch, and he shuddered, rocking his hips against hers. They'd promised her debauchery, implied if not explicitly, and Cruz felt poised on the edge of something vast. Not just claiming them both, but doing it in public—that fed into all the worst urges he pretended not to have.

No more pretending.

He smoothed his hand lower, spreading his fingers

wide over the curve of her ass and using the grip to haul her astride one of his thighs. "Are you wearing anything under this dress?"

"Not much." She dropped her free hand to the hem of her dress and tugged it up a single scant inch. "Want to see?"

He wanted to see. He wanted *everyone* to see, and to know they couldn't touch. Watching her face for any hint of unease, he fisted his hand in the stretchy fabric of her dress. "Lift your arms."

She obeyed instantly, with complete trust in her eyes, and Cruz undressed her slowly, letting the cotton rasp over every inch it exposed. Her thighs, her hips, the soft skin of her belly, the long line of her spine.

Up and up, and he wasn't surprised when Ace appeared at Rachel's back just before the dress cleared her breasts. Her nipples had contracted into tight peaks, and Cruz paused, dragging the hem back and forth a few times, teasing her.

She gasped, then moaned his name. Her hips shifted, grinding down on his thigh. Those sweet, barely there panties couldn't be much protection, so Cruz finished stripping her dress away before nodding to Ace. "Dance with us."

Ace didn't need much prompting. He never did. In the span of a heartbeat, he was pressed up against Rachel's back, forcing her higher on Cruz's thigh until she was up on her toes, riding his leg in earnest.

Rachel closed her eyes, leaned her head back against Ace's shoulder, and threaded her fingers through his hair. "I need you both so much right now."

They weren't the only ones putting on a show. Jas and Noelle had found a couch and were trading lazy kisses...with his hand lost under her skirt. Noah and Emma were straight-up fucking against the side of the cage, Emma's hands clutching at the metal siding as her mouth opened on a silent scream.

It was simple, just like Bren had said. Simple to cup her breasts, to catch those tight nipples between his fingers and tug at them until she whimpered.

Simple, but so satisfying. “Ace?”

“Yeah, brother?”

Cruz pinched harder. A whisper of pain, and it arched Rachel’s back in agonized pleasure. “Show me how you touched her this morning.”

Ace twisted his hand in those tiny panties and jerked. The lacy fabric ripped away, baring her pussy to his searching fingers.

She tipped her hips back, this time angling toward Ace’s touch. “Not like this morning,” she pleaded. “It won’t be enough, not right now.”

Christ, she was already wet. He could see the proof of it on Ace’s fingers as he stroked between her pussy lips only to spread them wide. She was flushed, too, so pink and pretty, her clit ready to be touched or licked or sucked.

Some other night he planned to get lost between her thighs, mapping every sensitive spot with his tongue, memorizing the topography of her pleasure. It would be the best damn recon he’d ever done, but it would take hours.

She couldn’t tolerate hours, not tonight. “How bad do you want it, honey?”

“Bad.” Her fingers traced around to his stomach, her nails scratching his skin as she reached for his belt. “But I’d do slow, just for you.”

“I know you would.” He caught her wrist and lifted her fingers, kissing the tips as Ace slicked lightly over her clit. “That’s why you get to choose. We can spread you out and lick and suck until we can’t make you come anymore...”

Her breath caught. “Or?”

Too far, whispered that tiny voice, the last gasping breath of sanity. It died as he met Ace’s gaze. Dark brown eyes stared back at him, devoid of shame or restraint, daring him to push farther.

As Cruz watched, Ace dragged his tongue over Rachel's earlobe. "I know that look, angel. He's about to say something beautiful."

Maybe to Ace, it would be. Holding the other man's eyes like a lifeline, Cruz stepped over the edge. "Or we can see how much of my cock you can take between those beautiful lips with Ace as deep as he can get in your pussy."

Rachel froze for an unending heartbeat, then bucked on his leg and shuddered. "*Yes.*"

There were couches everywhere, some filled with O'Kanes watching avidly. Cruz had never given less of a shit. He hauled Rachel up against him and crossed the four steps to one tucked back against the wall, cloaked in the illusion of shadow.

Everyone would be able to see. Cruz might forget, but he knew Rachel wouldn't. The exposure would magnify every moment of vulnerability, make her wild.

She was wild already.

He sank to the cushions with her on his lap and dragged her face to his for a rough kiss. She shivered against him, again when Ace slid his arms around her, but she didn't break away. Instead, she licked Cruz's lower lip and then teased him with the barest hint of teeth.

Cruz caught her face between his hands and held her there. "You're a brat with Ace, but you're so sweet and good for me, aren't you?"

"Always," she breathed. "I love the way you look at me, especially when you stop fighting yourself."

He'd touched her lower lip a dozen times, but now he pressed the pad of his thumb against it knowing he'd soon feel its silky softness rubbing along the underside of his cock. He still couldn't reconcile the dichotomy, how the desire to stroke her like this could coexist with the urge to see her lips stretched wide and helpless around his shaft as he fucked into her mouth with selfish hunger.

The paradox of wanting both should have swallowed the damn universe. But it didn't, because she wanted both, too.

He traced his thumb back and forth. "Find her something to kneel on."

Ace pressed a kiss to Rachel's shoulder and drew back, returning a moment later to urge Cruz's feet apart, wide enough to accommodate a cushion. Cruz edged the tip of his thumb into Rachel's mouth. "The more of my cock you take, the harder I'll let Ace fuck you."

She clenched both hands on his shoulders and whimpered around his thumb. Then she knelt on the floor with her hands folded in her lap—the perfect picture of lust and submission.

Her lashes fluttered, and she looked up to meet Cruz's eyes. "I told you before, I don't know how. And you said Ace would show me." The words were innocent on the surface, but a wicked awareness lurked beneath them.

She knew what she was asking. God save him.

God had better save him, because Ace sure the hell wouldn't. He groaned and knelt behind her, gathering her hair up off her neck. "You're not a good girl at all. You're a delicious, filthy girl who wants to lick my tongue while it's all over Cruz's cock. Does that make you wet and achy, angel?"

She slid one hand into his hair—and pulled hard. "I want to see if it makes you as hot as I think it does. And if it gets him off as hard as I know it will."

Ace smiled, and Cruz had seen that look before. It had curved his lips the first time Cruz had rasped out a command to help a woman suck his cock. Smug victory, followed by the words that had changed everything.

I thought you'd never ask.

Cruz spread his arms out on the back of the couch and focused on Rachel, on her sweet anticipation and her big, beautiful eyes. "Take out my cock, sweetheart."

She moved slowly, tugging open the button and then easing his zipper carefully down over the hard, prominent ridge straining against his fly. "Is this what you want?" she asked as she parted the denim and brushed her knuckles over his erection.

He dug his fingers into the leather cushions to keep from reaching for her—yet. "Take me in your hand," he commanded softly. "Stroke me."

Her eyes flashed with anticipation that turned to satisfaction when he hissed as she wrapped her fingers around him. "I like this." The words whispered over his exposed flesh. "So much power, and I can't even tell who has it."

Ace groaned, twisting her hair tighter around his hand. "You do, angel, start to finish. You've got so much power over the two of us, you should be drunk on it."

"Not drunk," she countered. "Happy." She squeezed her fist around Cruz's shaft and leaned in to lick the spot just below the crown.

It was almost too much. Pleasure prickled up his spine, but it was the *sight* that made him truly dizzy. Rachel, the flat of her tongue pressed against his cock, staring up at him with wide eyes while Ace gathered her hair around his fist.

And then Ace made it worse. Better. He covered Rachel's hand with his own, tightening her hold. "Not very obedient, are you?" he murmured, using his grip on her hair to drag her head back. "I think you should ask, angel. Ask for permission to lick his cock."

Her throat worked, and her eyes locked with Cruz's. "Please." Her other hand drifted up beneath his shirt. "Let me?"

"No," he growled. "Not until Ace does."

Her shudder melted into a moan. "Don't tease me

like that."

The corner of Ace's mouth lifted. Smug, all right, and he remembered the first night, too. He must have, because he edged Rachel to the side and bent low. "I thought you'd never ask," he murmured.

He slid his lips around Cruz's cock, taking half its length in one smooth glide.

Cruz groaned, his hips lifting into the unforgiving heat. Ace wasn't tentative or gentle. He went fast and hard, sucking while he worked Rachel's hand up and down the rest of Cruz's shaft.

She watched, fascination and arousal painted across her features. Then she nuzzled Ace's cheek, kissed his jawline, and licked his earlobe. When she spoke, it was in a heated whisper, so low Cruz almost couldn't hear it.

"Swallow him," she urged. "Show me how."

Ace lifted his head, his gaze never leaving Cruz's. "The trick is to get him all slick and wet first."

The words were as much for Cruz as for Rachel, a quiet nudge in the right direction. So Cruz gave him what they all wanted—the roughness of a command. "Do it, Rachel. Help him lick me."

She joined in eagerly, drawing her tongue from where her fingers wrapped around him all the way up. Another slow lick, and she met Ace's tongue, whimpering as he drew her into a wet kiss that enveloped the head of Cruz's cock.

Sweet *fuck*.

His hips lifted again, pushing toward their mouths, and the leather of the couch creaked under his clutching hands. "No one'll be swallowing me if you don't get to it," he grated out. Not that there wasn't a whole different appeal in the idea of coming like this, spilling across Ace's filthy smile and the sweet bow of Rachel's lips.

Christ, he was a twisted fucker, but the thought of it turned him on, fast and hot.

Then Rachel's lips parted. He sank into the heat of

her mouth, deeper and deeper until she gagged.

"Shh," Ace soothed, tugging her hair until she eased up a tiny bit. "Relax, sweetheart. It takes practice. Take him as far as you can again, until you're almost choking, and hold him there. Can you do that for me?"

She made a soft noise of assent and sucked again, gliding deep before drawing up short with a trembling moan that vibrated around Cruz, sweet and wicked, and he almost lost it. Ace murmured encouragement and held her there with one iron hand on the back of her head.

Then he lifted his gaze, and Cruz drew in a breath at the wildness there. "She's a good girl, isn't she?" Ace murmured. "Willing to choke on your dick to please you. Have you ever seen anything more perfect, brother?"

"No," Cruz answered honestly, freeing one hand to stroke Rachel's cheek. "Nothing could be."

She whimpered. Her hand flexed around him, fell away, and her head bobbed down. She swallowed him, the muscles at the back of her throat stroking as they worked.

Fuck. *Fuck.*

His vision narrowed, but Ace's words still hit him, twisting with the sight of Rachel struggling to swallow more of him. "Someone's been spending too much time with Lex. That's right, clever girl. Nice and slow..."

It was too fucking much. Cruz pulled Rachel up, his voice coming out low and desperate. "Do you want Ace inside you?"

She gasped for breath, and her voice was husky, hoarse. "Yes. I'm so empty. I ache."

"Ace will fill you up," he promised, dropping his free hand to tug at her nipple. Ace was already scrambling for his belt, tearing it open with shaking hands, and at least Cruz wasn't the only one fighting for control.

He wasn't the only one riveted, either. Cruz turned Rachel's face toward a nearby couch, where Lex and Dallas watched avidly. "And they're going to watch him do it."

Rachel half-laughed, half-groaned, stroking him as she stared back at their audience. "Lex is memorizing every second," she said. "She held me down, once, fucked me with her fingers. The whole time, she was whispering in my ear about all the things you and Ace could do to each other. I came so hard I almost blacked out."

Lewd words, but even with pleasure dulling his brain, Cruz saw the deeper truth there. Lex had been trained in battle strategy as surely as Cruz, trained to fight a war where lust and fantasy were her primary weapons. If she'd chosen dirty whispers to break through Rachel's defenses, the subject of those whispers was significant.

And useful. As Ace opened his pants, Cruz urged Rachel's gaze back to his own. "Maybe I should have her make me a list."

"You don't need one." She leaned down and rubbed her cheek against his shaft.

"No, we don't," Ace agreed, smiling as he ran one hand down Rachel's spine, smoothing over her ass and lower. Rachel arched and rocked back against him. "God, Rae, you dirty girl. So fucking ready."

"Hurry." Her hand skated down her throat, and she cupped her breast. "Please."

Ace gripped his shaft and looked to Cruz, and the power of the moment made him dizzy. Both of them were hungry, eager...and waiting for him.

He shifted his grip in Rachel's hair, twisting his fingers through the disheveled strands before closing his fist. Rough, commanding—all the things he'd promised himself he'd never be with her in those first days, when he'd thought respect meant deciding what she could want.

Respect was letting her want anything that got her off. Not just that, but giving it to her, in all its filthy, debauched glory.

He hauled her head back and forced her gaze to his. “Watch me,” he whispered. “Watch me while he fucks your pussy. I’m giving him to you, and I’m giving you to him. I decide how fast, how deep, how hard. I decide all of it, don’t I?”

“Y-yes.” She was barely breathing, just quick, shallow gasps of air. But her eyes—dark, wide.

Adoring.

He’d tear apart the world and everyone in it to give her what she wanted. But tonight didn’t require anything so extreme. It only required permission. “Take her, Ace.”

He did, plunging deep in one smooth stroke. Rachel shrieked, jerking in Cruz’s grip as she shuddered. Her eyes glazed over, but she didn’t look away, not even when Ace gripped her hips and held her steady for another thrust.

“That’s right.” God, he didn’t want to lose this intimacy. Not even the heat of her mouth around his dick was worth giving up the perfect view of everything she felt drifting across her face. Reaching out blindly, he grabbed both of her hands and guided them to his shaft. “Jerk me off, but don’t look away, Rachel. Do you hear me?”

“I hear—” The words dissolved into a sharp moan. “Fuck, I hear you.”

He was still wet from her mouth. She twisted her hands slightly as she stroked him up and down, keeping pace with the speed of Ace’s hard, steady thrusts. He wouldn’t last long like this, but he didn’t care. “Does he feel good inside you, sweetheart? Do you feel full?”

“So much.” Her voice hitched, and she jerked him harder. “I see it. How much you want this.”

“It’s all he wants.” Ace moved a hand up to twine with Cruz’s, tangling their fingers in her hair. “You’re all he sees, angel. All either of us sees, except for those moments when you shine so bright, you make us see each other."

Her eyes fluttered shut, and she snapped them open again immediately. The adoration in her gaze had deepened, melting into something that blazed even as it gentled. "I know. I feel it, too."

Ace tightened his grip, squeezing Cruz's fingers, and the first promise of release shuddered through him on the heels of Ace's rough whisper. "He wants to come all over your lips and tongue. He's too much of a damn gentleman to say it, but you'd let him, wouldn't you? You'd take it and love it, because it's him."

A flush spread up Rachel's chest. She made a low, shocked noise, and Ace hissed. "Oh yeah," he rumbled, sliding a hand beneath her. "Even hearing the words makes you squeeze me so fucking tight. Show him, Rae. Show him how you get off just thinking about licking the taste of him off your lips."

She came hard, throwing her head back with a cry that melted into lustful pleas—*now* and *more* and *fuck, yes.* But even as she shuddered apart in Ace's arms, her hands never stopped moving, sweet and a little rough, demanding that Cruz join her in ecstasy.

As if he could stop. Pleasure was alive inside him, throbbing harder and hotter until he bit off a snarl. And Rachel was lost, her eyes closed, but Ace wasn't. He caught Cruz's gaze, held it, all but commanding him to revel in the darkness, the reckless obscenity of the moment.

Release hit him, and Ace moved, bowing Rachel's head so the first spurt painted her parted lips. Her tongue glided out to slick over her lip, and she bent her head farther, closing her mouth around him in time to catch the next pump of semen.

If he'd had the biological ability, he might have come again.

"Good girl," Ace whispered, rocking his hips, riding her orgasm. "So hungry for him, aren't you?"

She didn't lift her head, but she reached back and dug her fingernails into Ace's side.

He hissed his approval, and the blood pounded back into Cruz's ears as Ace slipped his fingers from Rachel's clit and held his hand up to his mouth. "She tastes good, too," he drawled, dragging his tongue over the slick digits before swiping it around his thumb, until it glistened.

Even then, Cruz didn't realize what he was about to do. Not until Ace dropped his hand and stroked his thumb between the smooth cheeks of Rachel's ass.

She stiffened and raised her head. "Ace..."

He made a soothing sound. "It's your choice, angel. It's always your choice."

She shuddered and licked her lips. "I want it. I want everything."

"I know." Ace rubbed his thumb in slow, tiny circles that made Rachel shiver in Cruz's grip—or maybe it was his words that did it. Ace never ran out of words, and these...

"It'll take time," he was saying as he edged his thumb into her tight little hole. "We'll have to get you something shiny. Steel or glass. Spend forever working it into you, and you'll feel so full when we fuck you. But you'll get used to it, until you're begging for my cock in your ass. Or Cruz's."

Rachel whimpered. Her tongue lingered at the corner of her mouth, gathering the last remaining traces of Cruz's orgasm with a slow lick. He caught her cheeks between his hands and watched, entranced, as Ace pushed his thumb deeper and her eyes grew wide.

If Ace's thumb left her this dazed, Cruz could only imagine what the other man's cock would do. Or what they could do together, holding Rachel between them as they filled her. She'd let them. She'd let them do *anything*, and the dizzy power of it hit him in another rush, so wild and heady that all he could do was kiss her.

She clung to him, one hand in his hair and the other

wrapped around his arm, moaning into his mouth as her body began to jerk rhythmically. Ace, slamming into her with hard, demanding thrusts—that was all it could be.

And it wasn't enough. Cruz edged forward, sliding one hand down, over the trembling muscles of her abdomen and lower, to where Ace pumped into her, the girth of his shaft spreading her wide. Sinking his teeth into her lower lip, he centered his touch over her clit, stroking in time with her shudders.

Rachel bit him with a shriek, her teeth scoring his lip so hard he tasted blood. Judging by Ace's tortured noise she was coming hard, and the shaking didn't stop. Faster and harder, until he had to brace her body against the strength of Ace's thrusts as obscenities tripped from the other man's tongue.

But it couldn't last forever. Rachel was gasping, *sobbing*, and Cruz opened his mouth, ready to tell Ace that it was enough. Before he could speak, Ace threw back his head with a final, growling noise, sinking deep into her body and staying there. Cruz slowed his touch to a gentle brush, easing her through the last peak before moving his hand to her hip.

She swayed, then wrapped both arms around his neck and pressed her face into the hollow of his throat. Warm breaths gusted over his skin with every pant, until finally she began to settle, and her breathing slowed. Ace bent over her, pressing a kiss to the back of her shoulder before lifting pleasure-glazed eyes to Cruz.

This had always been the line for men in his squad. That polite edge of plausible deniability. It wasn't fraternization if you had a woman between you, because it wasn't about feelings, just a conquest you could brag about later. And you tried so hard, protested too much, stripped away anything warm and real because it was the only way to have even a little piece of what you wanted...

Fuck that life. Fuck those lies, the denial and shame.

With Rachel curled trustingly against him, Cruz let go of the last little bits of Eden clinging to him, wrapped a hand around the back of Ace's head, and pulled him in for a slow, tongue-tangling kiss.

10

AT SOME POINT, it had to get easier to face her father.

At least that's what Rachel told herself as she made her way through the busy market and toward the coffee shop where they'd planned to meet. She rounded the last corner, hoping she'd somehow managed to beat him there, but the sight of three burly guards put that hope to rest. Her father sat at a corner table under the outside patio, his customary cup of coffee before him and a bland look on his face.

If only she hadn't let Cruz and Ace lure her into spending that last lazy hour in bed. But she was helpless against their charms, not to mention the sheer warmth of affection in their kisses. She'd lain between them for far too long, her legs tangled with theirs, whispering secrets and encouragement between caresses. Relishing the soft glow of intimacy.

And now she was late. She smiled at Lou, the man who ran the bakery and coffee shop, and dropped into the chair across from her father. "Hi, Dad. Have you been waiting long?"

"No, we were a little late. Jerome's sector pass had been flagged." His gaze strayed unerringly to her throat, lingering for a moment on the beribboned chain before shifting to where the top edge of her latest tattoo was visible above her shirt. He pressed his lips together tightly but said nothing.

Somehow, she resisted the urge to cover her ink. Or the collar. "Not too much trouble, I hope."

Her father shrugged. "He stayed behind. It wasn't worth a bribe, not under the circumstances. Pete came with us instead."

She hadn't noticed the man standing behind the guards, but she waved at him now. Skinny Pete was one of her father's longtime employees, and Rachel couldn't remember a time he hadn't been around. "How's Mom?" she asked her father.

"Good. Sad you couldn't come into the city for a visit." He flicked up a finger, and Skinny Pete stepped forward to slip a paper-wrapped package from inside his coat. "She sent this for you."

Rachel didn't even have to unwrap it to know what it was. The scent of yeast and beer permeated the paper, and she smiled. "Soda bread. Tell her I said thanks."

"She misses you." Liam leaned back and studied her over the edge of his coffee. "It broke her heart that you chose not to come home, but she doesn't understand. You wouldn't be my girl if you picked the safe path."

"No, I wouldn't be." She was her father's daughter, dedicated to following her conscience, even when it cost her. She stretched one hand across the table, and her jacket sleeve rode up to reveal the ink on her wrist. "When Dallas took me in, when he gave me these cuffs, I made a promise. That's what this is. If I forgot all about it just because I have the chance to come back to Eden... What kind of person would that make me?"

"I know." He covered her hand with his own. "You've done more for the family than any of your cousins."

Her uncles had raised their children differently, had taught them to aspire to climb Eden's social ranks until they, too, were stepping on the faces of those beneath them. They weren't soft, not yet, but they were oblivious. "You've heard about the trouble Dallas is having, right? The knockoff liquor making its way into the city?"

"I've heard."

He said it carefully, but the slight edge of warning wasn't lost on her. He was wondering if Dallas had set the whole thing up as a way to bypass paying the Rileys their cut for import. "It *is* fake, Dad. Someone's bootlegging the bootlegger."

He studied her face for a moment before inclining his head. "One bottle came my way that didn't seem up to snuff...but that would just make it cost-effective as well as clever, wouldn't it?"

"You know Dallas better than that. He feels the same way about his booze that you do about your beer. He wouldn't put out substandard product."

"Then he has a problem. And so do we."

"Yeah." Rachel offered her father a lopsided smile. "He could use your help. No one knows the trade routes better. If anyone can find out how they're getting this shit into the city, it's you."

He inclined his head in acknowledgment. "I'll look into it, but I'd like you to do something for me in return."

"Anything."

"It's my understanding that Lorenzo Cruz is a full member of O'Kane's gang now. If things get dangerous, let him keep you safe."

For a few frozen seconds, she couldn't decide if the statement was as innocent as it sounded, or if he was looking for information and couldn't quite figure out how to ask. "You know Cruz? How?"

"I've encountered him," her father replied with frustrating vagueness. "And we have several mutual friends. I know his reputation is solid, and that he's a good man. A man I'd trust with your safety."

Her hand twitched toward the beribboned chain dangling from her collar, and she stretched her fingers flat on the table to still them. "He is a good man, and he'll watch out for me. We're together."

A pause. "I see."

"He's my—" Her what? Boyfriend? Lover? She reached up, after all, to toy with the ribbon and chain trailing between the open flaps of her jacket. "He and Ace gave me this."

Her father's eyes froze. "Ace. You mean Alexander Santana?"

Being ashamed wasn't the same thing as knowing someone wouldn't understand and dreading the inevitable confrontation. Rachel knew it, but her cheeks still heated. "Yeah, that's who I mean."

"Do you know what he was? What he *is*?"

"Don't, Dad."

"He slept with women for money and left their marriages in ruin." Her father's lip curled. "And you think I don't know the brothel owners in this sector take orders from him?"

Her discomfort melted in a flash of protective anger. "And I'm a criminal in exile. What's your point?"

"How did you expect me to react? Cruz is a decent man, but Santana..." His eyes—the eyes she'd inherited from him—went hard. "Don't ask me to think he's good enough for you. Or to understand why Cruz isn't enough."

The irony of it almost choked her. But trying to explain that Ace and Cruz had practically been together, even without her, would be useless. Her father would never understand because he lived outside of the law in

Eden, but he was still mired in its hypocritical moral system.

Sex was bad, wrong. And so was anyone who loved it as much as Ace did.

Rachel's chair scraped over concrete as she pushed it back and rose. "I have to go."

Her father sighed. Heavy, disappointed. "Don't be childish. I raised you to appreciate truth. Would you prefer I give you pretty lies?"

"No," she admitted, "but I don't think you want to hear the truth, either. Not really."

"Of course I do."

For one glorious, insane moment, she considered telling him everything. *Ace has fallen for him, too, and I think Cruz is headed the same way. I'm not the only one who wants Cruz, not the only one who wants Ace. We're all in, all together. Does that terrify you?*

Instead, she shrugged. "It's an O'Kane thing. You wouldn't understand."

A muscle jumped in his jaw, but her father was too rigidly controlled to lose his temper in public. "I'll look for the source of liquor within the city. You know I only have your best interests at heart."

And his own. "I know."

He rose, abandoning his expensive cup of coffee. "Be safe, Rachel."

"I will." It was stupid to keep trying, but she couldn't help it. "I'll be fine, Dad. I promise. I know you're worried, but Ace wouldn't hurt me."

The stern edges of his smile softened a little. "He'd better not. You're a Riley."

It was true, but not the whole truth. She was a Riley, all right, born and raised. But she was also an O'Kane now, a fact that felt just as vital, if not more so, because she had chosen it.

Hadn't she?

"Admit it," Ace drawled as they rounded the corner into the brothel district. "You've missed me, brother."

Jasper grinned and clapped him on the back. "Of course I did. Without you around, there's been no one to give me shit."

"It shows. Your head's three times its normal size. It's dangerous to let Noelle blow you so much when no one's around to deflate you."

"Smartass."

"Every day of my life," Ace agreed easily. Not hard to be generous when the world was such a fucking beautiful place. "Seriously, man, I know you're busy with all the lofty heir-to-the-throne shit, but I do miss you. Hell, *both* of you."

Jas nodded. "Noelle and I feel the same way. But you had things going on. It happens."

Ace's first clear memory of Noelle was watching her trail into his studio, all big eyes and wobbly legs, following Rachel around like a duckling who'd lost her mama. He'd had more than one sweaty fantasy about the two of them touching him or touching each other—and Christ, he didn't even know if the latter had happened.

Probably. Jas would tell him, if he asked. Or he might just smirk, and then Ace would have to punch his friend right in his manfully bearded jaw. "You didn't have to come with me today, but I'm glad you did. Gia's always more pleasant when I bring her hot cage-fighting studs to drool over."

"You mean you brought me along to distract everyone from wondering why you'll be keeping your pants on."

"Now who's a smartass?"

Jasper's huge shoulders rose and fell in a shrug. "It's good to see. You haven't been happy for too long."

Even a week ago, Ace would have argued with the

words. He'd spent months brushing off brooding moments with a laugh and a wink. He'd done it to Emma enough times, tugging her hair or poking her in the ribs. *Artists have moods.*

True enough, but most of his had been dark since the day he'd watched Rachel slip through his fingers and into Cruz's lap.

He stopped on the street in front of Gia's sprawling, three-story building and studied Jas's expression. The man saw more than anyone realized, maybe because they didn't expect a hulking, bearded fighter to have a sharp mind. And more—Jas didn't just care about other people. He understood them, sometimes better than they understood themselves.

God, maybe everyone understood Ace better than he understood himself. Everyone except Rachel. "You don't think I'm making a mistake?"

"A mistake? Hell, no." Jas wrinkled his nose. "Safe is safe, maybe, but it doesn't feel the same. Sometimes you have to take risks."

Jas had certainly taken them with Noelle. She'd tumbled out of Eden so untouched she'd nearly blushed herself unconscious at hearing the word *cock*, but she'd been as hungry for experiences as Rachel was—and as mired in shame and confusion as Cruz.

"They get past it, right?" he asked as he stepped up onto the curb. "All that bullshit Eden stuffed into their heads. It doesn't last forever?"

"Well, it doesn't just *happen*. And sometimes it shows up again when you least expect it. But it fades, yeah."

Well, thank Christ for that.

Ace turned as the front door swung open, revealing a stone-faced mountain of testosterone almost as huge as Jas. Every member of Gia's security team was hard as a rock with a face to rival Jared's—and had a brain just big enough to manage blind loyalty and the occasional dick stomping when a customer got out of line.

The man candy of the day ignored Ace and nodded at Jas, which said plenty about Jasper's growing reputation as Dallas's right-hand man. "The mistress is in the sitting room."

Ace could all but hear the capital *M.* This one probably knelt in front of Gia's chair to play human footstool in the evenings—a privilege for which more than one fancy man from Eden had paid handsomely. Ace breezed past him with another grin. "Come on, Jas. We don't want to keep her majesty waiting."

"So then I said—" Jeni cut off abruptly as they walked in, then belatedly swept her open robe shut, covering her bare breasts as if Ace hadn't seen them a dozen times before.

Unlike Jeni, Gia was fully clothed, though her silk gown was slit so high she was flashing her crossed legs to the top of her thigh. She quirked one perfectly shaped brow at Ace. "Alejandro, darling, your manners are as abhorrent as ever."

Only one other person had ever called him Alejandro—Eladio, the man who'd trained them. Hearing the name roll off Gia's tongue stirred the usual nostalgia, but Ace was in too good a mood to let it get to him. He crossed the room and swooped down to drop a kiss on Jeni's cheek before doing the same to Gia. "You'd be disappointed if you couldn't scold me. You remember Jas?"

Gia smiled, deploying the full-wattage charm that always meant she wanted something. "It's been too long, Jasper. Everyone's wild for me to lure you and Miss Cunningham to one of our parties, but Ace said it would be a waste of time to ask."

Jas acknowledged her words with a slight nod. "I'm not big on social events. But I appreciate the invitation."

"*Your* manners are delightful." She rose and gave Ace's cheek a fond pat. "If you'd come to my office with me, Jas, I can collect your money and write a personal invitation to your lady, just in case she'd appreciate one as well."

It was Jasper's turn to lift an eyebrow—at Ace. "You good?"

Gia's gaze sharpened, so Ace threw himself into her chair and waved a hand before she could get any funny ideas—or start asking questions. "Jeni will keep me company. We'll get through the long, dreary minutes, won't we, pet?"

"Sure, we will." Jeni let her robe fall open again and propped her hands on her hips. "It's been a while, after all."

Aw, shit.

Jas tensed like he was getting ready to seize Ace by the back of the neck and fling him off the path to certain self-destruction, and Ace couldn't even blame him. Jeni was gorgeous, and she knew it. Sleek curves, perfect tits, a pair of hips that could give Trix a run for her money.

Ace wouldn't even have to do anything to encourage her. In a few more seconds, she'd crawl into his lap and take him for a ride. A simple, friendly fuck, something they'd done a hundred times before, because he liked throwing cash at her and she liked how he hurt her just right.

It would feel nice. It would pass the time.

It would break Rachel and Cruz.

And yet, for one stupid second, he was tempted, because fucking up already felt inevitable. The longer he held out without disappointing them, the worse it would be when all those sweet, naïve illusions came crashing down.

Or maybe it was just the opposite. They'd grow bored with their crazy sex adventure, and whatever dumbass stunt Ace eventually pulled would be a relief. An excuse to get out, guilt-free.

Yeah, that seemed a hell of a lot more likely.

Jas took a step forward, and Christ, Ace was still staring at Jeni's tits like he had every intention of getting lost between them. So he shook his head, and he could feel the assessing weight of Gia's gaze burning into his back as he reached across to catch the edges of Jeni's robe.

"Just talking," he said, choosing his words carefully. The only people who gossiped more than O'Kanes were the people talking about them, and whatever he said now would be all over the sector by tomorrow. "Cruz and I have a thing with Rachel now."

"No shit?" Jeni absently tied off her robe this time, then dropped back to the arm of the chair she'd been occupying. "Huh."

Ace braced himself for teasing before glancing at Gia, but it was so much worse. Her brown eyes had softened, and she returned to her chair and bent to brush her lips across his cheek to hide her whispered promise. "*Hablamos más tarde.*"

We'll talk later.

A promise, or a threat—one Ace had every intention of avoiding, even if it meant avoiding *her*. The last thing he needed was Gia poking her too-perceptive nose into all his rationalizations.

Then she was gone, tucking her arm through Jasper's to steer him toward the door, her public persona so firmly in place Ace couldn't spot the edges. No one who looked at Gia would believe she'd once been as feral and snarling as Six, just like no one who'd met their mentor had believed he'd come from poverty and desperation.

Ace had never understood the fucking point. What was the benefit of climbing to the top of the damn pile only to pretend you'd always been there? No one who cared would ever believe you belonged, and no one who mattered would care.

Jeni eyed him curiously, then tilted her head with a squint. "It was Cruz, wasn't it? I should have known that crazy bastard wouldn't listen to me."

The words didn't make any sense until Ace remembered Cruz had spent the night of the party with Jeni—and that had been the night everything changed. "Lord, girl, what did you say to him?"

She had the grace to flush. "I told him if it was me? I'd steer clear of you two and your...thing. Sorry, but you know it's true. I mean, come on."

He scowled at her, but it was hard to put much force behind it when the outcome had been so spectacular. "I don't know if I should thank you or smack your damn ass."

She cracked a smile. "Careful. You're a taken man now."

Taken. That word felt far less awkward than *exclusive*, because at least it carried some deliciously filthy undertones. "Oh yeah, there's been some taking going on."

"Mm-hmm. Rachel's a lucky girl."

"I'm just as lucky." Ace summoned up a wicked leer for old time's sake. "I know who you're going to miss, pet, and it isn't me."

"Shows what you know," she sniffed. "That's exactly what I meant. Stuck between you and Cruz—there are worse places to be, that's for damn sure."

Jeni would know. She'd been his accomplice in luring Cruz to give in, after all, which meant Ace owed her for any happiness he managed to find. He rolled to his feet, leaned over, and kissed the top of her head. "You know you're always my girl. Anything you need, ever, you snap your fingers and I'll come running."

"Christ, don't get maudlin on me. It doesn't suit you." But she blinked anyway, her eyes suspiciously bright.

That was Jeni. Ruthlessly practical through and through, but she'd never let all that practicality kill her heart. He bumped her on the chin with his knuckle. "Hey, don't cry, pretty girl. I know it's hard not to, seeing as my dick's fucking amazing..."

She rolled her eyes and swatted his shoulder with a laugh that dissipated far too soon. "Is it good?" she asked finally, her voice small and low. "A different kind of good, I mean?"

"With them, you mean?"

"With someone you care about. Someone you love."

Jeni wouldn't appreciate his sympathy, so Ace smothered it beneath an easy smile. "It's always better with someone you care about. Maybe the more you care, the better it gets."

"Maybe." Jeni swatted him again. "You're terrible at this, you know."

"Probably," Ace agreed, then caught her wrist before she could smack him. "What am I terrible at this time?"

"Hiding when you feel sorry for someone." She shrugged. "Not that it matters. I'm doing just fine, thank you very much."

Jeni never hid much of anything. Not her cheerful lust, and definitely not her mercenary streak. Maybe she did with other clients, with the men who would never be anything more than a job. Maybe she covered boredom with fake enthusiasm and faker orgasms.

That had never been an option for Ace, not at the level he played the game. The women who had paid for his time couldn't be fulfilled by a fantastic fuck, no matter how creative he got with his dick. They wanted to be his muses, adored and seduced, the objects of obsession for the first time in their sheltered, neglected lives.

You couldn't fake that shit, not forever. You had to find a reason to believe it—and a way to survive when it fell apart.

Jeni stroked his arm and rested her cheek on his shoulder. "They're lucky to have you. Anyone would be. I wish you believed that."

"Of course they are," he whispered, but the words rang hollow. "I'm fucking fantastic."

Her lips brushed his cheek. “Don’t lie to them too much, love. Some people actually do want the truth.”

Rachel and Cruz were too whole for the truth. They lived in a world where love was simple, where you felt it or you didn’t, not where you turned some stunted version of it on and off like punching a pre-Flare time clock. “You’ve been doing this long enough to know better. People only want the truth when it’s pretty.”

She pulled back to gaze up at him, her blue eyes troubled. “Is that how you feel about them? That they’d better hide all their ugly stuff because you don’t want to see it?”

He flinched. Turned around like that, it sounded fucking awful. “Does Gia know you’re this damn smart? She’ll have you on the hook to help her run this place if you don’t lock those brains down, sweet girl.”

“How do you know that’s not my evil plan?”

It probably was, and Jeni was just the type Gia adored—smart-mouthed, tough, and too stubborn to let life run her over. For once, Ace choked back the urge to make a joke and seriously considered her. “Maybe it should be. Though we can find you another partner for shows at the Broken Circle, if you still want that money coming in.”

“I’ll think about it.” Another half-smile curved her lips. “Right now, I’m a little more concerned about you. As a friend, no funny business.”

“Don’t worry about me, pet.” Ace hauled her into a hug. “Rachel and Cruz want to fuck my brains out. Nothing short of another apocalypse could scare me away from that.”

Neither of them pointed out that it would damn near be an O’Kane apocalypse when things went nova. It would be bad, all right—pain and misery and heartache—but Cruz had made the only promise that mattered. He’d take care of Rachel’s heart, and she'd take care of his.

They could grind the broken pieces of Ace into sand on their way to happily ever after, as long as they made it there together, and Ace would settle for whatever bits of them he could get before they realized just how broken he was.

11

IT WAS AMAZING how quickly your concept of *home* could change.

A few short days, and Rachel was already thinking of the space she had occupied with Ace and Cruz as her own, as well. So when she caught herself barging into Cruz's room, she stopped short halfway through the door, mortified. "Shit. I'm sorry, I didn't even think—"

"It's okay." Cruz smiled as he rose. "You're always welcome here. You know that."

He'd been sitting at his table with an array of knives set out before him, along with several types of whetstones. Who the hell did that—just sat around, sharpening his knife collection like it was no big deal?

Cruz did, apparently, and the effect was ridiculously hot. "Uh, thanks," she muttered absently.

He pulled out the second chair in quiet invitation before returning to his seat. "I'm glad you came over. I was going to stop by your rooms after I finished this."

"Yeah?" She sat in the other chair and propped her elbows on the table. "What for?"

He picked up one of the knives and studied her over its flashing edge. "I heard you met with your father today. I figured I might have a few things to explain."

"Like how he hired you to be my personal bodyguard?" she teased.

He almost looked embarrassed. "Do you know about Cooper?"

She'd heard the name—from Bren, maybe, or Six. "Is he a friend of yours? From the city?"

"More like a friend of Bren's. He used to be Special Tasks, but now he..." Cruz smiled. "He collects people. Street kids, mostly, and orphans. But sometimes he takes a not-so-young orphan under his wing. Your father asked him to see if I'd look after you, and it seemed harmless to agree."

"It was." She climbed out of the chair, walked around behind him, and wound her arms around his neck. His hair smelled like his spicy new shampoo, and she leaned down to nuzzle his temple. "You *have* been looking after me. Not quite how my father meant, but that's what he gets for being pushy and interfering in my life, right?"

The knife whispered over the whetstone. "That's one thing that'll never change, Rachel. I've said it before, and I mean it. No matter what happens, I'll always protect you."

"I know." It was part of what made him *him*. "So. You have a reputation for helping people in Eden. Is that because of Cooper, or what?"

He shrugged it off, as if it was nothing. "It's not entirely selfless. Contacts are important. If I could gain someone's loyalty by helping him out... Well, I had a lot of resources. And most people in Eden have next to none."

"I came from there, too," she reminded him. "I'm familiar with how the military police usually operate, and helping out isn't it."

He snorted. "Because they're stupid."

He had put down the knife and the whetstone, so Rachel slid astride his lap, relishing the solid heat of his body against hers as she wound her arms around his neck again. "You were making people's lives better, being a hero. Don't downplay that."

"A hero, huh?" He smiled and lifted a hand to her cheek. "Just like you, sacrificing yourself for your family."

Maybe he expected her to brush it off like he had. Instead, she grinned. "Yeah, kind of. Just so happens, it worked out really well for me."

He stroked his thumb under her chin, tilting her head back to show off the collar. "You had a family worth standing up for. I had to betray mine before I found that."

If only he knew. She closed her eyes. "My father doesn't approve of our situation."

"Ah, hell." He folded his arms around her and threaded his fingers through her hair, guiding her cheek to his chest. "I'm sorry, sweetheart."

"It's not that. I would never expect him to understand. It's—" How could she explain the anxiety nibbling at the edges of her contentment? "Can I ask you something? Truthfully?"

"Always."

God, it was impossible to get the words out. She'd held them in for so long, terrified of what might happen if she gave them voice. "Is Ace in this? *Really* in it, I mean."

He didn't answer right away, and her worry intensified. When he did speak, the words were careful. "I think he's bringing everything he has to this relationship. I still don't know what that means in Sector Four. Hell, I don't even know what that means in Eden."

None of that mattered beyond the thin veneer of expectation, and O'Kanes excelled at bashing that to bits. "I don't know what it means to Ace," she clarified. "And I think that's what bothers me. There's so much he holds in, Lorenzo. I can sense it, but I can't see it."

"There's this." Cruz touched the collar again. "He's bad at words, but he's still talking to us. We just have to learn his language."

"I've been trying to do that for two years."

"He's been afraid, sweetheart." Cruz trailed his fingers down the chain falling between her breasts before looping it around his fist. "He's been protecting you from himself, and now he doesn't have to anymore because I'm here."

He said it with such confidence, and maybe it really was that simple. If they could show him what he meant to them, he would understand that the only person who needed to be protected from Ace was *Ace*.

She stretched her neck to one side, a physical reminder of the ribbon and chain secured around her throat. The collar was a promise, a vow, and Ace wouldn't have given it to her if he hadn't been ready to follow through on it.

So she shoved the worry down, locked it away. "Is he still out on rounds with Jasper?"

"They finished early." Cruz's smile turned dark, heavy with promise as he tugged on her collar. "He had a few other things to pick up from the person who made this. He asked me if I wanted anything special for you."

The prickle of awareness melted into a shiver. Everything about Cruz came down to this delicious contrast, how he could be utterly gentle and still gaze at her with this *intensity*. "Does that mean your answer was yes?"

"Maybe." He pressed his forehead to hers. "Do you need to take it easy tonight? Or are you ready for something a little more demanding?"

She bit her lip to hide a smile and curled her fingers

against the side of his neck until her nails bit into his skin. "You don't want to take it easy with me," she reminded him. "You want it hard, and so do I."

He hissed, one hand tightening around her hip. "I want to take it easy when it's what you need," he countered. "The rest of the time, I want everything."

"I won't break, Lorenzo."

"I might."

"Oh." That brought her up short. Everything seemed to be about her, what she could handle, and she hadn't stopped to think that maybe all his careful focus was as much for him as anything, intrinsically tied up with his need for control at all times. "I want everything, too. You know that. But nothing that could hurt you."

"I know," he soothed, smoothing both hands along her back. "Leaving Eden behind isn't easy. It's like taking shrapnel from a frag grenade. Even when you think you've dug it all out, sometimes you miss a piece."

Maybe that was what they'd always be—the walking wounded. "I don't want you to hurt," she whispered, leaning her forehead against his cheek. "I care about you. So much."

She felt his smile. "I know. You dug the first bit of Eden out of me. Remember?"

Only he could speak fondly of having her cut a tracking device out of him with no anesthetic. "I remember."

"Since then, I've been—"

Whatever he'd been doing remained a mystery, because the door rattled under two sharp knocks before Ace shoved it open. "Damn it all, you're both still wearing pants."

He was carrying a duffel bag that bulged at the seams. Recalling Cruz's words, Rachel blushed. "Are you moving in, or is that the haul from your little shopping trip?"

Ace flashed a grin that had Cruz's chest rumbling with repressed laughter. "Be glad I didn't bring the furniture, too."

"*Furniture?*"

The bag hit the floor with an ominous *thud*, and Ace swaggered over to the table. "Don't tell me Lex hasn't lured you back to Dallas's room to play with all his toys. She'll never stop pouting now that she missed her chance."

He looked so smug it was only a matter of time before he started thumping his chest like a caveman. Rachel arched one eyebrow. "Who says she did?"

Cruz's grip on her tightened. Ace only laughed and swept a few strands of hair back from her cheek. "You could bolt for the door, but Cruz really would tie you to his bed."

"I don't need to tie her." Cruz relaxed his hands and slipped them up, under the hem of her shirt. His fingertips were warm as he traced the line of her spine, lifting the fabric as he eased higher.

The quiet intimacy of it stole her breath. The air squeezed out of her on a low sigh, and she wrapped her arms around his neck again.

"See?" Cruz brushed his lips over her forehead. The shirt edged higher, caught between their bodies for a moment before Cruz pulled it up over her breasts. "You're not going anywhere, are you, sweetheart?"

Not if it meant leaving the circle of his arms, losing the heat of his skin on hers. "Never."

"Good," he whispered, still so soft. So gentle.

His arms flexed, and he ripped her shirt down the back and stripped it away from her skin. Rachel shuddered and let him drag the torn fabric off her arms. "I liked that shirt."

Ace tilted her head back with a hand caught in her hair, baring her throat for Cruz's mouth. "I'll make sure he buys you a new one. You know he sticks all the cash he wins from fighting in a box? Never saw him spend a damn dollar until he shoved it at me for your collar."

Knowing Cruz, he probably sent most of his money to his friend Cooper in the city, so they could keep on being big damn heroes in relative peace and quiet. But that was a conversation, a question, for another time. A time when Cruz wasn't rising from his chair with her still pressed to his chest.

He lowered her beside the bed, letting her slide against his body until her toes touched the ground. "I won't rip your pants. Take them off for me."

There it was, in a nutshell—Cruz would take, but only so much. The rest?

The rest, she had to *give*.

She glanced at Ace, who was hauling his shirt over his head. "Does he do this to you when I'm not around?" she asked softly, dragging open the button and the zipper on her jeans. "Rough and soft? Fast, then slow?"

Ace made an amused noise and stepped up behind her. "I think you're overestimating how many times I've gotten him naked without you around, angel."

"That's disappointing." She eased the denim off her hips with a little shimmy. "You could leave a girl her fantasies, for Christ's sake."

Ace took over, sliding the fabric down her legs as Cruz reached out to tilt her chin back. "Is that one of them? The two of us fucking?"

"Two hot guys, rolling around naked? Hell, yes."

His eyebrow quirked up, and Ace chuckled as he lifted one of her feet free of her pants. "Look at him, pretending he's never jerked off to the thought of Lex with her face between your thighs. Equal opportunity, brother."

"I don't know, maybe he hasn't." Cruz seemed to like softer women, ones who enjoyed submission more than fighting for control.

Women like her.

His smile confirmed it. He swept his gaze down her newly bared body and back up. His hand followed the same path, stroking down her throat, between her breasts and lower, coming to rest on her belly. "Sit on the edge of the bed."

She kicked her other foot free of her jeans and obeyed, moving just slowly enough to earn her a warning rumble and a soft swat on the hip.

Ace was still on his knees, and he looked as surprised as she was when Cruz dropped abruptly beside him, seizing the back of the other man's head with such deadly speed that their lips crashed together in time to muffle Ace's shocked noise.

Not that his shock lasted long. Before Rachel could do more than drag in an unsteady breath, Ace was kissing him back, licking and biting with a rough ardor that unfurled a tiny wisp of jealousy in the pit of her stomach.

It vanished in the next heartbeat, driven away by a low grunt and an answering groan that curled her toes. It wasn't fair that they could be this beautiful, that she could want them both this much.

Every way she could get them.

She slid to her knees next to them and echoed Cruz's earlier caress, easing one hand under his shirt as she skated her lips up the side of his throat, all the way to his ear. "Don't stop."

He groaned again, freeing one hand to wrap around the back of her head. He held her in place, forcing her to watch as he sank his teeth into Ace's lower lip and tugged. She gazed at their mouths, spellbound, until a flurry of movement—and a soft click—drew her attention lower.

Ace had one hand cupped around the ridge of Cruz's erection through his pants, and was unbuckling his belt with the other.

Rachel kissed the side of Cruz's throat again, then followed it with a sharp bite. "It's not just so I can watch," she whispered, "and I'm glad. I don't want you together to amuse me. I want you together because it feels good."

Cruz broke away with a hiss and dragged her head back so he could meet her eyes. "I told you to sit on the bed."

Her heart stuttered—until she realized there was no trace of anger or disappointment in his voice, only pleasure. Desire. "You did. I guess I got greedy."

He licked her lower lip, nipped it with just enough force to sting. "You don't have to disobey. Ace is going to spank you either way."

"I know." She laid her hand on his cheek and smiled. "But I like it when you growl."

His eyes gleamed. "You can watch me be a little rough with Ace. Or you can stay, and I'll be a little rough with both of you."

"You don't want me back on the bed?"

He twisted his hand, and her hair pulled tight, riding the edge of pain. "I want you to pick the one you want," he said, voice low and serious.

A clear exit, a way out—just in case. But Rachel didn't want it. "I'll stay." She dropped her hand to cover Ace's, gripping his fingers as well as Cruz's belt. "Right here."

He made that noise again—the one that wasn't quite a growl or a groan but made her shudder to her toes—and then he was kissing her, every bit as forcefully as he had Ace, with all the pent-up passion only the two of them could unleash in him.

And Ace knew. Rachel could feel it in the way his hand trembled beneath hers, the way he shifted his grip so *he* was holding *her*, and then his mouth was on her, too. Her shoulder, her collarbone, his tongue tracing meandering patterns until Cruz guided his head down.

Ace's stubble rasped over her nipple, followed by the softness of his lower lip and then his tongue, and Rachel's brain shorted out. She jerked her mouth away from Cruz's and hissed in a breath when he pulled her back, sliding his tongue between her lips to stroke hers.

His belt was hanging open, his jeans half undone, and she slipped her hand inside. He was hard, straining against the denim, and she wrapped her fingers around his length.

Cruz drew back, his teeth scraping her lower lip as he released her. "It's time to give her something sparkly, Ace."

Ace broke away, and Rachel stared up at Cruz, unmoving. "Was this his idea or yours?"

The corner of his mouth kicked up. "Ace has a thousand dirty ideas, but I pick when and how."

It was that simple, need converging until there could be nothing but pleasure. The three of them, each wanting what the others could give.

Or take.

She tightened her grip, and Cruz shuddered, thrusting into her hand. His gaze fixed on her mouth again, and there could be no doubts about the path of his thoughts.

He voiced the command anyway, using that implacable hand at the back of her head to guide her down. "On your hands and knees. I want your mouth, and Ace needs your ass."

"For something sparkly?" She murmured the words against Cruz's tight abdomen, more to feel his muscles flex at the warmth of her breath than to ask any real question. *What* didn't matter. She'd take anything, because Ace would never hurt her, not unless she wanted him to.

Cruz's cock nestled between her breasts, and she grinned up at him as she leaned lower. Lower, until she could run her tongue down the underside of his shaft without looking away. He shuddered, his hips jerking before he regained his perfect control.

It was Ace who answered her, returning to walk his

fingers down her spine before landing a teasing, open-handed slap on her ass. "Cruz has himself a dirty little fantasy, angel, but you'll have to work up to it."

"What kind of fantasy?"

"You know what kind." Ace smoothed his hand over her stinging skin before dipping lower. His fingers stroked between her legs, over her pussy, eliciting another shudder. "The kind where you're riding both of our cocks at the same time."

She squeezed her hand tight around Cruz's dick. It pulsed under her touch, and she swallowed a moan. "I could do it now." Barely a lie, and it wouldn't be one for long, not when she was sandwiched between them, every inch of skin touching theirs, inside and out.

"No." Cruz's voice was rough, but the fingers at the back of her head were gentle. "Tonight, you're going to take what Ace gives you. What I let him give you. Do you trust me?"

"With every breath."

Cruz folded his free hand around hers, guiding it up his shaft. "Then spread your legs wider. Ace?"

"On it." The teasing touch of his fingers vanished. Something else took their place, something cool. Hard. It stroked between her pussy lips and down to graze her clit. "We'll start you off easy. This isn't too big, though it might feel that way when it's nestled in your ass and you're riding Cruz."

A plug. She craned her head far enough to see the flash of silver in his hand a moment before it centered on her ass. It slid over her skin, slippery and warming rapidly, and he pushed it into her, slowly but firmly.

She told herself to breathe, but everything shuddered to a halt as the plug breached tight rings of muscle, unyielding and way too fucking big because she'd never done this before, never—

The discomfort melted into a shock of pleasure that raced up her spine. It dragged a stunned moan out of her burning lungs as the plug settled into place, heavy and foreign.

"There you go." Ace rubbed her hip with one hand and cupped her pussy with the other. "Talk to me, Rae."

She opened her mouth, but all that came out was another moan, this one pleading. Cruz tilted her head back and studied her with dark eyes. "You're all right, aren't you?"

Words didn't exist for how she felt, but she tried anyway. "It'll never be enough."

"I know." He pressed the slick head of his cock against her lips, tracing it from one corner to the other before rumbling another of those implacable commands. "Open for me."

Yes. She licked him again, this time in a slow circle around the crown, and closed her mouth around him. He shuddered and pushed deeper—not fast or rough, but steady, with his hand on her head to hold her in place as he pumped in and out.

Warmth blanketed her. Ace, leaning over her, his skin hot on hers and his jeans a taunting abrasion against the backs of her thighs. He braced one arm on the floor next to hers as his mouth brushed her ear. "Put your hand on mine. If something gets too intense, you squeeze three times. Understand?"

She slid her hand over his, wondering dizzily what they had planned, what could be so intense that she might need an out. Then Cruz tightened his hand, rolling his hips forward with enough force to thrust all the way to the back of her throat.

She gagged, caught off-guard not only by the suddenness of it, but by the way he shuddered then groaned when she didn't try to pull away.

Ace echoed the noise, his breath hot on her ear. "I've told him a hundred times that there's nothing civilized about a good fuck. Only what gets everyone horny."

God, *horny* didn't come close. It was such a weak

word for the ache that left her wet and fidgeting, bucking toward the hand that Ace dipped down over her hip.

Then his fingers made contact, and he hissed as he spread her pussy lips wide and pumped one finger into her. "If everyone feels good, nothing's bad. Not wanting it, not doing it... And you feel good, don't you?"

She had to pull back, just enough to breathe, and she squeezed Ace's hand, careful to do it slowly and only once, so they wouldn't stop.

They couldn't ever stop.

Cruz let her catch her breath before surging forward again. "So beautiful," he ground out, rocking back and forth, in and out. Fucking her mouth, each glide a little rougher, a little deeper. "You take everything I give you, so sweet and perfect."

For the first time, he didn't seem to be fighting it, just falling into her. And it was a gift—him giving them his control, if only for a while—so she sucked harder, followed him when he would have backed off to give her space and air.

All unspoken, but as loud and plain as she could make it without shouting—*more*.

"Tilt her head back," Ace said. Cruz did, guiding her with the fingers twisted in her hair, and Ace hummed his approval against her cheek.

She could see his face like this, his eyes. They blazed as he thrust forward again, the new angle easing his way. Cruz groaned helplessly as her lips stretched around the base of his shaft, and she swallowed him, desperate to keep him as deep as she could, until her need for oxygen trumped her need for him.

Maybe it never would.

He took the choice from her, pulling back to give her time to gasp in a breath, and then he was back, just as deep, only this time Ace drove two fingers into her, curling both with a low noise. "Do you feel it? How fucking tight you are when your ass is mine?"

His knuckles bumped against the back wall of her vagina with every stroke, shifting the metal buried in her ass. So full, but not full enough. Not yet. She clenched around his fingers and squeezed his hand again, her eyes locked with Cruz's.

He dragged her head back, his chest heaving. "Tell him what you want."

An impossible task. What she wanted was what she *had*, Cruz and Ace and this moment, forever. But needs? Oh, she had those. "I need to come. Please."

He nodded and guided her upright. "Turn around."

She obeyed, gasping when the change in position shifted the plug again. The wide, flanged end still outside her body felt odd, and she wiggled as she settled on her hands and knees once more.

It left her staring up at Ace's smug, lazy smile. "You like this too much," she whispered, matching his expression with a smile of her own.

"Like you don't." He traced her smile with one slippery fingertip before ducking his head to lick her lips.

"Not at all." She chased his mouth and bit him. "I love it."

Ace laughed and kissed her, teasing his tongue over hers as Cruz stroked the head of his cock between her pussy lips. He felt bigger than ever, poised against her, and Ace pulled back to grip her chin. "Look at me while he fucks that gorgeous cock all the way into you."

He'd spoken of intensity before. This defined the word, having Cruz, huge and hard as steel, ready to thrust into her as she gazed into Ace's eyes, eyes that could see through anyone, anytime. "I think I'm gonna come," she confessed.

Ace didn't look away. "Can she, brother?"

Cruz gripped her hip hard and pushed inside. Not far, an inch or two at most, and it still made her legs shake. "She fucking well better."

Harsh words. Demanding ones. Rachel gritted her

teeth and leaned against Ace, nestling her face in the crook of his neck. "You know how big he is," she said. "How full I'm going to be."

"I know." It was his turn to sink his fingers into her hair. They were different from Cruz's, long and clever, weaving between the disheveled strands. He cradled her with both hands, coaxing her head back up with his thumbs on her jaw. "No hiding it from me."

She met his eyes again, but couldn't resist teasing him. "Why not? You want to know how good this feels?" She lowered her voice to a purr. "Try it sometime."

But Ace only smiled, his gaze flicking up briefly. To Cruz, whose fingers clenched as Ace replied. "Oh, I plan on it."

Rachel's heart stuttered. "Can I watch?"

"Maybe." He lowered his lips, until they were almost touching hers. "Might be hard, though, if I'm inside you, fucking you while he fucks me. All of us fucking each other."

Cruz bit off a curse. His hips surged, driving his cock into her and driving her mouth against Ace's. They crashed together, the three of them connected by passion, by pleasure. By this craving that nothing seemed to sate.

It splintered through Rachel, igniting every nerve ending. She clung to Ace, her arms around his neck, her bare skin slip-sliding over his with every one of Cruz's rough, insistent thrusts.

Ace bit her lip, freeing one hand from her hair to reach down her body. He was the only thing keeping her in place, holding her up while Cruz slammed deeper with a hoarse sound. No words, not this time, just animal sounds as he lifted her hips and fucked her harder.

But Ace had the words. He always did. He fingered her clit, pushing her higher with slick little circles. "Just like that, angel. Come on that beautiful cock. Show him that you like to be taken."

"I love it." Her nails bit into his shoulder, his neck,

as the first waves of hot, clenching ecstasy washed through her, bathing her in fire. "I love you—"

He swallowed the rest of her sentence, his kiss frantic, wild. Not like he was trying to muffle the words, but like he was trying to steal them, lick them off her tongue and make them real.

But nothing had ever been *more* real. Every second of pain and laughter and longing had been leading her here, to this moment, and she embraced it. She slid her fingers into Ace's hair and held tight, even as she reached back with her free hand to cover Cruz's, and she clung to them both as pleasure swept her away.

Nothing had ever been more real.

12

THE ONLY THING better than watching Rachel shake her way to orgasm was doing it with the words *I love you* echoing in his head.

Ace was usually enamored of the visuals. The sweaty glory of sex and how it got messier as things heated up. Parted lips, swollen from sucking cock, and slick pussy, swollen from a firm fucking. Smooth flesh, pink from fingers and stubble and teeth, or bisected by artistic welts.

You could reconjure all the most beautiful depravity of any night by tracing the marks left behind. A carnal detective, recreating the scene of the crime.

But God, tonight the sounds were *killing* him.

I love you.

She had said it before with hate in her eyes, riding hurt and a broken heart. Now she'd said it with drunken passion, riding Cruz's dick.

Maybe someday she'd say it with nothing between them but quiet truth.

Not that he was complaining. Fuck, no, not when Cruz finished with a final thrust and another sound that shook through Ace. Tortured relief—not just an orgasm, but true fucking release. An entire adult life of denial, spent in one fury of wild-eyed passion, and suddenly it didn't matter that Rachel's words were still bouncing against the inside of Ace's skull. That his jeans were crushing a dick that had flown by *too hard* ten fucking minutes ago.

Cruz needed him right now, more than he ever had.

Ace coaxed a final shudder from Rachel and eased his hand away before he could wind her back up. "Don't you go flying again yet, angel. I don't care how good his cock felt." Words spoken to her but meant for Cruz, a reassurance of Rachel's enjoyment before doubt could close in.

She collapsed against him with a laugh, trembling, her cheek and temple damp on his shoulder. "I can't stop shaking."

"I know, Rae." Ace cupped the back of her head and smiled at Cruz. "You did a number on him, too. You should see the look in his eyes."

Cruz frowned. Well, he *tried* to frown, and Ace felt his smile widen to a grin when stone-faced Cruz stroked Rachel's hip with a soft look in his glazed eyes. "He never shuts up, does he?"

"Never." She kissed the side of Ace's neck with a pleased hum. "And his words are just like him. Every time he opens his mouth, something filthy and gorgeous comes out."

"Can't help it, lovers." He liked that word, the way it rolled off his tongue to curl around both of them. It let him pretend he wasn't gate-crashing a couple this time, a tourist in someone else's torrid love affair.

For now, at least, they were his. A matched set of

filthy-minded innocents who wanted to get dirty, and he wasn't about to waste a goddamn moment of it.

Cruz and Rachel were both dazed, so Ace slipped into the driver's seat. It wasn't hard—he'd had years of practice at nudging a situation without seeming to have taken control.

He eased Rachel upright, letting her fall back against Cruz's chest, and rocked to his feet. "If you two are all worn out, I'll have to take care of my own dick."

Rachel laid a hand on Cruz's cheek, then turned her face up to his with a questioning look.

Fuck if Ace knew what that question was, but Cruz's lips tilted up in a secret smile, like they had their own silent language. He made it look easy, and jealousy might have stirred if Cruz hadn't turned that smile toward him. "Get naked and get on the bed."

A command, without prompting. Halle-fucking-lujah.

Ace tore open his belt and damn near tripped in his haste to shed his jeans. Rachel laughed again, soft and hot, and tugged the denim down his legs. It put her mouth close to his neglected cock, and he spent a few seconds imagining her with those swollen lips around him, swallowing him with the same eager moans she'd given Cruz.

Patience. He had to fight the urge to grasp for everything, to exhaust them all in his quest to check off every fantasy on a list so long, Sector Four probably didn't have enough paper to contain it. If he wanted to make the most of every moment, he had to silence that mental countdown, the one that whispered to make the most of every hour, every minute, every second.

Fear lied. Rachel and Cruz weren't slipping away from him—not yet, anyway. So he stepped back, sprawled across Cruz's neatly made bed, and let his newly corrupted lovers come to him.

Cruz nudged Rachel forward, urging and permitting, all at once. She knelt over one of Ace's legs and braced her hands beside his hips.

That sweet little smile remained. "It's my turn, you know. Are you ready for all those dirty ideas you don't think I have?"

He'd never imagined her pure. Sweet, yeah. Trusting, sure. Maybe inexperienced, but not wide-eyed and innocent like Noelle had been in her early days. Only her endearing eagerness had saved Noelle from being a high-maintenance Eden virgin, and Ace had had his share of those.

But he wasn't dumb enough to admit as much to Rachel, not when a challenge could spur her to reach for extra-filthy heights. So he tugged at a strand of her hair with a teasing smile. "You? Dirty? I'll believe that when I see it."

She was on to his game—she had to be—but she played along. "It depends, of course, on what Cruz lets me do to you." As she spoke, she leaned down, just close enough for one hard nipple to graze the head of Ace's cock.

Hell, she had nice tits. Smooth, full. He could imagine pushing them together and fucking up between them until he came all over her throat, her collar. But that wouldn't help her flex her sexual power, and Christ, he wanted her to get real comfortable with that. So he dropped her hair and gathered the chain on her collar in his hand. "Yes, brother. What does she get to do to me?"

Cruz slid to the bed on his knees. A subtle position of dominance, towering over them as he stroked Rachel's back. "What do you want, sweetheart?"

She ran her thumb across Ace's lower lip, and then pushed deeper, into his mouth. "He spends so much time talking about his clever tongue," she whispered. "I want it."

Oh, that was even better than having her ride his dick. He bit her thumb before sucking on it, just like he'd suck on her clit.

If Cruz let him at her.

He flicked his gaze to the other man, but Cruz's expression gave no clues as he caressed Rachel. Her hair, her shoulders, one of those big hands disappearing down her back until Ace heard the distinctive *thwack* of an open palm against soft flesh.

Rachel jerked with a moan, and Ace's pulse sped, even faster when Cruz spoke. "Ace hasn't gotten to spank you yet. You can slide on up and ride his tongue. But if you do, he gets to do whatever he wants to your ass. Spank it. Flog it." He leaned down, his lips brushing her ear. "Fuck it."

Her long, surprisingly dark lashes fluttered over hungry eyes. "Anything."

Cruz smiled his satisfaction, close enough to permission for Ace to lock his hands around Rachel's waist and drag her up. Her knees landed on either side of his head, and she gasped and arched her back as he swept his tongue over her.

She swayed above him, her tits bouncing, her nipples tight, and for a heartbeat he wished he'd remembered to fish out her new nipple clamps. He'd gone overboard with the jewelry, throwing money at Stuart hand over fist, but it would be worth every credit when he got her spread out, jeweled chains dancing from her nipples and tugging on the sweet little piece that would hug her clit.

Next time, when he wasn't too busy licking her. He closed his lips around her clit and sucked. She cried out, falling back to brace her hands on his rib cage as she shook and trembled.

Too fast. He backed off, flattening his tongue to stroke, slow and soothing as he clutched her ass and pulled her closer. She relaxed, her tension melting away as she began to roll her hips against his mouth in a languorous, liquid rhythm.

The bed shifted, and Cruz dipped into Ace's field of vision. He caught the beribboned chain trailing between

Rachel's breasts and wrapped it around his fist, its length growing shorter and shorter until he tugged it taut. "Look at me."

Her head fell back, blonde hair sliding over her pale shoulders as well as Cruz's darker skin. She met his eyes, a pretty pink flush spreading over her face.

Ace thought life couldn't get any damn hotter. But it did. Cruz drew the chain up—not hard, just enough to urge Rachel to stretch her body, and lowered his mouth to her ear. "You wanted to ride him. Tell him where you want his tongue, and what you want him to do with it."

Her hips jerked. "I want his tongue on my clit, just like this—" The words hitched, and her voice dropped, low and husky. "And I want more. His tongue inside me, so he can lick the taste of you out of my pussy."

Jesus *Christ.* If he survived the night, he'd engrave the words on a fucking plaque for her. The perfect filthy moment of utter abandon, and as Ace speared his tongue into her, Cruz let out a choked noise.

That's right. Think about coming in my mouth. Think about coming inside her. Revel in it, even if it makes you feel dirty. Get fucking drunk on how much we don't care, how much we like it—

The only downside to having his tongue inside Rachel was that he couldn't say any of it now. Maybe later, after he'd jerked off all over the marks he was going to leave on her smooth ass. Or hell—he squeezed it, pushing his hands together, listening to her broken noises as the plug shifted—maybe she could take his cock tonight.

She'd take it if he wanted her to. She'd try anything, because she was perfect. She was fucking *perfect.*

And she was getting close, writhing above him as Cruz pinched her nipples between his fingers. Tight, and then tighter, and her inner muscles clenched as he dragged her right up to the edge of pain—and then over it.

She looked down at Ace, her eyes glazed with pleasure and more, with that dreamy look she got every time he laid her ink.

He licked his way back to her clit. Light, soft, flicking his tongue in a careful counterbalance to the roughness of Cruz's hands. Rachel cried out, quaking through an orgasm too fast to last long, but too hard not to leave her limp in Cruz's arms, dazed and spent.

Ace met Cruz's eyes, and they didn't need whatever secret, silent code the other man shared with Rachel. He lifted her, and Cruz figured it out fast enough, gathering her up against his chest as Ace rolled to his knees.

He'd brought plenty of options. Too many, maybe. Floggers that would caress, ones that would fall deep and hard, ones that would sting. A strap, too, wider than his belt and just as severe. His brain took a mental inventory as he watched Cruz ease Rachel to the bed, boneless and liquid and still so eagerly obedient that she sank into the ideal position, her cheek against the blanket, her knees under her, her ass in the air like an offering.

His hands itched to touch her. So he ignored that fucking anxiety, the taunting voice rising again, whispering for him to take everything now because there might not be another chance.

He eased into place beside her, smoothing both hands over the curves of her ass. "You with us, Rae?"

She smiled, slow and relaxed. "I'm not flying yet. I promise."

She would be soon. He jerked his head at Cruz, motioning for him to retrieve the abandoned bottle of lube, and pressed his thumb to the jewel nestled between her ass cheeks. "You look so pretty like this, angel. Decorated."

"I see what you like." She stretched gently, arching her back even more. "Dress me up and make me scream, huh?"

"You know it." Her skin was still a little pink from

where he'd grabbed her. He rubbed the marks, massaging his fingers from her hips to the tops of her thighs. Rubbing, squeezing, watching the color rise as Cruz returned to the bed.

Impossible not to savor the moment. Rachel, stretched out between them, her ass lifted, her expression blissful. It was easy like this. Easy to urge her arms up to the small of her back for Cruz to hold, easy to guide the other man's hand to settle between her shoulder blades. Ace liked chains, sure, but chains couldn't think or adapt, couldn't shift their leverage and move her into position, or turn steely at just the right moment to drive her wild.

"He's going to hold you here," Ace said quietly, brushing Rachel's hair back from her face. "You like that, don't you? Being helpless?"

She tried to stretch again, but Cruz's fingers tightened, and goose bumps rose on her skin. "Yes."

He knew. He'd always known, in his gut, in his *bones*. The reckless abandon that infuriated him when she flung herself at the world was beautiful like this. Trust, simple and pure, and it could only be better if they could convince her to save it for them alone.

Soon, Santana. Soon.

She was shivering beneath his touch now, her body tensing in anticipation. He shifted his hand lower, slipped between her legs to stroke her pussy. Once, twice, teasing up to circle her clit with just enough pressure to make her moan.

The sound still hung in the air when he raised his hand and brought it down the first time. Rachel cried out, arching away for a heartbeat before relaxing with a ragged breath.

Ace liked those sounds, too. So much that he did it again, on the opposite cheek, savoring the crack of his palm and the hitch in her breathing as much as the way her skin turned pink. The flush grew every time he struck her in a different spot, and Rachel squirmed in Cruz's grip as her cries and moans grew lower, more intense.

Her movements changed, too. Instead of tensing every time his hand fell, she arched into each blow. She rubbed her cheek sensuously against the bed, as if seeking more contact, more touch. More sensation.

"Hungry girl." He let the next land a little harder, pushing her toward the blurry edge of pain. "Holding you while you wiggle is getting Cruz hard."

Her hands flexed in the man's grip, and she licked her lips. "Tell me."

Cruz opened his mouth, but Ace forestalled him with another series of smacks, each hard enough to rock her body forward. "You want to see his cock, angel?"

"*Yes*. I want—" She wiggled again. "Let me."

Ace pumped two fingers into her, and *Christ*, she was wet, hot, and melting. Knowing the pain got her going was one thing, but feeling the proof as she clenched around his fingers short-circuited his fucking brain.

He tried to hide it, to sound casual, but his voice came out rough around the edges. As growly as Cruz usually sounded, and he didn't care. "Closer. Don't tell, beautiful girl. Beg. Beg for his cock, and for another chance to make him come all over your pretty face."

She turned her head and looked up at Cruz. "Please," she whispered—ready, eager. "I want you in my mouth while Ace fucks me."

You couldn't be on the receiving end of that stare and not feel like the luckiest bastard in all eight sectors. It sure as hell worked on Cruz—he didn't even glance at Ace for approval before shifting to kneel in front of her.

She reached for him immediately, wrapping one hand around the base of his cock with a satisfied purr. "Beautiful."

"No lie." Ace squeezed her ass before settling behind her and edging her knees apart. "Slide your other hand between your thighs, Rae. I want to see your fingers on your clit when I spank you again."

She didn't move.

Oh *hell*, no.

A growl slipped free as he wrapped one hand in her hair and dragged her head back until he could lean over and meet her eyes. "Is that how it is, Rae? He gets all the sweetness and I get the brat?"

"Could be." But she reached down anyway. She whimpered, her pupils dilating with pleasure. "How sweet do you want me?"

"I didn't say I wanted you sweet." He bent lower, so she'd feel every word as a tickle of warmth across her lips. "Cruz can keep it. I know what to do with a bad girl."

"Mmm. You make her come." She shuddered and licked his mouth, moaning as she pumped her hand up and down the length of Cruz's dick. "Make her beg."

"Uh-uh." He caught her wrist and—with a silent apology to Cruz—hauled her hand away from his shaft. "You can fuck yourself with as many of your own fingers as you can take, but bad girls don't get cock. Not in their hands, not in their mouths, not until their own fingers aren't enough and they promise to be very, very good so they'll get very, very fucked."

She groaned in protest. "Cruz—"

Ace pulled back and let her cast those imploring eyes on Cruz, and lust flared when the other man pressed his thumb to her mouth. "Maybe I'm not the only one going too softly with you. I know you want to be sweet. But you want what he gives the bad girls, too, don't you?"

"Every day." Her throat worked as she swallowed. "Every *breath*."

Cruz lifted his gaze to Ace's, and the world swam out of focus as Rachel trembled between them, soft and, yeah, sweet. He'd gone easy on her because, even now, even reminding himself every fucking second that this wasn't a dream—

It couldn't be real.

None of this could. Not Cruz wanting them both—wanting to share and be shared. Not Rachel, hungry for pain and dominance, starving for everything he'd always wanted to give her. Cruz might have been holding back out of shame, but Ace...

Sheer fucking disbelief.

Another twist tightened his grip in her hair. Rough—too rough, maybe, bringing tears to the corners of her eyes—but he leaned down and found her ear. "Eden. If it's too much, that's what you say. Eden. You understand?"

She nodded, short and quick, restrained by his hand in her hair. "I understand."

He released her without warning, letting her pitch forward, knowing Cruz would be there. And he was, catching her like they'd done this a hundred times. In tune now, on the same wavelength.

He spread one huge hand wide and pressed Rachel's cheek to the mattress. "I don't think the rest of your spanking's going to be very sweet," he said, and Rachel's answering moan was one of blatant, unguarded approval.

Of lust.

So it wasn't sweet at all. Ace straightened and ran his hands down her thighs to haul them even wider. She still had her fingers between her legs, three of them arousal-slicked and shaking, and Ace fell into the moment—the *thrill*.

She'd do anything to please him.

He covered her hand with his and forced her fingers deeper. "Don't you dare stop fucking this pussy. You don't get to suck Cruz's cock again until he's bored of watching you come. And you're going to come, aren't you? All over your own hand, again and again, because the only thing that'll get you off harder than this is when we do it to you at Dallas's next party."

Rachel sucked in a breath and tensed. "In front of everyone?"

"Oh yeah." He rocked his hand over hers, forcing the heel of her palm against her clit. "Noelle will be so fucking jealous, watching you squirm, watching you take it. Lex will be jealous, too—jealous of me."

"She can't have me." Rachel's husky declaration trembled, just like her fingers. "Only the two of you."

"That's right," Cruz said, low and intense, and Ace knew from the look in his eyes that there wouldn't be any wild parties anytime soon where Lex and Noelle crawled all over Rachel and made everyone's day. In time, Cruz might loosen up and roll with the O'Kane version of free love.

Or maybe not. Bren sure as fuck hadn't. A man who thought he'd slide a hand up Six's leg was risking life and limb, and Cruz might always be the same way—wildly, insanely possessive.

It was a whole lot hotter from the inside.

Rachel must have thought so, too. She whimpered again, obviously close to the edge, and Ace had waited long enough. She was warmed up, squirming, ready...

Theirs.

She moaned with the first strike, and this time he gave her no mercy. Just the heat and sting she craved, kindling a fire in them both which went far beyond the physical impact of his palm against her skin. Her cries rose this time, louder with every slap. Her legs shook, and her back arched as she worked her fingers in and out of her pussy.

"Harder," Cruz whispered, so softly Ace almost didn't hear him over Rachel's choked noises and the crack of his hand on her ass. But the word slipped under his skin, temptation and permission, because it didn't matter if he was on the edge. Cruz was right there, attuned to Rachel, observant and strong enough to protect them all.

So he gave her what she wanted. He gave her more.

Her shaking turned to shudders, and her scream drowned out everything else, buzzing in Ace's ears as she tipped over the edge.

Just like that, not being inside her was the worst decision he'd made in his entire fucking life.

She was coming so hard she was still shaking when he tugged her wet fingers away and gripped his cock. Her pussy was still clenching, too, hot and tight as he fucked deep, and she hissed in a choked breath as she slammed back against him.

She was whispering, too, hungry, pleading words that barely penetrated the haze of lust in his brain. Begging, just like she'd promised. Cruz lifted her chin up and cut off her entreaties with a kiss so soft and sweet, it made the words that followed even more obscene. "Open for me. Show me you want Ace to fuck you onto my cock."

She did, tilting her head like Ace had shown her so that Cruz could drive deep, and Ace's hands were goddamn *trembling* as he wrapped them around her waist just above the flare of her hips.

Cruz fisted his cock, rubbing the head against Rachel's lips as he pushed between them, and Ace used his grip to ease her forward, off his dick and onto Cruz's.

Rachel moaned and picked up the rhythm, shivering with pleasure as she rocked between them, welcoming them both into the blisteringly seductive heat of her body. He barely had to touch her—she'd fuck them both just like this, loving it because she was taking them.

But loving it more if *they* took *her*.

He let her sway forward one more time and moved with her, just a few inches, but it made all the difference when she tried to rock back. She was trapped now, filled no matter which way she moved, and Ace let her express her approval with a sharp, muffled squeal before tightening his grip on her and fucking her in earnest.

Fast, hard, plunging into her, and he had to cling to sanity the first time he drove her forward so hard she gagged on Cruz's cock. Walking the edge was one thing, but slipping over—

Her pussy felt like fucking heaven, squeezing down around him. But the goal was *her*, her pleasure, her fantasy, her desire to live and breathe the raw truth of possession, and he and Cruz couldn't forget that.

But Jesus, it was hard. Harder the second time she gagged and strained into it, harder when another thrust pushed Cruz past her gag reflex and she swallowed him, yielding and clenching and so full, Ace almost envied her.

It was Cruz who shoved them over the edge, dragging her off his dick by the hair. He dropped his other hand lower, over her clit. His fingers brushed the base of Ace's cock, and he and Rachel both moaned when Cruz rasped his command. "One more time, honey. Come one more time, and bring him with you."

"I—I *can't*—" A whimper cut through the words. Her chest heaved with panting breaths, and she grasped at them, one hand on Ace's hip and the other on Cruz's chest. "Please—"

Cruz let go of her hair and put his fingers around her throat, a sight that tightened pleasure at the base of Ace's spine. He was close, so close, and he shifted his grip, trying to fuck her to orgasm as Cruz growled in her ear. "You can, and you will. Let go. I have you."

The words melted her resistance, and she clutched at Cruz's hand, holding it in place as she cried out. The first convulsions swept through her, clamping her inner muscles tight around Ace's cock, and for the first time in his life, he couldn't think of an obscenity filthy enough to capture this moment.

Then release broke over him, and he couldn't think at all.

Pleasure pulsed through him, sweeping everything before it, everything but the visual. His hands digging into pale flesh as he ground deep and came, Rachel's blonde hair falling wildly around her shoulders, her head tilted back, her throat caught in Cruz's grip. And his other hand—

They were all getting off together, Cruz jerking his fist over his dick, Rachel writhing in their grip, Ace shuddering as she kept clenching, kept *coming*.

Maybe it was possible to fuck yourself to death. That would explain his current out-of-body experience.

They ended up sprawled across the bed in a tangle of limbs. Ace panted against Rachel's hair as Cruz stroked her body, and the only shock was when the other man managed to disengage long enough to get a warm, damp towel from the bathroom.

Even badass Cruz was walking a little shaky. That could make a man smug almost as fast as the way Rachel curled against him, tucking her head into the space beneath his chin.

Then she spoke—slow and dazed, soft with pleasure. "You think I was caught up in the moment, but I meant it."

His brain was sluggish. It took forever for him to figure out what she meant, and when he did, the import hit him all over again.

I love you.

He made a soothing noise, brushing her hair back from her sweaty cheek, touching her softly. "We've always loved each other, angel. Just promise me you don't hate me anymore."

"No." She smiled against his skin as Cruz smoothed the towel over her abdomen. "I was hurting and said stupid things, but I never hated you."

Ace kept touching her, teasing the strands of her hair straight while Cruz gently eased the plug free of her body. This was what he'd been missing, the lack that had crashed in on him that last time with Bren and Six. Watching Bren go soft around the edges as he ran his hands over Six's trembling form, every touch sweetly possessive and so painfully private Ace hadn't needed to leave. He'd disappeared while standing there, because the only way to get an invite to that secret world was to already belong there.

He hadn't. Not with Bren and Six, not with Noelle and Jas, not with Dallas and Lex. They could be generous and welcoming and reach out with every good intention, but they'd never see him in those first telling seconds.

Rachel saw him. So did Cruz. The other man proved it as he slid into bed, curling around Rachel's back. His other hand settled on Ace's waist, a possessive weight. Warmth and comfort. Acceptance.

Every needy, lost part of him wanted to call it love.

It would have been more comforting if he hadn't told Rachel the truth: it *was* easy to love him in the beginning. The countdown was back, clicking in his head with every thump of his heart, and the worst part was not knowing how long he had left, or how much more lost he'd be when time ran out.

jared

"SO. HERE WE are. Finally."

Jared had never seen Dallas O'Kane look quite this smug—which was a feat, considering he'd been to a handful of the man's parties and watched him play king to an adoring court more times than he could count.

Dallas leaned back in his chair, watching him with a mixture of curiosity and satisfaction, undoubtedly certain that this time he'd finally managed to lure him into the O'Kane web.

"Don't get too excited," Jared warned. "Ace said you were looking for information. I happen to have information."

"Do you, now?" Dallas grunted and reached for a silver cigarette case. "I wondered if he'd asked, to be honest. But I get it. You two have history."

"Enough for him to know that he can ask me anything, even though I might not be able to answer."

Dallas nodded his understanding. "But this time you can."

"After a fashion. One of my clients frequents an underground bar. A speakeasy." Jared smiled. Such a quaint word, an old one O'Kane might not even know. He enjoyed his freedom in the sectors, so much that the furtive language of Eden's more clandestine circles could easily elude him.

But Dallas surprised him, huffing out a laugh as he flicked open his lighter. "So it's Prohibition time in Eden, huh? Everything old is new again."

"Mmm." Of course he got the historical reference. The man might pride himself on his outlaw image, but he wasn't a stupid brute. "Imagine my friend's surprise when the bar was offering O'Kane liquor on her last visit."

Dallas's smile turned fixed. "That would be a surprise, unless Liam Riley happens to own the place. But I imagine his crowd and your crowd don't exactly mix."

"We travel in different circles," Jared agreed. "I was intrigued, so I dropped by the place the other night. The booze they're serving *definitely* didn't come from your barrels."

"Well, fuck." Dallas snapped his lighter shut, his cigarette unlit. "Someone's getting real damn cocky."

"Indeed." Jared shrugged one shoulder. "I suppose one could utilize a little judicious surveillance in order to find out where the shipments originate. If one were so inclined."

"I'm sure one could," Dallas replied easily. "And if it led to something, I'd owe you one hell of a favor. Unless you've reevaluated the sales pitch since the last time Lex dropped it on you."

In his more contemplative moments, he considered it. Joining up with the O'Kanes would ostensibly provide him with a place to belong, something he hadn't had since Eladio had died, and he and Ace and Gia had gone their separate ways.

But it wasn't quite that simple. He'd have to change his entire lifestyle, give up his work, and he wasn't sure he was cut out to trade satin sheets for switchblades. Life in the sector gangs was rough, and he'd had it way too damn easy for way too damn long not to hesitate.

So he deflected. "It's a generous offer. One I'm still mulling over."

Dallas watched him for a few seconds before leaning back to snag a bottle and two glasses off the shelf. "One of the first of Nessa's special batches," he explained as he poured two fingers' width into each glass. "She was fourteen when she barreled this. It should be a hot mess, not one of the best damn things I've ever tasted."

Jared accepted a glass. "The girl has skills. That much is undeniable." She produced smooth liquor, and she took the time to do it right, instead of loading her raw alcohol with colors and additives to approximate the flavor proper aging would have imparted.

"Her grandfather taught us both. I'm good. But she lives and breathes it." Dallas swirled the amber liquid in his glass and smiled. "Have you met Ford?"

"Haven't had the pleasure."

"He used to work in Sector Eight, pretty tight with Jim. But Jim didn't like his brains. He was afraid Ford might get *too* ambitious." Dallas took a sip of his drink and studied Jared. "Me? I think everyone's got their skills. And the more things change, the more we need men with different skills. I don't need another Ace, or another Jas. I need someone like Ford. Someone who can do shit the rest of us can't."

Jared barely managed to suppress a snort. "Like charm the French silk panties right off a politician's chatty wife?"

Dallas snorted. "I said shit we *can't* do. Plenty of sweet Eden girls like a bad boy. You know what they don't like?" He waved his glass in the air. "Thinking they're drinking the same shit as the unwashed masses. You think the liquor she barreled at fourteen is good? It's only getting better. Ford says we're wasting opportunities now."

The rest of the goddamn world wanted power, control...and Dallas O'Kane wanted the rich bitches' money. "You're an odd bird, O'Kane. I just want you to know that."

Dallas grinned. "Think about it. I figure I gotta make the hard sell myself this time, since Ace won't be climbing out from between Rachel and Cruz anytime soon."

Truer words had never been spoken. Jared had stopped off to see his friend before his meeting with Dallas, but he was nowhere to be found. "I'm happy for him. This is what he wanted."

Dallas clinked his glass against Jared's. "Wanna be real happy? Come to the next party and watch the three of them fuck."

One thing he had to admit—the up side to being an O'Kane was pretty goddamn far up. "A word of advice, if I may," Jared murmured. "Next time you want to sell me on joining your little organization? Lead with that."

13

IT WASN'T OFTEN that Six, Rachel, and Trix all had the night off from the Broken Circle. So when Trix invited her to dinner, Rachel jumped at the chance to spend a little time with her friends outside of work.

They ate at a small stand at the edge of the market district, enjoying their meal under a sky full of stars. A hot wind blowing from the south had turned the night unseasonably warm, and they lingered not only over dinner, but also during their walk back to the compound.

"I'm just asking, how big is big?"

Rachel covered her reddening cheeks with both hands. "I'm not going to answer that."

Six kicked an empty tin can out of their path and glanced at Trix. "She'll be as red as your hair if you keep going."

"It's a valid question," Trix protested with a grin. "Especially since some of us missed the show the other night."

Remembering what happened the night that Ace and Cruz had collared her made Rachel blush even harder. She toyed with the ribboned chain dangling from it, weaving it between her fingers as she recalled Ace's promise—or warning.

The only thing that'll get you off harder than this is when we do it to you at Dallas's next party.

She cleared her throat. "If you're so interested in Cruz's dick, I'm sure you'll get another chance to see it. Soon."

"Hallelujah." Trix looped an arm around her shoulders and leaned in for a conspiratorial whisper. "That man is too delicious to keep to yourself."

Six booted another can, and she was blushing now, too. Probably remembering another show, the one Rachel had put on with Dallas and Lex, the first time she'd thrown herself into the midst of true, unadulterated O'Kane sexuality. But she caught Rachel's gaze and grinned. "Forget about his dick, Trix. You really want to be jealous? Those Special Tasks guys have stamina."

Trix let her head fall back with a groan. "That might be the one thing I miss about Sector Five. The guys there were on some goddamn crazy stuff."

"What, like drugs?" Six's brow furrowed. "Since when do those make a guy fuck *better*?"

Trix said something in reply, but Rachel didn't hear her. A prickle of awareness raised the fine hair on the back of her neck, and she turned.

A van was idling on the street at the end of the alley, its windows blacked out by tint or paint. Something tugged at the edges of her consciousness, something *wrong*—

Not idling—in gear and waiting. She registered the engaged brake lights a moment before the side door opened, and three men jumped out.

Shit.

A voice echoed her thought. Six, sounding pissed as she spun to stand shoulder to shoulder with Rachel, heavy brass knuckles already glinting on her fist. "This damn sector's making me soft. I should have brought a gun."

"Bastards. They're going to regret this." Trix followed the words with another curse, her low voice almost eclipsing the vicious sound of her switchblade sliding open.

Rachel felt naked beside them, unarmed and unprepared. But she'd grown up in the dark corners of Eden, in rough places the city barely acknowledged. Street brawls were common, and she'd always held her own.

Her father had taught her a lot of things, but only after he'd taught her how to fight.

The men spread out, blocking one end of the alley, relaxed and cocky as only bullies could be when faced with presumably easy prey. Six spun abruptly and let out another string of curses. "Two more behind us."

No time to look. One of the men from the van lunged at Trix, grabbing for her wrist, and she lashed out, slicing his arm with a snarl. He didn't release her, so Rachel snatched up a rough, broken board leaning against the building beside them and swung it at the man's head. It connected with a sickening, splintering crunch, and he crumpled to the ground.

Another crack sounded behind Rachel, a thud followed by a bellow of pain as a man went flying past her, stumbling into one of his companions. The guy still standing in front of the van snarled and kicked them out of his way as he advanced on Trix. "I'll get this one. You get up and grab the damn blonde! And don't fuck her up—she needs to be alive."

The blood drained from Rachel's face, and she backed away instinctively. If they were after *her*, Christ only knew what they wanted. It could be a dig at Dallas or her father, and there was no way in hell she'd let either happen.

She almost tripped over the man Trix had cut. Blood flowed from his head, but the back of his waistband drew her attention. His shirt had ridden up, revealing the pistol tucked into his pants.

Rachel snatched it up and fired at the man going after Trix. The bullet tore into the right side of his chest, sending him staggering back with shock blooming on his features as he clutched his wound. One of the two remaining men bellowed a curse and lunged toward Rachel from the side. Six appeared out of nowhere, slamming into him hard enough to send them both sprawling.

With their easy prey turned vicious and the leader staggering, the remaining upright attacker whirled and bolted for the van.

Trix ran down the alley after him, pausing only to snatch up a broken brick. She threw it at the van, where it smashed against the driver's side window with enough force to shatter the safety glass into a haze of webbed cracks. "Hey! Get back here and take your street trash with you, motherfucker!"

Six rose from the still body beneath her and scrambled over to the man Rachel had shot. She shoved both hands to his chest, but the blood pumping from his wound had already slowed. "Shit. I didn't mean to kill that last guy, and this one's toast, too. Having someone to drag back to Cruz and Bren would have been useful."

"I don't know if it would have done much good," Rachel told her numbly. They had come after her, and there were precious few reasons anyone would risk that. "Do you recognize them?"

"Maybe." Six stood and wiped her bloody hands on her jeans. Several steps took her to the man Trix had stabbed, the one Rachel had hit with the splintered board. She turned him over with her boot and squinted down at his face. "There's something familiar about this one, but that doesn't mean much. Guys in Three will hire out to anyone with cash."

Rachel shivered, even in her lined jacket, and rubbed her hands over her upper arms. "Let's get the fuck out of here before the guy comes back with reinforcements. Dallas will want to know about this."

"And he'll want us all locked down." Six wrapped an arm around Rachel, squeezing her shoulders. "You okay?"

Not remotely. As a Riley, she could take care of herself, but she didn't have to like the violence. She never would. Her stomach roiled, and she crossed her arms over her midsection. "I want to go home."

Trix finished checking the final man's pockets. "He's got nothing. None of them do." She looked around the alley with a sigh. "You think it's related to the bootlegging?"

"Could be," Six replied, keeping her arm tight around Rachel. "Or it could just be random. People are poking at the edges, trying to see if Dallas is paying attention. Like those kids who robbed Ford's new assistant. Some people are just bad. The second they can't feel your boot on their neck, they act up."

It was more words than Rachel had ever heard Six say at once, maybe ever, and it tipped her hand. She was nervous, too. They all were, and for good reason.

Six might have been nervous, but she also spoke the truth. The attack could've come from anywhere.

Before Noah Lennox, Cruz had been confident he knew every way in and out of Eden.

Lord, had he been wrong.

The tunnels that ran beneath the city and out into the sectors were kept secret from most of the inhabitants on both sides of the wall. The military police knew of their existence, of course, and the Special Tasks teams were intimately familiar with them. Teams like the one Cruz and Bren had once belonged to used them to ghost in and out of the city, invisible to the people whose lives and well-being they were supposedly working to secure.

But the tunnels were even more extensive than Cruz had realized, and Noah knew how to access areas marked *incomplete* on every map they'd ever seen.

"My grandfather's work," the hacker admitted as he used a handheld tablet to descramble the lock on a door Cruz had walked by a dozen times without really seeing. Noah had revealed an access panel by prying away a plate that blended almost seamlessly with the white-washed cement wall, and the door itself was only outlined by a faint shadow—one of many in the poorly lit tunnels.

It whispered open on a silent mechanism once the code was complete. It was dark on the other side, and Cruz held up a flashlight as Bren guarded their backs. "Your grandfather?"

"Mmm." Noah unhooked his tablet and slid the panel back into place. "He helped design the city's networking, back when it was supposed to be utopia. Before the military—"

He cut off abruptly with a wary look Cruz's way. If Noah had access to Eden's files, he'd know where Cruz had come from. He might even think he understood what it meant to be from the Base.

No one understood. No one could, not even Bren. "Before the military took it," he finished quietly. Not that the General had ever framed it quite like that—rescuing an important resource from the chaotic panic of civilians sounded far more inspiring than outright theft. "I know what happened."

Noah cleared his throat. "Right. Well, long story short—my grandfather hacked the records. Erased plenty of places from the city plans, which means we should be able to get right on top of this speakeasy without anyone noticing."

"Provided Jared gave us accurate directions," Bren said.

"Provided that," Noah agreed, already moving deeper into the darkness, shining a tiny light ahead of him.

Cruz let Bren precede him before slipping through the door, which slid shut as quietly as it had opened. A surveillance mission hadn't been at the top of his list of things to do after coming back to the compound to find out that someone had tried to snatch Rachel off the street. He'd rather be back in his room, with her cuddled safely against his side. Preferably with Ace there, too, both where he could see them. Protect them.

But there were other O'Kanes guarding her back tonight. Mad and Ace were there, along with Zan, the quiet bouncer. And Six and Lex were just as deadly, not to mention a whole lot more likely to be underestimated by someone out to cause trouble.

Rachel was damn near as safe as she could be, and Cruz was doing the only thing that could truly make her safer—getting the intel they needed to end this shit.

Knowing that didn't make it easier to be gone, something Bren would understand. "How was Six after the fight?"

"Angry," Bren answered. "Mad at the assholes who attacked them, and mad at herself for not managing to take one alive."

Taking someone alive was harder than simply winning a fight, but Bren knew that, and undoubtedly Six did, too. They were all lucky that *alive* had been one of the requirements the kidnappers had been operating under—though Cruz's fingers curled into a fist at the thought of what often happened to prisoners who needed to be taken alive.

Cruz forced himself to exhale, to relax his hand. Calm and reason, that would keep Rachel safer than rage. "I'm assuming she told you what she remembered. Did any details stand out?"

"They were looking for a quick pickup." Bren grinned, wide and feral. "And they weren't ready for three O'Kane women to fight back."

No, they wouldn't have been, and Cruz shared Bren's smile. "Poor planning on their part, then."

"And poor planning means bad intel."

Noah bit off a curse from the other door, his face eerily lit by the glowing tablet screen. "Speaking from personal experience? It takes an act of fucking God—or access to secret Council files—to get reliable intel on the O'Kanes. Bren has one of the most complete files I've ever seen. Took me forever to figure out half of it was faked."

"Serves you right for snooping." Bren jerked his head toward the door. "Through this one, then the tunnel to the left, yeah?"

"Dead on." Another few seconds of cursing, and Noah opened the door. The tunnel on the other side had lighting strips along the top of one wall. The floor sloped gradually upwards, toward a dead end with another door. "I'm sure you guys know this tech better than I do," Noah said, swinging his pack around before tossing it to Bren. "But I made some upgrades to the facial-recognition algorithms. It's always iffy with pictures taken in the dark, though, because intensity and contrast—"

"Clear pictures are better," Cruz cut in. Noah was terse as hell until you got him rolling on some fine point of technology or code, and then the man couldn't seem to run through words fast enough. "Got it."

Bren slung the bag over his shoulder. "Call it, Cruz—you want to plant the tracker or deploy the drone?"

Cruz grinned, and for a moment it was like a decade had fallen away, like he and Bren were on just another mission, ready to give each other a hard time right up until the bullets started flying. "You're out of practice,

Donnelly. Stick to the easy shit and leave the tracker to me."

"You saying I've gone soft?"

"Maybe."

"Whatever," Noah interjected as the door slid open. "You're both crazy scary motherfuckers, so get out there and do your thing."

Cruz slipped through the door, into the darkness of an abandoned office. This section of Eden was mostly warehouses, empty caverns of space that had once held surplus supplies looted from cities within driving distance. But Eden churned through resources faster than necessary, and didn't trust a populace that got poorer every year. Anything of value had been moved to a more secure location years before Cruz had run his first mission.

Short-sighted. Stupid. No wonder men like Ashwin Malhotra no longer considered loyalty to Eden their first priority.

Bren held up one hand in a silent gesture—*stop*—and cocked his head. Activity bustled on the other side of one thin wall, the sounds of wood scraping and glass clinking. He scanned the room, pointed two fingers to his eyes, then indicated the far side of the warehouse.

With one finger, he quickly sketched a box in the air. *Window.* At Cruz's nod of understanding, he slung the bag containing the surveillance drone off his shoulder and melted into the shadows.

The window wasn't large, but Cruz didn't need it to be. It squeaked slightly when he lifted it the first two inches, but through the gap he could hear the men in the alley, talking over an idling engine. No shouts—they wouldn't want to call attention to what they were doing any more than Cruz did—but they weren't good at stealth.

Cruz was. With the tracker and the rest of his tools secured to his belt, he opened the window all the way, slipped through it, and lowered himself silently to the ground. Gravel stirred beneath his boots, just a whisper, and he dropped to a crouch in the shadows and looked to his right.

The truck was facing him, parked at a crooked angle, as if backed up to the door by someone without much skill. Even better for Cruz—they'd swung the truck doors open to unload the merchandise, blocking their view of the narrow space between the vehicle and the building.

He could have strolled in and slapped the tracker into place in broad daylight.

Not that he was careless. Too much was riding on this for any accidents. Cruz stayed low, inching along the side of the building, thankful that Eden didn't waste energy on streetlights here. He made it within a few feet of the front fender before dropping to roll under it, careful not to disturb any stray garbage. He was close enough to hear the men clearly now, and all it would take was one slip—

"I can't believe they go through this shit so fast."

"No kidding. Good thing for them it's cheaper than the real stuff."

A snort. "You been in this joint? They charge *more* than the real stuff. Didn't think that was possible."

"Fancy fuckers," a third voice replied as Cruz dug out the tracker and affixed it to the undercarriage. "Money makes 'em stupid."

"Amen." Bottles clattered, followed by a vicious curse. "You drop that, and the boss'll have your ass."

"Hell, you think I'm scared of—"

The third man, the one with an unmistakable thread of intelligence running through his voice, hissed. "Shut the fuck up. You know the MPs have eyes and ears all over the goddamn place."

It was truer than they'd ever know. Bren might have already deployed the surveillance drone, which would send video back to Noah's tablet as long as he stayed within range—a limitation the official drones didn't share. By the time Cruz crawled back through the window and into the tunnels, the hacker would be cleaning up whatever shots he'd managed to get of these men's faces. If he was fast, he'd be comparing them to Eden's files.

The drone would tell them who, and the tracker would tell them where. Knowing both would give them time to do real surveillance, to plan an attack that wouldn't just lop off a few branches, but tear the whole messy operation up by the roots.

Cruz made sure the tracker was secure before crawling back to the wall, but he was still three feet from the window when the truck doors slammed behind him.

No time for careful. He hoisted himself and went through the window headfirst, biting off a curse when his shoulder smashed into the cement floor. Not the most graceful roll, but he managed to come up on his knees, crouched just low enough to watch the men pull the delivery truck past the window and out of the alley.

He turned and found Bren standing there, grinning. "Now who's out of practice?" he asked, tossing the bag to Cruz. "Come on. Let's see if Noah's turned up anything yet."

"Impossible," Cruz retorted, but a few minutes later he was standing next to Noah, eating his words for a second time.

Noah was fast. He was good. Scary good, because Cruz had known techies who could make computers sing, and they would have been hard-pressed to pull a clean image and a facial match out of thin air, much less using a portable tablet and home-brewed algorithms.

Noah didn't just have the faces. He had dossiers, and a serious expression that spelled trouble.

With dread building in his gut, Cruz lifted a brow and tried to sound casual. "And?"

Instead of speaking, Noah handed the tablet to Bren.

He stared down at it for several endless moments before shaking his head and passing it on to Cruz. "One unidentified...and two known associates of Liam Riley."

Fucking hell.

14

DALLAS HAD THROWN the gang into lockdown mode, which usually led to a lot of pissed-off O'Kane women, resentful of the restrictions on their freedom.

Tonight, three of their own had been attacked. Tonight, lockdown had led to drinking.

Ace heard the voices from the first floor of the living quarters, the kind of wild feminine laughter that only seemed to happen when men weren't around. Ace had gate-crashed enough girls' nights to know just how ribald a group of women could get *before* they broke out the liquor.

On any other night, that would have been reason enough to climb the stairs to where Lex and Noelle had claimed Dallas's party room for a different sort of debauchery. But tonight—

Tonight, he really needed to see Rachel.

Nessa's voice rose as he approached the door, edged

with liquor and laughter. "—so then he was like, 'most women only get off from anal sex—'"

"Wait, wait, no—" Noelle gasped, barely getting the words out around her giggles. "He said that while he had his hand in your pants?"

"Yeah, but I didn't let him keep it there after that," Nessa retorted. "Maybe that works on women who've never stuck their *own* hands in their pants. But even then, fuck. If he gives up after thirty seconds with his fingers, what are the odds he knows what to do with his dick?"

"Zero," Trix declared confidently. "Well, maybe two percent—but only because he could've gotten lucky and hit the right spots by accident."

More laughter, as Noelle and Six started to argue over whether two percent was too high or not high enough. Ace paused in the shadow of the doorway, peering in. Most of the women were there—even Amira, with tiny Hana nestled in a clever sling and sleeping against her mother's chest.

Rachel sat there right along with the rest of them, a drink in her hand and a bright smile on her face. But the smile was fixed, nothing like her usual, gentler expressions, and it didn't quite reach her eyes.

She was trying. Lord, she was trying, because she knew this was for her benefit. The stories, the drinking, the women gathered together—they were here for Rachel, to have her back, to make it clear she'd never be alone.

So Rachel would be here for them, because that was who she was. Giving until it broke her.

Fuck that.

Ace swung into the room, grinning. "Okay, ladies, I'm here. The party can start now."

"Uh-uh, no penises allowed." Amira threw a pretzel in his direction. "Not even yours."

"I'm wounded," he retorted, swooping down to kiss

her cheek. He spared a moment to stroke Hana's dark hair and trace a fingertip over her tiny little ear.

Babies were a new addition to the O'Kane compound—unsurprising, considering the danger of their lives and how much it cost to get reproductive drugs that made them possible—but Hana was enchanting when she wasn't screaming or puking. Small and perfectly formed and capable of a surprising range of emotion between her papa's big blue eyes and her mama's pretty smile.

Hana stirred, and Ace stroked her cheek again. "Hey, peanut."

"Oh, that's cheating," Noelle groaned. "Being adorable with the baby is out-of-bounds. Lex, make him stop."

"Can't." Lex arched an eyebrow as she reached for a half-empty whiskey bottle and refilled her glass. "Adorable is Ace's middle name."

"You know it, sister." Ace offered Noelle a wink, grabbed the bowl of pretzels, and parked his ass next to Rachel. He threw an arm around her, too, trying to make it look casual even as he tucked her close to his side. "So, Nessa. Tell me more about this ass-lover so Bren and I can round up Jas and Mad and kick him into next year."

"Oh, God." Nessa shot him both middle fingers. "This is why I never get laid, seriously."

Rachel poked him in the side. "Being an idiot isn't an ass-kicking offense."

"Being an idiot to an O'Kane woman about sex is," he retorted.

Hana fussed a little louder, and Amira squinted at Ace as she eased her daughter from the sling. "He who wakes the baby holds the baby, Santana."

Maybe he shouldn't have been pleased, but Ace still smiled as he held out his hands. "Give her here. She loves me just as much as the rest of you do. As she should, because I'm damn lovable."

Amira settled the infant into his arms. Ace shifted

her carefully, tucking the blanket more snugly around her body. He'd been scared of holding her at first, terrified of breaking her. Everyone had been, except Jas and Six, who'd grown up on farms where Eden didn't bother with birth control in the water. Babies meant workers on the farms—everywhere else, they were just more mouths to feed, a drain on resources.

That's what they were in Sector Four, too, but *damn*, they were cute.

Rachel finished her drink and slid her finger into Hana's outstretched hand, like it was the most natural thing in the world. The baby gripped it and cooed, eliciting the first real smile Ace had seen on Rachel since walking in.

It slayed him.

"She's sweet," Rachel said quietly. "Reminds me of my baby cousins."

Ace had only had one "uncle"—a man who may or may not have been related to him—but that grumpy bastard sure as hell hadn't reproduced. "Do you have a lot of them?"

"More than my share," she admitted. "In my old neighborhood, babies were a sign of prosperity. The bigger the family, the better off everyone knew you were because it meant you could afford to pay the bribes *and* take care of them all."

Eden supposedly had limits on children for the same reason they pumped birth control into every source of water they could reach. You could only balance so many rich people on the backs of the poor, after all. It figured they broke the rule as fast as they could make it, as if that extra bribe money would do them shit-all good when they were outnumbered ten to one and everyone was hungry.

They'd never realize it, though, not until it was too late. Ace had nailed enough wives and daughters of councilmen to know those fancy bastards couldn't see what was going on right under their noses—or in their own beds.

Hana made a pleased, burbly sound and waved her little fist with Rachel's finger still firmly in hand. Ace hadn't known about her cousins. He hardly knew shit about her life before, because it wasn't the sort of thing you asked about. Life in Eden was bad—and if hers hadn't been, why grind salt in the wounds by reminding her she could never go back?

A safe enough rule, but it felt shallow now. Not because he thought he should ask, but because he honestly wanted to know. "What about your family? Did you have brothers or sisters?"

Rachel's smile went rigid again. "No. Pregnancy was hard on my mother, so there's just me."

And she'd been exiled, taking the fall for her father's bargain with Dallas O'Kane. *Way to go, Santana.* He couldn't even manage basic human bonding without the verbal equivalent of kneeing someone in the guts. Cruz should have been there, petting her or holding her or saying all the right things.

Too bad Cruz was out exercising one of his ten thousand other skills, and Rachel was stuck with Ace. The guy you called when you wanted to get inked or fucked.

Lex poured refills all around, and Rachel eagerly wrapped her trembling fingers around the glass and downed it all at once.

Silence fell, a little awkward until Jade rose and glanced at Amira. "Do you mind if I hold Hana?"

"Go ahead." Amira tilted her head. "I think it might be time for Rachel to get some rest, anyway. It's been a long damn day."

"I'm fine," Rachel protested.

"You're tired," Noelle countered as Jade gathered the baby out of Ace's arms. Nessa collected Rachel's glass and kissed her cheek, and before Ace knew it they were both upright, with half a dozen women flashing him meaningful looks when they thought Rachel wouldn't see.

So much for rescuing Rachel from the clutches of well-meaning sisterhood. *We gave you your chance,* all those pointed looks practically screamed, demanding that he step up and make this work. And it shouldn't have been so fucking hard—he knew how to soothe a woman, how to make one smile.

A random woman, maybe. Not the woman he loved.

Shit.

He had to try, so he slipped an arm around her waist and guided her toward the door. "Come on, angel. Walk with me?"

"I'm—" She swayed, stumbled, and stepped on his foot. "Christ, I'm a fucking mess, aren't I?"

What would Cruz have done?

No question, really. Ace hoisted Rachel in his arms, cradling her against his chest as he started toward his room. "No, you're a tough-ass woman who had a fucking awful day."

She curled her fingers in his shirt with a moan. "It's so much stupider than that."

"So tell me, honey. Talk to me."

She turned her face into the hollow of his shoulder. "I can't."

His heart hurt like hell. Maybe he'd sprained it, trying to do something beyond his abilities. Loving wasn't any easier than fighting—it took training and skill, and he was shit with both. But she sounded so lost that he kept trying, shoving through the ache. "You can tell me anything, Rae. I swear it, okay? On my life. On my ink. Hell, on my dick."

Her sudden laugh huffed against his skin, and she lifted her head. "I'm sweet. That's what you always say. Cruz, too."

"Because you are," he said, and knew it was wrong the second the words left his lips. Not because they weren't true, but because there was a rawness in her eyes, a fear he should have seen. "But that's not all you are."

"I wasn't that at all. Not today."

He bit his lip on the instinctive protest and concentrated on navigating the stairs. At the bottom, he let her slide slowly to the floor and cupped her face, tilting her head back. "You kicked ass today, because someone was trying to hurt you and your friends. What's not sweet about that?"

"I don't *know*." She tried to turn her head, but he held her tight, and she closed her eyes. "Sometimes it hits me, and I remember. I'm not here because someone wanted me to be an O'Kane, but because Dallas and my father made a deal. I'm here because Eden had to have someone to punish."

"Bullshit," Ace said, the word rough enough to have him wincing. He pressed his forehead to hers and softened his voice. "So you got the ink by saving us from Eden. Then you made us love you. *You*, not your daddy, not your big sacrifice. You walked in here, drank your double shots, and belonged more than most of us ever could."

She melted against him with a soft sigh, her cheek to his and her mouth close to his ear. "Say it again."

No playing stupid, because he knew the words she wanted. They were easy because they'd been true forever, and hard as hell because they had never mattered this much before. "We love you," he whispered. "I love you."

Her arms locked around his neck. "I protected my friends. Myself. And I still hate it. I *hate* what happened."

"Hey, I know. I know, Rae." He smoothed his thumbs under her eyes. "Some people kill easy. Some feel like shit. Some can't do it at all. I hate that you had to, but only because it's hurting you. And it has nothing to do with how sweet you are."

"I'll be better tomorrow," she promised. "I'm drunk and stupid, that's all."

"You're tired." He dropped a kiss to each eyelid before brushing his lips against hers. "And maybe a little drunk, yeah. Ready to tumble into bed, angel?"

"Mmm." She opened her eyes, looking blurry and dazed. "Maybe I shouldn't have had that last drink."

And maybe it was exactly what she'd needed. Sweeping her up into his arms was easy this time, and she nestled against him like she belonged there. "It's okay, honey. I've got you."

"Stay with me," she mumbled, soft and slurred.

"Always, angel." Or at least until Cruz came back to say all the right things.

Rachel woke up with a splitting headache, in a room she'd never seen before.

It had to belong to Ace. Mounted canvases hung on every wall, surrounding her in blazes of vivid color. But instead of the relatively smooth surfaces she'd seen on the pre-Flare artwork collected by Ace or Lex or Dallas, these pieces had been piled high with paint. It had dried on the surfaces in raised ridges and whorls, creating a three-dimensional effect that made her itch to touch them.

Between the paintings were shelves and racks of chains and floggers and toys, and she blushed, hot and sudden, as she averted her eyes. It was too intimate, being in Ace's bedroom for the first time, even without the blatant reminders of all the things he could do to her—and Cruz—in it.

She crawled out of the bed, dragging a sheet along to wrap around her body. She lifted a hand to one of the paintings, an innocuous blur of blue and green and yellow, just as a door to her right swung open. Ace walked out, his jeans low on his hips, his skin still damp.

He rubbed a towel over his hair before tossing it over a nearby chair. "I didn't think you'd be up yet. How's your head?"

"It's been better." She turned and caught sight of a bench—much like one Dallas had in his room. She'd seen it in action exactly once, and remembering it was enough to make her blush even harder. "I, uh—I've never been in here before."

His gaze followed hers, and a slow smile curled his lips up. "It's new. I told you there was furniture."

"When were you planning on showing me?"

"Eventually." He hooked a hand under the canvas and lifted it off the wall. "Did you want to look at it up close?"

The painting, not the bench. "It's beautiful. Everything you do is beautiful."

"Not everything." He laid the painting on the nearby table and frowned at it as he ran a finger over one of the raised swirls. "I couldn't get the colors right on this one. It was easier in Eden. I always knew I'd be able to get the supplies I wanted. I did this one before I really learned to work with what I have here."

"I like it." Her hand brushed his as she traced the swooping lines of paint. "Will you show me sometime? How you make them?"

"Sure. You could look at—" He cut off, and for a second he looked self-conscious. "Nah, you don't need to go clomping around in my workroom. You need food. And a bath."

She opened her mouth to protest, only for her stomach to rumble loudly. "I could eat," she said instead, covering her mortification with laughter. "Breakfast in bed?"

Ace laughed and leaned in to kiss her cheek. "The bathroom's through there. Clean up and crawl back into bed. I'm gonna go raid the kitchen."

"Okay."

The bathroom was huge—and still steamed up from Ace's bath. Rachel cut on the water, slipped into the stall, and leaned against the warm tile. It reminded her of being in Cruz's shower with Ace before, listening to him whisper about touching himself through fantasies of her.

Do you know how many times I've jerked off in the shower while imagining your hands on my dick?

She sucked in a breath, dipped her head under the water, and reached for the shampoo. She scrubbed quickly, before the memories of that morning could sweep her away into some deliciously distracting fantasies of her own. But when she climbed out of the shower and wrapped herself in a clean, fluffy towel, distraction was exactly what she found.

There was another door on the far side of the bathroom, this one open just a crack, but wide enough for her to see a paint-splattered table and walls. When she nudged the door open, she saw the shelves beyond, lined with tubs of paint and jars of water. Half a dozen empty buckets were stacked against the wide table, and on top of it—

Two half-finished paintings. The one on the left was of a blonde woman lying on her side in bed, almost all of her naked flesh on display. There were two lotus flowers and a wild tangle of vines running up and down her back, ending above the lush curve of her ass.

The tattoos were Rachel's, and so was the fuzzy profile of the figure's partially turned head.

The other painting was of Cruz, just as naked, but standing strong and proud. His likeness was less complete, more detailed around his tattoos than anywhere else, but mostly shadows and lines that suggested his massive physical strength.

The emotion in the paintings was more straightforward than in the abstract textured work he usually did, but it was no less complex. His longing and affection were plain, but it was all tinged by a darkness she couldn't quite understand. There was a certain distance in the paintings, as if the whole point was melancholy admiration for the subjects...because you could never, ever hope to touch them, not really.

"The world through my eyes." She hadn't heard him come in, but his voice came from just behind her, and his fingers traced a path down her back, over the tattoos he'd placed there. "Vain, huh?"

"I guess that depends." She reached out and lightly echoed his caress on the painting of her. "Are these about your work, or about me and Cruz?"

"Your guess is as good as mine. It's not the same as giving someone a tattoo. I use my head for that. With the paint..." He caught her hand and tugged until she collided with his chest. "Maybe I use my heart. Or maybe it's just pretty colors."

"No, not that." She turned in his arms and looked up at him. "The way they make me feel, there's *something* there."

"Yeah?" He settled his hands on her hips and smiled. "Then tell me. How do they make you feel?"

He wouldn't like the truth, but she couldn't bring herself to lie. "Sad. You painted us like—like we're far away. Like we're not with you."

"You *were* far away when I started them."

That was fair enough. "Mmm, but not anymore." She stretched up and kissed his chin. "Guess you'll have to start new ones."

"Guess I will." A tilt of his head and his mouth found hers, but he only lingered for a few seconds before spinning her toward the door. "Now you're going to get your deliciously naked little ass out of here before I forget I was going to feed you."

"Can't. I'm starving." She made a beeline for the bed and slipped beneath the covers as he swept up a battered paper sack from the table. "What'd you bring us?"

"Warm biscuits, to start." He sprawled across the bed and arched an eyebrow at her. "Do you know what's happening in the downstairs kitchen as we speak?"

Of course she did, because she actually saw the sun rise sometimes. "Lessons. Six has been teaching everyone to cook like her mom did." She nudged him with her foot. "You'd know these things if you got up before noon once in a while."

He mock-glared at her as he passed over one napkin-wrapped biscuit, still warm and rich with the scent of sugar and raspberries. "Noelle sent that. Got it from Lex, I think. I don't know anyone else who manages to get fresh jam on a regular basis."

Rachel broke off one flaky edge and popped it into her mouth. The sweetness of the fruit exploded over her tongue, tempered by the slightly salty biscuit. "I tried to grow some strawberries on top of the warehouse once. I got a few, but nowhere near enough to cook them down into jam."

"Maybe you need more space." He unpacked more items from the bag—a few apples, another napkin wrapped around crisp bacon, and a couple hunks of cheese. "Jade and Six were talking about taking over the new warehouse roof for a giant garden. It'd take some work, but I guess Jade really wants something to do now that she feels better."

"I could help." His hair had fallen over his forehead, and Rachel bit her lip to hold back a smile as she brushed it away.

His gaze went soft and warm as he chased her hand and kissed her fingertips. "It's too cold to plant, but Cruz might let us out of bed by springtime."

"You don't want him to. And neither do I."

"Maybe not." His expression turned serious, eyes locking on hers. "I don't think either of us want you off the compound again until this bootlegging shit gets straightened out. Not after yesterday."

Guilt slammed into her. She didn't have any problems lying, apparently, because she still hadn't admitted the truth about the attack. "You should be worried, maybe," she muttered. "I'm pretty sure they were after *me*."

Ace rolled to his knees, his body tense, his eyes hard. "What?"

"Get up and grab the damn blonde! And don't fuck her up—she needs to be alive." Rachel parroted the words. Her lips were numb, so she licked them before meeting Ace's eyes. "Doesn't sound too good for me, huh?"

"Jesus Christ, Rae." He caught her face between shaking hands. "You told Dallas, right?"

"Six was there. She told Bren, Bren told Dallas. That's the way it goes." Her stomach twisted, and she touched his hands before dropping her arms to her sides. "I didn't want you to know."

"*Why?*"

Because it was dangerous, letting the slightest thing go wrong. Things were still so new, tenuous, and if she didn't keep them perfect, if she gave him an excuse, an out—

Ace had bailed on her once. He could do it again, and this time she wouldn't be the only one with a broken heart. She had to think about Cruz, too.

It felt unfair, a little too much like betrayal, sitting around and wondering when Ace would leave them. It *was* a betrayal. But the fear was there, a cold knot in her stomach, undeniable.

Inescapable.

"You worry," she heard herself saying, "and there's nothing to worry about. I'm staying put. No more chances."

"No more shows, either." It was Cruz's voice, tired and serious, coming from the doorway. "That's straight from Dallas."

"I don't need the money." No, she needed the freedom, to know that she was finally doing something instead of waiting for life to happen to her. But there were other ways. "No more shows."

But Ace had gone rigid. "She pulls down money hand over fist. What the fuck did you find last night that's so—?"

He cut off abruptly with a sideways look at Rachel. Cruz sighed, shut the door behind him, and slowly crossed the room. "She knows it's not good," he told Ace without releasing Rachel's gaze. "I asked Dallas if I could tell you first. But when you're done eating, he and Lex need to speak with you."

He'd gone into the city to pull surveillance with Bren and Noah, and now he was looking at her like the world was crumbling. "Just say it, Lorenzo."

He showed her instead, slipping a tablet from inside his jacket. A smaller model, no bigger than his hand, but the picture on the screen was crisp and bright.

She would have recognized the man anyway. His features were unmistakable, even if she hadn't spent the better part of a decade looking at him every day. Even if she hadn't seen him only days before. "Skinny Pete. He works for my father." The implication was stark, unforgiving, and her fingers clenched around the edge of the tablet. "He was at the drop?"

"Unloading the liquor," Cruz confirmed. "Supervising, I think, though I'd need to hear his voice to be sure."

It was a setup. That was the only thing that made sense. "Someone's trying to pit Dallas and my father against one another. Start a war."

"Maybe." Cruz sat on the edge of the bed, dropping one hand to squeeze her leg. "No one's jumping to conclusions, especially after what happened yesterday."

Liam Riley wasn't a saint—far from it—but the attempted kidnapping made one thing painfully clear, even in the whirling confusion of Rachel's mind. "Whatever kind of game he was running, there is no goddamn way my father would risk my safety. None. Which means there has to be someone else in play."

"Then we'll find out who." Cruz said it as if it was already fact, with such confidence that she didn't doubt it for a moment. In Eden or in the sectors, no matter where he was, he was going to be a hero.

Their hero. She slid her hand into Ace's and squeezed. "It would have to be someone who'd know how to get to Skinny Pete," she noted. "I guess Dallas has already called my father out for a chat?"

Cruz nodded. "And gotten an answer. He'll be here this afternoon. I don't know if you want to be at the meeting..."

"No." There was no way they'd be able to hash things out with her sitting there. "I'll need to talk to Dallas and Lex beforehand. Make sure they understand."

The rest was out of her hands.

15

CRUZ KNEW THE explosion was coming, he just didn't know what would set it off.

Ace was brooding. Angry. Cruz could read the signs, because reading people had been part of his job. Flat eyes. Compressed lips. Tense muscles. Arms crossed, posture closed off.

Unsubtle. Cruz doubted that was an accident, since not one of those signs had been evident before Rachel had pulled on her clothes and left to meet Dallas and Lex.

Cruz could have followed. He needed a shower and a few hours of sleep before Rachel's father showed up, and both would be easier to get in his own rooms, free of Ace's clenched jaw and tight sighs.

But they were unsubtle, as close as Ace came to deliberate vulnerability. So Cruz stripped, stepped into Ace's spacious, tiled shower, and considered how easily the three of them could fit in there. Rachel caught between them, wet skin slippery with suds as they lifted her—

"You could have told me, brother."

Cruz rinsed his hair before glancing over his shoulder. The shower was so deep it didn't need a door to keep the spray from the rest of the bathroom. Ace had hung a curtain anyway, and he pulled it aside now as he stood there, still shirtless. Still frowning.

It was a magnificent sight. The ink alone would have made him stand out, but for all his joking about being a lover instead of a fighter, Ace had a lean, beautiful body. Not bulky or overly cut, but muscular and tough. Hard in all the right ways.

"Cruz." Ace's frown deepened, though something flashed through his eyes—appreciation of Cruz's distraction, even a hint of dark satisfaction. Fair enough, since lust came so easily now, fraternization be damned.

But there was pain under his words, so Cruz forced himself to pay attention. "What didn't I tell you?"

The wrong answer. A furrow formed between Ace's brows as he crossed his arms over his chest again, flexing and hard and damp from the tiny droplets of water splashing off Cruz's shoulders. "So you weren't holding back, it just straight up never occurred to you. It still hasn't."

Still vague, but a swift process of elimination brought him to the only thing that might matter to Ace. "That Rachel was the apparent target of the kidnapping?"

"*Apparent?*" Ace slapped a hand against the mosaic tile, his eyes burning. "Someone says *grab the blonde*, and you don't think maybe that's information I should have?"

Cruz shoved his damp hair back from his forehead and faced Ace head-on. "It wasn't information you could use," he said bluntly. "Would knowing have changed any of the decisions you made last night?"

"Maybe," Ace snapped. "Knowing *she* knew might have. Why didn't you take five minutes to warn me?"

"Because I assumed she'd tell you!"

He hadn't realized he was throwing a verbal sucker-punch until it landed, and then he hated himself for it because for one terrible second, Ace was as naked as Rachel at her most vulnerable. Those dark, expressive eyes shuttered with pain, and Ace was already turning to leave when Cruz grabbed his arm.

Ace tried to rip free with a growled curse, but one jerk and he crashed back against Cruz's chest, slick skin slapping together. "Don't. Don't run."

"Fuck you, brother." Ace drilled his elbow into Cruz's ribs. "And if you think I won't knock your balls up into your ears because you've got a hard-on from staring at me—"

Cruz shut him up by slamming him into the opposite side of the shower hard enough to drive a grunt from them both. "You won't. You're too busy feeling sorry for yourself."

He expected retaliation this time, and he twisted before Ace managed to break his nose with the back of his skull. But Ace was *fast* when he was pissed, and he wrenched out of Cruz's slippery grip and knocked them both backwards.

Cruz's back hit the wall beneath the shower spray. Ace pinned him there, smacking the showerhead to one side so the water bounced off the tile and soaked his jeans. "I'm just remembering my place," he hissed, wrapping a hand around Cruz's dick. "Not tactical decisions. Not emotional support."

Ace stroked upward, and this time Cruz whacked his own head against the tiles, groaning as the slick, rough touch sparked pleasure up his spine. Ace was still pissed, still furious, but there was a different kind of heat in the growl of his voice, along with an undertone of pain so sharp and vulnerable, Cruz couldn't have pushed him away if he wanted to.

Not that he wanted to.

"Yeah, that's right." Ace pumped harder, his face inches from Cruz's. "I'm the one who makes it okay for you to shove your cock so far down her throat she can't breathe. I'm the one who makes it okay to fuck her so hard she feels you for days."

The words landed painfully, just as Ace had known they would. Because Cruz could protest, could claim *Rachel* was the one who made it okay by wanting it, but she'd been telling him what she wanted all along and Cruz hadn't heard—or hadn't believed.

He'd needed another man to tell him it was true. Fucking hell, he was a bastard.

Rage burned in his chest, as hot as the desire. Ace read it in his eyes and laughed, slowing his strokes, squeezing Cruz's shaft. "Yeah, that's right. Not so fucking honorable after all, are—?"

Cruz grabbed him by the throat and rolled them, putting Ace against the wall again, still grinning, still gripping Cruz's dick, because the flash of temper proved his fucking point.

When he crashed their mouths together, Cruz told himself it was the only way to shut the other man up. And for a second, he thought even that wouldn't work, because Ace jerked away, and Cruz knew words would follow, words that would rip him open, show him for what he was. Dark and bent and anything but heroic.

"Get your hand on my fucking dick already," Ace snarled instead, before sinking his teeth into Cruz's lip. He tasted blood, sharp and metallic, and growled against Ace's mouth as he fumbled with the fly of his soaked jeans.

The fabric wouldn't give, so Cruz ripped off the button. Ripped the zipper, too, and he didn't give a shit. Nothing mattered but crossing every line that was left and spiking the same furious lust in Ace's blood that raged through his own.

It was fast. Rough. Ace's tongue slicked over his, thrusting into his mouth in challenge, and his hand sped up like they were in a fucking race. They were under the spray again, hot water pounding against Cruz's shoulders, sliding down his arms, the steam turning everything slippery and hot.

He tightened his grip on Ace's cock, working him from root to tip as he shifted his mouth to the other man's ear. "You're the one who makes it all about her. When do you start telling me it's okay to shove my dick down *your* throat until you choke on it?"

He'd expected shock. God knew why, because Ace just laughed, low and taunting, his breath hot on Cruz's cheek. "Like you could choke me."

Joking, like he knew it could never happen, because Ace had been careful not to touch him without a woman around. Jeni, Rachel—that safe buffer standing between them, the plausible deniability that must be eating Ace up from the inside out, because Cruz knew what it felt like to be the intruder in someone else's epic love.

He caught Ace's wrist, pried the other man's fingers from his cock, and slammed his arm back against the mosaic tile. He ignored the grunt of protest and caught Ace's other arm too, pinning both against the wall as he sank to his knees.

He'd sucked cocks before, but not in a long time, and not like this, with a man he cared about staring down at him, naked disbelief over crazy, soul-deep longing.

Ace swallowed, his wrists flexing in Cruz's grip, and he knew it was serious when the first word out of Ace's mouth wasn't an endearment or a tossed off *brother*. "Cruz, you don't have to—"

"Shut up." He had to release one wrist to grip Ace's shaft again, and he glared up at the man with the same forbidding look that always turned Rachel sweet and pliant. "For once in your goddamn life, Santana, just *shut the fuck up.*"

It could have been the look or the words or the fact that Ace couldn't tear his gaze from Cruz's lips. Whatever it was, it was a goddamn miracle, because Ace kept his mouth shut as Cruz opened his.

It wasn't smooth. Christ knew he didn't have Ace's practice—he didn't even have *Rachel's* practice—but from the stunned expression on Ace's face, it wasn't going to take finesse. Just passion and enthusiasm, and he had plenty of both.

He had attention to detail, too. He'd already begun to map Rachel's responses. Now he made note of Ace's, cataloging how fast and how deep, when he should suck and how firm a grip he should use. And Ace didn't speak, but he was still talking, with hissed groans and grunts, with the free hand that dropped to Cruz's head, fingers pressing hard against his scalp.

Next time would be better. He'd know how Ace liked to be touched, and Rachel would be there, too. Maybe chained, forced to watch, getting wetter and wetter as she watched Ace's cock disappear into Cruz's mouth.

The fantasy spun out as easy as breathing, and with Ace's harsh words echoing in his skull, he made himself revel in every detail with the same loving attention he was lavishing on Ace's cock.

Rachel—naked, her arms above her head, her legs spread wide. Decorated, because Cruz could see the appeal now that Ace had opened his eyes to it. Jewelry sparkling from her tight nipples, her clit, her ass. But nothing in her pussy, because she'd be watching Ace's cock, watching Cruz slick his tongue up and down, just like he was doing now, watching him suck the head until it glistened, and she'd feel empty, needy. Desperate to have him inside her.

But that was Cruz's fantasy. Hers would be deeper, darker. Ace and his flogger, driving her outside herself when pain bled to pleasure. And people watching—that was what she needed most. An audience, someone to witness her vulnerability, her submission, her bliss.

Maybe Ace was right, and they were still relying on him to push them where they knew they wanted to be. But he wasn't a corrupter, slinking into their lives and forcing them into sin. He was a liberator, reaching inside them to draw out what they really needed.

Just like he did when he laid someone's ink.

That was Ace's purpose—pulling truth from darkness and giving it form. A thankless job sometimes, especially when someone wasn't ready to face that truth. So Cruz sucked and stroked until Ace lost it and came with a stuttered groan, then rose with Ace's taste lingering on his tongue and wrapped both of their hands around his own straining cock.

"I'll tell you what I want to do," he rasped, pressing his forehead to Ace's as the first shiver of pleasure whispered up his spine. "And you don't need to make it okay."

He only got half of the fantasy out before Ace made him come, but improvising would be part of the fun.

Ace could usually finish a back piece in a few marathon sessions, but Zan would be the exception. Not because he couldn't take the pain—the man could sit like a stone through shit that had badass cage-fighters punking out after a few hours—but because his back was so massively *huge*.

The scope of the project made Zan the perfect distraction while Dallas was facing off with Liam Riley. Ace rarely involved himself in political shit anyway, and Zan was like Flash—his idea of diplomacy was shooting someone in the face instead of the back.

Sometimes Ace missed the days where that was the only kind of diplomacy the O'Kanes had to worry about.

Political power was all well and good, but there was a refreshing honesty about solving your problems with your fists or your gun.

And if he told himself that enough times, maybe he wouldn't feel like he was hiding from Rachel's daddy.

"I'll have to sketch this one first," Ace said, rolling his stool around so he could see Zan's face. "It's just too much to design and outline in one session. We'll nail down what you want today, though."

"Just don't leave me hanging with something that looks stupid half-finished," Zan grumbled, then grinned. "And make sure you spell everything right, for fuck's sake."

Ace laughed and flipped open a sketchpad. "Like you'd notice."

"I have mirrors, and I can read backwards." He paused. "And if that doesn't work, I'll get Rachel to check it out for me."

So they'd been a *thing* long enough for the teasing to start. Ace had been waiting, watching his O'Kane brothers and sisters circle. No one would poke at something fragile and risk damaging it, but they'd sure as fuck give him hell if things looked solid from the outside.

Ace's insecurities felt more ridiculous by the day, so he flashed a smile and did what he always did. Played it cool. "You gonna make her choose between your back and my dick? I don't like your odds, brother."

Zan laughed. "Neither do I, Santana. Neither do I."

At least he had that going for him—a dick so legendary, no one doubted its power. "So tell me what you had in mind for—"

Zan tensed before the bells over the front door jingled, and somehow Ace knew who it would be. Because it was the last thing he could handle right now, and because it was fucking inevitable—his past had to roll back over him eventually.

He spun his stool and found himself staring at Liam Riley.

The man removed his hat to reveal impeccably trimmed black hair shot with gray, especially at the temples. "Mr. Santana."

Liam didn't look much like Rachel, not in the obvious ways. His hair was darker, his features sharper. Harder. And it didn't matter that they shared the same remarkable eye color—meeting Liam Riley's gaze brought back the conversation he'd had with Cruz after their shower.

Do you believe her father didn't do it?

I believe she needs to believe that. But I can think of three perfectly reasonable justifications Liam Riley could have for arranging his daughter's kidnapping. Removing her as a potential hostage before he starts a war. Getting her out of the crossfire without tipping Dallas off to an upcoming fight. Or using her kidnapping as an excuse to start one.

So you think he did*?*

It's not that. Honestly, it doesn't seem like Riley's style. But that has nothing to do with whether he's capable of it.

Looking into Liam Riley's cold, hard eyes, Ace wondered if Cruz had gone far enough. Even his reasons had assumed Liam wouldn't take unnecessary risks with Rachel's safety. Ace still remembered the trembling girl whose bar code he had obliterated, removing her chance to return to the safety of Eden line by line because this man had valued his business over his daughter.

They were all giving Rachel's dad too much fucking credit.

"Forgive the intrusion," Liam said with a pointed look. "May we speak? Privately."

Zan hadn't moved. Probably wouldn't without Ace's signal, and for a second he toyed with the idea of letting him sit there, a wall of surly-tempered muscle at his back. It would piss his visitor off, that was for sure.

That would make it easier. Pissing Rachel's father off in advance, so he could pretend whatever came next wasn't about him.

Ace jerked his head toward the door. "Why don't you go find some food, Zan? Bring me back something, too. This won't take long."

"Sure thing, Ace." Zan moved slowly, lingering at the door for just a moment before letting it swing shut behind him.

Liam smiled a little. "I have to hand it to O'Kane. That's one area in which he excels—instilling loyalty in his men."

"Being worthy of loyalty is always a good start."

"So it is." Liam laid his hat on one of the rolling carts that held ink and supplies. "But I suppose your statement was more of a veiled insult than an observation of truth."

"Fair enough." Ace rocked to his feet, bringing himself eye level with Liam. "Maybe I should cut through the bullshit, then. You wouldn't be here if you didn't know."

"About you and Rachel. And Lorenzo Cruz, evidently."

"Evidently." Ace quirked an eyebrow. "Is he getting a father/son talk, too?"

"No bullshit, huh?" Liam looked around the room before turning the same critical eye on Ace, his veneer of polite civility gone. "You're a wreck, kid. You always have been, and I'm not talking about the whoring. Everyone's got to eat, and a man does what he has to do. But you're *messy*, Santana. Wherever you go, you leave a trail of broken shit behind you."

It was just what he'd asked for, the truth laid out between them. And what was he supposed to do? Deny it? His biggest claim to fame in Eden was destroying marriages—sometimes even ones he'd never touched. "Hazard of the business. Doesn't matter if you're selling sex or drugs or booze. Vice is messy."

"True. And, unless my daughter is paying you to warm her bed, utterly beside the point."

"Then what is your point? Because mine was that I left that shit behind me."

"Maybe you tried. Maybe you even got it done." Liam's jaw clenched. "But Rachel deserves more than maybes."

It wasn't supposed to hurt. He'd expected it, practically provoked it. No father from Eden could possibly approve of an O'Kane, and this father was never going to approve of him.

It wasn't supposed to hurt. But then, he wasn't supposed to agree.

"Rachel deserves everything she wants," Ace said, spacing out the words, making them as clear and sharp as the pain in his chest. "And that's what I'm going to give her, whether you like it or not."

"And when it ends?" Liam asked softly. "This is her home—as you say, whether I like it or not."

When it ends. He had to fight back against the words, because if he didn't, it meant he believed those, too. "Maybe you should be more worried about what you'll do when it doesn't."

The man sighed and picked up his hat. "You don't get it, kid. I don't hate you. I pity you." His voice turned to steel. "But I love my daughter more. If you hurt her, I will kill you."

Ace let him get to the door before asking the last question, the one that would drive the knife home and twist it until he bled out. "Is that what you told Cruz?"

Liam paused with his hand on the push bar and barely turned his head. "Why would I?" Then the bell jingled as he shoved through the door.

lili

THE FIRST TIME Lili saw her father hit her mother, she was fifteen.

Exactly fifteen, in fact, because it had been the evening of her birthday. She'd sacrificed the chance of a morning spent with her new piano—an extravagant gift that had arrived the previous evening—to supervise her six younger brothers and sisters while her exhausted mother oversaw the preparations for the evening's fancy dinner.

Lili would have just as soon skipped the party and the cake in favor of letting her mother stay in bed. The poor woman had a three-week-old daughter and a body worn down by constant pregnancy, but Lili had never seen her counter her husband's wishes. If the leader of Sector Five wanted to celebrate his eldest child's birthday by enacting some touching farce with the family he barely knew, Anna Fleming would make it happen.

And she had. The Fleming family sat down with its patriarch, who had invited three of his business partners—and a cadre of tattooed bodyguards who lined the walls as if Mac was in danger from his own family.

It happened over wine, before the cake. Her father had asked her to play them a song on her new piano, because the one thing he'd always encouraged was her music. He liked the conceit of having a talented, cultured daughter, as if it meant a damn when that daughter had never left the security of his fenced-in estate. But she'd obliged, because that was the only time she felt alive. The moment her fingers found the keys, the ivory cool under her fingers, her heart beating faster in anticipation of that first note.

It hadn't been perfect. The keys felt different than the piano she'd learned on, but even the missed notes hadn't bothered her, not when the sound was so rich, so full. She'd fallen into it, unaware that her father had risen and crossed to her side. Not until the last note echoed in the room, and he shattered the peace of her spell by dropping a heavy hand to her shoulder.

But when she looked up, her father was beaming at his second-in-command, a humorless man in his mid-thirties who oversaw all of the Fleming factories. "See what a prize I'm giving you, Logan?"

That was how Lili learned who her husband would be.

Her fifteenth birthday had taught her many things. That gifts were traps, and that getting older meant adding to the list of things you had to endure. It taught her that her father could backhand the mother of his children so hard he split her lip and bruised her jaw, and no one would twitch so much as a finger to help her up from the floor—especially if she deserved the blow for daring to suggest fifteen was too young for marriage.

But it was during the weeks leading up to her wedding that Lili and her mother both learned the most important lesson of Sector Five: no husband was unbearable when you had unlimited access to drugs.

Lili kept hers lined up next to the kitchen sink in neatly labeled bottles, the end result of five years' worth of experimentation in the best ways to detach. Nothing addictive, of course—it would be incredibly gauche for her to dabble in the common drugs her husband and father peddled on the street—but a single pill from the right bottle could grant sleepy peace or pleasant indifference or even icy numbness.

It had been a long time since she'd felt anything but icy numbness.

She was reaching for that bottle when the front door slammed open. Her fingers closed around the plastic, the tablets rattling in her suddenly shaky hand. It was too late for breakfast but too early for lunch, and Logan rarely made an appearance for either in any case.

"Pour a few drinks, Logan, and we'll toast our success." Her father, his voice smug and pleased.

Footsteps in the hallway. Lili was still in her nightgown and robe, her hair around her shoulders and her feet bare. Unforgivable enough in front of only Logan, but potentially disastrous if he'd brought her father and a business contact home for a celebratory drink.

But she didn't panic. She had vague memories of how fear felt—a quickening pulse, a tightness in her chest, thoughts that seemed to race. But that was the beauty of numbness. She had all the time in the world to float across the cool tiles, and no shame at all at the indignity of hiding from her husband and father in the pantry.

She pulled the slatted door shut as Logan rounded the corner, his expression as stern as ever in spite of whatever news her father felt compelled to celebrate. The liquor cabinet stood across from the pantry, its shelves lined with expensive bottles displayed like works of art.

Logan appreciated having his property exhibited to

best effect. Especially his wife.

"You'll understand if I don't stock your specialty," Logan said, the words filled with a pleasure his hard features didn't reflect.

And the words themselves made no sense at all until a third man stepped around the corner with a laugh. "That's what I like about you Sector Five bastards. None of this sanctimonious fuckery about a quality product. You save the good shit for yourselves and fuck the little guy."

Lili's father snorted. "If the little guy wants quality, he can damn well get rich enough to buy it."

Logan poured liquor into a glass—O'Kane liquor, by the looks of it—and handed it to her father. "And if he prefers quantity—or can be encouraged to require it—far be it from us to deny him."

"Mmm." Mac clinked his glass against the third man's. "I'm so glad you understood what an opportunity it would be for us to collaborate on this. You're a visionary, Mr. Tierney. Much more forward-thinking than O'Kane."

"He'll be too busy going to war with Liam Riley to do much thinking. Pete passed the word—Liam's already been summoned for a meeting. I'll be on Dallas O'Kane's throne inside a week. And maybe on that woman of his, too."

"The bitch from Sector Two?" The slur fell from Logan's twisted lips as he shook his head. "I'd put her down, if I were you. No whore tricks could be fancy enough to risk one of Cerys's vipers in your bed."

Pain throbbed in Lili's hand, and she realized she'd clenched her fist around the bottle until its hard edges dug into her palm. She loosened her fingers—carefully, so carefully. She kept her breathing careful, too. No sudden gasps. Nothing.

Being the daughter of a man like Mac Fleming meant hearing things. Being the wife of a man like

Logan meant knowing things. It was part of the life, the dark corners you pretended weren't there. Innocence was her only defense against suspicion, because if they ever suspected you'd heard too much—

Lili thought about her mother, crumpled on the floor, blood splattered on the front of her perfect dress. She thought of the bland look in the eyes of her father's men—in *Logan's* eyes—all of them staring politely past the woman sobbing as she struggled against dizziness and pain to rise.

If her father ever realized she'd overheard him plotting against another sector leader, having her jaw cracked would seem like a mercy. So she'd forget. She'd be numb. She'd be innocent.

She'd be ice.

16

IT WAS THE first time Rachel had ever been bound to a chair.

Cruz stroked a finger over one wide leather cuff, tracing along its edge and up to the inside of her arm. "Is there any practical reason for these to be here?"

Ace wasn't listening. He was wholly, completely focused on the curve of her ribs, beneath her breast, his gaze a mixture of admiration and something just short of worship.

Rachel answered for him. "People squirm. But that's not why they're there."

"You're not squirming," Ace murmured, proving some words penetrated. "How you doing, Rae?"

He'd barely gotten started. The scrape of needle over flesh was still stinging and sharp. "It's not so bad."

"Good. Make it through the outline, and we'll make you squirm plenty."

His hair fell over his forehead, and he stared up at her through it with eyes that burned with the same carnal promise as his words. It accomplished what the needles hadn't yet—it made her fidget, jerking her wrists against the tightly buckled leather.

Apparently satisfied, Ace smoothed a gloved hand over her stomach with a soothing noise. "Not yet, angel. You don't want fuzzy lines, do you?"

"Then stop teasing me."

"He doesn't know how to stop." Cruz tilted her face toward him with a gentle hand under her chin. "Especially not with you."

Cruz's gaze was just as steamy, just as fraught, but he looked at her differently. So solemn, serious, even at times like this.

Rachel couldn't help it. She smiled.

Cruz touched his thumb to her mouth, the corners of his own lips lifting slowly. "How does it feel?" he asked as the buzz of the needle resumed.

"So far? Irritating." She whispered the words against his thumb. "But it's still good, because I know what's coming." The giddy rush.

"Do you?" He leaned closer, his breath warm on her cheek. "He has you strapped in this time. Helpless."

She always was, whether she was shackled or not. That was why the bondage didn't matter to her one way or another, because what really held her captive was the sheer force of their desire. It pressed in on her already, stilling her movements when Ace's machine focused on the skin stretched taut over one of her ribs.

Pain flared, and she sucked in a quick breath before swallowing—hard.

"I know," Ace said softly, running his fingers over the spot. "Just a few lines up this high. But you're good, aren't you? Like a rock. Jas whines more than you do."

"The big ones always—" Rachel's words cut off with a hiss. Ace had moved on to a less sensitive area, but it was like that one moment of pain had set her entire body on alert, and there was no going back. The next touch of the needle screamed, and she bit her lip.

Cruz cupped her cheek, his skin hot on hers, his hand large enough to cover the side of her head but still so painfully gentle. "How does it feel now?"

"It doesn't tickle," she managed.

"I'm sure it doesn't." With her body sensitized, his fingers rasped tauntingly over her skin as he smoothed that huge hand down to rest across her throat. "That's not what I asked, sweetheart. Tell me what you feel."

Hot. Her left side was on fire, and that heat had begun licking through her, spreading even faster at the gentle pressure of his hand around her throat. "It hurts," she murmured. "*God*, it's going to be so good."

"Only if you can stay still." Ace repositioned once more, hitting another spot that stung, the needle breaking the skin over and over. "Can you do that, Rae? Even with him touching you?"

"Yes." The answer came without thought, her voice dreamy and slow. This was always how it started, with a clumsy tongue she couldn't quite control.

Cruz slid his hand lower, circling one broad fingertip around her nipple. "Maybe I should test you. See how much you can take without moving."

"He wants to play with you." Ace's voice was rough around the edges, ragged, like the pain as he traced across her ribs again. "You should have heard the shit he was saying to me in the shower yesterday. Your city boy's got a massive hard-on for all sorts of filthy goodness."

She barely bit back her moan. "You took a fucking *shower* together?"

"Whoops." The pain eased for a second as Ace rolled the stool up to the reclined head of the chair. "Don't blame him, I'm the one who started the half-naked fight."

Cruz grunted. "I was totally naked, as I recall."

"Details." Ace leaned over her, the fall of his hair

tickling her forehead. "All I'm saying is, it wasn't premeditated. But if you feel left out, we can reenact it tomorrow."

It was impossible not to imagine it. Hell, even a saint would have—skin against skin, wet and muscled. And the *noises*—

Jesus Christ.

A shiver of heat low in her body had her squirming again, and she stretched up, trying to reach Ace's mouth.

"Uh-uh." He hovered just out of reach, a wicked smile her last glimpse before he vanished back down her body. "Patience, angel. But if you need a distraction, why don't you ask Cruz about a few of those ideas he whispered in my ear while I was jerking him off?"

"Shit, you're *evil*." Her skin prickled as the tattoo machine began to buzz again, mirroring the anticipation vibrating through her. She turned her head to Cruz, who waited until the needle had jabbed into her skin before smiling and catching her nipple between his thumb and finger.

Gently, still gently. But his eyes held hers, gaze intent. "Are you ready?"

She froze, even held her breath, and nodded.

All that gentleness turned to steel as he pinched tight. It hurt more than the constant, repetitive sting of the needle because it was more intense, a rush of sensation instead of a slowly rising wave. She steeled herself not to move as the pain crested, then subsided in a haze of relief so sharp she whimpered.

Silver caught the light, drawing her attention as Cruz lifted his free hand. A nipple clamp, like the ones everyone knew Ace kept in his studio. But these were different, a fact Cruz confirmed as he gently drew the magnetic cross bars apart and fitted the circle around her nipple.

"He got these just for you, you know." When he released the tips, the magnetic bars flew together, pinching almost as tight as his fingers had. "I made him show me everything. It'll take months to try it all, and every last piece he chose while thinking about using them on you."

It was unexpectedly sweet, the thought of Ace poring over items until he found exactly the ones he wanted, the ones that made him think of her. "Why?"

Cruz tugged at her other nipple, sending a shiver through her as he teased it tight enough to fit the other clamp in place. "Are you going to answer her, Ace?"

He grunted, not glancing up from her side, but she swore he looked self-conscious. "Hell, I don't know. Because it was different. It was..."

He trailed off, and Cruz brushed the collar around her throat. "It's a commitment."

It was *hers*, something he'd never given anyone else. "Thank you."

Ace rallied, flashing her a dirty smile as he reached for fresh ink. "I don't know why you're thanking me. You're strapped in my chair, under my needles, wearing nothing but tiny lace panties and sexy little nipple clamps. It's my best fucking day ever."

By the time it was over, Rachel had no doubt she'd be saying the same.

Cruz leaned over her, one hand trailing almost absently down her leg as he studied the beginnings of the tattoo. The bright blue of the marker was giving way to smooth, perfect black lines—her angel, caught in a joyful, dizzying dive, and Ace had captured everything she'd wanted. The rush, the freedom, even the paradox of lust and innocence, as the wind caught at the angel's modest gown, tugging it tight around a body bent in a sensuous, blissful arc.

"It's going to be beautiful," Cruz said, stroking his fingertips higher. "Perfect."

Everything Ace created was, whether he realized it or not. "What colors?" she asked, staring down at his hands as he moved the needle across her skin.

"Come on, Rae. You know what angels wear."

"Oh." White, the color that hurt the most. Ace had explained the reason to her before, but she'd been flying high already, fuzzy-headed and practically writhing from the dreamy heat of arousal.

"Mm-hmm." He rested a hand on her stomach. "Don't worry, it won't be *all* white. And I'll go easy on you...until you're begging me to go hard."

The heat of Cruz's palm settled across her thigh, his fingertips brushing the edge of her panties. "I think she's ready to do that now."

Rachel caught herself before she twisted up toward Cruz's touch, but she couldn't hold back her moan.

He made her wait. One endless moment, then another, with Ace burning lines of shivery pain into her skin and the clamps taunting her nipples with an ache too soft to be anything but pleasure. His gaze caught hers, held, and his thumb swept one slow line over her skin.

"What am I going to find when I move my hand?" he murmured. "Are you wet already?"

"*Yes.*" A confession and a plea, all at once. She was torn between the anticipation of his touch and the pain dragging at her as Ace worked on her ink, and if one of them didn't give soon...

Cruz shifted his hand, brushing her abdomen as he slid down, down, down. Under her panties, over her pussy, fingers curling to cup her possessively. "Does he know what he does to you? Have you ever told him?"

She almost nodded, then stopped. Had she? It had always seemed so damn obvious that there was no way Ace couldn't know. But she'd never said the words because it would mean another layer stripped away, one more vulnerability on top of so many more.

"Ace turns me on," she said instead. "He always has. But that's not why I want him so much."

Cruz rocked his hand slowly, the heel of it a heavy pressure above her clit. Not direct enough to satisfy her, but enough to stoke her need, to deepen it. "Why do you want him?"

She couldn't have held back the truth, even without the encroaching haze of pleasure and pain colliding. "It's not the sex. I want *him*. The things he doesn't show anyone else."

Cruz held her open with two fingers and edged the third inside her, another shallow tease. "I'm lucky. I get to see all those things every time he looks at you. Especially when you're like this..."

"Like—" The word died as a pulse of pleasure rocked her, and Rachel shuddered, breaking her stillness. "Sorry, I'm sorry—"

"Cruz." Ace's voice held a warning, and the buzzing stopped. "I don't do wobbly lines, so if you can't keep your fingers out of her pussy—"

"She can do it." Cruz slid his free hand beneath her head, pressing his forehead to hers. His finger pushed deeper, broad and stretching all on its own, and even more overwhelming when he eased back and worked a second in alongside it. "Just this," he whispered against her lips. "You'll do it for me, won't you? Stay so very still, so I can feel how your pussy clenches when he hurts you."

There was no fucking way. The penetration alone was enough to tip her down a slippery slope of sensation, and if he kept talking, she'd never be able to stop.

But for Cruz, she'd try. She'd do anything.

Rachel balled her hands into fists and nodded, her lips brushing his. "I can."

"I know." He settled his arm more heavily across her body, pinning her in place. Ace started again, working his way down her side inch by dizzying inch.

The pain hit her in waves that left her pussy clamping around Cruz's fingers with each harsh crest. She hadn't been aware of it before, not exactly, but there was no escaping the sensation now. Every ripple drew him deeper, until it felt like he was fucking her, even though he hadn't moved his hand at all.

He moved his mouth, though, along her cheek, straight to her ear, where he groaned. "You're doing so well, sweetheart. Staying so still. If you can hold it a little longer, we'll let you come. Do you want that?"

For a heartbeat, she was scared to open her mouth, scared that letting go just enough to answer would open the floodgates and she'd lose all control—

Except she didn't have control. Cruz did, and he always would. So she sucked in a shaky breath and released it on a sigh. "Yes. I want it."

"Look at me, Rachel."

He had his hand in her hair, and it pulled as she turned her head to obey. Every line of his face was hard, as sharp as the needles piercing her skin, and his gaze trapped hers. Held it. "Tell me the truth. Am I still being too gentle with you?"

"I don't want gentle." The words came in a dreamy rush, truth bypassing any part of her brain that might have constructed a lie. "I want you to *need* me like I need you."

His fingers flexed inside her. "I always do."

"It's more than that," Ace said, the rasping edge of his voice a tangible caress. "Need's a given, brother. She wants you to take."

Take. Her inner muscles gripped Cruz's fingers, so tight that he didn't even have to move for the contact to blaze through her.

He sucked in a breath, his hand tensing at the back of her head. "Then we'll take you. Just like this. Tied down, trembling and wet, already close to coming." She whimpered as he slipped his fingers free, and again when he brought them to her lips. "This is one of his fantasies, you know. Fucking your mouth while you're bound. I wonder how hard you'd squeeze me then."

The way he said it kindled the fantasy in her, too,

and she opened her mouth to lick his fingers. Bound and used. It could have felt dirty, shameful, but all she could think about was whether Ace would tremble at the touch of her tongue. What kinds of glorious things he'd say as he fucked deep into her throat.

With the machine still humming along, she didn't realize the pain had stopped. Not until Cruz gripped her chin, his fingers still pressing down on her tongue, and turned her head.

Ace was looking at her. Staring, really, his hand hovering six inches over her skin, the tattoo forgotten as his gaze fixed on her mouth, her lips.

When Cruz pumped his fingers deeper, Ace choked on a strangled noise.

She had to have him. Now.

Rachel twisted, straining against the leather cuffs with a pleading hum, and she knew she'd won when he cut off the machine and rose so fast the wheeled stool went skittering into a nearby shelf and toppled with a clatter.

Ace didn't seem to notice. His hands shook as he ripped open his belt and unbuttoned his jeans. His cock was already hard, lovingly outlined by the faded denim, and she licked her lips as the quick rasp of his zipper shivered up her spine.

She couldn't look away from his hands. Cruz had moved, but she didn't know where until his fingers hooked under her panties, dragging them down her legs, leaving her naked. Bare, but not vulnerable, not until he stepped between the leg-rests on Ace's clever tattoo chair and pushed them wide, spreading her legs with them.

It was instinct to try to draw her legs back together, but Cruz's grip was implacable, holding her in place as his breath tickled over her. "I never asked why you did this," he murmured, brushing his fingers over her bare pussy. "For the shows?"

She struggled not to arch her hips to his touch. "At

first. But I like it."

"I bet you do." Ace drew her attention back to him with a hand on her cheek, and his cock was so close, the head almost, *almost* resting on her lips. "You like to feel exposed, don't you, Rae? More than the pain, more than the rough fucking...you want to be just like this. Spread open and naked where everyone can see."

How could she not get off on the power of being desired like this? "I'm not untouchable anymore," she whispered, stretching out in an attempt to close the distance between them. "So touch me."

His hand fisted in her hair, jerking her head back with delicious roughness. "No, not until Cruz gets his fingers inside you again. Tell him you want them. Tell him you want him to feel how tight and wet your pussy gets when I'm giving it to you fast and hot."

She'd wanted it ten minutes ago. A lifetime. "He knows how hungry I am. How much I ache."

Ace rubbed his cock against her lower lip. "Then tell him for me, angel. So I can hear those filthy words from the mouth I'm about to fuck."

Holy shit. "Cruz," she managed to rasp, though she couldn't quite tear her gaze from Ace's set, determined features. "I want you to fuck me with your hand. Not so you'll know how turned on I am—you already do—but so you can tell Ace. Because I won't be able to."

Cruz didn't answer with words, filthy or otherwise. He answered with action, pumping two fingers into her, giving her a scant moment to savor the pleasure before his tongue found her clit.

It hit her with a shock, like the time she'd tried to replace the solenoid in Dallas's favorite car without unhooking the battery first. She jerked against the cuffs with a cry, and Ace took advantage of her parted lips, fucking deep as Cruz lashed his tongue over her a second time.

So *different* like this, everyone and everything moving after staying so still. Rachel focused on gliding her tongue over Ace's shaft, quivering when he growled his approval and thrust deeper, his gaze never leaving hers.

And his words...

"Every time," he hissed, rocking back and forth, taking her with all the greedy need they'd both been holding back. "Every time I get your beautiful fucking skin under my needles and watch you get all wet and soft, this is what I imagine. Fucking you until you come all over this chair so hard, I can never give another tattoo without getting turned on."

She'd been so distracted she hadn't noticed the rush creeping up. It was on her now, full force, the cascade of endorphins that left the world fuzzy and gray around the edges. It had happened to her during tattoos before...but never like this.

It freed her from the last of her inhibitions. She sucked harder and rocked her hips against Cruz's fingers, his tongue.

She was dizzy by the time Cruz lifted his head, his beard scraping her inner thigh as he slicked his thumb over her clit. "This is your fantasy, Ace. What happens next?"

Ace eased free of her mouth, shifting his grip from her hair to her throat. His palm covered her collar, pressing it into her skin as he tightened his hand, not cutting off her breath—not quite—but still a dominating weight. "After she comes on your face, I mark her again by coming on hers."

The words did what the hand around her throat couldn't, and she panted for breath. "Please. Please, *fuck—*"

Cruz stole what was left of her oxygen with a third finger, and they weren't just inside her this time, stretching and still. He played with her, worked them deep, and Ace's face filled her vision, his hot smile, his free hand sliding up and down his cock as he held her tight. "You're so damn wet, aren't you? I love the sound of him fucking your pussy with those big fingers. Does it hurt a little?"

"No." Nothing hurt anymore. Everything was red-hot, glowing with a pleasure she'd only flirted with in the past. "I want more."

"Dirty, perfect girl," Ace whispered, leaning close, his eyes lost to darkness. "You'd let him do it, wouldn't you? You'd let us work you over for hours, until you could take his whole damn hand."

The sheer animal urge to bite him overwhelmed her, and she gave in to it with a moan, locking her teeth at the corner of his mouth. He groaned and pressed closer, grinding into her teeth until she tasted blood—

Cruz sealed his lips around her clit and sucked hard.

She came even harder. The back of her head hit the chair as she tried to chase the orgasm, drawing out every blinding moment. But she didn't have to, because every clench of her inner muscles around Cruz's fingers sent new pulses of pleasure rocketing through her.

She vaguely heard words, sounds—their voices, full of pleasure and approval. She might have screamed, loud and long, because the vibration was what followed her down into the darkness. Her whole body was alive, singing, and she never wanted it to stop.

Ace put his dick away.

Not the most comfortable choice, but a big part of his fantasy included having Rachel aware enough to appreciate the big finish. He took her fuzzy-headed floating as the compliment it was, and decided the rest of the outline could wait. Another round with the needles would just send her flying again, and that wouldn't work.

He had a whole different big finish in mind now.

They got Rachel untied, and Cruz settled into the

chair with Rachel curled against his chest while Ace smoothed med-gel over her tattoo. The unfinished outline was lopsided, one wing missing, the angel's dress fading into nothingness. His streak of artistic perfectionism wanted to kick his ass, but then Rachel moaned and shifted languidly, and his brain shut down with a single half-hearted promise.

Later.

She stirred again, rubbing her cheek against Cruz's skin. "We moved."

Ace kissed the back of her shoulder. "You said you wanted more. That wasn't the position to give it to you."

She smiled lazily. "You two would find a way."

"Not for this." Cruz slid his hands down to cup her ass. "Not the first time we're both inside you."

The smile melted into a soft, pleading noise, and she dug her fingernails into his arms. Ace met Cruz's gaze and found shared purpose there, a second of communion hotter than having his hand around the other man's dick.

No conflict, no complications. They knew what Rachel wanted, and they wanted to give it to her. "Ace first," Cruz said, taking control of the moment with an ease that would have made Ace smug in any other instance. Any time he wasn't thirty seconds from working his way into Rachel's virgin ass.

She turned her head and looked back at him, her hazel eyes gone dark with arousal. "Is this part of your fantasy?" The words held a teasing lilt, and she arched her back, lifting her ass to his view. And because God hated him—or loved him—Cruz shifted his grip, digging his fingers into her ass and spreading her cheeks.

Rachel was on display in the lewdest, most gorgeous way possible, and Ace's hand shook as he tried to get the damn lube open. Not because of the fantasy, but because of the sure, certain fucking knowledge that Rachel and Cruz could be bundled up in snowsuits, snoring and maybe drooling, and they'd still be the hottest damn thing he'd ever seen.

Not exactly poetry, but maybe it would be enough. They would never turn to him for protection or support, never expect him to say the right thing when they were hurting. But they trusted him with the most naked parts of themselves, with their base, unfettered *need*—

No, it wasn't poetry. But Rachel whimpered when he pressed the slick head of his cock against her ass, rubbing and taunting with just enough force to let her feel it before easing back, and it didn't need to be poetry, because it was *art*. Fucking into her a little at a time, knowing which words to growl, which to whisper. He gave her encouragement as he worked her open, stretching her bit by bit, an act that could have been as shallow as lust and getting balls-deep in a tight, hot ass—

But it never was. It was living raw and to the edge of who you were, stripping away all the layers of bullshit that kept you alive in the unsafe parts of the world. It was the sound she made as he finally took his first shallow thrust—sharp and relieved, as if he'd broken open her world.

Rachel wanted to be herself, strong and powerful, making all of her own choices. Cruz understood that. But he still didn't understand this, the moment when Rachel's choice was to have no choices, to be taken, tenderly used, lovingly violated.

Cruz could give her love and all the right words, but at least Ace could give her this. His hand around her throat, his cock buried in her tight, tight ass, his mouth on her ear as he ground her clit down against Cruz's jean-clad cock. "You feel that dick? You want it inside you, don't you? One's not enough for you anymore."

She lifted one hand to his wrist, wrapped her fingers around it with a trembling moan. "Not when I can have this instead."

Ace withdrew, ignoring her groan of protest, and jerked her back, manhandling her into position until she was straddling Cruz's knees. "Open his pants," he ordered, taking back control. Here, now, there was no room for Cruz's brand of gentlemanly filth.

Rough and brutal, that was the only thing they'd never given her—and Ace didn't know if he should pray for Cruz to be a quick learner, or pray for him to never get it. As long as Cruz hovered on the wrong side of that line, they'd always need Ace.

And Rachel needed this. Her hands shook with excitement as she fought with Cruz's belt, her breath coming in short pants, and Ace slapped her hip. "Get out his cock and ask for permission to ride it."

"Please," she said eagerly as she eased the zipper down and reached into his jeans. "Let me—let me ride you—"

Ace used the hand across her throat to haul her back against his chest and slid the other down to lightly slap her clit. "That sounded like a demand to me."

"Oh, fuck." Rachel shuddered, her eyes unfocused as she looked down at Cruz. "Can I—that's what I meant. Can I ride you? I'll make it good, I swear I will."

Cruz pressed his thumb to her lips, rubbing back and forth so gently that it made his words all the more lewd. "What do you think, Ace? Am I still being too easy on her?"

"Fuck yeah." Ace rubbed his fingertips over her, reveling as her hips jerked every time he brushed her clit. "If I were you, I'd make her say, *please, Sir, shove that big manly cock into my tight, hungry pussy*. But that's not your style, and that's not what it's really about, is it, Rae?"

"I—I don't *know*." Her skin heated as she writhed between them, captive and captivated, and her next words came on a whisper that sounded like a confession. "I love it like this. When you tease me until I can't stand it anymore, and it doesn't matter what I say or how much I beg."

Because it wouldn't be submission if she could say a magic word and get exactly what she wanted. There was no trust in that, no real satisfaction. Begging was her final grasp for control, and being denied was permission to let go and float on freedom.

Cruz's gaze clashed with his, and maybe he *did* get it. His thumb slipped from Rachel's lip, and his hand traced down the center of her body until his fingers tangled with Ace's. They stroked her together, driving another whimper from her lips. "It doesn't matter," Cruz repeated, the words rough-edged and harsh. "Because you'll get what we want to give you, when we're ready for you to have it."

The tiniest question lingered under the words, and Ace answered it with his lips against Rachel's temple. "The begging's just a bonus. A hot, sexy bonus."

"Oh *God.*" Her hips bucked against their hands, and she dragged in a sobbing breath. "Please, please—I need it. I need you both—"

She was past the point of grace. Ace had to help her lift her hips, but then he held her there, shaking and pleading as Cruz stroked the head of his cock over her, up to her clit and back, poised to push into her…

He waited. Looked to Ace and *held*, every muscle tight with anticipation, with the struggle it must have been to give up control, even in this tiny way.

Ace had never needed control, not the way some of the other guys did, but that didn't make it any less hot to have the two of them hovering on the edge, waiting for a release only he could give them.

He nodded, and Cruz thrust up, driving into Rachel as Ace dragged her down to meet him. She went tense, rigid, then ground against Cruz with a startled, shuddering cry.

Coming already, and hard, judging from the way Cruz's head tilted back, pleasure twisting his features. And it would have been better to drag it out, make her come around him again and again, but that was the problem with being an artist. You could bleed out every feeling inside you, splash it across the canvas in an orgy of creation, but in the end you'd still be staring at an imperfect reflection, so fixated on the flaws that you could never share in the joy of discovery.

Rachel was made of joy. She was overflowing with it, shaking as Ace spilled more lube over his hand. The bottle slipped to the floor, but he focused on stroking his cock and positioning it, savoring the way she moaned when she realized what was about to happen.

It was clumsy and a little uncoordinated, and he shuddered as he buried his first two inches in the impossible clenching heat of her ass, but *God,* you couldn't see the imperfections when you were part of the art. Everything was slick and hot and good, and he leaned over to grip the head of the chair, burying his face in her hair as he flexed his hips again. "Fucking *hell.*"

"Now." Rachel's fingers brushed his cheek, and she breathed his name. "All of you."

All of him. All of his cock, surging into her, all of his control, slipping away. He couldn't even find a profane word to say, because Cruz had shifted his grip to Ace's ass, and Rachel was crushed between them, so tight and hot and wet and warm and any of those would be perfectly serviceable filth if he let them roll off his tongue with the right undertone of approval, but when he parted his lips, the only thing he could manage was another groan.

Cruz slid into the silence, driving up into Rachel with a grunt. "Do you still want more?"

"Always, love." Dreamy words, shivery and appreciative. "Everything I can get."

"Then tell him." He freed one hand to tangle in the chain swinging from her collar, twisting it tight to tilt her head back. "We both know what he likes. Filthy, dirty, hungry begging."

But she didn't beg. "The first time I saw you was in this room," she murmured softly. "You were covering my bar code from the city, and you made me forget that I was all alone."

Ace sank his hand into her hair and turned her head, just far enough to press his forehead to her temple. "You were never alone, not after that day. I took your bar code and gave you ink."

She rocked, down and back, against Cruz and then Ace. When she spoke again, her voice had gone low and husky, thick with pleasure. "You took my heart, too."

He didn't deserve it. He never had, not when she'd held it out the first time, not when he'd smashed it without noticing. He didn't deserve her now, like this, moving between him and Cruz, giving them both everything, because the sweetest, most reckless gift she'd ever given Ace was a second chance to crush her.

He couldn't promise not to hurt her, but he could promise something else, the safety net that had brought them together, the one reason he wasn't just a reckless asshole playing cruel games.

No one deserved Rachel, but Cruz came close. So Ace put his trust in him, following the other man's movements as they drove Rachel up and up, until she teetered on the edge of another orgasm, one that threatened to sweep them all away.

Ace found her ear with his lips and whispered the most important truth, the one he'd cut out his own heart to protect. "You'll never be alone again."

Cruz would keep that promise, even if Ace couldn't.

17

CRUZ HAD TO give Dallas O'Kane credit—for a man with a reputation for having a short fuse and zero subtlety, he had a hell of a lot of patience.

Noah had followed the tracking signal to the main warehouse the first night, but Dallas had held back. With the tracer in place, they had an opportunity the Sector Four leader couldn't pass up—the chance to make a list of every outpost, every delivery, every person or place who'd had a damn thing to do with making or taking the bootlegged liquor.

When O'Kane set out to send a message, he didn't do it by half.

Jasper finished a cigarette and crushed it beneath his boot as he stared at the unassuming building down the street. "You think this is really it? The hub?"

"That's what the travel pattern indicates." Cruz glanced up from the bag of supplies at his feet, his gaze settling on Dallas.

Their leader wasn't looking at the warehouse. He was facing in the opposite direction, studying the wide road just behind him—the road you could follow straight north to Eden's walls.

The dividing line between Sectors Four and Five.

Mad was watching Dallas, too. "Having second thoughts, boss?"

"Not many," Dallas replied, turning to face them. "If Fleming knows what's going on, this'll bring the war out into the open. If he doesn't? The bastard's got way bigger problems than me."

"He knows." Bren's flat observation was certain, sure. "Shit like this doesn't go down right under his nose without one of his enforcers rooting it out. And someone bootlegging O'Kane liquor? He'd fucking die of glee."

Dallas snorted. "If it wasn't his idea to begin with. His or that piss-face second of his."

"Beckett," Noah said, not looking up from his tablet. "Logan Beckett. The man's fucking cold. And I'm not talking cold like he gets things done. I mean he's a goddamn sociopath. He's the one who came up with the shit that makes their drugs addictive."

"Charming," Jas said sourly. "You got the blueprints yet, Lennox?"

"I'm loading them up for everyone now."

The datapad strapped to Cruz's vest vibrated, and he pulled it free and studied the schematic Noah had sent. It outlined the building's support structure. Bren had already gone over it and marked the sweet spots—the areas in the foundation where they were going to place the bags of explosives at Cruz's feet. Old-fashioned dynamite on timed charges. Blow them in the correct sequence, and the whole fucking building would fold in on itself like a house of cards.

Dallas O'Kane had patience...until he didn't. And then he burned shit to the ground.

Cruz lifted the bags, passed one to Bren, and shouldered the other. "I'm ready."

Jasper ejected the magazine from his pistol, reinserted it, and chambered a round. "We clear on the plan?"

Bren smiled, his typically perverse humor surfacing. "Yes, Dad. We're clear."

But Jas eyed him grimly. "Get in, get to the basement, and do your thing. Leave the fighting to us."

"We went over it a hundred times, McCray. We'll handle it."

"Good." Dallas dropped a hand to his holstered gun and studied them all for a silent moment. "In and out, boys. Noah will handle access. We've got five minutes to secure the building, fifteen until the charges go off. Do *not* get caught in there when this shit blows, you hear me?"

"It'd be ugly," Jasper agreed. "We're bringing the whole damn thing down. That's the message." He started for the building, and Cruz followed with the rest.

The whole night was a message—a coordinated strike against the bootleggers' hub of operations along with every outpost the tracker had led them to. The leaders probably wouldn't be around. They'd scatter, but they wouldn't be able to hide, not with Liam and Dallas working together.

Cruz just prayed they'd keep working together. For Rachel's sake.

The street was deserted, as if its usual late-night occupants had sensed trouble and scurried away to hide from it. But even hidden away, they had to be watching. Cruz could feel the eyes on him, the sensation of being watched prickling up the back of his neck.

Soon, Mac Fleming would know exactly what had happened at the edge of his sector.

The front door to the building was newer than the rest of it, probably solid-steel core. Impervious to breach and secured with an access panel, a more robust version of the one he and Bren had found on that very first shack out in the middle of nowhere. Noah studied it for several seconds before pulling a flat, black case from his back pocket.

He flipped it open to reveal a grid of small, metallic dots. They almost looked like stickers, the kind a child would play with, except Cruz was intimately familiar with their real nature and purpose. He clenched his hands into fists as Noah peeled them out of the case, one by one, and placed them at the four corners of the panel.

He stepped away even before Noah motioned them back and pressed a tiny button on the outside of the case. The dots began to glow and then exploded in a sizzling shower of sparks. The lock clicked open with a heavy *thunk*, and Jasper and Mad shoved through the door, weapons in hand.

An alarm began to ring throughout the cavernous structure, joined by the sound of raised voices and shouts of warning. Cruz ignored the noise and headed straight for his objective—an office off the left side of the main room.

The clatter of gunfire echoed behind them as Bren hurried through the dark office and kicked open the door at the back of it. He activated a small, handheld light that illuminated stairs leading down into a heavier darkness.

The basement.

Cruz waved him onward, tensed for the sound of footsteps behind them, but none came. Their training had served them well.

The sub-level of the building was a confusing warren of storage and office space. Bren moved silently through the near darkness and skirted one half-wall before coming to a stop beside a fat concrete pillar. He dropped his bag, unzipped it, and dragged out a heavy-duty drill exactly like the one Cruz had in his bag. He worked fast and steady, laying out his supplies before beginning, the way a cook might gather ingredients before tossing them all into a pot to boil.

He set the hollow carbide-tipped drill bit against the concrete, and a low buzz filled the dank air as Cruz took up his position on the other side of the pillar. Twin holes, drilled on either side, filled with three sticks of dynamite each, wired to a primer charge controlled by an electrical detonator.

It took twenty-eight seconds to drill the hole, place the dynamite, and attach the wires. By the time Cruz adhered the detonator to the concrete precisely six inches above the hole on his side of the pillar, Bren had already dragged a pre-cut roll of shielding fabric from his bag.

They wrapped the pillar in silence, and Cruz secured it. Dallas was determined to send a message, but not at the cost of innocent bystanders' lives. The sheeting would limit the range of the blast, keep it focused to the pillar itself. No mess, and no mistakes.

They had already hit the third support column and were starting in on the fourth and final one when the muffled sound of gunshots died down above them.

Bren looked up and shook his head. "Took them long enough."

Longer than it should have, but Bren knew why as well as Cruz did. Dallas had no problem killing the men trying to infringe upon his territory, but he wouldn't take the easy path and tell himself he'd had no choice. When they brought this building down, Dallas would know who was in it and who wasn't—no accidents with wives or sisters or desperate children who'd been pressed into working.

They drilled the final holes, and Cruz reached for the explosives. "What do you figure Fleming will do when this place caves in?"

Bren snorted. "Pitch a hissy fit worthy of any cranky toddler."

"And when he's done kicking his heels on the floor?"

"Who the fuck knows? Come at us, probably. A crazy bastard like Fleming can only run the slow play so long before he needs a little blood-and-guts gratification."

It could mean a sector war—a *real* one, the kind of messy bloodshed that hadn't happened in years. That sort of battle would spill past the O'Kanes and Fleming's men, dragging everyone in both sectors into a fight that would end with one side's death, or with Eden coming down hard on all of them.

There was no safety in that option. Ace would be in the thick of it. Rachel, too, when it came down to it, though Cruz couldn't stand the idea of encouraging her back into the city. He needed them both where he could see them, touch them. Protect them.

"We could take care of that," he said, keeping his voice carefully casual. "It'd only take one bullet."

"Maybe, but without clear evidence that Fleming moved against us first, a strike like that would make the other sector leaders nervous. We can't have *everyone* against us." Bren leaned around the pillar with a serious look. "You've got to trust Dallas, man."

Cruz flexed his fingers and looked away, staring at the tangle of wires instead of his friend's face. "It's fucking terrifying, isn't it? Having to decide who's worthy of your loyalty?"

"At first. It gets easier."

Cruz managed a smile as he finished wiring up his side. "Can't get harder, I guess."

Bren barked out a laugh as he double-checked his detonator and secured it to the concrete. "Famous last words."

When they had wrapped the final charges, Bren zipped up both nearly empty bags and hoisted them onto his shoulder. They made their way back through the basement and up to the main floor.

Dallas stood in the center, arms draped over his

chest, watching as Mad riffled through a crate of liquor bottles. He scowled when he caught sight of Bren and Cruz, jerking his head toward the exit. "I considered looting the place, but Nessa would stab me if I brought her the shitty grain they're using. Set the charges and let's get the fuck out."

"Yes, sir." Bren dragged the control box from one of the many pockets on his vest.

The moment he clicked the yellow arming button, an explosion rocked the floor beneath them.

Something had gone wrong. Cruz's brain tried to process the possibilities as the floor shuddered beneath them and his ears rang with the painful aftermath. Dust billowed up, damn near blinding him, too, but he was still alive, which meant all of the explosives couldn't have detonated—

The building kept shuddering. Kept groaning. Dallas staggered and Cruz lurched, landing painfully on his knees as he watched the far side of the floor crumble away, taking Mad with it.

Jas was already on his feet, running toward the crater and listing walls that used to be the rear right quadrant of the building. "Bren, what the fuck?"

Bren was just as fast. "I don't *know*! The detonator must have shorted out—"

Too much of the structure had gone down on top of Mad. Digging him out of the rubble from here would be hard. Doing it before the rest of the fuses blew—or Mac Fleming responded to the first one and swept down on them—would be fucking impossible.

His brain struggled to the realization, but his body was already shifting position. Up to his feet, stripping away his heavy gear because he had to *go*. "The tunnels! Lennox—move your ass."

Noah's bootfalls thudded behind him as Cruz sprinted out the door, around the corner to the access hatch set into the cracked pavement of the alley. They'd already removed the rusted bolts—just in case they needed an escape route—and shimmied the heavy steel plate loose. Cruz pried it up as he ruthlessly ordered his thoughts.

No room for panic. No room for any emotion but calm. He could find the closest point to the cave-in, open the secured door with Noah's help, and work from there. But he couldn't do it if his mind acknowledged the ticking clock, so he locked that away.

He had time. All the time in the world.

He jumped the last few rungs of the ladder down into the tunnel, ripping a light free of the pocket of his cargo pants as he landed. He'd committed the tunnel schematics to memory, more out of habit than anything else, and now he was damn glad he had.

One hundred meters due north, second branch to the left.

All the time in the world.

Noah started swearing before they reached the door—and its ominously dark panel. "The power supply's been disrupted."

"Can you open it?"

He bit off another curse and smacked the wall beside the panel. "These locks re-sequence when they lose power. I won't be able to override it again without cracking it, and brute force'll take twenty minutes. Minimum."

There was another way, a destructive last resort no one was supposed to know about. Cruz had learned about it during his training on Base, and employing it now would reveal exactly how much knowledge he possessed about Eden, the sectors...and everything that lay beneath them.

"Out of the way." He slapped his emergency light to the wall. Then he jerked a multi tool out of another pants pocket, flicked it open, and pried away the recessed plate beneath the panel.

A bevy of wires greeted him, a rainbow of colors oddly out of place in such a cold, sterile construct. Blue, red, green, yellow, white. Ace would probably have other names for them, prettier ones that would distract from the horror of the situation.

Cruz only had a blade.

One by one, he stripped away the plastic coating, keeping the wires carefully separated as he worked.

"No, you can't do that." Noah stopped just short of grabbing his wrist, but his hand hovered there. "You can't overload these. You think I haven't tried? You'll jam the damn lock for good."

Not if you did it right. Cruz rattled off the sequence he'd learned all those years ago, vaguely surprised by how easily it all came back to him. "White and blue to yellow. Yellow to red. Red to green. Any other combination won't work. It'll fry the circuit, but it'll disable the lock first."

Boots pounded toward him from the far end of the tunnel. "Why isn't this fucking thing open?"

Dallas. Noah answered him, repeating his caution about the danger of fucking around with the circuitry. Cruz blocked it all out as he held his breath and twisted the first wires together.

"Bren—"

"Shh." Bren cut off Dallas's question. "He knows what he's doing."

Dallas cut through Noah's protest with a curt noise, and put his trust—and Mad's life—in Cruz's hands. "Get him out of there."

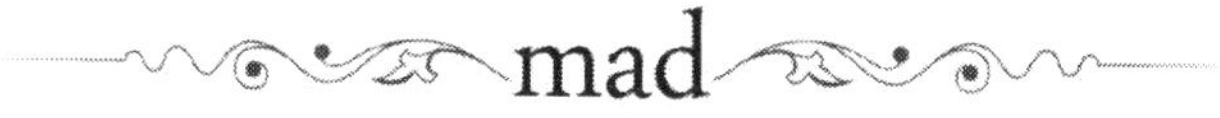

mad

MAD HATED THE dark.

He hated the silence of it, the emptiness. It wasn't natural. Outside, under the night sky, the world gave him a hundred subtle sources of sound and endless pinpricks of light. God had never intended for man to have to survive alone in the darkness.

He hadn't meant for man to survive underground, either. Mad could feel the weight of the earth pushing in around him, and not just because a few chunks of building had landed on him in the aftermath of the explosion.

Lucky. He'd been so, so lucky. The floor had crumbled and carried him down, but he'd managed to roll before the ceiling followed it. Trapped in claustrophobic darkness was still better than crushed to death, even with a body bruised and his head throbbing with the kind of pain that would have Doc in a panic.

If he ever saw Doc again.

If he ever saw *anyone* again.

He couldn't think in the dark. He couldn't breathe in it, either. That was the only sound left, the dim, faraway rasp of air flooding his lungs and rushing out, and it was probably his imagination that it felt thinner every time his lungs expanded.

"It's all right, *mi hijo*. We're going to get out of here."

No, no *they* weren't. But she sounded so confident every time she said it, because Adriana Rios had grown up as the daughter of the prophet, Sector One's adored, benevolent princess, and she refused to believe in a world where love didn't conquer all.

"Here." Something brushed the backs of his fingers, a phantom touch that crawled over his skin. "Squeeze my hand. Can you do that for Mommy?"

His hand would be larger than hers now. God, it almost had been then. He hadn't been thirteen years old in decades, but he'd never forget the shame of clutching at her hand like a little boy when he was old enough to be a man. Maybe if he'd been a better one, she would have walked out of that cramped cellar with him.

But he could feel her now. Hear her. Maybe that meant his time had run out. The first explosion must have been a misfire, but the next ones wouldn't be. There'd be no time to dig Mad out, and Bren or Jas or *someone* would do their fucking duty and drag Dallas to safety before it blew. The end was rushing toward Mad, and his mother had come to take him home.

The next rough voice dispelled that perversely comforting thought. "You treat him like a child, Adriana."

"I don't want you," Mad whispered, and he didn't care that he was talking to empty air. Sound filled the silence, whether it was the rasp of his own voice or the murmuring of ghosts.

But not this ghost. Not him.

Rubble crunched under boots, and Mad felt hot

breath on his face. "Live or die," his grandfather whispered. "It isn't in human hands. Your fate is God's to decide."

God hadn't thrown Mad and his mother into a dark room. God hadn't held a gun to Mad's head, grinding it so hard against his temple he still had the scar, swearing to Adriana that he'd kill her son if she didn't convince him to slice off her finger.

Her fate had rested in the prophet's hands. In human hands.

Mad's fate rested in human hands, too—but not in his grandfather's. Not this time.

Rolling over meant a moment of dizziness, but Mad forced himself to his knees, and then his feet. Panic made his heart pound. Pain made his head swim. The bomb had to blow, any minute now, any second—

The blueprints Noah had flashed at him floated through his head. They'd considered coming in through the tunnels, at first, before discarding the plan as too complicated. But they were there, a way out, if he could just move his feet—

—if Dallas remembered the tunnels—

—if someone got there in time to open the doors—

"I'm not a Rios," he told the ghosts, ignoring the insanity of talking to them at all. The first step nearly sent him sprawling, but he found the wall and oriented himself, struggling to remember the path he had to take. Away from the explosion, away from the wreckage.

Toward his brothers.

He wasn't a Rios. Wasn't even a Maddox, though that was the name he'd taken as his own. He took step after staggering step because he knew Bren wouldn't have dragged Dallas away. Dallas wouldn't have let him.

Mad had faith. The door would open.

"You can do this." His mother's voice—calm, level. No hint of the terror she'd tried so damn hard to hide from her little boy.

The door would open.

He wiped sweat from his forehead, only to realize it was too sticky, too warm. Blood, and he could taste it on his lips when he wet them. Every step hurt. It would be easier to lie down and close his eyes.

But the door *would* open.

He reached the far side of the basement and slammed into it, sagged against it, pressing his forehead to the cool steel. If he had a light, if his head hadn't been swimming, he could have tried to pry the panel off this side, struggled to figure out some way to force it open.

All he could do now was believe. Put his faith in O'Kane hands.

Empty space opened up in front of him. Light flared, hurting his eyes, but he was already falling, not toward the light but away from it, dizzy and weightless—

Strong arms caught him, and Bren's familiar voice rumbled, "Fucking hell."

The light swung back, illuminating Dallas's face as the man dragged him down the tunnel, his growled words chasing Mad into a different kind of darkness. "Let's get the fuck out of here."

18

RACHEL WOKE TO the sound of screams. Terrified, horror-stricken screams that raised goose bumps on her flesh and made her bolt upright in bed. "What the *fuck* is that?"

Cruz had snapped to instant alertness, but Ace was the one who rolled from the bed with a muffled curse, diving for his pants. "I knew I should have stayed with Doc."

Mad. Cruz had told them about the explosion and the resulting cave-in, but nothing he'd said would explain the barely human noises echoing through the walls. "Is he—?"

But Ace was already gone. Rachel reached for her discarded dress, dragged it over her head, and followed him.

Mad's room was only two doors down, a vast suite that encompassed almost as much space as Ace's did. The door to the hallway was hanging open, and Rachel could hear Ace's voice already.

"*Está bien, 'mano. Estas bien. Estas a salvo en el Sector Cuatro.*"

Mad answered in Spanish, the panicked, pleading words spilling from him so quickly that Rachel couldn't understand a single one.

Then she reached the open door and got a good look at Mad, backed up against the wall, face twisted in horrified terror, and she was suddenly, selfishly *glad.* Whatever hell he was caught up in wasn't a place she ever wanted to go.

A disheveled Doc stood by the bed, a rumpled blanket tangled around his feet as he dragged open his black bag. "I tried to calm him down, but it's like he can't even hear me."

"No drugs." Ace shoved Doc to the side and knelt on the bed, covering Mad's white-knuckled fists with his own. "Come on, Mad. Don't make me break out more Spanish. You know my accent sucks." When Mad continued to shudder, Ace twisted and found Rachel. "Lights. Turn on all the lights."

She hit the switch beside the door, then rushed into the bathroom and did the same thing. Every light she could think of, even the open closet and the small lamp on his bedside table. "What else can I do?"

"Wait." Ace hauled Mad away from the wall, ignoring the flash of anger and the dangerous snarl. Rachel's heart shot into her throat as Mad twisted fast, slamming Ace onto his back and grabbing his throat in a brutal grip.

Ace flung out one hand, palm toward the door, and Cruz froze, body rigid with tension. "Ace..."

"Not you," Ace rasped, and she wondered how close Mad was to choking him. "Not Doc. Talk to him, Rachel."

She hesitated, torn between complying and tearing Mad's fingers away from Ace's neck herself, even if she had to break them. Then she moved slowly, sinking to the edge of the mattress.

She took a deep breath and focused on the pulse throbbing at Mad's temple, but her first words were for Cruz. "Go get Dallas and Lex. Hurry."

He held for another few seconds, his breathing as rough and unsteady as Mad's. It wasn't until Ace said, "Brother, *go*," that she heard the whisper of footsteps behind her.

Mad was oblivious, his bare, bruised chest heaving with every breath, his dark eyes seeing nothing.

Rachel struggled for words. "I don't know what happened," she said softly, "or what you're seeing right now. Where you are. But I know you'll never forgive yourself if you hurt Ace. Let go, Mad." She gingerly brushed a lock of hair behind his ear. "You have to let go."

A shudder. Mad turned his face. Just a little, his cheek brushing her palm, his breath skating over her skin. Ace squeezed her leg, silently urging her to continue.

She did. "Poker. You promised to start up a game with me, remember? Let's make Ace and Cruz play with us, take all their money. Doc, too. I bet you'd like that."

The fingers around Ace's throat loosened. Ace sucked in a breath, but he didn't roll away. Instead, he grabbed Mad's hand and held it, clutched it tight even as Dallas and Lex spilled through the door. "If you want to stay lost in the dark, you're shit out of luck, brother. O'Kanes don't play that game."

"Fucking hell." Lex climbed onto the bed and wrapped both arms around Mad with no fear, no hesitation. Exactly like she did everything else. "Honey, are you okay?"

"No." The word creaked out, low and raspy, and Mad moved like his whole body ached, lifting off of Ace one careful inch at a time.

Cruz snatched Doc by the shirt. Ignoring the man's

grunt of protest, he dragged him to the side of the bed. "Check Ace out."

"Cruz, I'm f—"

"*Now.*"

For once, Doc seemed completely sober. He examined Ace quickly, then shook his head. "Bruising. Nothing's broken."

"Clear out," Lex said firmly, and Rachel realized others had begun to gather in the open doorway and the hall beyond.

Ace opened his mouth to protest, took one look at Lex's expression, and eased from the bed. "Come on," he said, holding out a hand to Rachel. "Dallas and Lex have this."

The roughest thing about Ace wasn't the grave, worried expression he wore, or the angry red marks on his skin that would soon deepen to a vicious purple. No, it was the sadness lurking beneath it all, a desolation that made her chest ache anew.

As soon as they'd retreated to the safety of Ace's room, Rachel slid her arms around him and buried her face against his shoulder.

"It's okay," he whispered, leading her to the bed. He didn't even kick off his pants, just rolled onto the mattress with a groan and held out one arm to her.

"Adrian Maddox," Cruz said as she slid under the covers beside Ace. Cruz remained next to the bed, his gaze fixed on empty air. "Adrian *Rios*. I knew he was Gideon Rios's cousin, but I never connected him with the civil war in Sector One."

"It was a long time ago," Rachel murmured. And a time best left forgotten—except when it reared up to snatch Mad in its jaws once again.

"Not long enough," Ace countered. He shifted closer as Cruz stretched out on his other side, but for once he was sheltered between them. Protected. "It's easier to snap him out of it if someone can understand him, but my Spanish has always been shit. It drove my mentor crazy. Like it should be in my blood or something."

"You did good." Rachel rubbed her knuckles over the reddened skin of his throat, a featherlight touch meant to soothe. "Better than anyone else could have. You knew what he needed."

"I guess." He closed his eyes and leaned into her touch. "It's happened a couple times before. Never this bad."

Cruz laid his arm across Ace, settling his hand on her hip. "He hit his head pretty hard. It probably made the disorientation worse."

"He'll be all right," Rachel told them. Sure, certain, because it had to be true. Seeing Mad in this kind of pain hurt too much.

"Yeah he will." Cruz tightened his fingers on her hip, his palm a comforting weight as he carefully changed the subject. "I think my mother was from down south, across the old border, but I never learned to speak anything but English. Didn't fall within likely mission parameters, and I had other aptitudes."

Rachel had been separated from her family in adulthood, after spending her entire life basking in their attention and love. She couldn't imagine growing up knowing they were out there, but not knowing *them*. Not even definite details. "I'm sorry, baby."

"It wasn't that bad," he said quickly. "I was in the most comfortable position on the Base. One of the elite soldiers, but not..."

"Not what?"

He stayed silent, his fingers stiff until Ace slid a hand on top of his. "It's okay if you can't tell us."

"Not can't. Shouldn't, maybe." Cruz stared at the ceiling. "They trained me from birth, almost literally. My mother probably lived on the Base. She might have known who I was, but she never let on. That's how strong the loyalty is. You have your place, your orders, whether you're a soldier or a child or a cook or a whore. The mission comes first."

Even worse, to suspect his mother was that close and never know for sure. "What's the mission?" she asked carefully. "What could be that vital? To protect Eden?"

"That's what Eden thinks. Maybe it started out that way. But I'm not the most dangerous kind of soldier the Base created."

Flat words, matter-of-fact, but they sent a frisson of warning shivering up Rachel's spine. "What does that mean?"

"The spooks," Ace said. "He's talking about the mind-fuck spooks. Didn't you have those stories in Eden?"

"Never."

"They can read your minds and make you disappear out of your bed." Ace snorted. "My uncle used to tell me the spooks would know if I stole from his cashbox. Because if I had some psychic warriors, that's what I'd do with them—send them after punk teenagers who'd pilfered beer money."

Ace was joking, but Cruz was so still. So very still. "They're not psychic. But their brains function on so high a level that the difference can seem negligible."

That was something she *had* heard, rumors that no one believed but that refused to die anyway. "Genetic modification," she mumbled. "Engineering super soldiers. The city abandoned that project before it even got off the ground."

"The city did," Cruz agreed. "The city forgets it doesn't control the Base. In fact, it started the other way around."

The military coup was a fact of history, either a glorious victory or a tragic abuse of power, depending on who you believed—schoolbooks, or the old timers who would only talk of such things in hushed whispers at the tail end of boisterous parties, when they thought all the children were already asleep in the other room. Even now, there were those in the poorer parts of the city, the areas that weren't supposed to exist, who maintained that the Council was little more than a sham, a pretty lie to keep everyone complacent while the men with the guns and tanks ran the real show.

Cruz seemed to be implying something else entirely. "If they're not under city control..."

Another endless pause. Cruz rubbed his thumb over her hip in small, endless circles, as if the touch grounded him. "You don't know what it's like to leave the base and see Eden for the first time. We lived in barracks, without families, without luxury. We went on missions to other cities in the area to destabilize threats and steal resources. We fought and we bled and some of us died, and Eden burns through resources like the flares never happened."

The waste was enough to drive anyone mad, even if you hadn't spilled and shed blood to secure it. But there were no words, no comfort she could offer that she hadn't already, so she squeezed his hand.

Ace found the words. He always did. "It's fucking bullshit. You know how many of us never got to have parents? And you could have, and they just... What, thought they'd make you too soft?"

"Families divide loyalty," Cruz replied, not sounding upset about it. "All relationships do."

"Not here," Rachel said. "Family *is* loyalty. That's what being an O'Kane means."

"When things are going well," he agreed easily. "And when they're not? If you had to choose between Lex and Dallas? Or Dallas and Ace?"

"That wouldn't happen." She met Ace's gaze and held it. "Sticking together is the most important thing. It's bigger than any of us. I get it now, what you've always tried to tell me. You have my back."

Ace's eyes were normally dark, an unrelieved brown a few shades deeper than his hair, but in the shadows of the room they seemed swallowed by blackness as he touched her cheek. "In all the ways I can, no matter what."

She trapped his hand against her cheek. "What about you? Where do you come from, Alexander Santana?"

"Seven blocks southeast." His lips curled up. "Unlike the rest of you, I'm a Sector Four native."

As if she'd been talking about geography. It was a deflection, pure and simple, and it cut through Rachel like a rusty blade. All this time, everything they'd shared, and here it was again. The part of Ace he held back.

A part she could never touch.

Maybe the pain showed on her face. His hand slipped away and he turned his gaze back to the ceiling, and more words came. "I did my time in Eden, though. Not as much as you two, but probably softer living. I even had an apartment for a while, one of those nice ones on the river. Couldn't really leave it, since I didn't have a bar code, but it was swanky."

Rachel swallowed hard. "You don't have to tell us."

"It's not a secret. It's just..." He laughed, tight and a little pained. "My poor ego. Ultimate hero lover boy here is hot as fuck, but he's a tough act to follow."

Cruz frowned, lifting himself up on one arm to study Ace. "None of what I did took thought or initiative. I followed orders, for the most part, sometimes very unheroic ones."

"Same here." Rachel shrugged. "My family had plans for me. I never embraced them, but I never fought them very much, either."

"I guess." Ace's sudden smile held the wicked edge she loved, the one that said, *I'm about to be bad, and you know you want to be bad with me.* "I do have one secret. Only Jared knows the truth. You know about the home-wrecker paintings?"

Who didn't? Ace had acquired his reputation for sin long before becoming an O'Kane. "Sure. There was always gossip about your patrons in Eden."

"Yeah, well, there are a hell of a lot more paintings floating around than I ever had patrons. Once or twice a year, Jared helps me sell one to some nitwit with more money than brains. You wouldn't believe what they'll pay to own a piece of the scandal."

It was just ridiculous enough to be brilliant. Rachel stared at him. "You're kidding, right?"

"Nope. I did one for a patron—my first patron—and it really did cause a huge damn scandal. But after that..." He shrugged. "My mentor told me not to repeat *that* mistake. But plenty of Eden's finest fancy ladies like to pretend I did."

Even Cruz laughed as he relaxed back to the bed. "That's incredible."

"I know," Ace replied. "I'm amazing."

Flippant words, an easy match to their laughter. But something about the way Ace looked left a tense knot in her belly that refused to ease. His usual charm had been subsumed by an intensity that seemed out of place, even on a night like this.

Only maybe it wasn't. Mad had almost died, and witnessing his resultant trauma had been painful enough without his hand around her throat. Everyone was on edge.

So she snuggled closer to Ace, tucked her face into the hollow of his shoulder, and told herself things would be better in the morning.

Ace didn't know how old he was. He had vague memories of a mother who had died when he was young. Old enough to walk and talk and love drawing, but not old enough to understand why his mother hadn't come home to slap a meal on the table, or that she was gone for good.

It was a nice, juicy sob story. Better when he omitted the uncle who'd swooped him up off the streets before he'd been there more than a week, and Ace had never been above a little creative license.

Words had never been his thing, but he could use them for that much. Hair falling over his forehead, eyes big and sad. He spun out the story of little orphan Alexander drawing on his cheap sketchpad with his chubby fingers, oblivious to the fact that his mama was never coming home, and panties melted away like snow in July.

Fuck, he was a piece of work.

He hauled another oversized portfolio folder off the shelf and tossed it onto his desk with enough force to send the cup holding his colored pencils rattling to the floor.

"Hey, now." Emma stood in the open doorway, one eyebrow raised. "You want to *not* trash the place, Santana? What the hell are you doing here this early, anyway?"

Good fucking question, especially since he'd left Rachel and Cruz curled up together in his own damn bed. Not that it had been possible to crawl out from between them without waking Cruz—the man snapped to high alert at a whisper—but Ace had simply tilted his head toward the bathroom. Cruz had nodded, rolled over into the empty space Ace had left behind, slung an arm over Rachel, and gone back to sleep.

Of course he had. Cruz could roll into any empty space and fill it up just fine, because he was fucking perfect.

"*Ace.*" Emma's brow plummeted into a frown as she stared at him. "Are you all right?"

"I'm fine," he grumbled, slapping open the portfolio. The top sketch fluttered toward the floor, and he caught it with one hand. A half-formed design for a tattoo stared back at him, sketched with adolescent clumsiness but clear emotion. A grim reaper, his scythe dripping blood, his skeletal face twisted in a chilling laugh. "I'm just looking for something."

"Bullshit."

He finally gave her his full attention, fixing on her worried expression. "Shit, what are *you* doing out of bed? I figured Noah'd be burning through adrenaline for half the night."

She propped her hands on her hips. "Don't change the subject. What gives?"

Emma had been easier to deal with in the beginning. So bright and eager, but sweet, too. Already a damn good artist, showing up with a stack of beautiful sketches, most of them better than Ace's uncle had ever dreamed of being, but she hadn't been pushy about telling him what to do.

Sometimes he missed those days. "You're a pain in the fucking ass, you know that? If I want to ransack my studio for no goddamn reason, I will."

She snorted. "Get pissy with me if you want, but I still think you'd be better off using your words."

The hurt and anger pulsing in his chest found a focus—if not a target. "The only words I've got are the filthy ones. I've never fronted about that, so I don't know why in hell you all expect better."

"You've always been hardest on yourself." Emma tossed her bag on the desk with a sigh. "How can you be so damn generous with other people, and then treat yourself like such shit?"

Because he deserved it. Because Rachel had asked a soulful question about Ace's past, and for a second he'd actually imagined trying to say it all.

I was a whore when you were still a kid, but I wasn't even a good one because I'm a self-obsessed narcissist who mostly just wants to have fun with his dick. And while Cruz was off bumping off bad guys and saving babies, I was playing temperamental artist fuck-toy to a bunch of women Noelle used to have over for tea and dinner parties. Boohoo, isn't my life sad.

At least Ace the tragic orphan had had a mother. An uncle. He'd had a mentor who'd given him a profitable skill set and a sense of connection to his ancestors and his heritage. He'd had Jared and Gia, who'd been his family long before the O'Kanes.

And he'd had Dallas. Lex. Jas and Mad and Nessa and everyone who had joined over the years, an ever-expanding network of family who loved him unconditionally, even when he was selfish, even when he was a narcissistic asshole who only wanted to have fun with his dick.

Cruz had nothing. Fucking *nothing*. No parents to teach him to love, no family, no warmth and tenderness. He'd had rules and regulations and brutality.

All of Ace's excuses for not being able to love looked pretty fucking flimsy with Cruz standing there, getting it done.

Ace flipped through a few more sketches without really seeing them, just to have something to do with his hands. "Maybe I know I have it coming. Ever considered that?"

"Of course I have. It's the obvious answer."

The next sketch crumpled as his fingers tightened. "Obvious, huh?"

"Yeah, to anyone who knows and loves you."

"You think you know me, kid?"

She leaned forward and braced her hands on the far edge of the desk. "Don't be patronizing, Ace. I know you better than you think, because I watch you every day. I see what you do when you're not thinking about what you *should* be doing."

His heart jackknifed halfway to his throat, but he made himself lean in until they were face-to-face. "And what's that?"

"You care," she answered softly. "You love, Ace. Maybe harder than anybody else I've ever met."

"I love easy," he corrected, grinding the words into his own heart like a reminder. "I love fast. I love everyone. But it's not hard, and it's not deep. It never was, and it's never enough."

Emma straightened with a groan. "I know that look. Don't, okay? Whatever you're gonna do, just...wait."

"I'm not *doing* anything," he snapped, but the words fell flat, like the lie they were. He was spinning out of control, panicking as hard as he had the last time he'd shattered Rachel's heart. Only this time there wasn't any comfort in telling himself he was doing the right thing by walking away, because this time there was no right thing.

He flipped over another stack of sketches, and there it was.

The paper was old, faded. So was the drawing. He could have been six or seven. Maybe five, maybe eight. The years were blurry, but the memory never was. He could remember the scratched table, so small his paper had covered almost the entire surface. He could remember the pencils—his mother had done six months' worth of extra mending to afford them, sitting up by the light of the cheap, stinking candles and sewing until her fingers were numb.

Five in all, but the true miracle had been that three were color. Blue, orange, and green—those had defined the art of his childhood, because they were the only colors that had existed for him.

God only knew where he'd seen a dragon, not that the sketch beneath his fingers was a very good rendition of one. Wobbly lines, no shading, terrible proportions. But he'd labored over it for hours, ignoring the empty gnawing in his stomach and the growing darkness, coloring in each individual scale with a mixture of blue and green. Laboring over the orange flames shooting from a mouth lined with giant, pointy teeth.

Ace traced his finger past the fire, down to the awkward figures half-sketched at the dragon's feet. A woman and a boy, though you couldn't really tell from the unfinished outlines. He'd been working on that part when his eyelids got too heavy, desperate to finish before his mother came home.

A dragon to protect us, Mama.

While he'd been trying to capture the fall of her long, black hair, she'd been bleeding out in an alley, an accidental victim in a shoot-out between rival drug runners. It had happened all the time before Dallas wrested Sector Four from the grip of his predecessor. Ace's story had never been special, except for its relatively happy ending.

The dragons he'd tattooed onto Cruz's skin were sophisticated. They were elegant, beautiful, a crowning fucking achievement of ink in black and gray, and they were just as childishly hopeful as this drawing.

A dragon to protect me.

Ace had heard the warning under Cruz's words, even if Rachel hadn't. Relationships divided loyalties. A world where Rachel had to choose between Dallas and Ace was almost unfathomable.

A world where she had to choose between Ace and Cruz was damn near inevitable.

Ace was like that faulty stick of dynamite that had nearly obliterated Mad last night, no matter how much he tried to keep his shit under control. No one knew exactly when he was going to blow. He didn't even know. He just knew it was coming, one way or another, and that he'd been lying to himself all along.

Being in love with them both didn't change anything. Ace fucked up. It was what he did, who he was. When he detonated everything they'd built together, Cruz would protect Rachel. Rachel would protect Cruz. No one would protect Ace.

But he'd known that. Hell, he'd counted on it. Little orphan Ace, abandoned again. The best sob story yet.

If he didn't get out before they claimed the last shreds of his heart, he might not survive long enough to tell it.

19

THE DAY AFTER the explosion—and Mad's subsequent nightmare—was arduously long. Rachel slogged her way through it, yearning for a cold beer, a soft bed, and some comfort from her two favorite men.

Only Cruz was in his room when she came in after her shift pouring drinks at the Broken Circle. She kicked off her shoes, crawled onto the couch next to him, and curled up against his side. "This day sucks."

"Yeah, it does." He slipped an arm around her, tugging her closer as his lips brushed the top of her head. "But Mad's doing okay. He came to Dallas's meeting to hear what Noah had to say."

"How'd it go with Fleming?"

"I'd say he heard Dallas's declaration of war loud and clear." Cruz snorted. "Noah thinks quick on his feet. He convinced Fleming that he'd rigged one of the blasts to go early to try to take out Dallas."

It was audacious—and just crazy enough to play well for an egomaniac like Fleming. "Noah's got a set of brass ones, doesn't he?"

"Without a doubt. He gave your father some equipment to help him track down Skinny Pete. A few more days, and we should have the whole organization wiped out." He squeezed her shoulder. "Your life can go back to normal."

His touch kindled a peaceful warmth that had her leaning in closer, her lips curving up into a smile. "I could do without the danger and violence, but I kind of like our new normal."

"Me, too," he said, leaning in.

His lips had almost reached hers when an abrupt knock pulled them apart. Ace was already coming through the door, his usual easy smile looking fixed. "Hope I'm not interrupting."

Rachel shifted on the couch, drawing her legs up to make room for him. "We were waiting for you."

But Ace swung a chair out from the table instead, spinning it around so he could straddle it. "Good. Because I've been thinking..."

Mild words, innocuous, but Cruz went rigid next to her. "About what?"

"About this." He waved a finger, taking in the three of them.

If it weren't for Cruz's sudden tension, Rachel could have told herself this was a good thing. Talking, maybe even about cementing their relationship into something deeper. But in so many ways, it felt like Cruz knew Ace better than she did.

This was wrong, all wrong.

Ace was cool, relaxed. She'd seen him like this a hundred times, his legs casually sprawled, his tattooed arms folded across the back of a chair. He looked like he was getting ready to share a funny story, not rip their world apart.

But that was exactly what he did. "I was just thinking, it's been really good. And maybe we should go out on a high note instead of riding it into the ground."

The words echoed in her head, like the garbled sound of rain hitting a tin roof combined with the low murmur of voices in a faraway room. No matter how much her brain tried to make sense of it all, turn it into something intelligible, she kept coming around to the fact that he couldn't have said what she thought he said.

And yet she knew he had.

"Go out," she repeated flatly.

Cruz tightened his hand on her hip. "What are you doing, Ace?"

"I'm being responsible. Thinking about the bigger picture." He met Rachel's eyes. "Do you really want to keep going until you hate me again?"

"This time is different." She heard her own words like they were coming from that far-off room, not her own damn mouth. "I don't understand."

"Cruz does," Ace said without releasing her gaze. "He knows about divided loyalties."

Cruz sat beside her, still as stone except for the fine tremor in his hands, and that tiny concession of control drove her from numb to furious in a heartbeat.

It would never be enough. No matter how much they opened to him, no matter how much they gave, Ace would always find a way to withdraw. It didn't matter whether it was out of fear or boredom—or if he was telling the truth when he said he didn't know how to love. The end result was the same.

Agony. Loss. The sharp, driving pain in her chest that couldn't quite drown out the anger, because this time he wasn't just hurting her. He was hurting Cruz, too.

"No." She climbed off the couch and stood directly in front of Ace's chair. "If this is what you want to do, I can't stop you. But you don't get to blame it on us, because all we've done is try to love you."

Ace didn't flinch. "I warned you about that, you know. It's only easy to love me in the beginning. This way you won't have to keep trying."

"That's bullshit. Cowardly, straight-up fucking bullshit, and you know it."

"Rachel." Cruz slid his arms around her, tugging her back a step, and Ace's gaze finally shifted, skating down her body to lock on the hands spanning her waist.

A muscle in his jaw jumped, the only indication of tension he'd shown. "We all got what we wanted, right? You got me out of your system, and Cruz figured out how to loosen the hell up. We can all walk away friends, or we can wait until this whole fucking thing crashes and brings half the gang down with it."

Part of her wanted to scream at him. The rest of her wanted to cry. She had to bite the inside of her cheek to stop the questions, the demands. The pleas.

Nothing had gone wrong, that was the hardest part to wrap her bruised heart around. Ace was bracing for an impact that hadn't come, maybe never would...but he was bailing out, all the same.

Her pain left her harsh, bitter. "I remember now. Words don't mean anything until you want them to." Rachel took another step back. "And when you're done, you throw them away like everything else."

Ace rose and shoved the chair back toward the table. "Keep the collar, brother, until you can find her one that can be from just you. And when you're ready for marks, you know where to find me."

Cruz's fingers curled into fists. "You think you're that disposable?"

"Oh, I know I am." He swung toward the door. "You'll thank me later for making it clean."

Clean. An odd word, out of place, because even if he was okay with how things had turned out, even if he wasn't bleeding inside, shouldn't he have been a little sad? It was a bittersweet ending, at best, but Ace was strolling toward the door as if nothing had happened.

As if he'd never told her he loved her.

The clasp on her collar was too small to manipulate quickly, so Rachel yanked at the delicate webbing of chain until it fell away. It felt heavier in her hand than it had around her neck, and heavier still when she flung it at Ace's back.

He'd already half-turned when it smacked into him, hitting him on the shoulder and sliding toward the floor. One hand came up as if by instinct, catching it against his hip. "It doesn't change anything. We're O'Kanes. I've got your backs."

"No, you don't," Cruz growled, stepping past Rachel. "The only back you're guarding right now is your own, and if you take another damn step without admitting it to all of us, I'll—"

"You'll what?" Ace interrupted with a lazy smile. "Drag me into the cage again? Beat me down in front of everyone because I wouldn't keep sucking your dick when you only ever wanted her?"

"Stop it." Agony squeezed its way up out of Rachel's chest, threatening to close her throat. "Both of you, just stop."

"He's not going to listen," Cruz said, the words soft and deadly. "He'll poke and push and shove my face in everything that scares me, but when we get to the part that makes *him* nervous? He'll throw us both away as fast as he can. And if he'd do that, he doesn't deserve you."

"I think she told you to stop, brother."

"I think she told you to stay."

Ace balled up the collar and tossed it onto the bed. It sprawled across Cruz's neatly tucked covers, a tangle of broken memories in black and silver. "Then neither of us deserve her. At least I'm man enough to admit it."

"Yeah? Well, I'm man enough to *try*."

Her sorrow and desolation condensed into helpless, burning tears, and she pressed the heels of her hands to both eyes to hold them at bay. If they kept talking, the pain and anger roiling through the room would take over entirely, and things would happen, things they couldn't take back. "Stop it." She dragged in a breath that turned into a sob. "Please."

"Okay, okay." Cruz's hands slid over her arms, warm but almost tentative. "I'm sorry."

The door clicked open, and there was the pain, blooming heavy in Ace's voice. "That's right, brother. Don't forget that you're still the hero."

The door slammed behind him, and Rachel's tears spilled over.

"I'm sorry," Cruz repeated, still rubbing her arms, still tentative. "This is my fault. I started this. I thought—"

"No." That was the worst part, the part that killed. The part that left her aching, body and soul.

Neither of them had fucked up.

The only thing they hadn't done was push Ace to come closer, to reveal more of himself. If it was anyone's fault, it was hers, a sin of omission. She'd been so scared of pushing him away that she'd accepted all of his easy smiles, his ready deflections, even when she'd glimpsed the darkness lurking beneath.

So scared of pushing him away, and now he was gone.

"Rachel?"

Cruz held out his arms, and she fell into them as another sob wracked her. "It's all right," she murmured as he cradled her against his chest. Stupid, for her to be comforting him while he held her like a child, but it was all she could think to do.

So she hid her face against his cheek and whispered it again. If she said the words often enough, she could convince herself. Cruz.

She might even make them true.

Right when he'd stopped bracing for the end, Cruz slammed into it.

It hurt. It *ached*, like something in his body had actually broken on impact. Watching Rachel cry through the night had hurt the worst, but the tangle of emotions went deeper. There was his own pain at Ace's rejection, twisted with the fear that showing too much of it would make Rachel feel worse. And, beneath all of that, guilt—guilt that as soon as he'd lost Ace, some part of him had started counting down the moments until Rachel drifted away, too.

She didn't deserve his doubts. They came from a dark place, one that wondered if he'd only been a consolation prize all along, if Ace had been his ticket into heaven. Hell, Ace didn't deserve it, either, even if he was an asshole. Ace shouldn't have been a step to Cruz's happy ending, he should have been *part* of it.

He would have been. He had been, only Cruz had been too awkward with his own feelings to say so, and now Ace would never believe it. Too little, too late.

"Hey, you were military, right?"

Cruz glanced up from the engine parts spread out before him and found Zan giving him a contemplative look. The massive bouncer had dropped by the garage and offered to help Cruz reassemble one of the motorcycles they'd rescued from Three, but this was the first thing the man had actually said to him that didn't involve carburetors or wrenches. "Yeah, pretty much raised military."

Zan studied him. "You ever train outside Eden?"

Distraction only worked if you let it, so he wouldn't think about last night. Wouldn't wonder if something in the story of his past had been the final push that had shoved Ace away. "Sometimes."

"Did you go to a place called Groom Lake? It used to be part of an Air Force installation before the Flares."

"I've heard of it, but no, I haven't been there. The inter-base command structure fell apart pretty fast after the lights went out."

Zan took a long drag from his cigarette and spoke through the cloud of smoke drifting from his mouth. "People used to think the government was experimenting on alien aircraft there, you know. Called it Area 51."

It was almost enough to make Cruz smile. "Are you so sure they didn't? The military has experimented with a lot of things they'd never admit to publicly."

"Crazier shit has happened, I guess."

"You wouldn't believe me if I told you."

"Try me sometime." Zan chuckled. "I've seen some wild things out here in the sectors."

"I bet you have." Cruz rose and circled the bike. "I think we're ready to—"

The words froze in his throat as Ace pushed through the door.

That tangle of emotions constricted into a tight ball of anger, anger that burned toward rage as Ace crossed half of the distance between them without giving any indication that things were wrong. He was playing the game for all he was worth, wearing his *nothing really matters* smile like armor, and all Cruz could think about was Rachel's voice breaking as she fought through her tears to reassure him.

Maybe Ace had a little survival instinct, though, because he stopped just out of reach. "Hey, Zan."

"What's up?" Zan laid down his wrench, swiped one grimy hand across his forehead, and glanced at Cruz. "I got a thing. You square?"

"We're square." Good, he hadn't forgotten how to make his voice nice and empty. Easy, just like Ace. "Thanks for your help."

Zan ambled out, and Ace tilted his head with a grin. "He's probably off to tell Dallas that you're about to break all of his artist's fingers, so you've got about five minutes, tops."

"I'm not going to break your fingers." To prove it, he unclenched his fists. "But I am going to ask you a question, and if you don't answer it without the bullshit, I might break your face."

Ace's smile slipped away, but he couldn't hold his tongue. He could never hold his damn tongue. "So much for the hugs and hand jobs, eh?"

Cruz crossed the space between them so fast, the passage was a blur even to him. The world shifted to flashes of sensation—the tensing of his muscles, the relief of movement. Of *reaction.*

He slammed into Ace's chest, and the impact drove him back against the wall. Ace didn't fight back, only stared at Cruz from two inches away, his eyes dangerously blank.

"Why?" Cruz ground out, laying both hands against the wall on either side of Ace's head. "Why did you do that to us? To *her*?"

"Hey, that was the deal, right? You promised me you could handle it if I couldn't. You said there'd be someone there for her, no matter what."

Words whispered in the heat of the moment. A tactical decision. Ace had been paralyzed by the fear of hurting Rachel, and Cruz had told him what he needed to hear. *It won't matter. One way or another, she'll be okay.*

He'd said it knowing the most likely alternative was for them to move forward without him. If Rachel had fallen into Ace, Cruz would have let her go. For her happiness, for *his*—watching the two people he cared most about in the world drift away from him together would have been hellish.

But not as hellish as watching them fall away alone.

"It wasn't a deal," Cruz said, fighting his rising anger. "It was a promise."

Ace shoved at his chest. "Then keep it. Take care of her."

"If things went wrong, Ace." Cruz shoved back. "Things didn't go wrong. You got scared, or bored, or who the fuck knows. I gave you a chance, and you turned it into an excuse."

Ace pushed harder this time, with enough force to send Cruz staggering back a few paces. "Are you done with the fucking lecture, brother?"

Brother. Ace threw the word around like it came free, promising intimacy he would never really feel. Or maybe he did, and that was the first mistake Cruz had made—assuming Ace's usual affections ran shallow, and the glimpses of real emotion Cruz had grasped at had been something more, something just for them.

Ace loved everyone in the gang just enough to feel real—and no one enough to *be* real.

Cruz knew shit about love, but he knew it wasn't abandoning the people who needed you. "You broke her heart." *You're breaking mine.*

For a heart-pounding moment he wondered if that was what Ace needed to know. That he wasn't handing over victory to a rival, but leaving two people devastated in his wake. Cruz opened his mouth to tell him, to make himself say the words, no matter how clumsy—

"Better sooner than later," Ace drawled, a hard, biting edge to his voice. "At least now you know how to fuck her."

For the first time in his adult life, Cruz lost control of his temper.

The first punch snapped Ace's chin to the side. The second slammed into his ribs. That was all he got before Ace started fighting back.

They'd gone at each other once before, in the cage, for an audience. Cruz could barely remember why, except that Rachel had been wounded and Ace had been to blame, and he'd still been a chivalrous knight in his own imagination, slaying dragons for his damsel.

But it had never been about her. Not in the ring, where they'd pounded each other against the steel cage until anger had led to a simmering tension Cruz barely knew how to process. And not now, when they smashed into each other, too pissed off to fight effectively, slamming each other into walls with the sort of full-body contact that twisted in Cruz's gut.

He'd wanted Ace there, that night, wanted to fuck him, wanted to hit him, wanted things more inexplicable and indescribable than both. He'd *wanted*, and wanting had changed everything.

Knowing what he was losing changed it again.

There was no finesse in this fight. No rules. Ace got him with a vicious jab to the ribs before barreling into him, carrying Cruz back against the opposite wall with a force that rattled the workbench and jostled a box of screws to the floor.

Cruz blocked his next swing and shoved away from the wall, winding up to nail Ace again.

A feminine hand wrapped around his arm, long nails digging into his skin as Lex's face penetrated the haze of his tunnel vision. "All right, knock it off right now before I take a lead pipe to you both! Jesus fucking Christ."

His hand itched with the need to connect with Ace's face, but if he swung and took Lex with him, he really would be feeling a lead pipe—or Dallas O'Kane's boot on his face. He let her drag him back a step and looked away from Ace's bleeding nose.

"Santana," Dallas barked. "Cruz is new, but you know the damn rules. You got shit to deal with, you take it to the cage."

"I didn't—"

"Shut up. I'm not joking, Ace. Drag your ass to my office, and do not open your damn mouth until I get there."

After Ace stomped off, Lex growled and smoothed her hair back into place as she faced Cruz. "O'Kanes don't fight each other, not outside those steel bars. We fight, we fall."

Cruz remained silent, and Dallas leveled a finger at him. "We don't have time for this bullshit, so you listen to what she says, or you're gonna be hauling trash in Three while the guys I can trust deal with this attack. Understood?"

An ultimatum on obedience, and it was still a struggle to nod. "Understood."

Dallas turned to Lex. "You got this?"

"Yeah, I'm on it."

The leader pivoted and strode after Ace, leaving Cruz to the mercy of Lex's stare. Cruz met her gaze for a few seconds before deliberately dropping his attention to his bruised knuckles. "It won't happen again."

"Right." She stepped closer, gingerly prodded his split lower lip, and sighed. "Oh, honey. We've got to talk about your methods of coping with grief."

It hurt like hell, but he refused to wince. "I think that was anger more than grief."

"Eh, you're full of shit. Sit down." She retrieved a bottle of water from the electric cooler against the wall and handed it to him. "For the lip."

He didn't even choose to sit, not really. Adrenaline faded, and he let gravity carry him to the sagging couch. "I'll be fine, Lex. I'm more worried about Rachel."

"You and everybody else." She sank down beside him. "Me? I'm worried about you and Ace."

Cruz lifted the bottle to his lip and said nothing. What was there to say? Lex knew people from the inside-out, so she probably saw the truth—whether Cruz wanted her to or not.

Lex rubbed her hands on the legs of her faded jeans. "If there's one person in this gang that I just *get*, without even having to think about it? It's Ace. So I understand why he'd flip his shit and bug out on you and Rachel. I'm not saying he did the right thing...but I get it. What it really means."

"That we're not worth the risk?"

Lex cast a somber look his way. "Not even close. It means he's so crazy in love with you both that it's all he can see—how fucking *flawless* you guys are. It's not a long way from there to wondering why you'd want to waste your time on someone like him."

Cruz rubbed a hand against his chest, and it didn't help. That ache was back, worse than before. "I can't tell him if he won't listen."

"Sound travels faster than a good left hook, last time I checked."

"The right sounds might." The right words. If he was anything close to flawless, he'd know what those were.

"Yeah," she agreed, then slapped him on the leg. "That big damn heart of yours? You'll figure it out."

Cruz twisted the top from the water and drained half of it, buying time and gathering courage. There was one question he didn't want to know the answer to—the one that would break his heart with or without Rachel. "What if he only loves her?"

Lex rose and shoved her hands in her back pockets before turning and fixing Cruz with a thoughtful look. "What if he doesn't?"

The front door slammed open, crashing back against the wall, and Jasper strode in. "We've got trouble."

Lex's easy demeanor vanished. "What kind?"

"Big fucking group of guys smashing their way through the market." His lips pressed into a thin line. "Looks like someone didn't like having his booze blown up."

"Back office." She jerked her head in that direction and spun to face Cruz, and only the tight set of her shoulders betrayed her sudden tension. "A street brawl.

That's straight-up old school. Kind of quaint."

Not quaint at all in the parts of Eden where Rachel had grown up. It was exactly how her father and their rivals had settled things—man to man, fists and blood. Guns ran too much chance of bringing the military police down on all of them, but a quiet, vicious fight...

His blood was pumping again, his body alive at the opportunity. To hit something, to vent his anger and hurt and frustration. To have an excuse to bloody his fists and exhaust his body and deaden his heart.

Cruz flexed his hands and smiled. "You coming with us?"

"A bunch of shitheads causing trouble in *my* sector? I wouldn't miss it."

dallas

THE PEOPLE OF Sector Four had long memories.

It had been years since Dallas had faced a real challenge to his authority, even longer since something like this. An honest-to-Christ street fight, and the people of his sector still knew how to get the fuck out of the way. The O'Kanes strode through empty streets on their way to the market, and Dallas could feel the heavy weight of hundreds of eyes.

Not everyone in Four loved him, but most of them would be rooting for him. The devil they knew.

This time would be different, and not just because Lex stalked at his side, brass knuckles glinting on her fists. He might regret not fighting her on this point, even though Lex was deadly when she wanted to be, and half the sector knew what Six could do to a man with her fists. Denying the women the right to defend their territory would discredit the ink he'd given them, and it sent a message he couldn't get behind anymore.

The sector wouldn't change until Dallas changed it. For Lex, he would. For Lex, he'd fight to his dying breath to make a world where she could do anything.

Today was about keeping the power to make that world happen.

They heard the crashing and laughter from one street away. Boards breaking, glass shattering—and even if Dallas hadn't been determined to put this bastard down, the waste of it would have tipped him over the edge into rage. A careless bit of destruction could mean the difference between a crafter's survival and starvation. The senseless loss aside, a starving man couldn't pay his dues.

Stupid. Fucking stupid, and when he broke free of the last building and stepped into the market square, he got a good look at just how destructive some stupid motherfuckers bent on making a point could be. "All right," he shouted, giving it enough force to roll across the empty space. "I'm here. Is one of you fuckheads in charge?"

The man who strolled around the edge of old man Miller's food stand had red hair and a wiry build. His features were thin, as well, angular and hard, marred by a vicious scar that cut across his right cheek and up through his eyebrow. He carried a battered club in one hand and had two wicked blades strapped to one leg. "That would be me."

A vaguely familiar face, but that only meant Dallas had seen him somewhere before. Someone he'd met in person or seen in Eden's files—half the sectors fell into that category. He didn't know *who*, but he could guess at *why*.

The whiskey. Nessa's instincts, Ford's business savvy, Dallas's ruthlessness. He'd built an empire—a name—and if this guy couldn't play off it, he'd try to straight-up take it.

Dallas kept his expression lazy as he quirked an eyebrow. "And you are...?"

The man swung his club in an equally lazy arc. "The new king of Sector Four."

Cocky fucking bastard. "Not yet, you're not."

"His name's Tierney." Cruz stepped up next to Dallas. "Another associate of Liam Riley's."

Then Rachel's father had a serious personnel problem—one Dallas had already seen coming. Liam's belief in family and blood was noble and all, but constantly overlooking your ambitious, competent employees in favor of screw-up nephews didn't buy a lot of loyalty when other opportunities presented themselves.

"Former associate. I remember this one," Bren added. "He wanted to branch out into liquor, but Riley shut him down. He pressed the issue, and Liam gave him the boot." He tilted his head and grinned. "And the scar."

"Smart of Liam," Dallas drawled, putting an extra bit of lazy disdain into the words. "Tierney's not so good at the liquor business, is he?"

The man tensed. "I worked hard to build it. *Years*, and you tore it down. Guess I'll have to take yours."

"Guess you'll have to try," Dallas corrected, reaching out a hand. Lex slapped his club into it, and he hefted it, testing the weight as he gave himself one final moment to second-guess the fight.

He could have done it fast and dirty, thrown Bren up on a roof with a sniper rifle and come in, guns blazing. Unsporting against a bunch of sorry fuckers armed with bats and knives, but no one had the power to take Dallas to task for picking the safe route of a bully. He didn't owe the chance at bloodshed to anyone, not anymore.

But guns were dangerous in a brawl. Bullets went wide. Found friends, family. Found innocent bystanders. Kids. This was the risk he took for everything they gave him, the protection his sector's inhabitants bought with their money. O'Kanes lived the comfortable life because they were the ones who would bleed when that life was threatened.

So it would come down to what it always did. Fists and strength and beating the life out of your enemy, because Sector Four was only safe as long as everyone knew in their guts that Dallas O'Kane was so damn strong, he didn't need the easy path.

Besides, swinging his club at Tierney's head would be a real, honest-to-God pleasure.

20

THIRTY SECONDS INTO the fight, Ace wanted to kick back and laugh himself sick. It wasn't like the fight really needed him, not now that Dallas had let Lex off the chain.

The bastards from Eden couldn't handle ladies kicking their asses.

It was nice to know he could still feel the urge to laugh. Not much had seemed funny in the past forty-eight hours. But watching Lex duck a punch before swinging to connect with her attacker's baffled face was gold. Pure fucking gold.

A blow to the shoulder spun him around in time to throw a punch of his own. His brass knuckles weren't as fancy as Lex's—they weren't even his—but they broke bone just as well with enough temper behind them, and Christ knew he had that.

The fight was chaos. Ugly, fantastic *anarchy*, and it

didn't matter that the O'Kanes had started off slightly outnumbered, not with Cruz and Bren cutting twin paths of destruction through the tangled horde of attackers.

More than one person broke under Cruz's advance, bolting for an exit only to be smacked down by Flash or Zan. One idiot ran toward Six, and Ace tried to remember his first sight of her—a tiny brunette with skinny arms and a sharp, delicate face. If you'd never seen her in the cage, maybe she looked like an easy target.

She let the poor bastard take a swing at her before executing a block that turned into a throw, and then she was on him, her knee at the small of his back, her knife at his throat, her contained fury burning so bright the next man pivoted and ran back toward Cruz.

He got his face pounded, too.

A fucking garbage can sailed through the air, narrowly missing a man striding toward Lex's back, his features set with fury, as it clattered to the ground. Emma swept it up and used the heavy metal can's momentum to her advantage, cracking it into the side of the man's head.

That was his girl.

One of the guys Bren had left in his wake tried to roll to his knees. Ace booted him back to the pavement and snatched the knife out of the sheath strapped to his thigh, coming up in time to sink it into the shoulder of someone hauling back to punch him.

The man screamed with pain, lashing out fast enough to catch Ace aside the head. His ears still ringing, Ace got in two more punches before a third finally laid the man out. He spun toward the sound of Flash's furious shout and came face-to-face with someone familiar.

Skinny Pete, Rachel had called him. The bastard who'd been so close to her family he'd taken her to school. A virtual uncle, someone who should have had the sense to be loyal.

He didn't look so loyal now, sneering at Ace, blood

dripping from a busted nose and a cut on his temple. "O'Kane collects trash." He spat blood at his feet. "Even little whore boys."

There'd never been a time when those words had stung. He felt more moral conflict over selling his art than he ever had selling his body—but someone from Eden would never understand.

So he smiled. "Someone's mad they couldn't afford me, huh?"

Skinny Pete snapped his arm out to his side, low toward the ground, opening a wicked-looking telescoping baton. "Rumor's out about you and Liam's girl. That kinda thing doesn't stay secret for long."

"I don't listen to rumors." Without taking his eyes from Pete, Ace swooped and wrenched the bloody knife out of the unmoving man's shoulder. "They're almost never right."

The fucker was fast. A flick of his wrist, and pain exploded across Ace's unprotected side—searing at first, followed by a dull ache that throbbed in his ribs.

He wasn't messing around, so Ace didn't either. Ignoring the pain, he pushed forward, slashing at Pete's ribs. The other man twisted, leaving the knife to slice through his shirt. The man raised his arm again, but only as a distraction. He swung a punch that glanced off Ace's jaw and knocked his teeth together painfully.

Fuck, he'd had enough of being punched in the face today.

Not that he could afford to think about Cruz, not with Skinny fucking Pete doing his damnedest to put him in the ground. Ace channeled the pain, the hurt, the twenty-four hours of outright *misery*—

Dallas probably wanted this bastard alive to hand over to Liam. But his entire existence was Liam Riley's fault. Rachel's father was careless with his people. Careless with the ones that *mattered*.

Skinny Pete was one mess Ace wouldn't leave behind

him.

Ace saw the next feint for what it was. He ignored it, waiting for the pull back, the wind up, the split second of vulnerability.

A split second was all it took, if you knew how to use it.

When it came, Ace launched a distraction of his own, a page right out of Six's *How to Terrify Men* handbook. He went for Pete's balls and didn't care when his knee smashed into a hip instead of the man's undoubtedly tiny dick.

It didn't matter. His knife was already headed for Pete's throat. The blade found its mark, blood spurting as it sliced deep, and Pete's eyes bugged out as he staggered back.

Sorry, Dallas.

But he wasn't sorry, not until Pete slumped to the pavement and Ace saw Cruz standing there, his gaze wild around the edges. He hopped over Pete's body and almost slammed into Ace, but stopped short of actually touching him.

For one crazy second there was no fight, no dying bootlegger at their feet. There was nothing but naked worry in Cruz's eyes, and an intensity Ace had never expected to see directed at anyone but Rachel.

Too much intensity. Cruz was completely focused, oblivious to the fight still raging around them, oblivious to the man coming up beside him, knife already raised.

Ace didn't think. He shoved, knocking his shoulder into Cruz's chest. Shock distorted the other man's face. Shock and pain, and in the heartbeat before Cruz tripped backwards over Pete's sprawled body, Ace realized that might be the last thing he saw.

The knife sliced into him.

It hurt. *Christ*, it hurt, making his bruised ribs feel like an itchy tickle in comparison. Burning agony exploded through him, worse when the man crashed into him and the knife twisted, and he was going to die, because that's what happened when someone stuck a blade in you and twirled your guts around.

Death. Nothingness. *Numbness*. God, he would welcome that part, if he could just get Cruz's wounded expression out of his head. But it was all he could see, fuzzy and pulsing as the light faded, and closing his eyes didn't help him because it was everywhere.

Cruz and Rachel hurting. Hurting forever. Because of him.

Maybe he was already dead, and this was hell.

Noelle was losing her shit, and Rachel couldn't seem to focus long enough to calm her down.

Her mind flitted from thought to thought, darting between worry and the certainty that surely the universe wasn't fucked up enough to take anyone from her right now, not after everything that had been said and done. Then it was right back to worry, because she knew better. Life didn't come with guarantees.

Hell, sometimes it barely came with first chances, much less second ones.

She tried to distract herself by straightening stacks of first aid supplies—gauze pads, bandages. Tubes of med-gel. Anything to keep her hands busy, her mind blank...and off of the fight raging mere blocks away. Sometimes she thought she could hear them, even from here. Shouts, cracking bone, cries of pain, the muffled thud of fists against flesh. But there was only nervous silence in the bar as everyone who had stayed behind waited for their family to come home.

Please come home.

Finally, she snatched up a bottle of water and pressed it into Noelle's hand. "Jas will be fine."

"I know." She clenched her hands around the bottle

as if it would hide their trembling. "So will Dallas and Lex. And Ace and Cruz. And Six and—"

"Everyone," Nessa cut her off, throwing an arm around her shoulders. "Trust me, girl. You guys are new to this, but I used to have to watch them roll out all the time. Hell, before Dallas got control of the sector, it could be damn near every week. They got this."

It was truth. It should have settled the panic churning in the pit of Rachel's stomach, but it didn't. Anxiety swam in her gut like acid, and she could barely stand still.

Jade folded her hand over Rachel's and squeezed briefly. No words, no empty condolences. Just a moment of solidarity that slipped away as someone shouted outside.

The door slammed open. Mad came first, carrying one end of a makeshift stretcher. Cruz held the other. He was shirtless and covered in blood, and he wore an expression of such devastated shock that she knew. Before Mad turned, before she could see who was lying on the stretcher, she *knew*.

The room exploded in a flurry of shouts, but the noise faded into a dull, faraway din as Rachel watched them lay the stretcher across the end of the stage. People rushed past her, and she barely felt them as she focused on Ace's ashen face.

His shirt had been stripped away, as well, cloth balled up against his abdomen and soaked through with too much blood. She watched—numb, empty—and then somehow she was on her knees by the stage, reaching for him. She couldn't remember moving, only the spark of something desperate kindling in her belly.

She had to take care of him.

"What was it?" Her voice, clipped and calm, drifting up from somewhere.

"Knife." Cruz's voice wasn't calm. It was raw, like he was coming apart, and his next words told her why. "He shoved me out of the way—I almost got hit in the back."

Rachel peeled back the wadded-up shirt, and a wave of nausea washed over her. "Doc's on his way. Someone go find him. *Now.*"

Mad turned and ran.

"Rae."

Ace's voice was weak, thready with pain. His fingers were sticky with drying blood as she wrapped her hand around his and leaned closer. "Just hang on, okay? We're here."

His eyes didn't open, but he squeezed her hand. "Emma. Promise me. Only Emma."

It took her a moment to figure out what the hell he was talking about, and when she did, she burst into tears. "You motherfucker." Only he would be worried about her goddamn tattoos when he was lying there, dying right in front of her.

He shook free of her hand and reached for her side, smearing blood across her shirt. "Let her finish it, angel. Don't fall forever."

Not in a million years. She'd wear his half-finished ink in her skin until she died, a mark and a brand and a reminder that she, too, was undone. Incomplete.

Doc burst through the door, bags in hand, already barking orders. "Donnelly, where's my IV access?" He halted by the stage, cursed viciously, and tore off his jacket. "Stabbing?"

"Straight blade. Five or six inches." Cruz didn't relinquish his place next to Ace until Bren nudged him aside, and even then he stayed crouched on the stage, his face blank. "It wasn't clean. The bastard twisted it good before I got to him."

"I'll have to open him up." Doc pulled the cloth away from Ace's belly and swore again. "Not much opening to do."

The world went white around the edges, and Rachel swayed. Trix steadied her with both arms around her.

Doc tore open one of his surgical prep packs. "Want to help me with this, Ra—" The words cut off with a cough as he glanced up at her. "Never mind. Sorry."

Jade appeared at Doc's side, her hair tied back from her solemn face. "I can help."

"Good. Everyone else, get the fuck out."

Rachel stood, rooted to the spot, until Trix steered her toward the back door. "Come on," she whispered. "Let Doc take care of Ace. Cruz needs you, too."

Cruz. If she was reeling from the trauma of seeing Ace laid out and bleeding like this, how bad did it have to be for him? To not only see it happen, but to have it come as Ace was protecting him?

She circled the stage and fell into his arms.

"I'm sorry." His voice broke. "God, I'm sorry, Rachel."

They made it as far as the back hall, and she slumped against the wall while the others filed past them. She wrapped her hands around his forearms, stared at the splashes and smudges of blood—*Ace's* blood—on his bare skin. "He'll be okay. All Doc has to do is stabilize him, and Dallas will get a regen tech out here to do the rest."

Cruz shuddered. "It shouldn't have happened. I was distracted. And—Christ, Rachel, we fought. I was punching him before this started. I was—"

"Shh." She slid her hands up to frame his face, stared at her own terrified misery reflected back at her. "This isn't your fault."

"I should have protected him." Cruz clasped her waist, but his fingers were too tight, digging in until it hurt. "I can't just wait. I have to do something. I have to—" His hands flexed, and he released her abruptly. "Christ, I'm sorry."

"Cruz—" She bit off the words. There was nothing she could say to soothe him, no comfort except for her touch...and Ace's survival.

21

THINGS WENT FROM bad to worse.

Doc stood there, his hands clean but his shirt still bloody. His words ran together, and Rachel struggled to make sense of them, even though his first were the ones that kept ringing in her ears.

It doesn't look good, O'Kane.

"...managed to repair most of the damage, but the deep vessels in his liver must have been compromised." Doc rubbed his eyes and sighed. "He's oozing blood, and I can't stop it. He's stable enough for now, but if you want him to last the night, get that goddamn tech out here."

"Jas is working on it," Lex told him.

"Working on it?" Cruz hadn't gone more than a few steps from Rachel, but nervous energy kept him pacing back and forth. "I thought you *had* a tech."

Dallas cast a look at Rachel and then shut Cruz down with a curt, "Jas is on it."

"No, I'm not," Jasper said from the open door to the dancers' dressing room. "She's not coming."

Rachel shuddered, the words propelling her up and off the couch. "*What?*"

"What the fuck does that mean?" Dallas growled at Jasper. "I pay her ridiculous fees, and that means I want her ass here when one of my people needs her."

"It's Fleming," Jas answered hoarsely, dragging his hands through his hair "Payback for the warehouse. I hit up all my other contacts—I even went out to Two. I couldn't find anyone else."

"Because he'll hold back the drugs they need if they give in. Fucking *hell*." Dallas paced away from them, his shoulders rigid, every step measured. "I should have seen this coming. The bastard has no honor."

Rachel clenched her hands to still their trembling, but it didn't help. The stark, brutal reality of the situation was there, laid out before her like a nightmare, and she couldn't wake up.

She couldn't fucking wake up.

"How long?" Lex asked flatly.

Doc shook his head.

She advanced on him. "Operate again. Fix the bleeding."

"The damage—"

"Fuck the damage. I'll go drag Fleming over here and give Ace *his* goddamn liver, you watch."

"I can't!" Doc exploded. "I don't have the equipment or facilities for this kind of procedure. And frankly? I don't have the skills either. It's out of my hands, Lex."

Rachel stepped between them, harnessing every last bit of composure she still possessed to speak past the choking lump in her throat. "There's nothing you can do for him?"

The man froze. For once, his expression of cool arrogance was gone. He stared down at her, anguish and remorse darkening his features. "I can end the pain."

Red clouded her vision, something deeper and more visceral than rage, and she slapped him.

"Rachel!"

She reached for Doc's throat, but an arm went around her waist, hauling her back. "Stay with us, sweetheart," Dallas murmured against her ear.

Stay with them. The world was spinning away, slipping through her fingers, and all she could imagine was Ace gone. Day after day of loss, of emptiness.

Of watching the light in Cruz's eyes die, too, a little bit at a time.

"I can't." The words ripped free of her burning throat, carried on a desperate sob. "I can't do this. I can't—I *can't*—"

"I can get a regen tech." Cruz stared at the open door, into the looming darkness beyond, his eyes blank and unseeing.

Jas flinched as if Cruz had struck him. "I tried, man. I swear to Christ, I did."

Cruz turned slowly, but his gaze skipped over Jas and settled on Rachel. Her pain was echoed there, shared and multiplied. "I can get a tech," he repeated.

"How—?" Dallas started.

"Don't ask, because I can't tell you." Cruz touched Rachel's cheek. "Trust me, O'Kane. This is a favor you can't afford to owe. You can't even be here. The only one it's safe for is Bren."

Rachel reached for him, clenching her fists in his borrowed shirt. "*No*, Cruz. You can't go. Please don't leave me."

He framed her face with both hands and pressed his forehead to hers. "I don't have to go anywhere," he whispered hoarsely. "But you do. Go back to the barracks with everyone else, and trust me. Can you do that for me, angel?"

Angel. It shredded her, because it was more than an endearment. It was a plea, Cruz's way of saying that he had to do this, because he needed Ace as much as she did.

Loved him.

She took a deep breath—and nodded. "For Ace," she said quietly. "For you."

Cruz placed his call and made his promise, and then there was nothing to do but wait.

Wait, and finally tell Bren everything.

"He took Miller's spot as head of Military Police after Miller went down for the trafficking," he explained as they stood in the empty parking lot together. "I don't know why the Base sent him, but it must mean something. He's Makhai."

"Shit." Bren lit another cigarette. "No wonder you couldn't tell Dallas."

"Yeah." Even the people who believed the rumors were better off not having them confirmed. Especially someone in Dallas's position. "Eden should be worried, Donnelly. He's not just a soldier I happen to know from the Base. He's my contact."

A muscle jumped in Bren's jaw, the only outward sign of his sudden, palpable tension. "That's a dangerous fucking game, Lorenzo, and it doesn't belong in Sector Four. We'll all get dead."

"Do you trust Coop?"

"Coop's not planning a rebellion," Bren whispered. "A *revolution*."

A dangerous word. The kind that could get a sector firebombed. But for all that he trusted Bren's instincts, his friend would never understand the Base. If the Makhai soldiers had decided Eden wasn't deserving of their loyalty, they had the skills and power to make a rebellion swift and successful.

If revolution was coming, Cruz wanted to know.

A black car turned the corner up ahead, and Cruz straightened. "The favor I owe him will be between us, soldier to soldier. No O'Kanes, no Ace. I knew what I was doing when I made the call. And if you tell me you wouldn't have done worse if Six was bleeding out in there..."

Bren didn't hesitate. "I would have burned the world."

So would Cruz. And he'd be twice as dangerous, because he had two reasons to strike the match.

The car pulled into the lot in silence, and Cruz watched as Ashwin Malhotra slipped from the driver's seat. The back seat held three heavy silver briefcases Cruz recognized as the portable regeneration kits, but there was no sign of the regen tech.

Of course there wasn't. She wasn't here willingly.

Ashwin passed them the cases, then closed the car door and walked to the back of the car. "She sees no one. Hears no one. No threats, and no payment. Those are the terms, soldier."

"I've cleared everyone else out," Cruz replied, keeping his voice flat. Emotionless, as if he wasn't negotiating for Ace's survival. "I'll explain the situation to her."

Ashwin's hand hesitated on the trunk release. "That would put her life at risk. Unacceptable."

And to a Makhai soldier, the lines were perfectly clear. He'd calmly kidnapped the woman from her secure lab, had transported her blindfolded and bound in the trunk of his car toward an unknown fate that must have her paralyzed with fear—and he'd take her straight back to Eden if Cruz did anything that might endanger more than her emotional well-being.

Practicalities. Black-and-white variables. That was what a man like Ashwin Malhotra saw, and Cruz had drifted farther from that world than he'd realized.

It was hard to shut himself down. To consider the options. Every time he tried, he saw Ace's horrified face as the knife twisted in his gut. He saw the pain in the other man's eyes. The blood on his own hands.

He saw Rachel's heartbreak when he'd called her *angel*.

"We could leave her in the room with her supplies and a note," he said finally. "But how do we know she'll help him?"

"It's who she is." He opened the trunk.

The woman inside lay still, unmoving except for her quick, shallow breaths. Her hands were secured behind her back, and the blanket around her had fallen away to reveal pajamas. A pair of noise-blocking headphones had been secured to her head with the blindfold covering her eyes.

Then she shifted, and the delicate lace edge of her sleeve rode up to reveal two bar codes on the inside of one wrist.

Bren exhaled sharply. "Motherfucker. That's not just a tech from Eden. She has Special Clearance."

Cruz shifted his gaze to her face again. Her features were obscured by the blindfold, but even in the darkness he could pick out enough identifying characteristics. Regen techs were rare. Regen techs with Special Clearance...

"Dr. Kora Bellamy," he whispered. She was young but brilliant. She'd put Cruz back together more than once in the short time she'd been caring for the elite soldiers, always with a kindness and compassion he didn't often see.

She'd be terrified. She'd be upset. But if he shut her in a room with Ace, she'd get past all of those things and do what she always did.

Preserve life.

Ashwin pulled her up out of the trunk. She began to thrash, only stopping when he set her down and squeezed his hand around the back of her neck. Not hard enough to hurt, but she stiffened and stilled with a whimper.

Then he led her into the club.

Bren held back. "Nothing like this comes for free. You know that, right?"

He knew it better than Bren did, because he knew Makhai soldiers had a code, one that transcended military protocol and city laws. Nothing transcended a promise between soldiers. When the time came to pay the price, Ashwin would be ruthless in collecting.

As long as Ace survived, Cruz would pay. "Let's hope he doesn't ask me to set the world on fire."

"And if he does?"

For the first time since he'd left the Base, Cruz didn't feel pulled in opposite directions. Blood had a way of simplifying things. He'd do his best for Dallas, for all the O'Kanes, but his loyalties would never be divided again.

Rachel and Ace were his. If that meant razing everything in his path, it would be worth it. As long as they were alive. As long as they were safe.

"Cruz?"

"If you see me reaching for a lighter, start running."

22

HELL SHOULDN'T HAVE been so comfortable.

Ace was warm. Peaceful. Pain had been replaced by a bone-deep lethargy, the kind of exhaustion so far beyond tired that he drifted there for minutes or hours, wondering if opening his eyes was worth the trouble.

Probably not. This had to be a dream, because he wasn't alone. A solid wall of muscle radiated heat along one side of his body, and the other side was pressed up against soft curves. A pair of entwined hands rested on his chest, and sleepy whimsy imagined them guarding his heart.

If he really was in hell, this was a trick. Rachel and Cruz had slipped from his life, shoved out of it before they could walk away, and this moment could never be more than a fantasy. A dream. A cruel taunt, reminding him of what he'd lost, what he'd never been worthy of trying to take.

But if he kept his eyes closed, he could pretend. Just for a little while longer.

"His breathing changed," a feminine voice whispered, the words seeping through the layers of cotton around his mind. "Should we go get Doc?"

"Not yet. Let's see if he wakes up first."

What a shitty trick. It didn't even sound like Cruz and Rachel. Comfortable illusion shattered, and there was no point in trying to reclaim it.

Ace turned his head and opened his eyes, blinking until a pale face framed by brunette hair swam into focus. He parted his lips to ask where he was, but his throat was so dry he only managed the first word in a rusty whisper. "Where...?"

Soft fingers framed his face. "Shh, you're okay. Jas will get you some water. You've been asleep for a long time."

The bed shifted, and Ace twisted his head in the opposite direction. Jas was reaching for a bottle of water, the worry etched on his face already giving way to a grin. "Here."

The water helped. Ace drank half of it in slow sips before sinking back to the pillows, struggling to hide the ache of loss as Noelle smoothed the blankets back into place. It wasn't fair to feel so empty with the two of them beaming at him like he was their own personal miracle.

Maybe he was. But not enough of one.

"What happened?" he asked finally, glancing back to Jas. "Is everyone else all right?"

"Fine. Cuts and bumps, nothing a little med-gel couldn't fix. We won, by the way."

"Of course we did." He owed it to them to find a smile, so he squeezed Noelle's hand and gave her a grin. "Did Dallas get a chance at that bootlegging bastard, or did Lex get to him first?"

"Dallas killed him." Noelle curled up at his side, her hand settling on his chest again. "Lex knows the value of a symbolic victory."

"Yes, she does." Jasper hesitated. "How do you feel?"

"Tired." He stretched, flexing his feet and taking mental inventory. His last clear memory was being stabbed, but aside from a general ache, no part of him hurt much worse than the rest—which meant Dallas had opened his cashbox and purchased Ace a new lease on life. "Dallas called the regen tech and her magical silver briefcase, I'm guessing."

"Not exactly. I called, but she wouldn't come." Jas looked away. "Fleming pulled a power trip. He figured he'd punish Dallas one way or another, I guess."

It didn't make any damn sense. He slid his hand over his abdomen, searching for a wound he already knew he wouldn't find. His fingertips found only smooth skin—*too* smooth. "Dallas obviously found someone who was willing to show up. If he had to ask Jared or Gia, I can deal with the payment."

"Cruz called in a favor."

Ace stared at him, his heart suddenly thumping. How big a favor did it take to make Jasper look that wary? "From where?"

Jas shook his head. "He wouldn't tell us. All he said was that it would be too dangerous for us to know."

"He went a little crazy," Noelle whispered. "It was bad, Ace. We thought..."

She didn't finish, but she didn't have to. They'd thought Ace was going to die. He couldn't blame them. He'd thought it, too. By all rights he should be dust on the wind, but Cruz was a hero, and a hero never let anyone slip away.

Noelle kissed his cheek and climbed from the bed. "I'm going to go find Doc. If he says it's okay, we can get you some real food."

Ace watched her leave the room, a smile curling his lips in spite of himself. If anyone had told him a year ago that he'd be harboring a sincere fondness for a councilman's daughter, he would have laughed himself sick.

Women from Noelle's world had traded Ace between them like a dirty secret, but she'd rejected the lessons of that life with a courage that made them all look a little cowardly. Ace was twice a coward, because he couldn't even ask the question burning a hole in his chest. "Alright, brother. I suppose picking her up off the street wasn't your *worst* idea."

"Not by a long shot." Jas sat up and swung his legs over the side of the bed. Turned away, but Ace didn't need to see his face to understand the gravity of his words. "You fucked up."

Which time. But if he said it like that, Jas would think he was joking. There was no reason to assume he wasn't. Everyone knew he couldn't be serious.

He had to prove them wrong. He had to try. "I know."

"No, you don't. You didn't see them, man."

"Then tell me."

"Rachel lost it," he said simply. "When we thought we couldn't get a tech out here for you, Doc started talking about putting you down like a fucking dog. She tried to strangle him. But the surprise was Cruz." He shifted on the bed, turning to face Ace. "I thought he'd lock it down, you know? Try to prop Rachel up, get her through it. But he couldn't."

"He would have." It was impossible to imagine an alternative, a world where Cruz didn't do all the right things for Rachel. She was the one who mattered to him.

Deserved him.

Jas snorted. "Tell me, you say, and then you don't listen when I do."

He closed his eyes, wry laughter rattling up through his chest. "Because it sounds a lot less fucking manly to say *make me believe.*"

"Truth. And I've got another one for you—if they couldn't get it through your skull, then I don't stand a chance."

"I'm scared," Ace admitted, and then groaned. "Fuck, Jas. Why in hell do they have to be so *perfect*?"

That brought a chuckle spilling out of his friend. "I'm just spitballin' here, man...but have you considered that maybe they're not, only you're too fucking in love with them to notice?"

No, he really hadn't.

Ace struggled into a seated position. The room spun woozily for a second, and fuck if he knew why. Maybe he was still light-headed from his injury. Maybe Jas had just upended his world. He only had one lifeline left, and he lunged for it as everything else fell away. "If they were that worried, why aren't they here?"

Jas's smile faded. "Because you told them they didn't belong here."

Despite her bone-crushing exhaustion and the mysterious regen tech's assurance that Ace would be fine, Rachel slept fitfully. Not deep enough to dream, but nightmares dragged at her anyway, bloody and desolate. Every time one began to seem too real, too focused, the heart-pounding fear jerked her up out of a shallow doze.

She was staring up into the darkness, trying to fall asleep again, when the door opened.

"Ace is fine," was the first thing Cruz said, even before he eased the door shut. He continued as he approached the bed, toeing off his boots and stripping his shirt over his head. "Doc's with him now, but Noelle said he was awake and talking and seemed good."

Relief surged through her, even more gut-wrenching than the terror. "He's okay?"

"He's okay." Cruz slid into bed and reached for her, and the tremor in his hands made his calm words a lie. "I didn't go see him. I didn't know if..."

"Yeah." They weren't invited, pure and simple. Ace

could insist nothing had changed, that the gang came first, but the truth was it would be a long time, if ever, before the pain settled. O'Kane for life—that was the promise, the oath, but it didn't make things effortless or easy.

Cruz exhaled slowly, but the tension didn't leave his body. "I don't know what to do. I fixed what I knew how to fix, but it wasn't enough. There's nothing left to fight."

"You keep going." The words rang hollow, thick through the tears closing her throat and burning in her eyes. "One foot in front of the other."

He gathered her closer, fingers sifting through her hair as he guided her head to his bare chest. For a long time all he did was stroke her hair and drag in deep breaths, both of them silent in the lonely darkness.

When he finally spoke, it was barely a whisper. "I was afraid you wouldn't want me without him. But when I saw that knife go into him, I got it. I really got it. You're enough for me, you'll always be enough. But that doesn't mean we're not less without him."

That was the heart of all the messy confusion, wasn't it? From her father's angry questions to Ace's inability to truly believe they held a place in their hearts for him. She should have been more open with her words, her feelings, but fear had held her in its paralyzing grip. And now it was too late.

"I'll always love you, Lorenzo. It's not about whether what we have is enough, or needing more," she agreed. "It's about needing *him*."

"At least he's alive. I just hope—"

He cut off as someone knocked at the door. Just two hollow thuds, but then the door swung open and Ace stood there, weaving a little on his feet. "If I wait for someone to answer, I'll probably tip over."

Rachel's heart lodged in her throat. She sat up slowly and tried to tell herself that his arrival didn't necessarily mean anything had changed. Maybe he wanted to apologize for how things had gone down. Maybe he wanted to thank them.

It didn't mean anything.

Ace swayed, and Cruz rolled from the bed and made it halfway across the room before stopping. "Should you be out of bed?"

"Probably not." Ace met Rachel's gaze. The terror in his dark eyes was stark, unhidden. Far too much emotion to be anything safe or simple. "Is there still room in that one?"

The blaze of hope inside her chilled as it crashed into the aching remnants of her shattered heart. "If you want to be in it. That's the real question, isn't it?"

"Not for me," he said bluntly. "I know about fucking, Rae. But all I've ever known about relationships is being paid to fake them. What I wanted never really mattered."

Truth, finally. The kind of honesty she'd always craved from him, even if the words were edged with pain.

Cruz must have heard the same thing, because he crossed to Ace and got a shoulder under one of his arms. "Let go of the doorframe before you break it."

Even with the support, he wobbled as they made their way to the bed. Rachel slid over to make room as Cruz urged him down. "Come here."

Ace stretched out with a wince, his hand going to his side. "Don't turn on the lights. I'm not ready to see what my tattoos look like."

As exasperating as it was, the hint of vanity almost made Rachel smile. "Shut up. You're lucky to be alive."

"So I hear." He looked at Cruz, who was still looming next to the bed. "How much did you give up for me?"

Rachel didn't know the answer. Cruz had been stubbornly silent on the topic, but even she knew it was a lie when he shook his head. "Nothing. Someone owed me a favor."

"No." She'd had enough hiding and half-truths to last a lifetime. "No more lies, or we might as well just let it go now."

"What'll happen if I tell him? If I tell him I risked everyone in the damn sector, everyone in *all* the sectors. That I promised the scariest man any of us will ever meet an open-ended favor, and in return he kidnapped the most prized doctor in Eden and brought her here in the trunk of a fucking car?" Cruz slammed an open palm against the headboard and leaned over them, his gaze a little wild. "What will you do if I tell you that, Ace? Will you finally believe I fucking love you? Or will you figure out a way that it's all about her?"

Exactly what she'd demanded—the truth—but Ace stared at him for a long time before speaking, his tone full of confused wonder. "You're fucking crazy, brother."

"Not crazy." Rachel touched his hand. "He loves you, that's all. Just like I do."

"That just makes you both crazy," Ace retorted. But he curled his fingers around hers and held on as Cruz settled on the bed.

When they were under the blankets with Ace between them, Cruz laid his hand over theirs. "Your turn, Rachel. Tell us something true."

She didn't stop to censor herself. "I don't want to spend the rest of my life holding back, or being scared to say how I really feel in case it's too much for either of you. I want to be *me*."

Ace tightened his grip. "I'm going to fuck up a lot, because I don't know how the hell to do this. I feel like an asshole asking you both to put up with it."

"You didn't," Rachel shot back. "We decided we wanted to, because you mean so much. It's a choice. Don't take that away—from yourself or from us."

He took a deep breath and turned to face her, his forehead almost touching hers. "Ask me again. Ask me where I came from."

It still hurt, the way he'd brushed off the question before. "Will you answer me this time?"

"I'll answer any question you ask."

He always had—technically. Giving her tiny bits of the truth while keeping most of what mattered hidden. "Where do you come from?"

Ace caught her hand and guided it to his side, over the tattoo Mad had translated for her all those years ago. "*En el orgullo, fuerza.* Strength in pride. Eladio Zamora plucked me, Jared, and Gia off the streets. He trained us. Taught us different things. Jared and Gia were brilliant, cold. They could make people feel without feeling. But I was always..." A short, pained laugh. "I was messy."

In every way, maybe, good and bad. "Is that why you left Eden?"

"I didn't, not soon enough. I wanted to be amazing, like Jared. I wanted..." He let his hand fall away, leaving hers splayed across his ribs. "It's some kind of twisted. The closest thing I had to a father was my damn pimp, and I couldn't even make him proud. Guess I should be glad I didn't end up like Gia, half in love with him."

"If he wasn't proud of you for using your heart to find your way, then he was the crazy one." Rachel closed the distance between them and pressed her forehead to his. "And you are amazing. I wish you could see that."

"I'm sorry." Ace's voice cracked, and he drew in a breath. "I'm a bastard. And a fuckup. And a temperamental artist."

He was all those things—and none of it was an excuse. "You told me once that letting someone who had hurt me back into my life made me too brave for my own good."

"Because I'm a coward." He closed his eyes. "It's been so long since I wanted someone to really see me, and you're both so good. I thought I could walk away before you realized I wasn't."

The words scraped her already raw emotions. "No matter what it did to us? How much it *hurt*?"

"I thought you'd get over it. You had each other."

"You panicked," Cruz said quietly. "And I get it. Do you think I never watched the two of you and wondered? You had history I'd never understand."

Ace winced. "No, but—"

"Do you think Rachel never watched us and wondered if she'd always be on the outside because brotherhood matters so much to O'Kanes?"

A pause. Ace drew back to study her face in the dim light. "Did you?"

"Of course I did." They had built a friendship and a connection in no time at all, and it terrified her. "Maybe I still wonder. Sometimes it feels like I'm a complication you don't need."

Cruz slid his hand around the back of her neck, his fingers a soothing, comforting warmth. "That was the trade-off, Ace. You could have had us both, all of us. All that filthy sex, all that love. But we pay in honesty. And if you can't do that, all we end up with is heartbreak and jealousy."

Ace swallowed hard. "Could have had?"

The moment of truth, where she had to decide whether to open her heart again or shut him out for good. In the end, there was only one choice she could live with, one chance for the kind of happiness she'd glimpsed.

"Can have," she whispered. "No secrets—you promised me that too, Ace. Remember?"

"I remember. I'm sorry, Rae. I'm so fucking sorry."

So was she. As much as he loved to call her fearless, she'd been anything but. And that terror—the terror that Ace was going to leave her—had kept her from loving him the only way he deserved. Fully, madly. Completely.

"So am I," she whispered. "I'm sorry I hurt you. But we'll fix it." She caught Ace's chin and stared into his eyes. "You have to promise to try, Santana. I mean it. If you can't believe in us, I'd rather hear it now."

Ace stared back, and he still looked scared, but there was more than fear in his eyes now. There was hope.

"Faith in you is never the problem. Not until you tell me I'm worthy of you. That's the part I'm trying to figure out."

For once, she didn't try to hide, either. There was no guarding her heart, there never had been, because between Ace and Cruz, there was no part of it they didn't touch. "Then trust me. If I'm so damned special, *believe me*."

"And me." Cruz rose up on one elbow to stare down at them both. "But I want more than that. No more collars. No more rules. If you can't believe words, I'll say it with ink."

Stunned, Rachel blinked up at him. It was insane to jump to ink when Ace could barely bring himself to hear them...or was it? Maybe he needed tangible proof instead of reassurances, and there was nothing more tangible than a mark.

Ace watched almost warily as Cruz brushed his thumb over Rachel's cheek before pressing it to Ace's lips. "But before you agree, you need to know I'm done denying what I want. Both of you are mine. And if it comes down to ink, Rachel isn't the only one I want wearing my marks."

Heat flooded her at the prospect—but there were so many ways and reasons to call someone yours. Not about dominance, but belonging. "We'll mark each other."

"Ink is for life," Ace said hoarsely. "You won't be able to get away from me. Even when I'm an asshole."

Cruz made a rumbling sound that was almost a laugh. "You're always an asshole. Maybe we just like you that way."

Because he was so many other things, too—passionate, dedicated, fiercely loyal. "You don't need to change, Ace, just stop hiding. Let us in."

Ace slipped his fingers behind her head and tugged, dragging her into a kiss with Cruz's thumb between their lips. His tongue touched hers, wet and rough, then retreated. She followed, desperate for another taste of him to sate the hunger gnawing at her. Not for sex, not exactly, but for this sort of open intimacy. A closeness she'd craved for years.

Then Cruz's fingers were in her hair, too, hauling her back. Not far, just enough for him to claim Ace's mouth, and Rachel's hunger spiked. She watched, heat pulsing low in her body at the quick flashes of tongue, and Ace's low, rasping growl.

So she kissed him again, sliding her lips over his jaw, his throat, up to the spot below his ear.

"Let us love you," Cruz rumbled, cupping Rachel's head. "You wouldn't let me hide from who I was."

"Because you're fucking perfect," Ace groaned. "And I'm—"

"A hero," Cruz interrupted, raising his head to catch Ace's chin in his hand. "You took a knife in the gut for me, and Jesus *Christ*, Santana, if you ever try that again, I swear to God..."

"You'd kidnap another doctor and put me back together." Ace twisted free of Cruz's hand, turning to nuzzle Rachel's cheek. "I get stabbed, and he still one-ups me in the hero department. You got your saint, Rae. Just...promise me you need a sinner, too."

"I always have," she whispered. "More than you know."

Ace kissed her again, dragging her close enough for his denim-clad erection to grind against her hip. He hissed out a breath and seized her lower lip between his teeth. "How much sinning are you gonna let me do?"

She slipped her hands under his shirt, up over his miraculously, blessedly unmarred skin. "Use your imagination."

"No." Cruz grasped the edge of Ace's shirt and helped her pull it up. "Ace isn't the only one with an imagination. I think this time we get to use ours."

She caught his gaze, then his meaning. Ace was accustomed to seeing himself as the seducer, the corrupting force bringing them together. The one they turned to for guidance in the heat of the moment, and he filled the role because he felt it was expected of him, even when he wanted something different.

Not this time.

As Cruz dropped the shirt off the side of the bed, Rachel came to her knees and pushed Ace to his back on the mattress. "Don't move," she whispered.

His eyelids drooped as he watched her, his gaze hot. Hungry. "Dirty girl."

"That's right." She straddled his thigh, pushing the oversize T-shirt she wore—Cruz's shirt—up around her hips.

Cruz stayed stretched out alongside Ace, but his hand slipped down, lingering over the place where newly healed skin marred a vivid tattoo done in black and gray and vivid red—a skull and roses and a dove that was missing a wing now.

Then his fingers crept lower, grazing the button on Ace's fly. Cruz toyed with it and smiled up at her. "Take off that shirt, sweetheart."

She obeyed, but lingered over the task long enough to tease all three of them with a slow unveiling of skin.

"She's beautiful, isn't she?" Cruz said, popping Ace's jeans open. "And you walked away. You think you could have survived watching her from across the room, never getting to touch her?"

Ace tangled his fingers in the blanket, his chest lifting with his harsh breath. "No."

"Good. Because there are all sorts of things I'd miss." Rachel brushed one hand over the growing bulge of Ace's erection and trailed her other hand up to the hollow of his throat. She stroked his skin, marveling at the way his pulse jumped, then laid her fingers on his lower lip. "Your smile the most, I think."

His lips parted beneath her touch. He licked her fingertip, growled, and caught it between his teeth. The spark of it licked through her, too, left her fidgeting on his thigh.

Cruz dropped his hand to cover hers, squeezing it around Ace's cock. "What else would you have missed, sweetheart?"

Whispers and groans, hot breath and soft touches. Both of them, sighing her name and each other's. Silent passion. Rough caresses. The mad, heady rush of arousal, not tempered by affection and tenderness, but stronger because of it.

This. She didn't realize she'd said it aloud until Cruz guided her hand up, sliding her fingers along her inner thigh and higher.

"Show him," he commanded, coaxing her to cup her pussy. "Show him how hot you get, even just looking at him."

She took over the movement, parting her outer lips to tease her clit, and closed her eyes at the shock of pleasure that raced through her. Then she heard the rasp of a zipper, and opened her eyes again just in time to see Cruz wrap his hand around Ace's dick.

"That's all it takes," Cruz whispered against Ace's cheek. "She loves you when you're filthy. We all love you when you're filthy. But that's not all we love about you."

Ace groaned, thrusting up into Cruz's hand. But when he reached for Rachel, Cruz released his cock and grabbed his hand, forcing it back to the bed. "No, you get to watch."

"Fucking hell," Ace hissed, clutching at the blanket. His gaze dropped to Rachel's fingers. "I want to get her off."

"You do." She canted her hips, opening herself to the ravenous craving in his eyes before sliding her fingers deeper with a sharp sigh.

"Watch her," Cruz told Ace, gripping the other man's cock again. But not stroking, not pushing him toward the edge. Cruz held Ace in a tight grip, his gaze heated as he sought Rachel's eyes. "You want to be inside her, don't you? Feel her pussy clenching around you, so hot and wet."

"I didn't die, did I?" Ace ground out. "Of course I fucking do."

"Too bad." Cruz released him and sat up, sliding his hand along Rachel's leg and up her body. "I don't think she's done taking what *she* wants yet."

Rachel bit back a whimper. She let instinct guide her instead of thought, hooking her fingers in the loosened denim Ace wore. She lifted up and dragged his jeans down to his knees, far enough to bare his muscled thigh, then moaned as she settled on his leg again, skin to skin.

Ace groaned, flexing his leg, rubbing up against her as much as he could. "Fuck, Rae. You're so wet."

"Make me wetter." She rocked, grinding harder. "Tell me what you see."

Ace shuddered. "My lovers."

"That's right." Cruz dragged Rachel's hand toward his lips. His tongue swept out, licking her wetness from her fingertips, and he made a low, approving noise. His other hand slipped between her legs to stroke her pussy, sending shivers of pleasure up her spine as he toyed with her clit.

Oh God. She rolled her hips up to his touch, watching Ace's face as she moved. He reached for her again, and this time Cruz let him settle those strong hands on her legs, his thumbs stroking high on her inner thighs.

Cruz growled his approval against Rachel's temple as his fingers worked into her, deep and a little rough, stretching her. "He loves to watch you. He's painting you in his mind, over and over. Give him a memory, sweetheart. Give him you."

She wanted to wait, to drag out the sensation, to have him watching her like this forever. But Cruz curled his fingers inside her, the heel of his hand pressing hard against her clit, and she lost it. She shivered through the orgasm, crying out again when Cruz bit her throat, marking her with his teeth the way he'd soon mark her with ink.

When she stilled, Cruz eased free of her body and leaned forward, pressing her against the heat of Ace's body as he glided slick fingers over the other man's lips. "Taste how sweet she is. You want to be inside her, don't you?"

"Fuck, yes." Ace held her gaze as he licked Cruz's fingers.

So many things she wanted to do, but it was all too intense to slow down. She slid back, pulled Ace's jeans the rest of the way off his legs, and sank to the bed beside him. Pretty words bounced around her brain, seductive and sexy.

They vanished before they could reach her mouth. "So take it," she whispered instead, winding her hand in his hair.

Ace rolled on to her. Rocked into her. It was nothing like the other times they'd fucked, no precise choreography or endless taunting, just his hips pinning her to the mattress as he worked his cock into her with slow, steady thrusts.

He braced his hands on either side of her head and lifted his upper body, his gaze locked to her face as he pushed deep. "You were never the one falling," he whispered. "I was. I've been falling forever."

Not anymore. She wrapped her legs around his waist and framed his face with her hands. "We've got you, baby."

"We've got you," Cruz echoed, coming to his knees behind Ace. "All you have to do is decide you want us both."

Ace's breathing hitched. He groaned. Reached down. Hooked an arm under Rachel's leg and hauled it higher, spreading her wide, and she gasped as he pushed deeper.

"Do you want that, angel? Want him to fuck me while I'm fucking you? All three of us fucking each other?"

More than a fantasy—a way to show him the truth. She gripped his shoulders, her nails digging in to his skin, and looked up at Cruz. He stared back, love in his eyes, and relief, and sharp anticipation.

It lingered as he reached for the lube, as he stroked a hand down Ace's back and lower, until his fingers brushed Ace's shaft as he thrust into Rachel again.

"You don't come until she does," he said, easy words with the sharp edges of a command, and she knew the moment he pressed his cock against Ace's ass because his body went stiff above her, his arms trembling.

And Cruz held him there. Held them all there, anticipation twisting higher with every panted breath, until Ace dropped his head forward with a groan. "Goddamn it, brother, just fuck—"

Cruz thrust forward, driving a cry from Ace's throat, driving Ace into Rachel. The force of it pushed them up the bed, and she whimpered as she braced her hands on the headboard.

It was a position meant for a slow grind, and she embraced it. Using the headboard for leverage, she pushed back. Every nerve ending blazed to life, bringing into sharp focus the tiniest details—the delicious weight pinning her to the bed, muscles in Ace's stomach flexing against hers. The quick rush of Cruz's breath as he shifted position slightly.

Ace's mouth found her jaw. Her cheek. His own was unshaven, three days' worth of stubble rasping over her skin as he sought her ear. "Is this how you feel when you're trapped between us?"

"Yes." It was reflected in his eyes, the same emotion. That it was all so good he might not survive it, and he didn't care, because for once everything was *right*. Exactly the way it needed to be.

Complete.

Cruz bent forward to grasp the headboard, every beautiful muscle in his arms flexing as he set their pace. Slow. Deep. Ace was already close, his body tense, trembling. He buried his face against her chest, breath falling in hot pants. "Don't let me go. Don't—"

"Shh." Cruz laid one hand on Ace's head, but his gaze locked with Rachel's, full of love and determination but also a silent plea. This was what *he* needed, to be the one who made it okay for them to fall, because he'd always hold them.

She picked up the rhythm, rocking up with the slight retreat of his hips, following the searing heat of Ace's body as he moved between them. Over and over, as the slow build slipped away from them, replaced by a desperation that left them rough. Grasping.

The first clenching waves washed through her. Rachel shuddered and cried out as she reached for them, her shaking hands slipping over sweat-slicked skin. Ace came with her name on his lips, whispering against her skin before he closed his teeth on her throat.

A possessive gesture of dominance. A helpless moment of surrender. It couldn't be both, but it was, because *they* were both, and more. Everything for Cruz, who stiffened with a growled curse.

His hands dropped from the headboard to the mattress, his trembling arms barely holding the bulk of his weight off their bodies as he shuddered. And he stayed like that, above them, around them, a solid wall of muscle and strength who'd tear apart the world to keep them safe, or maybe even just make them happy.

Rachel couldn't breathe, and she still protested when he rolled to the bed beside them. "No, not yet—"

"Shh." Ace moved—not enough to pull away from her, just enough to shift her to her side, and then Cruz was tight against her back, his legs tangled with theirs, his arm across their bodies, his breath hot on her nape.

Close, so close she could feel their hearts pounding in

time with hers. "This," she whispered finally. "This is what makes me whole. Without both of you, there's a part of me that's missing."

Cruz kissed her shoulder. "Me, too."

"It's more," Ace whispered hoarsely. "It's... When I was a kid, my mother couldn't afford art supplies. But she saved everything she could and got me these pencils, orange and green and blue. And I loved them. You can do a lot with orange and green and blue. I knew there were other colors, I saw them all around me. But that was my world. Orange and green and blue."

The undercurrent of pain in his voice tore at Rachel, but she ran her fingers through his hair and kept silent. Let him talk.

He slid his fingers up her arm and caught a lock of her hair, wrapping it around his finger. "When I got that first box of twenty-four colors, I didn't know what the fuck to do with them. Seeing color doesn't mean you know how to use it. I kept leaning on orange and green and blue, because even if it wasn't everything it could be, I knew I could make it work."

He'd done far more than that—she had the ink to prove it—but his words weren't about how practice made perfect. They were about fear, and the comfort of old habits. "Ace?"

He smiled, brushing his thumb along her lower lip before twining his fingers with Cruz's. Their joined hands settled on her bare hip, warm and heavy. "You two are all the colors I've been missing," Ace whispered, closing his eyes. "I'm going to make gorgeous fucking art with you."

The pain was gone, leaving a languorous contentment in its place. "It'll take a while," Rachel murmured, her lips against his. "Maybe forever."

"That's what I'm counting on, angel."

kit rocha

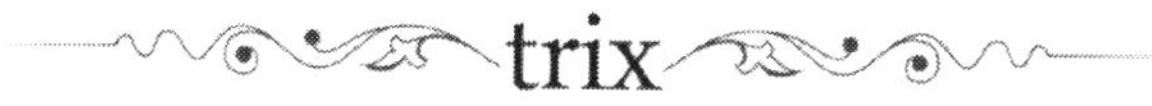

trix

THE NIGHT WAS quiet, clear, and cold enough for Trix to be glad not only for her coat, but for the solid warmth of the man beside her. "Thanks for walking with me, Zan."

"Any time, darling." Zan shoved his hands into his pockets and eyed the empty streets. "Not that many people are out tonight. I'd say Dallas made his point about who still runs things."

His bloody, emphatic point. "Not like he had a choice."

"Hell, no. It's been coming for a while." He shrugged one big shoulder. "That's the price, right? You can be easygoing most of the time, but when it's time to teach a lesson, you better make it stick."

That was the thing Mac Fleming never could understand. His lessons had always been swift, brutal—but unpredictable. With Mac, a personal betrayal or a casual, ill-considered comment could have the same violent result.

No rhyme, no reason. And the bastard had reaped what he'd sown.

She asked the question burning in her gut, because she knew Zan would answer it honestly. "Do you think Fleming will let it go, or come after Dallas?"

"Doesn't matter," Zan replied without hesitation. "Dallas won't let it go. It's going to be war, one way or another. Only question is who hits first. And who hits hardest."

Trix managed not to wince. "I left Sector Five behind for a reason. I guess I'm not excited to have it all back in my face, is all."

"I know." Zan slung an arm around her shoulders. "We won't let those drugged-out bastards fuck with you. You're an O'Kane now. Don't forget it."

What would he think if she told him the truth—that even having the collected might of the O'Kanes at her back couldn't protect her from the biggest threat in Five. "Thanks, Zan. That means a lot."

"Any time, girl. Now where are we—?"

It happened so fast. Screeching tires, a burst of gunfire, and Zan hit the wall, his hand still on the butt of his holstered pistol. Trix was already reaching for him when she caught a flurry of movement out of the corner of her eye and realized this wasn't a drive-by, not at all.

An arm slid around her waist and yanked her off her feet. She fought, kicked, and one lucky blow connected. The man dropped her, and she slammed painfully to the pavement on her knees.

Zan. He was still, dreadfully still—but if she could reach his gun—

"Not a chance," a low voice growled. A hand closed around her wrist, wrenching her arm back so brutally, tears sprung to her eyes. "You killed enough of us last time around. Cy—get the drugs."

No. She thrashed against the man's steely grip, but he held tight and dragged her toward a van on the corner. The side door slid open with an ominous shriek, and he shoved her toward it.

More hands came out of the darkness. They closed on her clothes, on her arms and legs, dragging her into the vehicle. She got one last glimpse of Zan, sprawled in a growing pool of blood, before the door banged shut and tires squealed.

"Here," a rough voice barked, and the arm holding her tightened. He pushed a plastic inhaler against her nose, and she knocked it away.

She yanked one hand free and reached for the switchblade in her belt, but it tumbled away when the man they called Cy slammed her hand against the van wall.

Another hand covered her mouth, rough fingers crushing her lips against her teeth until she tasted blood. The inhaler jammed tight under her nose, and tears streamed out of her eyes as Trix held her breath.

Never again. She'd sworn it, through every last night sweat and muscle spasm. Every gnawing ache. No more drugs, not for *anything*—

Her burning lungs yielded to the need for air, and she breathed in. It hit her almost immediately, and her head began to swim with hazy flashes of color and snatches of thoughts.

Revelations, really, only every time she tried to hold on to them, they slipped away. The answers to her predicament were there—the answers to the *world*—but she was too fucked up to see them.

It was the story of her life.

The pressure on her face eased, along with a little of the rush clouding her brain. She dragged in a sob. "What do you want?"

They ignored her.

Someone shoved her against the floor of the van.

Bare metal and bolts dug into her cheek as someone else wrenched her arms back. Rope cut into her wrists, and a blindfold settled over her eyes, rough fingers catching her hair as they knotted it at the back of her head. She floated there, the rumble of the van's engine vibrating through her, rattling her teeth.

Then the van lurched to a halt and the door slid open. "Come on," a man growled, dragging her by the arm. The harsh glare of streetlights filtered in through the edges of the blindfold, and she dove toward the light only to be yanked back. She stumbled, hit the jamb of an open doorway, and then darkness closed in around her.

The darkness had a *smell*—antique wood and cigar smoke and money. It was burned into her brain, right alongside all her bleakest memories, and Trix dug in her heels, despite sliding across slick tile, because now she knew.

She knew exactly where she was.

Another shove, and she landed hard on a chair. She tried to stand up, and someone backhanded her across the face, snapping her head back. The taste of blood filled her mouth, but it didn't hurt, and that scared her more than anything.

Almost anything.

She could hear them breathing, but nothing else. Not until a careless hand ripped away the blindfold, taking some of her hair with it.

She barely noticed, not with a nightmare swimming into focus two feet away.

Mac Fleming had always been handsome. Put together. He wore an expensive business suit with the rumpled ease of a man used to taking beautiful things for granted, but there was nothing attractive about the darkness in his eyes.

They narrowed slightly. Widened. A cruel smile curved his lips as he set aside his drink. "Well, now. This is an interesting turn of events."

She tried to channel Lex, to think of something witty and cutting, the perfect *fuck you.*

In the end, she stared at him.

It only made his smile widen. "It's like looking at a ghost. I have to say, Dominic. It seems like your vengeance will fit rather neatly with mine."

She followed his gaze. Dom stood on the other side of the room, leaning against the wall with a smug, shit-eating grin on his face.

Trix. They'd kidnapped *Trix*, some sort of payoff for Dom, and Fleming hadn't known what he'd really be getting. Not until now.

She licked her lips and sat straighter in the chair. "It's been a long time, Mac."

"It has, hasn't it?" He leaned forward, cupping her bruised cheek. His thumb swiped across her lower lip, wiping away blood with a smile. "Welcome home, Tracy."

ABOUT KIT

Kit Rocha is actually two people—Bree & Donna, best friends who are living the dream. They get paid to work in their pajamas, talk on the phone, and write down all the stories they used to make up in their heads.

They also write paranormal romance as Moira Rogers.

ACKNOWLEDGMENTS & THANKS

We owe a ridiculous amount of thanks to a ridiculous number of people—Vivian Arend, Alisha Rai, Lauren Dane, Victoria Dahl, Carly Phillips, Sara Reine, Marie Hall, Deanna Chase, Minx Malone, Roxie Rivera, and the filthy ladies of TLTSNBN. We could not have done this without every single one of you guys cheering us on. Thank you so much.

We also need to thank our beta readers, Jay AhSoon Samia and Tracy Meighan, for being so damn awesome it hurts. Lillie Applegarth, Sasha Knight, and Sharon Muha have all helped us make this book its best, and we're so grateful for their help.

And last—but, as always, first in our minds—huge thanks to all the readers who have embraced the O'Kanes. Should the end of the world arrive, Dallas has a round waiting for all of you.

Turn the page
for a sneak peek at

1

LOGAN BECKETT WAS one sincerely unsettling motherfucker.

Finn recognized the irony of the sentiment. Next to Beckett's tailored suit, polished shoes, and clean-shaven jaw, his own three-day stubble and bloodshot eyes weren't exactly a character recommendation. The battered leather boots didn't help. Neither did the tattoos—Mac Fleming made a big deal about how his sector was *civilized*, and Finn had always figured the tattoos reminded him of Dallas O'Kane.

Reminding Fleming of Dallas O'Kane wasn't the way to get ahead in Sector Five.

Beckett knew that. He knew how to fake civilized like it was going out of style. Perfect clothes, perfect grooming, perfect loyalty. Hell, he even had a perfect wife—Mac Fleming's eldest daughter, the ultimate accessory for an ambitious man eager to take on a leadership role in the family business.

What he didn't have was a shred of humanity in his cunning gaze. Finn wasn't exactly in a position to throw stones there—he'd done shit that had given him horrifying dreams, and a few things so bad the dreams were better company than the memories.

But goddamn, at least he *had* nightmares.

"You heard me," Beckett said smoothly. "As of now, nothing recreational hits the streets without additives."

Fuck, Finn hated the additives. The people who wanted oblivion were already wasting their money and lives, and they were doing it willingly. Drugs didn't have to be a messy business anymore, because science had taken addiction out of the equation.

Beckett was putting it back in. With interest.

Arguing with the bastard was pointless, but Finn still tried. Not because he thought it would help, he just liked irritating him. "Doesn't that make shit more expensive?"

The man sighed. "In the short term. But once all of our customers are equally dedicated, price increases will be well-tolerated."

Equally addicted, you mean. "And if someone doesn't want to get that dedicated? Are we not selling the regular stuff at all anymore?"

"Of course we are. If the price is right." Beckett shuffled some of the papers on his desk and stifled a yawn. "I don't want any of the small-time dealers handling it, though. The bastards can't be trusted."

Maybe not by him. Finn crossed his arms over his chest, forcing Beckett to stare at the lines of ink winding up his arms. "They'll do what I tell them to do."

Beckett sat slowly back in chair and studied him. "At one time, I would have agreed."

Not an unreasonable doubt. At one time, Finn hadn't been slowly undermining the whole damn sector. "You saying I can't keep my boys in line?"

Beckett smiled. "Yes, that's exactly what I'm saying."

A chill slithered up Finn's spine. Christ, that smile

was creepy. It was off, like the man knew how to move all the right muscles, but didn't have anything to back it up. The only emotion lurking behind those cool blue eyes was anticipation.

Victory.

Something was really fucking wrong. Beckett might hate Finn, might sneer down his nose and drop barbs into every conversation, but he never crossed the line into outright disrespect. *Someone* had to do the man's dirty work.

Finn tensed, fighting the gut instinct to go for his gun. Shooting his way out of Five was a suicide mission—and a last resort. So he played the game, twisting his features into a scowl. "If you have a problem with how I run shit, maybe you should just lay it on out."

That chilling smile grew as Beckett leaned forward. "All right—" A quick chirp from the small tablet on his desk interrupted the words, and he glanced over at it with a sigh. "Mac wants you in his office."

"Guess you'll have to give me that job critique later." Finn rolled out of his chair, his hand still itching for his gun. The spot between his shoulder blades itched just as much when he turned his back on Beckett, even though he'd stopped caring about taking a bullet in the spine a long time ago.

Hell, he'd stopped caring about damn near everything a long time ago.

Mac's office was the last place Finn wanted to be. The man had been unlivable since Dallas O'Kane had thwarted his attempt to set up a puppet as the new leader of Sector Four. He'd spent an entire afternoon raging, swearing he'd call the sector leaders together and accuse Dallas of violating his territory.

Which he had. O'Kane and his men had blown up a warehouse on the edge of Sector Five. Under any other circumstances, that might have brought retaliation from the other leaders. But Mac had been financing bootleggers who'd been doing a little violating of their own when it came to O'Kane's territory.

No high ground there.

Finn had barely taken three steps out of Beckett's office when Ryder fell in beside him, a deeper-than-usual frown creasing his dark face. "We've got trouble."

Great. Just fucking *great*. "Does it have anything to do with why Beckett was looking so damn pleased with himself?"

"If he's happy, it won't be for long." Ryder cursed under his breath, vicious and low. "That asshole O'Kane kicked out of Four is gonna get us all killed."

"Who, Dom?" More evidence of Mac's slipping grasp on reason. Dominic wasn't even a useful asset, just some stupid, bitter brute whose explanations for why Dallas O'Kane booted him got more ridiculous every day. No useful intel, no brains. All the bastard ever did was spew bile about his former boss while Mac hung on his every word. "What the hell did he do now?"

"Not what he did—what Mac did *for* him." Ryder shook his head, his shoulders tight. "The motherfucker kidnapped one of 'em. Don't know what she is to Dom, or why he wants her, but she's got the ink."

Finn stopped so fast his boots squeaked on the hardwood floor. "Wait, back the hell up. Mac did what?"

Ryder spun around, his expression grave. "He snatched an O'Kane right out of Sector Four, and we're all fucked. We're in it now, whether we want to be or not."

Jesus fucking Christ.

Finn stared at his closest friend—his *only* friend—hoping for one crazy second that it was all a twisted joke. But Ryder stared back, grim and angry, and Finn flashed back to the last time he'd come face-to-face with Dallas when someone had endangered one of his women.

He'd almost gotten his head blown off.

"So that's it," Finn said. "This is how we go down. Riding Fleming's hate right into our graves."

Ryder arched one eyebrow and tilted his head down

the hall in the direction of Fleming's office. "Talk him down. Tell him we'll fix it before things go too far."

How were they supposed to do that, drop the girl at the edge of the sector and hope she didn't blab? That was assuming any bird with O'Kane ink wouldn't turn around and go for their balls.

No, Finn had been laying this groundwork for far too damn long. Chipping away at Mac's base of power, delivering frustration instead of victory. He'd known it would all blow up in his face eventually.

Hell, he'd counted on having a front row seat. He hadn't bothered with an exit strategy, because he hadn't wanted one. He deserved the fall that was coming.

Ryder didn't.

Finn grabbed his friend's arm and hauled him into the nearest empty room, slamming the door behind them with the bite of temper. This was why making friends was stupid. Caring about people complicated shit.

Finn had never planned on liking Ryder. The other man was nothing like him. He was smart. Ambitious. He'd rocketed up the ranks of Mac's organization through wits and stubbornness, somehow always finding that line Finn wove back and forth across, the one that made a man decent, even if he was ruthless.

He held up both hands now. "Whatever you're about to say—"

"Shut up." Finn braced his hand against the door, as if he could hold it shut if Ryder really wanted to get through. Not that Finn wasn't tough, but Ryder had always been in a different league. A better league. Everything about him screamed polish, from his fitted leather jacket to his tattoos—high quality black and gray etched into his brown skin, the kind of artwork Finn couldn't have afforded when he got his first ink.

Ryder had never belonged in a hellhole like Five, so Finn was going to get him out. "There's no fixing this. O'Kane will burn us to the ground, but you're new enough to make it out first. So you need to take that girl over to Four and buy your way into O'Kane's good graces."

"I can't."

"Yes you can. I'll distract the guards, and you—"

"I can't leave," Ryder repeated flatly.

Final fucking words, and they were out of time. Mac would send someone to fetch him if he didn't arrive like a good guard dog, and he couldn't *make* Ryder save himself.

Finn's good intentions had never been worth much.

Exhaling roughly, he jerked open the door. "Fine. Do you know which woman he grabbed?" *Please don't let it be Lex.*

"I don't know—some redhead."

Fuck. Damn close to four years, and it still felt like getting kicked in the gut. Thank God redheads were rare—he'd known just a handful, and only one who really mattered. Maybe he'd never be able to think of red hair without imagining her the last time he'd seen her, sprawled lazily across his bed, floating on the rush, her long red hair a tousled halo around her pale face.

He hadn't given her the drugs that killed her that night, but he'd given her enough over the years to have no illusions about his involvement. Her death was on his shoulders, her blood on his hands.

He could almost feel it as he reached Mac's office. He was shocked not to see his fingers dripping red as he reached out to rap on the heavy oak door and waited for permission to enter.

Instead, the door slammed open to reveal Dom's glowering face. "Don't get any bright ideas," he sneered. "That bitch is mine." He shoved past Finn and stomped down the hall.

Finn tilted his head, and Ryder headed after Dom with a short nod.

Bracing himself, he swung into Mac's office—and stopped cold.

Tracy.

It couldn't be. Finn blinked and let his gaze sweep over the redhead, trying to discount that first disorienting impression. She was tied to a chair, the plastic ties digging into skin marked by O'Kane ink. She was disheveled, her clothing askew, ripped in places, her hair wild. Killer curves, a pointed chin, a split, bloody lip that someone needed to die for giving her—

Icy, blue-green eyes. *Familiar* eyes.

Tracy was alive.

She stared back at him—frozen, barely breathing—and Mac stepped into the silence with a quiet hum of approval. "She looks good, doesn't she?"

Finn barely heard him. Barely saw him.

Fucking hell, *Tracy was alive.*

She sat there like a statue or a ghost or a fucking hallucination until Mac brushed her cheek. When she flinched away, he grabbed her by the hair and jerked her head back.

Finn's fingers flexed, and he could already feel Mac's throat beneath them. He'd crush the fucking life out of his boss and consider it his best day ever. "Get your hand off her."

"I don't think so." Mac bent low, putting his face close to hers. "She stole from me."

That got her attention. She turned her head so fast she almost bumped into Mac. "I did not, you lying asshole. You gave me those drugs."

It made a sick sort of sense. The leader of Sector Five didn't mess with common girls. Only the best for him—young, pretty, drugged out of their minds. Eager to do anything and everything to stay that way. It was a soft, blissful life, a *short* one, which meant Mac was always on the prowl for a replacement.

He would have taken Tracy just to prove he could. "You told me she overdosed."

"I honestly figured she had." Mac studied her. "But you sold it all and ran, didn't you, love? Over to Sector Four."

So casual. Curious, but only vaguely, as if he didn't care about the answer one way or another but was simply going through the motions. Finn knew better. Mac had staged this melodramatic reveal just for him, and this was just the opening act.

Finn had to get them both out of there before Dom came back for the big finale. "Yeah, she ran straight into Dallas O'Kane's arms. Is this really how you want to start a sector war?"

"War was inevitable, and it's already begun," Mac said absently. He was focused on Tracy, staring at her like he was trying to decode an unfamiliar language. "We all thought you were dead. Finn, too. You walked away and never looked back—that's stone cold, darling. Color me impressed."

Her jaw clenched, her gaze clashing with Finn's before she looked away, and it didn't matter that four years had passed. He knew what she'd been thinking the day she'd walked out of Sector Five, out of his life. Once Mac set his sights on a girl, her opportunities narrowed to two—survive as long as she could as a high class junkie whore, or die trying to get out.

Tracy had picked the path that wouldn't take him down with her.

Finn rolled his shoulders, letting himself really feel the familiar weight of his shoulder holster. His gun was right there in easy reach. Two big steps, and he could have it shoved under Mac Fleming's jaw. He owed Tracy that much.

Christ, he owed her everything.

"You cost Dom his O'Kane ink," Mac continued, his voice taking on a wicked, sharp edge as he pulled her hair harder, pulled until a whimper escaped her. "Have you seen his scars? He's eager to show them to you. Every...single...one."

Finn didn't choose to move, but then he never made choices when it came to Tracy. Every damn time she had brushed his life, he'd stumbled forward without control or reason.

He didn't stumble now, just took those two steps and dug the barrel of his gun under Mac's chin. "Let her go. Now."

Mac's eyes went wide before narrowing as he barked out a laugh. "You stupid bastard."

Finn ground the gun deeper into the man's flesh, pressing up until Mac had to stretch onto his toes. "I'm not telling you again. You can let her go back to Sector Four and fuck what Dom wants, or I'll blow off the top of your head right now."

Mac stared back at him, his eyes burning with outrage. "Do it. Neither one of you would make it out of here al—"

Finn squeezed the trigger. One shot, and it splattered Mac Fleming's fucking brains all over his office.

It was loud, reverberating through the room as Finn watched his boss fall to the floor. Putting another round in his head as insurance would have been smart—just to be sure he was well and truly beyond saving, even with regen tech—but Mac's last words had been truth.

If Finn wanted to get them out of Sector Five alive, he didn't have bullets to waste.

Coming in fall of 2014

Beyond Shame

Beyond Control

Beyond Pain

Beyond Temptation
(novella – available in the MARKED anthology)

Beyond Jealousy

Beyond Solitude
(novella – first published in ALPHAS AFTER DARK)

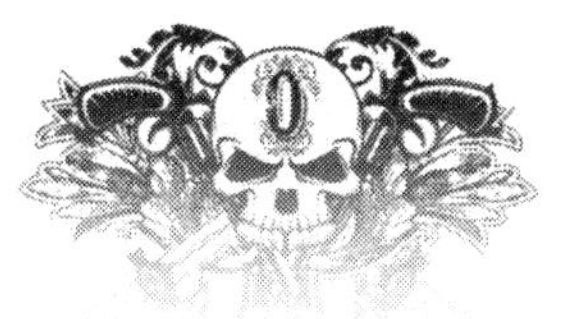